DEATH ON THE R

DEATH ON THE ROMNEY MARSH

Deryn Lake

A John Rawlings Mystery

For Chris,
   Sincere thoughts and thanks
for your years of friendship.
   With love,

   Deryn Lake

Hodder & Stoughton (Dina)
                              x

Publication Day,
1st January, 1998.

Copyright © 1998 by Deryn Lake

First published in Great Britain in 1998 by
Hodder and Stoughton
A division of Hodder Headline PLC

The right of Deryn Lake to be identified as the Author of
the Work has been asserted by her in accordance with the
Copyright, Designs and Patents Act 1988.

10 9 8 7 6 5 4 3 2 1

A CIP catalogue record for this book is
available from the British Library

ISBN 0 340 67428 8

Typeset by Palimpsest Book Production Limited,
Polmont, Stirlingshire
Printed and bound in Great Britain by
Mackays of Chatham PLC, Chatham, Kent

Hodder and Stoughton
A division of Hodder Headline PLC
338 Euston Road
London NW1 3BH

For LINDSEY DAVIS
with affection.
Olé.

Acknowledgments

As ever, people have been so kind and willingly given their time to assist me with this book. First, I must thank Mark Dunton of the Public Record Office who, on his day off, helped me go into the archives and find the Cipher of 1757, used by the secret agents of that time. Not only that, he also unearthed the facts behind the workings of the Secret Department and the Secret Office, to say nothing of discovering the legendary Dr Willes, Bishop of Bath and Wells and Decipherer to the King. Next I would like to thank Lt Colonel Henry Dormer, former mayor of Winchelsea, who opened up the town's museum especially for me and also loaned me a precious book on Winchelsea's history. I am most grateful, too, to the Reverend Lindsay John Hammond, Vicar of Appledore and also of the remote churches of the Romney Marsh, who helped me so much with the background to St Thomas à Becket, Fairfield, and St Augustine, Brookland. As always I am in the debt of P.C. Keith Gotch of the Metropolitan Police Thames Division for discussing the state of the victim's body with me. Keith is a mine of information and I am very lucky to be able to call on his expertise. Finally let me thank Maureen Lyle and John Kerr, who stoically tramped the Romney Marsh with me, even through the snow. It was on a photograph taken by Maureen that Kenny McKendry based his wonderful cover illustration. Thanks to Kenny, too. Last but not least my gratitude to fellow writer Keith Miles, always ready to help and advise.

Chapter One

As soon as the Magistrate had taken his seat, those who crowded the public benches did likewise. 'Bring up the prisoner,' called Joe Jago, the clerk of the court, and there was a general drawing in of breath as a handsome lad with straw coloured hair, well set-up in his person, and with nothing to condemn him except the dirtiness of his face, was brought to stand at the bar facing the clerk and, on a higher level, the Magistrate, John Fielding himself.

'Read the charge,' ordered the Beak.

'That the prisoner, Nathanial Hicks, did on Epiphany Day, throw at a cockerel at a fair, thus breaking the directive of the Justices of the Peace as given last 1st March, 1756.'

'How plead you?' the Magistrate asked crisply.

Hicks looked round the court and gave what John Rawlings, apothecary of Shug Lane, present at this hearing, could only think of as a small snigger of satisfaction. 'Guilty,' he said, and from certain quarters there came a murmur of amused admiration at his bravado.

The Apothecary shuddered. He lived in an age of horrible cruelty which sickened him, and he could only be glad that people like William Hogarth, the artist, were making a positive stand against the monstrous treatment meted out to defenceless animals by so-called humans. To him, the good-looking young man standing at the bar now wore an evil leer.

Mr Fielding's words ripped into the ensuing silence. 'Orders have been given to prevent that barbarous and inhuman custom, for I should blush to call it a diversion, of throwing at cocks on Shrove Tuesday and other festive days. What cowardice in a brave nation, to see a fellow of six foot high throwing a monstrous stick at a poor inoffensive animal, tied to a stake to prevent its escape from the wanton cruelty of its unequal adversary! How inhumane the devices of the boys to whom these creatures belong, who have been seen to put them into hats, after the poor animals' legs, thighs, etc. have been broke, to have their brains knocked out. Surely this is highly inconsistent with that charity, compassion and benevolence,

1

which foreigners observe to be the characteristics of our country. Query, would not these tall young fellows before mentioned make a more comely figure with a musket on their shoulders? For we are now a nation at war and let that not be forgotten. I sentence you to three months in Newgate, Nathanial Hicks, and may the press gang be waiting at the door when you come out.'

'Huzzah!' shouted the Duke of Richmond patriotically, and there was a further murmur, this time of approval. The mood of the court had swung. What right had able-bodied young men to be hurling missiles at cockerels when they should be doing so at the French? Amidst hisses, the glowering Hicks was led away, and the afternoon's work continued.

The Apothecary ceased to concentrate, thinking instead about the extraordinary fact that Britain was once more engaged in hostilities, not only with its neighbours across the Channel but also with Austria and Russia, banded together in a formidable alliance with Sweden and Saxony. The whole sorry business had started the previous August, 1756, when Prussia had resisted Austria's attempts to regain Silesia, lost to the Austrians eleven years before. After that opening defensive action there had been a rush to join one side or the other, each country entering for its own hidden reasons. Yet here in London, other than for more visible signs of the press gangs round the riff-raff hostelries, the public at large were hardly affected by the outbreak of war and life went on very much as it had before.

On this particular day, however, it being a vaporous February, the streets of London dank with fog and the squares and crescents hushed and silent, lying beneath shrouds of ghostly mist, the *beau monde*, those butterflies of society whose pleasure it was to parade forth in bright colours to see and be seen, were for once quite noticeably absent from the walkways of the capital. Normally, people of rank and quality sallied abroad before the hour to dine, observed loosely at any time between two and five, to visit shops, auction rooms, coffee houses, or to call one upon the other. But this specific afternoon, the risk of exposing their fine garments to the damp spirals of clinging haze had clearly sent them into mutual alarm, and they had consequently sought to waste their vapid time elsewhere. Thus when John Rawlings had set foot in the Magistrate's court, located next door to the Public Office in Bow Street, he had found it packed with sightseers. For watching justice

2

meted out by a blind man was considered good sport by those with little else to do with their lives. Shaking his head with a certain wry amusement, John had squeezed his way along the back of the three wooden benches which ran on either side of the courtroom on the ground floor and found himself a very small perching place.

Above his head, the gallery was crammed, and the Apothecary had recognised several faces, particularly that of the Duke of Richmond, who had grinned and waved his tricorne hat. John waved back, but no further exchange of greeting had been possible for it was at that moment that the Principal Magistrate, Mr John Fielding, known to the masses as the Blind Beak, the switch that he always carried into court to help him find his way twitching before him, made his entrance. Everybody rose as with the aid of his clerk, Joe Jago, the Magistrate had walked to his high chair and sat down.

From his uncomfortable vantage point, John had gazed with affection at the man who over the last three years he had grown to respect and admire almost more than any other. It had been a death that had brought them together in the early summer of 1754, the death of a young woman whose body John had found in the pleasure gardens at Vaux Hall. He had been briefly suspected of the crime but had gone on to become John Fielding's friend and confidant, and help him bring the real killer to light. Since then he had assisted the Blind Beak twice more, and was now fondly regarded as an unofficial Beak Runner, that name given to those officers of the court whose duty it was to apprehend criminals. Yet by calling, John was a herbalist who practised his trade from his shop just off London's Piccadilly.

The Apothecary shifted in his cramped position, then realised that Mr Fielding was speaking again.

'As there are so many members of the public gathered here today, may I take this opportunity to remind you of the situation regarding the joining of His Majesty's forces and marines. Volunteers are given £3. However, the press gang's quarry are all able-bodied, idle' – the Magistrate paused and let his sightless eyes, hidden from view as always by a black bandage, turn in the direction of the gallery and benches – 'and disorderly persons who cannot, upon examination, prove themselves to exercise and industriously follow some lawful trade or employment, or to have substance sufficient for their support and maintenance. Those sought for impressment are males aged between seventeen and forty-five, who are fit and stand not less than five feet four inches in their stockinged feet.' The Blind Beak rose to reveal that he himself stood well over six feet tall. 'I thank you for your attention,' he said by way of dismissal. 'The court is adjourned until tomorrow.'

As he proceeded out, so too did the onlookers, jostling in the entrance that led them to Bow Street. John went with the throng, his intention to walk the few steps back to the Public Office and from there climb the stairs that led to Mr Fielding's private apartments. For tonight he had been invited to dine with the Fielding family; a small one consisting of the Magistrate, his wife Elizabeth, and their adopted daughter Mary Ann, who was in reality the couple's niece. Quite how this adoption had come about John had never been certain, though he had a suspicion that the child might have been born out of wedlock to one of Mrs Fielding's sisters.

He was thinking about this when he felt a hearty clap on his shoulder, and saw that Charles Lennox, Duke of Richmond, was waiting in the fog to have a word with him.

'Rawlings, my dear soul, how are you?' Not bothering to wait for a reply, the nobleman rattled on, 'This war business is mighty upsetting, ain't it? Quite put me out of countenance, so it has. I've been asked to volunteer some of my manservants for the army. Damned inconvenient, in view of my plans.'

'What plans?' asked the Apothecary with a sudden lurch of his heart.

The Duke winked a dark, saturnine eye and for a moment looked exactly like his ancestor, Charles II. 'Marriage,' he whispered loudly.

John Rawlings quite literally felt sick, having nursed for some considerable time a passion for the beautiful actress Coralie Clive, a passion never consummated but for all that strong enough to make him feel ill at the thought that she might be about to marry Richmond, another of her many admirers.

'Who is the fortunate woman?' he managed to ask, his voice a croak, at least to his own ears.

Charles Lennox winked again. 'I'd best not say, as yet. The fact is that I still haven't proposed to her and I think she should be the first to know, don't you?'

The Apothecary fought an overwhelming desire to hit him. 'Then let me try to guess,' he said, forcing a laugh.

4

'I shan't tell you, even if you're right.'

'Do I know her?' John persisted.

'Maybe, maybe not,' the Duke teased, clearly enjoying himself.

'Oh, come now, surely you can trust me to keep your secret.'

'I judge everyone by my own standards, my friend, and consequently rely on none. Anyway, why is it so important to you?' He narrowed his eyes and stared at the Apothecary suspiciously.

John could feel himself growing wretchedly uncomfortable beneath Charles's perceptive gaze and was positively relieved when somebody bumped against him, clearly not seeing him in the haze.

'Beg pardon, Sir,' said a woman's voice.

'Not at all,' he called after her retreating figure.

The Duke, seizing his opportunity to end a conversation which had clearly become tedious to him, said, 'Well, I must be on my way. Dining with Marlborough, y'know.'

John, still gazing after the female, who had by now vanished in the mist, wondering whether she looked vaguely familiar, turned back to his companion and stared him straight in the eye. 'Is Coralie Clive your intended, Sir?'

Charles Lennox guffawed. 'Oh, so that's the way of it, is it? I suspected as much. No, she ain't. But you're a brave man to chance your arm there, my friend. Miss Clive thinks more of her acting than she does of any chap alive.'

'I know,' said the Apothecary ruefully.

The Duke threw an arm round his shoulders. 'But I wish you well of her. One of these days she'll come round to realising what she's missing.'

'I sincerely hope so.'

'But until she does, may I give you a word of advice?'

'Please do.'

'Play the field, my friend. It can be a very exciting pastime.'

'I might just do that,' John answered as he gave a polite bow of farewell and made his way into the Public Office.

As always, John Fielding received his guest in his spacious salon, its curtains closing out the February fog, a fire of both coal and wood driving away any bodily chills. The Apothecary gladly took the seat opposite that of his host and accepted the glass of hot punch which Mary Ann, sitting on the floor by her uncle's feet, poured out for

5

him. She was a pretty little thing, very composed and self-sufficient, and at the age of almost thirteen starting to lose the roundness of childhood, exhibiting clear signs of the beautiful woman she would one day become. John, who had always liked her, considering her well behaved and unspoiled, gave her a warm smile.

'Oh, Mr Rawlings, I do like the way you do that,' said Mary Ann, impulsively rising to give him a kiss on the cheek.

'Do what?' asked the Apothecary, puzzled.

'Smile. Your mouth goes quite irregular when you do so. Up at one side only. It is most amusing.'

'I'm glad that I please you.' He made a small bow from where he sat.

'You are quite the prettiest man alive,' Mary Ann continued, laughing.

'Enough!' said John Fielding, though his voice was not angry. 'You are an impudent imp. Begone, before you feel the palm of my hand.'

The child laughed all the more, obviously not in the least afraid of her uncle or his empty threats. 'Very well. Good evening, gentlemen,' she said saucily, and left the room, staring at John over her retreating shoulder.

'She's growing up,' commented the Apothecary.

'A mite too quickly.' The Blind Beak sighed. 'Elizabeth says that the child is turning into a fine beauty. Is that so, or is it just an aunt's fond wish?'

'No, it's true enough. Another few years and you'll have every suitor in London knocking on your door.'

'Perish the thought. But enough of the girl. How are you, Mr Rawlings? How do you fare?'

'Well enough. Though I declare that I long for a little excitement. Do you realise, sir, that it is almost two years since that sad business at The Devil's Tavern?'

'Is it really? Good gracious!'

John nodded, even though his companion could not see him, once again endorsing the fact that everyone who knew him treated the Blind Beak exactly as if he were sighted.

'I realise that much has been happening at the Public Office, what with your many reforms, to say nothing of the criminal cases. But meanwhile I have been living quietly, compounding my simples, instructing my apprentice—'

'How is young Nicholas?' Mr Fielding interrupted.

'Never better, Sir. Recovered from the difficulties of his early years and completely restored to the full vigour of youth. Though he will always be thin, in my view.'

'And his work?'

'Excellent. He has a natural feel for the use of herbs. You did me a service on the day you introduced him to me.'

The Blind Beak nodded. 'I am very glad to hear it.' He sipped his punch and then relapsed into silence, sitting so still that he looked almost as if he had fallen asleep. But this was an old trick of his and John, observing his host closely, was certain that behind the calm façade one of the most active brains in the kingdom was working hard. Eventually the Magistrate spoke again. 'We must all keep vigilant, Mr Rawlings.'

'What do you mean, Sir?'

'I speak of the political situation. Britain has entered this war ostensibly because our Hanoverian monarchs have been linked to the Hohenzollerns of Brandenberg – the Prussians, in short – by more than one generation of dynastic ties. However, that is not the real reason at all.'

'No?' John knew better than to voice any opinion of his own at this stage of the discussion.

'No. The true motive of the British government was to go to war to stop the growing imperialism of their old enemies across the Channel. Both the French and British navies have long been vying for control of the seas, while higher powers struggle for mastery of the newly discovered territories in the East and West. In short, both sides have been spoiling for a fight and now the opportunity has been given to them.'

'I understand that. But why should that make us go on our guard?'

'Beware of spies,' answered the Magistrate succinctly. 'They'll be swarming across that small stretch of water which divides us by the boatload, mark my words. Adding to the number already here, of course.'

'Already here?' repeated the Apothecary, his incredulity obvious.

The Magistrate lowered his voice and leaned forward, gesturing to John to do likewise. 'I am perfectly serious, Mr Rawlings. I have recently had private communication with Mr Todd of the Secret

Department, whose contention it is that a powerful spy is even now working out of London.'

The Apothecary's lively eyebrows shot upwards.

'It is his belief that the man has been in town for some time, before hostilities even, and that his activities are masked by a most respectable position in society,' the Blind Beak went on.

'But why should a French spy – he is French I presume?' – Mr Fielding nodded – 'be active in peacetime?'

'Because there is much that takes place. Deployment of troops, designs of government, to name but two. It would be a spy's duty to discover as much as he could about such things and report his findings back to his masters. Of course, in contrast, there are some foreign agents residing here who do little other than take their money. Mr Todd referred to them as "the sleepers".'

'Are you saying, then, that there is a network of spies in this country?' John asked in astonishment.

The Blind Beak refilled both punch glasses as adeptly as if he could see. 'Perhaps a network would be stating the case too strongly. Shall we simply say a skein of people, probably unaware of each other's existence, who for some reason or another, maybe a straightforward lack of funds, have agreed to act as lookouts for our enemies across the Channel.'

The Apothecary drank deeply. 'I am amazed. I had no idea.'

Mr Fielding laughed his melodic laugh. 'You hinted earlier that you were bored, my friend. So here's a task for you. Find a spy and tell the Secret Department of it. But be warned, don't make a fool of yourself in the process.'

'What do you mean?'

'During the time of the Jacobite rising, a cousin of my father's believed everyone he met to be a traitor and spent his entire life reporting his friends for Jacobite activities. In the end, they got so angry with him – for these people were all quite innocent, let me hasten to assure you – they bundled him off in a hackney coach, threw a hood over his head, stripped him naked, and left him tied to the railings in Hyde Park for all the world to see.'

The Apothecary pulled a wry face. 'What a terrible fate! I have taken due warning.'

'Quite right,' said the Blind Beak, and stood up to escort his guest into dinner, led by the servant who had come to announce that the meal was served.

*   *   *

It wasn't until he was in the confined space of a sedan chair, one of the few playing for hire on such a foggy night in town, that John felt the object in the pocket of his cloak. It had not been there earlier when he had walked from his shop to Bow Street, of that he was certain. But now, drawing it out in the dimness, he saw that it was a letter and could just make out the words 'Mr John Rawlings, Apothecary of Shug Lane', written in a fine flowing hand on its exterior. Wondering when it could possibly have been thrust into its hiding place, and whether Mr Fielding knew anything about it, John closed his eyes, aware that he would make nothing of it in the dark interior of the chair and that he must wait until he got home.

He lived in Nassau Street, in the parish of St Ann's, Soho, sharing a home with his adopted father, Sir Gabriel Kent and, in the custom of the time, his apprentice, Nicholas Dawkins, a boy of exciting ancestry who claimed descent from a member of the court of Tsar Peter the Great, and who had consequently earned himself the nickname of the Muscovite. This entirely male household was strengthened even further by a complement of male servants.

'A maid could never protect her virtue in such surroundings,' Sir Gabriel had announced firmly, though from whom he had not specified.

However, there was nothing austere or staid about either the house or its occupants, Sir Gabriel himself being considered one of the finest-looking men in town and his son a positive bird of paradise in his love of high fashion. Indeed, clothes were the Apothecary's weakness, his tailor's bills accounting for nearly all his spending money. Yet, other than for this foible, he was an industrious young man who worked as hard as any at his chosen profession, and accusations of being empty-headed were never made against John Rawlings by those who knew him well.

Picking his way through the fog, the linkman, carrying his torch of pitch and tow and walking just ahead of the chair and its two sturdy porters, turned into Gerrard Street and from there into Nassau Street itself, where the chairmen set down their burden outside number two.

Paying all three of them off, John hurried within, anxious to see the letter and learn, perhaps, how it had so mysteriously arrived in his pocket. But he was forestalled on his way to the small salon.

9

The door to Sir Gabriel's library opened and Nicholas Dawkins, his thin face animated, appeared in the entrance.

'Ah, I thought I heard your footsteps, Sir. I have something of interest to impart to you.'

'It would seem you have a secret admirer, John,' called Sir Gabriel's voice from inside the room.

Drawing the letter from his cloak, which he handed to the waiting footman, the Apothecary resigned himself to reading it later, and followed Nicholas into the library.

A bright fire, its flames leaping into the chimney, glowed hot in the grate and before it, on a card table, stood a chessboard. The Master's father and the young apprentice had obviously been locked in a battle of wits when they had been interrupted by John's return.

'Indeed, my dear,' his father continued, 'it appears you have made such an impact on the poor woman that she called at your shop, incognito of course, in order to speak with you.'

'That's right, Sir,' added Nicholas enthusiastically. 'She did do so.'

John stood looking at them, smiling at their little caprice, glad, as always, to be home with the man who had brought him up since he had been a child begging on the streets of London, and with the apprentice whom John had rescued from a similar fate.

Sir Gabriel waved a long, thin hand, a dark, almost black, sapphire ring glittering as he did so. 'Help yourself to some port, my boy. I find it a very fine vintage and would like your opinion of it.'

'Thank you,' said the Apothecary, and, having poured some of the deep red liquid into a crystal glass, took a seat by the fire.

Tonight his father was déshabillé, clad in a black velvet nightrail and a white satin turban, a black brooch completing the somewhat awesome ensemble. For Sir Gabriel was famed throughout town for his individual taste in clothing, always wearing that particular colour combination, except on festive occasions when he changed the theme to black and silver. Even his jewellery reflected Sir Gabriel's taste for the stark, though lately he had been seen sporting a dark purple amethyst on his fob chain, the furthest he had ever gone to introducing colour into his attire. Though this evening he wore no wig, John's father usually stepped forth in an old-fashioned high storey, with long curls flowing over his shoulders. Indeed, if one mentioned the words bag wig in Sir Gabriel's presence, he would visibly pale and talk of modern monstrosities. Yet despite his individual and decidedly eccentric style, Sir Gabriel Kent was considered one of the most fashionable men alive, and there was many a younger man who regarded him with a jealous eye.

In contrast, Nicholas Dawkins wore the sensible garb of an apprentice, even though John, his Master, would have allowed him some leeway in this matter when it came to the hours of relaxation. But the young man would have none of it, still grateful that the Apothecary had granted him indentures when once Nicholas had stolen in order to feed himself. When he had signed his agreement with John Rawlings, in which Nicholas had promised not to fornicate, marry or run away, to behave with propriety at all times and never visit a brothel, he had taken the matter very seriously. As far as the Muscovite was concerned, even though he was a zestful nineteen, he had to discipline himself into accepting the rules of his position, despite the fact that as he walked around London on his Master's business, young maidens cast warm glances at his black hair and handsome russet eyes. Indeed, sometimes Nicholas felt more than inclined to wink back at one of them and take the consequences of breaking his vow. Now, though, he stood respectfully behind his chair, waiting to be spoken to, those kind of thoughts a million miles away.

John turned to him. 'So what's all this about a woman visiting my shop?'

Nicholas's eyes glistened with the joy of telling his story. 'Well, Sir, she came in about half an hour after you had left for Bow Street. She asked for you but I told her that you were dining with Mr Fielding and—'

'Did you know her?' the Apothecary interrupted.

'She wore a mask,' put in Sir Gabriel, steepling his fingers and smiling meaningfully.

'Serafina!' John exclaimed. 'Playing a game with me, no doubt.'

'But, Sir, it *wasn't* the Comtesse de Vignolles,' Nicholas put in. 'I would know her anywhere. This was a stranger, no one I had ever clapped eyes on before.'

'I see. So what did she do when you told her I had gone?'

'Hurried away and said she would catch you up. I had already informed her that you intended to go to the court first, so she said she might join you there.'

11

'And then?'

'That was the last I saw of her.'

Sir Gabriel interjected, 'What age was this woman, Nicholas? Could you tell?'

The Muscovite's light brown eyes gleamed once more. 'Oh, yes. I observed her as closely as I could, Sir Gabriel. Beneath the hood of her cloak I would say that the lady's hair glistened silver, whilst on that part of her face visible beneath her domino, I observed white enamel. Therefore, unless she was wearing a wig, I would say she was in her fifties, possibly more.'

'An older admirer then,' commented John drily. He sat silently for a moment, deep in thought, then he said, 'By God, I do believe that she *did* catch up with me after all.'

Sir Gabriel raised a fine eyebrow. 'What do you mean, my son?'

'Simply, that I found this letter in my cloak whilst travelling back from Bow Street.' He raised the paper aloft from the arm of his chair. 'I thought at first it was a jest of Mr Fielding's but I remember now that a woman bumped against me in the fog. She must have slipped the letter into my pocket as she did so.'

'There's only one way to find out for sure, Sir,' answered Nicholas, brimming with excitement.

John broke the seal and read aloud.

My dear Mr Rawlings,

Forgive me for this Unorthodox way of contacting You. I had Hoped to see you in your Shop but none the less had prepared this Note lest you be unavailable. I have Travelled to London in the Hope that we could talk, but now that you must Read my Words I hardly know what to Say to you. But yet I am Compelled to come to the Point. The Fact of the matter is, my very dear Sir, that I Fear my Life to be under Threat. Somebody is trying to Poison me, I feel sure of it. Yet, when I look Back on my Past I can quite Understand why in view of the Hatred I have Engendered. Oh, my dear Friend, I beg you, if you value an old Acquaintanceship, to help me. In short, I Implore you to come here and Advise me what to do. I sign Myself only as One to whom you once were more than Kind.

A Voice from the Past, Petronilla's Platt, Winchelsea, Sussex. (A few miles west of the ancient Town of Rye.)

There was silence in Sir Gabriel's library, broken only by the distant murmur of the servants' voices from below stairs.

'Well, well,' said John's father thoughtfully. 'What an intriguing situation. Will you go?'

The Apothecary smiled crookedly. 'Only this evening I was complaining to Mr Fielding that I had had no excitement since that unfortunate affair in The Devil's Tavern. It would seem that fate overheard me.'

'Do you want me to take a letter to Master Gerard tonight?' asked Nicholas eagerly, quite enjoying those times in the shop when his master was absent and he, in company with an elderly apothecary who helped out when John was not present, ran the place.

John's smile broadened. 'Can't wait to see the back of me, is that it?'

The Muscovite, who did not truly relish being teased, flushed. 'No, Sir. I like having added responsibility, it's true. But I miss your company when you are away.'

'A grand compliment,' remarked Sir Gabriel, sipping his port.

The Apothecary nodded. 'Which I much appreciate. Anyway, don't let us disturb the old fellow now. If I leave the day after tomorrow we can contact him in the morning.'

'I suppose it doesn't occur to you,' asked his father, only half joking, 'that you might be walking straight into a trap?'

John looked at him sharply. 'What makes you say that?'

'If it was somebody's aim to lure you to Winchelsea for a purpose best known to themselves, they couldn't have succeeded better. After all, who is this Voice from the Past? And what guarantee do you have that it is a woman? The female who delivered the letter might merely have been a decoy.'

'Would you like me to go with you, Sir?' asked Nicholas keenly.

'Not you, nor anyone else either,' the Apothecary answered, giving his father a meaningful look.

Sir Gabriel inclined his head. 'I bow to your bravado, John. I am sure that you know what you are doing.'

'I most certainly do,' the Apothecary answered firmly, and poured himself another glass of port, wishing that he actually felt as assured as he appeared.

Chapter Two

Having received an immediate reply from Master Gerard that he would willingly assist his fellow apothecary while he took leave of absence, John sent one of his father's footmen to The Borough by hackney coach to enquire as to the best way to travel to Winchelsea, that ancient town founded in 1288, one of the famous Cinque Ports. It was from The Borough that stagecoaches and post chaises, commonly known as Flying Coaches because of their ability to travel sixty miles in one day, set out for Kent, Sussex, Surrey and Hampshire, plying for hire from the old inns of Southwark. Other destinations were catered for from various hostelries situated throughout town, the famously regular York service leaving from The Black Swan on Holbourn Hill. Winchelsea itself was not directly served, however, the nearest point of disembarkation being Hastings.

'The carrier said to go there and hire another vehicle, Sir,' John was informed.

'I see. So at what time do the Hastings coaches depart?'

'The stage leaves at midnight and sounds mighty uncomfortable, Master John, travelling most of the hours of darkness as it does. Though there's another service that leaves at midday and puts up at Lamberhurst overnight. However, the flying coaches leave at six in the morning and guarantee to get you to Hastings that same day, stopping at Sevenoaks for comfort and a horse change and at Lamberhurst for dinner. They mostly leave from The White Hart.'

'Then I'll spend the night there. I would prefer that to rising at some ungodly hour and making my way across London.'

Having so decided, the Apothecary dined early with Sir Gabriel, leaving his apprentice to close the shop for the night, packed a large valise with a goodly selection of clothes, travelling light being quite foreign to his nature, then put some herbs specifically for use in the treatment of poisons into his medicine bag. This done, John kissed his father on the cheek and stepped into the hackney coach that had been hailed from Gerrard Street, to set off with a certain amount of nervous excitement on his journey to meet the Voice from the Past.

Like many of the other old inns of the seventeenth century that still stood intact, The White Hart was a galleried building constructed round a cobbled courtyard in which coaches gathered whilst awaiting or discharging their passengers. Below the galleries were stables for the horses, troughs and bales of straw, and even a few chickens scratching about, half-heartedly pecking for seeds. There was also dung, around which John picked his way carefully in the poor illumination thrown by the flickering lanterns hung round the quadrangle. Inside, however, The White Hart was resplendent with light, bustle and noise, typical of a place at which journeys begin and end.

Having booked a room on the first floor with a window overlooking the courtyard, John, who had intended to retire early, found himself unable to resist the jolly hubbub coming from the parlour and put his head round the door to see what was going on. Instantly, smoke from both pipes and fireplace assailed his nostrils, while his eyes were dazzled by the sparkle of flames and the glow of candles, to say nothing of the brilliant emerald green of the coat worn by the man who was at the very centre of the commotion. For, with a raised glass in his hand and a broad grin on his rubicund features, a great lummox of a fellow, affability flowing from his every pore, was holding forth.

'So I says to this woman, "Ma'am, t'was not I who farted thus but mine horse . . ."'

There was a howl of hysterical laughter, much encouraged by the fact that a great pitcher of wine was being passed round.

'So then she says to me, neat as you please, "Nay, Sir, t'was neither of you – and I should know for sure." I should know for sure! Have you ever heard the like?'

He drained his glass, slapped his thigh, and wiped his eyes with a spotted handkerchief in what appeared to be one continuous movement. John found himself laughing with the rest, not at the joke, which seemed both meaningless and crude, unless he had missed some salient point, but at the sheer joviality of this hearty hulk. Seeing the Apothecary smiling, the other man walked forward, hand outstretched.

'Ffloote, Sir,' he announced. 'Two Fs.'

'Rawlings,' John replied. 'One R.'

16

Ffloote stared at him blankly for a second, then appeared to have a seizure. 'One R! Oh, I like that, so I do. You're a wit, Sir. A regular wit.' He bent double, guffawing.

The Apothecary, grinning broadly by now, despite the stupidity of the conversation, shook the offered fingers, the smallest of which was the size of a full-grown carrot. 'It is a great pleasure to meet you, Sir.'

'All mine, all mine,' Ffloote answered, recovering a little. 'Come, let me buy you a bottle of wine.'

'I think perhaps just a glass will do. I'm travelling early tomorrow so must try to avoid a thick head.'

'Nonsense,' replied the other. 'I'm off at first light myself. But I've never let that deter me from my pleasures. We only live once, you know. Women and wine, my life employ.' He sang a snatch from *The Beggar's Opera*.

John laughed despite his misgivings. 'I can't promise you that I will finish it.'

'That's of no consequence, my friend. I am here to help you,' Ffloote answered, and winked a little dark eye, much obscured by the many bags and pouches in which it lay concealed.

Despite the general awfulness of the fellow, the Apothecary found it impossible to do anything but warm to him. He was so vulgar, such an archetype of the sort always to be met in coaching inns or places of assembly, particularly when one had thought of spending a quiet evening alone, that Ffloote seemed almost unreal, a caricature of himself. As a serving girl came through the door, the Apothecary silently wagered that his new companion would slap her heartily on the rear and, sure enough, Ffloote, with a great bawl of laughter, did just that. The girl, to her credit, did no more than pout and walk away, resisting the temptation to empty the pitcher of wine she was carrying clean over her assailant's head.

'Sweetmeat,' Ffloote called after her jocundly, but the girl had moved out of earshot and John was able to distract his attention by asking a question.

'Are you journeying far, Sir?'

'Not really. The Sussex coast, you know. I live in Winchelsea. I'm known locally as the Squire. Ha ha!'

He erupted into pointless laughter once more, his wine-laden breath puffing directly into John's face. But the Apothecary was too astonished to notice, staring at his companion open-mouthed.

17

'Winchelsea did you say?'

'Yes. Why so surprised?'

John recovered himself. 'Because, as chance would have it, I am travelling there myself. To a house called Petronilla's Platt. Do you know it?'

'In the High Street, you mean? Yes, I most certainly do. Recently rebuilt, though there's been a cottage on that site for centuries.'

'It may sound strange but I have no idea of the identity of my hostess. Are you acquainted with her?'

For the first time since John had met him, Ffloote stopped smiling and sighed explosively. 'Rather an odd woman actually. Can't say I've had much to do with her. I believe she was left the place by a cousin. She's only been there a year.'

John felt a prickle of excitement. 'Do you know her name by any chance?'

Ffloote frowned, his florid face creasing till his eyes vanished almost entirely. 'Let me see now. Roe, Roach, something of that order. My wife would know. But she ain't here, is she?' He nudged the Apothecary violently, then laughed again, bringing John to the conclusion that the man had the most economical sense of humour he had ever come across. Then, just as suddenly, Ffloote's face took on a foxy expression, signalling quite clearly that he wanted to find something out.

'Why d'ye ask?' he said. 'Ain't you been advised of the lady's details? Bit rum when you're going to call on her, what.'

John, who had been half expecting this, answered glibly, 'She's a distant relative of a friend of mine, and he refers to her simply as Aunt Crotchety, because of her disposition I presume. Anyway, to cut a long story short, I've been asked to attend her in my professional capacity. I'm an apothecary and the lady has requested a decoction of herbs to settle her colic.'

'Long way to go just for that,' Ffloote answered, his tiny eye beady.

John who had over the past few years developed a range of expressions to suit most occasions, contrived to look honest and slightly sheepish all in one. 'Fact of the matter is I wanted to get out of town for a while.' He waved a hand in the air. 'Reasons of my own. So to visit Aunt Crotchety was a good excuse to let the dust settle.'

'Let the dust settle!' Ffloote roared, his face convulsed with mirth once more. 'I see you're a man of the world, my dear Sir. To say nothing of a young rip. Glad to make your acquaintance, so I am. Name in full is Sir Ambrose, plus the last part. You must call during your visit. Wife would be delighted to meet you. Now *she* suffers enormously with her health. A martyr to the headache, you know, is poor little Faith. Perhaps you could help her, Mr Rawlings. Didn't catch your first name.'

'John, Sir.' The Apothecary produced a card and placed it in Sir Ambrose's enormous fingers. 'I will certainly do what I can to assist.'

'Well said, well said,' Ffloote replied. 'I hope I'll have the pleasure of travelling with you tomorrow. The post chaise leaves at six. The carriers know me of old and always keep me a place, so I usually look round for three others with whom to share the cost.'

Having little option but to agree, John forced a smile, hoping as he did so that Sir Ambrose was the type who fell asleep as soon as the wheels started turning. 'I'd be delighted,' he said half-heartedly.

'Good fellow. Have another drink. I intend to sit up all night. Waste of time going to bed. I can sleep on the journey.'

The Apothecary's spirits rose again. 'Thank you very much but I really must refuse,' he said politely. 'I've had rather a hard day. So if you will forgive me . . .'

Ffloote grinned widely, displaying a set of minute teeth. 'No stamina, you young people,' he said waggishly. 'That's the trouble with the youth of today. Now I was brought up to drink and gamble all night and it never did me any harm.' He thumped his chest, producing a spluttering cough. 'Fit as a fiddle, me.'

John looked apologetic. 'I am sorry to disappoint but the fact remains that I need my sleep. I shall see you tomorrow at six.'

'Don't be late,' warned Sir Ambrose. 'The coach leaves dead on time. They've a fierce reputation for speed and the postillions wait for no one.'

'I'll remember,' said the Apothecary, and, giving a formal bow, thankfully left the room.

It started to rain during the night, indeed a veritable torrent of water fell out of the sky, waking the Apothecary and sending him to the window to look out on the courtyard, which now resembled a lake, the drains being quite insufficient to deal with the flood. The lights from the hanging lanterns, reflected in the water, looked like little yellow stars that had fallen out of the sky, brought down by the downpour, while all the coaches had drawn up under the galleries for shelter. John could dimly make out the shapes of the coachmen preparing to leave, their hats pulled firmly down, and pitied the intrepid souls who would shortly have to set out, braving the weather as well as all the other perils of the road.

John slept only fitfully after that, and at five o'clock a pallid girl, yawning and looking totally exhausted, brought him a jug of hot water for his shave, shouting at him as she departed that breakfast was below if he was prepared to pay for it. Being a member of that school of thought who believed no day should commence without a hearty meal, the Apothecary prepared himself at speed and went downstairs to tuck into eggs and sides of ham and pickled herrings. Creeping cautiously into the dining parlour, John was greatly relieved to see that Sir Ambrose Ffloote was not present, presumably having finally fallen asleep where he sat.

And indeed his first glimpse of the Squire endorsed this theory. Bleary-eyed and unshaven, his wig askew, Sir Ambrose staggered through the deluge and into the courtyard, heading purposefully towards the post chaise in which John had already secured himself a place.

He stuck his head through the window, water dripping from the brim of his hat and running down his nose. 'Ah, you're here, my young friend. With whom are we travelling? Got to keep the cost down if we can.'

'Nobody's arrived as yet,' the Apothecary answered. But even as he spoke, a small neat figure, spruce of appearance and smartly turned out, the very antithesis of Sir Ambrose, stepped from a hackney coach and advanced towards the post chaise. He glanced briefly at the notice: 'For The Safe and Reliable Conveyance of Travellers, the Hastings Fast Coach. Dines at Lamberhurst. Horses changed, Bromley and Sevenoaks. Fare 9d a mile.'

'Have you a seat left?' the newcomer asked one of the two postillions, who were huddling beneath the galleries, large cloaks and oilskins over their green jackets.

'Two places still available, Sir.'

Sir Ambrose heaved himself aloft. 'I want to sit at the back where I can snooze. Best take it before that fellow gets his damned buttocks on it.'

No chance of that, thought John, but said nothing.

A second later the stranger had his foot on the step and was climbing in, glancing round the coach's interior as he did so.

'Good morning, gentlemen,' he said politely, removing his hat. 'It seems I am to have the pleasure of travelling with you.'

'Sir Ambrose Ffloote,' the Squire announced ungraciously.

'John Rawlings,' said the Apothecary, making as best a bow as he could in the cramped conditions.

'Florence Hensey,' replied the other, returning the salute.

'Eh?' exclaimed Ffloote, opening one eye.

'Florence Hensey, Sir.'

The Squire guffawed earsplittingly. 'Florence, did you say? I always thought that to be a woman's name. Damme, so I did.'

John squirmed as the newcomer said patiently, 'Alas, it is a family tradition, Sir. The second child, be it male or female, is always called Florence. It has been a subject of much embarrassment during my lifetime.'

'Sounds foreign to me,' continued Sir Ambrose unrelentingly.

'My grandmother was Italian,' Hensey continued.

'Oh, well, that explains it,' the Squire answered, and firmly shut his eyes, thus indicating that he had no further wish to converse.

A postillion tapped on the window. 'Begging your pardon, gentlemen, but we must set off punctual if we're to make any speed in these bad conditions. Are you willing to share the fare three ways? Unless another passenger comes in the next few minutes, we've no choice but to go.'

'Damned expense,' muttered Sir Ambrose, without raising his lids.

'It suits me well enough,' said Florence Hensey courteously.

'I would rather leave on time,' answered John.

'Then we're off,' stated the man. 'Maybe we'll pick someone up at one of the stages. All right, Will,' he called to his fellow rider, who mounted one of the second pair in the four-horse team.

John stared through the large front observation window, Mr Hensey sitting beside him, thinking how the rain had driven all the fun out of the occasion. For normally at one of the coaching inns each departure was a small excitement. Friends, come to bid farewell to loved ones, would weep and wave handkerchiefs; horses would stamp and snort and try to lift the hostlers off the ground, stoutly resisting their every effort to turn out the team. Pedlars would fall over one another in their last-minute attempts to sell wares for the journey. And all the vagabonds of town would come to join the general pandemonium and see if there was a pocket to pick while they were about it. But today nobody stirred and the Apothecary felt a sense of anticlimax as the flying coach, its high back wheels whirling, splashed over the courtyard cobblestones on the start of its journey to the old seaside town of Hastings.

'Quite monstrous weather,' said Mr Hensey, raising his voice above the sound of Sir Ambrose's snores, an accompaniment that had begun the very second they started to move.

'I was just thinking the same.'

'I doubt we shall complete the journey in the usual time.'

'Probably not. I think I shall spend the night in Hastings if we are late, then travel to Winchelsea tomorrow morning.'

'May I help you in recommending an inn?'

'You know Hastings well then, Mr Hensey?'

'Yes, I do, very. And it's doctor, actually. Allow me to present myself.'

Fishing in an inner pocket, John's travelling companion produced a card and handed it to him. The Apothecary, looking at it with interest, read 'Florence Hensey, Doctor of Physick, 16 Liquorpond Road, Holbourn'.

'This is a happy coincidence,' he said, producing his own card, 'for I am an apothecary.'

Dr Hensey took it, read it, then extended his hand. 'A pleasure to meet you, my very dear Sir. The miles will fly by indeed. Normally I tend to remain quiet on a journey lest my fellow passengers regale me with tales of their illnesses.'

John smiled. 'I know exactly what you mean. And I simply cannot recall the number of times I have been called upon to deal with travel sickness.'

'I, too,' answered the doctor, his eyes gleaming with the pleasure of exchanging banter with a fellow practitioner. 'Tell me, what do you prescribe?'

'Peppermint oil in a little sugared water. And you?'

'The same. Though occasionally slippery elm, depending on the amount of flatulence involved.'

'A thing not to be recommended in the close confines of a flying coach,' said the Apothecary, grinning.

Dr Hensey wrinkled his nose. 'I shall never forget travelling to York with an old lady who suffered from uncontrollable wind. I swear to you, Mr Rawlings, her fellow passengers were fit to choke, for the weather was too inclement to permit ventilation. Do you know, Sir, it was almost a relief when a highwayman pulled us up and turned everybody out.'

John smiled, not believing a word of it but enjoying the story, and in this light-hearted manner the time passed quickly. As the post chaise slowed down and he looked at his watch, the Apothecary saw that two hours had passed, slightly longer than the postillions had hoped for, and they were drawing to a halt at The King's Arms in Bromley in order to change horses. Sir Ambrose woke instantly and lumbered out, presumably in search of a bog house. John and Florence, more decorous about their requirements, were for all that glad of a stop. Having answered nature's call, they had just time to down some ale in The Ram, one of the rooms put aside for travellers, having hurried in there after hearing roars of laughter coming from The Union, another such room. Thus, having successfully avoided Sir Ambrose, the Apothecary and the doctor made their way back to their conveyance, only to stop short and stand staring, despite the rain.

'They've found another passenger and she's in my seat!' John exclaimed.

'I'm sure she'll move when it's explained to her,' Dr Hensey answered, then suddenly looked knowing. 'Though, on second thoughts, perhaps I should join Sir Ambrose and leave my place for you. I take it you're not a married man.'

'She may be a married lady,' the Apothecary answered, and laughed, reading the doctor's mind.

'Well, whatever, she's a fine-looking woman.'

'She most certainly is.'

Suddenly aware that she was being scrutinised, the newcomer turned and gazed straight at the two men who stood surveying her, water pouring from their headgear, making them look utterly ridiculous. Then she smiled and inclined her head in a bow, the feathers on her hat sweeping down as she did so.

'Gracious me,' said the doctor.

John did not speak, anxious to get closer and see if the stranger was really as lovely as she appeared to be through the glass of the window. Stepping to the door, he pulled the handle down and allowed Dr Hensey to precede him into the carriage.

The man of medicine handled the situation with great aplomb.

23

'Madam.' He bowed in the doorway. 'Pray forgive me while I push past you to take my place in the back. It is my companion, Mr Rawlings, who is fortunate enough to be sitting next to you.'

She turned to the doctor. 'I do hope I have not taken anyone's position.'

'Not at all,' Florence answered with a smile, and went to the rear seat, a far inferior place, for it faced the back of the front seat, which was positioned so that its two occupants could look out of the large fore window, quite a private way of travelling and certainly not one aimed at general conversation.

The woman looked straight at John. 'I must apologise for causing a disturbance. The fact of the matter is that I was travelling on a stage coach that cast a wheel late last night. I decided to stay here and this morning pick up what transport I could to Hastings.'

Wonderful eyes with flecks of green and brown in them, clear as a brook and almost transparent, were staring into his, and John became tremendously aware of a small heart-shaped face, hair the rich bright shade of amber, and finely curved eyebrows sweeping up over eyelids pale as moonstones. Stuck in the doorway as he was, the Apothecary made a low bow and hit his head on the jamb as he straightened up. The girl smiled and held out her hand.

'Henrietta Tireman.'

John fought for dignity. 'John Rawlings, Madam.' He kissed the outstretched fingers, then was forced to sit down hurriedly by the arrival of the Squire, who pushed him unceremoniously from the rear. Sir Ambrose hurled himself within, then stopped and gaped at the newcomer.

'Well, I'll be damned. If it ain't Henrietta. What are you doing here, my dear?'

'Why, Sir Ambrose. What a surprise,' Miss Tireman replied, her voice just the slightest bit clipped. 'I have been visiting an aunt in town and was to have returned home last night had there not been an accident with the stagecoach.'

John opened his mouth to offer the Squire his seat, since he and the lady were acquainted, but a sudden pressure from Miss Tireman's leg, hardly proper but for all that very pleasant, made the Apothecary shoot her a covert glance. A slight roll of her eye told him everything, so he remained studiously silent.

24

'Stagecoach's loss, our gain,' answered Sir Ambrose, leering a little.

'Indeed,' called Dr Hensey from the back. 'It seems we two must sit together, Sir. I shall probably join you in a snooze.'

'You may do as you please,' answered the Squire ungraciously. He took his seat.

'Thank you,' breathed Miss Tireman as the postillions cracked their whips and the new team of horses headed off into deepest Kent.

'Not your ideal travelling companion, I take it?' asked John, the clatter of the wheels drowning the sound of his voice.

'I find the man has all the charm of a haystack,' came the forthright reply. 'We are neighbours, alas. Part of the social life of Winchelsea, such as it is. I come across him at every gathering and am running out of excuses to escape the amorous advances of the old wretch.'

John stared at her. 'Do *you* live there as well?'

Henrietta's crystal eyes once more looked directly into his. 'Yes. Why do you ask?'

'Because I am also on my way to Winchelsea.'

'What a strange coincidence. Who are you going to see?'

'That's just the point, I'm not really sure.'

She gazed at him blankly and suddenly, and for no reason, John found himself recounting the whole story of the woman who had bumped into him in the fog, and how he had answered the summons to help the Voice from the Past.

Henrietta Tireman's attractive lips parted slightly, vividly reminding John of a child listening to a fairy tale.

'How thrilling!' she said eventually. 'I would never have thought Mrs Rose to have had an exciting history. Particularly one that involved a man as young as yourself.'

'Mrs Rose?' the Apothecary repeated, ignoring the innuendo. 'Do you know her?'

'You said the mystery woman lived in Petronilla's Platt, didn't you?' John nodded his head. 'Well, then it must be her. She comes to church every Sunday and is one of my father's parishioners. He is the Reverend Richard Tireman, Rector of St Thomas the Martyr, by the way.'

'I look forward to meeting him. So what does this Mrs Rose look like?'

'The name clearly means nothing to you?'

'No, it doesn't. The Voice from the Past must be using a pseudonym.'

'Better and better!'

Henrietta was looking more like a delicious child with every passing moment, and John found himself most attracted, not only because of her looks but also her enthusiasm.

'Well, she's no young beauty, that's for sure. In fact I would imagine she has seen fifty at the very least. And yet there *is* a beauty about her, a kind of faded charm, like a sampler that has been left too long in the sun.'

A thought pierced the Apothecary's mind. 'Is her hair silver and does she wear face enamel? My apprentice described such a woman visiting my shop.'

'Yes, that's her. So you *do* know who it is.'

'I think perhaps I might.'

'Well that,' said Miss Tireman, 'is a very satisfactory conclusion.'

The weather worsened as they proceeded, for now not only was there a downpour but a howling wind to hamper the horses further. Staring through the window at the miserably hunched postillions, whose very backs spoke volumes about their extreme discomfort, John's heart went out to them, and he determined to speak to his fellow passengers about a good tip when they finally reached their destination.

The flying coach had arrived at Sevenoaks, where there had been another change of horses, almost an hour later than planned, still before them another seventeen miles and a full three hours' run to the village of Lamberhurst, where they were scheduled to dine. Sir Ambrose had wanted to stop for refreshments but had been outvoted by his fellow passengers, a fact which had left him much disgruntled and determined to grumble throughout the next leg of the journey.

'Damned if I'll see my bed tonight. What is the world coming to? They shouldn't advertise as flying coaches if they go slow as the common stage.'

'Come now, Sir Ambrose,' Dr Hensey had said soothingly. 'Nobody can control the weather. The poor devils are going as fast as they can without tipping us into the ditch. Have a little patience, I beg you.'

26

'Patience be blowed! I expect service for my money. Besides, my man Withers is meeting me at The Swan in Hastings with the carriage at half past six.'

'Well, he can wait surely.'

'Of course he can,' put in Miss Tireman firmly. 'He's a very patient soul. He has to be working for him,' she added in an undertone. In her normal voice, she said, 'In that case may I crave a ride with you, Sir Ambrose? I'm afraid Papa needed our conveyance for parish visits. He told me to hire a man and a trap when I got to Hastings.'

From the back, Sir Ambrose could be heard taking snuff, then sneezing. 'Of course you can join me, my dear. It would be a pleasure,' he said through the folds of his handkerchief.

'And I trust you will extend the same kindness to Mr Rawlings. He too is bound for Winchelsea.'

There was a harrumphing sound which the resourceful Miss Tireman took to be an affirmative answer. 'Oh, thank you,' she gushed, nudging John in the ribs, another unladylike gesture but one which he enjoyed enormously. In fact, he thought, it was most delightful sitting next to her in the gloom like this, smelling her perfume and seeing her enchanting profile etched against the glow of the carriage lamps, lit early because of the wretchedness of the day. And then, unbidden, into the Apothecary's mind came a picture of Coralie Clive's dark beauty, of the flash of her emerald green eyes, and he sighed that even though they hardly saw one another, the actress should still have the power to haunt him.

'Not much further,' said Henrietta.

'We're very late though.'

'We should have arrived to dine at just after one o'clock. Now it's nearly three. However, I'm more concerned with my stomach than with the hour. I'm simply longing for something to eat. It seems a very long time since breakfast.'

'It does indeed,' answered John with feeling.

Half an hour later they rattled over the cobbles of The Chequers, an inn famous for welcoming travellers since the 1400s, set in the remote Kentish village of Lamberhurst. With great relief, the party descended from their carriage and made for the dining parlour, where all of them, including Miss Tireman, partook of a hearty repast. And it was there, just as the Squire was downing port as if it were the last drink he would ever have in his mortal life, the Apothecary and the doctor joining him, though somewhat more abstemiously, that news of further mishaps on the road reached their ears. One of the postillions, having asked permission to join them at their table, informed them that trees had been blown down all along the route and that he was forced to take a diversion through Tenterden.

'And how do you know this?' asked Dr Hensey.

'The coachmen and postillions eat together in their special parlour, Sir. The man on the up journey, as it were, has just told me he has had to go miles out of his way.'

'This is very inconvenient. I have to see a patient in Hastings tomorrow.'

'An appointment you'll keep, Sir. If we work our way over the Romney Marsh to Winchelsea, we can drop the other passengers off then creep round the coast road to Hastings.'

'But whatever time will we get there, man?'

'That I can't guarantee, Sir. But get there you will.'

'And what about my man Withers?' asked Sir Ambrose, genial again after downing port.

'We can give him a message when we drop off the doctor.'

The Squire rubbed his hands. 'Well, we may see our beds tonight after all.'

Henrietta gave a little shiver. 'It will be dark soon.'

John turned to her. 'Does that worry you?'

'Not really. It's just that I don't relish the thought of driving over the Marsh in the blackness. It's a bleak, desolate place at the best of times.' She turned to the postillion. 'Is there no other way?'

'I'm afraid not, Miss. It's the Marsh or nothing. The other road is impassable. I couldn't risk the horses taking a tumble over some fallen tree trunk, d'ye see.'

'Yes, I do. Very well, then.' She got to her feet. 'Gentlemen, if you will excuse me. I'll go and refresh myself for the rest of the journey.'

'Lovely girl,' said Sir Ambrose, watching Miss Tireman's departing back. 'I've known her since she was a child. Not so lovely as her sister Rosalind, mark you. Now she really is a sensational beauty. And got herself a great match as a result.'

'Really?' John was only half listening, still enchanted by the recent presence of Henrietta.

'Yes, damme. Daughter of a country parson marrying the Marquis of Rye. Have you ever heard the like?' He did not wait for an answer, raising his glass on high. 'Well, here's to the rest of the journey, my friends. May we cross the marshland without mishap.'

'I'll drink to that,' said Dr Hensey, mopping his brow anxiously.

The Apothecary returned to earth. 'So will I. To the Romney Marsh.'

'And all its mysteries,' added the Squire with a chuckle, and drew off the remains of his glass.

Chapter Three

They left The Chequers in a sea of spray, and plunged into the early dusk created by the lowering cloud cover. Staring through the window, John saw that the rain was finally beginning to ease off and the wind die down, so that now the wayside trees no longer bent and groaned over the road but stood straight and somehow menacingly still. Mist began to rise from the fields and swirl eerily about. It was the sort of evening that would make even the most foolhardy think twice about going out, and the superstitious firmly lock their doors and remain within.

'Hobgoblin time,' said Henrietta Tireman.

John looked at her. The outrageously feathered hat and the charming elfin face beneath looked vulnerable in the coach's dimly lit interior, and it was as much as he could do not to take her small gloved hand and hold it in his.

'Surely you don't believe in such things,' he answered.

'No, of course not. Not during the hours of daylight, anyway. But on several occasions when I have been returning home late, I have crossed the Romney Marsh after nightfall and felt afraid of things unseen.'

'And of things seen too, I should imagine. Wasn't the place rife with smugglers at one time?'

'Very much so. They used to export sheep or fleeces, quite illegally of course, and bring back French brandy, tea, silks, all sorts of things. The whole black trade had been going on for years.'

John looked thoughtful. 'We're both speaking in the past tense. So I presume the trials and executions of seven years ago really *did* put a stop to smuggling for good and all. Or am I being naïf?'

Henrietta gave him a smile like quicksilver. 'My dear Mr Rawlings, one will never put a stop to anything in which there lies a profit. Indeed, for a while, relative peace and calm descended but now I have heard that the past tense has yet again become the present. A certain Dick Jarvis, bastard son of the infamous Kit, alias Gabriel Tompkins, leader of the Mayfield Gang and involved in God knows what other mischief to boot, has returned to emulate his scoundrelly sire and is working the Marsh once more.'

John laughed aloud at her turn of phrase. 'Is he, by God! Well, let's hope we don't run into him.'

Henrietta laughed too, though not quite so heartily. 'I believe that despite his many other faults, Dick's father was not known for his cruelty. Let us hope his son takes after him.'

'But surely the outbreak of war will put a stop to the fellow's schemes. He's not going to find it so easy to get his wool over to France with the French and English navies baring their teeth at one another across the Channel.'

'On the contrary, I expect his trade will increase.'

'Why do you say that?' asked John, astonished.

'Because he will be seen as a useful form of transport for both spies and their secret correspondence. If letters go direct there is no fear of them being intercepted.'

The Apothecary frowned. 'That's the second time this week that someone has mentioned spies to me.'

'No doubt you'll hear the word frequently from now on. In times of hostility all the secret agents come crawling out of the woodwork, do they not?'

'Yes, I suppose you're right.'

John and Henrietta sat in silence for a moment, thinking about the times that lay ahead, wondering how and when the savagery of war would end. And thus with their thoughts miles away were startled when the postillion riding the second team turned and tapped on the window with his whip.

'Are you gentlemen armed?' he called through the glass.

'I am,' John answered, 'but I don't know about the others.'

He moved in his seat, pulling back the curtain which separated the two places, drawn earlier by the Squire when he decided to have yet another doze and consequently cutting Dr Hensey off from his other companions.

'Are you both armed?' he called into the dimness.

His fellow travellers woke up abruptly, the doctor giving a small snug snore which he disguised with a cough, Sir Ambrose bellowing, 'Who's there, dammit? What?'

'It's John Rawlings,' the Apothecary answered quickly before the Squire leaped to his feet in alarm. 'The postillion has just asked if we are carrying weapons.'

'I am not,' answered Dr Hensey firmly. 'It is my vocation to heal not to harm.'

'Well, I'm armed to the teeth,' Sir Ambrose rejoindered with satisfaction. 'Always travel with a pair of pistols, to say nothing of a sword. Why does he want to know?'

John turned back. 'Yes, we are. Why?' he called through the glass.

'Just heading through Tenterden, Sir. Rum place. Used to be a haunt of smugglers and there's word amongst the carriers that they're coming back. A stagecoach was stopped here a few nights ago, and it wasn't by highwaymen.'

'Tally ho,' said Sir Ambrose, leaning forward so that his face appeared between John and Miss Tireman. 'Let the bastards just try, that's all I ask. Shoot their heads clean orff, so I will.'

In the dimness John felt rather than saw Henrietta's grin and would have laughed had not every effort gone into keeping upright on his seat as, with a crack of whips, the two riders urged the horses to a frenzied pace as they charged through the small town, determined to stop for nothing.

'Oh, my goodness, I'm sorry!' exclaimed Miss Tireman, as she was hurled against him, displacing the Squire who went sprawling on to the floor.

'My pleasure entirely,' said John, and used the excuse to hold on to her tightly as the flying coach lived up to its name and crashed over the main track between the dwellings.

For a few frantic minutes, the occupants of the post chaise were thrown about like toys in a box, then the pace slowed and there was a cry of triumph from the two postillions.

'We're through! But keep your weapons handy, gentlemen.'

'Where are we going now?' called John.

'We'll pick our way round Shirley Moor, then on to Appledore, Sir,' the postillion answered over his shoulder.

'Will somebody help me up?' said Sir Ambrose plaintively, and for the first time since they met the Apothecary felt sorry for him, quite unable to get his balance and rolling round the carriage floor like an upturned beetle.

Dr Hensey recovered his equilibrium. 'My dear Sir, pray allow me to give you a hand. You have sustained no injury I trust.'

'M'leg feels a bit the worse for wear. I think I cracked my knee as I went down.'

Somewhat reluctantly, his better nature winning the day, the Apothecary released his hold on Miss Tireman and went to the Squire's rescue, somehow heaving him up and back on to his seat, all the while travelling at a lively pace across the rough terrain of the marshlands.

'Permit me to examine the injured limb,' said the doctor, which the Squire, with a great deal of grunting, allowed him to do.

Henrietta looked up at her companion. 'Mr Rawlings, if we drive over bumpy ways again, may I trouble you to hold me as you did before. I am quite certain it was your strong arm that prevented me ending up alongside Squire Ffloote. A fate I would not prefer,' she added in a whisper.

'I should be delighted,' answered the Apothecary enthusiastically, and made a concerted effort to send Coralie Clive packing to the deepest recesses of his memory. Looking over the back of his seat, he saw that the doctor was now applying some lotion to Sir Ambrose's knee, prior to swathing it in a bandage. Meanwhile, the Squire was groaning a great deal and taking nips of brandy from a hip flask.

'Very civil of you, Sir. Very civil,' he croaked, the first polite thing that John could recall him saying to the dapper little man of medicine.

'No trouble, Sir Ambrose, I assure you. You have been badly shaken,' Dr Hensey replied.

'You must come and dine with me and m'wife, so you must. How long will you be staying in Hastings?'

Dr Hensey shook his head. 'I'm not sure, Sir. I have to attend a rather difficult patient, an extremely querulous invalid. The old lady will permit no other physician near her except myself. Depending on her condition, my visit could be as brief as a day or as long as a week. I am in the lap of the gods.' He spread his hands.

'Write to me when you know,' ordered Sir Ambrose, grunting as Dr Hensey deftly fastened the Squire's breeches back into place. 'You shall be entertained royally. Indeed you will.'

'Most kind, Sir. Most kind,' the physician answered, and John could not help but be glad that Sir Ambrose was treating Dr Hensey with a degree of politeness at last.

He turned back to Miss Tireman. 'This looks like marshland to me. Why is it called a moor?'

'Heaven alone knows, for it's full of drainage ditches as you can see.'

And sure enough, illuminated by the light of a fitful cloud-flurried moon, John observed that the territory through which they were passing was slashed with ribbons of gleaming water, a maze of trenches used by the smugglers of earlier times to outwit pursuit, vanishing into them as Hereward the Wake had once done in the Fenlands of East Anglia in order to elude the Norman invaders.

'The weather's going to change,' announced Miss Tireman.

John, having successfully imprisoned poor Coralie in a deep dungeon at the back of his brain, gazed at her entranced. 'How do you know?'

'It often happens in Kent, and in Sussex too, when one gets near to the coast. The cloud is thinning all the time. Soon it will be gone and it will be bright moonlight. Just you wait and see.'

'What time do you think we will get to Winchelsea?'

'About half past seven or thereabouts. In time for supper.'

'I wonder if Mrs Rose will give me any?'

'I should call on her tomorrow morning if I were you. Book yourself a room at The Salutation, Mr Rawlings. You will be comfortable there. Besides, they are known for their excellent food.'

'Is the inn far from the Vicarage?' John asked boldly.

'There is no Vicarage,' Miss Tireman answered, smiling to herself.

'Then where . . . ?'

'I live in the Rectory, Mr Rawlings. And, no, it is but a short pace from The Salutation.'

'Then I hope to have the pleasure of calling on you.'

'Had you not invited yourself, I would have invited you,' Miss Tireman answered, then closed her eyes, signifying that the conversation was at an end.

The village of Appledore safely negotiated, the postillions set out on what John could only think of as a somewhat perilous route, for now they had left all habitation behind and were winding along a track through the marshland. Even a road covered by fallen trees would have been preferable to this, he thought, for other than a glimpse of an occasional isolated farm or remote inn there was no sign of life whatsoever. Suddenly he felt desperately alone, as if he were the only person left awake. Behind him, the snores of Sir Ambrose and Dr Hensey blended together in a strange duet of falsetto and bass, while beside him Henrietta Tireman slept as neatly as a dormouse, her head tipped over on to his shoulder, her body relaxed next to his. Even the postillions, weary now with the extra miles of their detour, seemed in a world of their own.

Henrietta's prediction about the weather had proved correct. Overhead an almost full moon shone brightly, the clouds blown away to reveal a mass of glittering stars in the jet black firmament. The rain had stopped completely, the wind was at dead calm. It was a landscape of unreality, drawn from legend. No human entity, or so it seemed to the Apothecary, was left alive. And then he saw something so incredible that he blinked his eyes in disbelief, while down his spine ran a chill of unease.

A man stood in the grasslands beyond the track, ignoring the sheep which grazed at his feet in the moonlight. A man in clothes so fine that one could have laughed at the incongruity of his setting had not the stillness of his stance struck such an awful note of fear. Behind the man and slightly to his right was an ancient church, oddly shaped and somehow hunched against the darkness. Before and all around him curved the marshland ditches, winding gashes of silver sparkling in the moonlight. John stared until his eyes hurt, wondering what any human being could be doing on such a night as this, so distant from habitation and standing so terrifyingly still. And then the Apothecary laughed harshly and Henrietta Tireman stirred beside him.

It was a scarecrow who stood there, he could see that now, the elegant clothes tattered and torn by the elements. Even the lace-trimmed tricorne hat, pulled well forward to hide the fact that the dummy had no face, had a slightly battered look. And yet its lifelike quality was extraordinary. So much so that John realised his heart was pounding and his mouth had gone dry with fright. As the coach continued down the track and the scarecrow passed out of sight, the Apothecary stared back over his shoulder for a final glimpse through the small window set in the door. But to no avail. The unearthly vision had vanished into the night.

Just under an hour later, by dint of making the best time they possibly could, the flying coach crossed the river Rother by ferry and passed rapidly through Rye, the noise of the cobbles beneath the horses' feet waking up the three sleeping passengers. And shortly afterwards they came to Winchelsea and were put down outside the church, John alighting first to help Miss Tireman and

Sir Ambrose down the step. Dr Hensey stuck his head out of the window.

'Goodbye to you all. It really has been a pleasure to travel with you.'

Thinking the man either a saint or an extremely tactful liar in view of Sir Ambrose's initial rudeness, John made a respectful bow. 'Do look me up when you are in London, Sir.'

'I intend to ask you to compound some physicks for me.'

'I will be delighted to do so.'

The Squire broke into the conversation, jovial now that he was back on home territory. 'Gentlemen, forget London. You shall meet again when I invite you to dine. Dr Hensey, please write to me as soon as you know your plans.'

'I certainly will.'

The chief postillion, who by now looked ready to drop with fatigue, said, 'We must go on, Sir. Neither horse nor man is fit for much more.' Then he brightened as John Rawlings handed him a generous tip on behalf of the departing passengers, a douceur to which Sir Ambrose had liberally contributed. 'Well, goodbye, lady and gentlemen, we're at your service at any time should you require us.' And they were off into the darkness, leaving the three remaining to make their own way to their final destinations.

'If you will wait while I secure a room at The Salutation I'll walk you home, Miss Tireman,' said the Apothecary hopefully.

'Nonsense,' answered the Squire genially. 'It is no trouble to me. The lady's route is the same as my own.'

Henrietta smiled her mecurial smile. 'Gentlemen, I need bother neither of you. My Papa is always in church at this hour of the night, leading evening prayers for those who wish them. So, as we are almost at its very door, all I have to do is go down the path. That being the case, I'll bid you both farewell.'

She curtsied and would have turned to go had not John taken her hand to kiss it. 'I shall call on you if I may,' he said.

She bowed her head so that her ridiculous feathers brushed her shoulder. 'I hope I shall be in, Sir,' she replied, and, with only the merest backward glance, made her way into the ancient portals of St Thomas the Martyr.

Chapter Four

It was the lucent sunshine of a late February day that woke John Rawlings the following morning. Leaping out of bed with one of the hare-like bounds that so often characterised his gait, the Apothecary threw back the shutters and stared out over Winchelsea, taking in the details of the houses and the pleasing symmetrical pattern in which the town was laid out. Then, almost of their own accord, his eyes were drawn towards the imposing church, and his thoughts straight to the delectable Miss Tireman. Had she, John wondered, located her father and returned to the Rectory in safety? Then he frowned as a picture of Coralie Clive came to mind and smiled sweetly at him.

'Don't start any of that,' John grumbled aloud. 'You've played fast and loose with me for too long, my girl. It's time for fresh fields and pastures new.'

The vision pulled a face and vanished, and the Apothecary turned to see the chambermaid standing in the doorway with a jug of hot water, staring at him, mouth agape. The girl hurried in, put the pitcher down, and fled, not stopping even to say good morning. With a grin, John turned to the mirror and started to shave, noticing as he looked at his reflection that his cinnamon hair had started to get long again, thus making it difficult for him to wear a wig. With a shrug he decided against putting it on, thinking that after all he was in a country town and the fashion codes of the metropolis no longer applied. None the less, he completed his rural ensemble with a very handsome burgundy velvet coat before sauntering down to breakfast.

Delighted to find that the landlord clearly shared the Apothecary's views on a hearty repast being the only way to start the day, John tucked in to a great plate of pickled sea trout and prawns, fresh caught that morning, or so he was informed, followed by a bowl of beef broth, and rounded the meal off with a gammon of bacon and three helpings of bread. With this he drank several cups of tea, thinking that it had probably been acquired through the good offices of Dick Jarvis, tax on the commodity being extremely high. Then, much refreshed, John set out to solve the mystery of the Voice from the Past.

He felt fairly certain that he knew who it was, matching the description Miss Tireman had given him against people of his old acquaintance. Yet still there was an element of uncertainty and danger about the whole situation, and John felt a shiver of excitement as he left the inn by the front entrance and made his way down Castle Street to the High Street.

Before he left London, the Apothecary had consulted one of his father's many guide books, on the subject of the historic town of Winchelsea. He had read the following: 'At some Unknown Date in our History, five Towns in South-East England banded together to form the Famous Cinque Ports. These Towns were Hastings, Romney, Hythe, Dover and Sandwich, and it is Believed by your Writer that the confederation could have begun as Early as the Reign of Edward the Confessor. By the Thirteenth Century, the Antient Towns of Winchelsea and Rye had been Added to Their Number.'

This information continued with a vivid description of how the fleet of the Cinque Ports had ruled the high seas, had given King John a navy, had indulged in piracy and private wars, all of which had struck the Apothecary as highly colourful. But these glories of the thirteenth century had been ended at a single stroke by an implacable enemy. In October 1250 the town had been partly submerged by an exceptionally high tide which 'flowed Twice without Ebbing with a Horrible Roaring and a Glint as of Fire on the Waves.' Thirty-seven years later the town suffered a similar fate and was practically submerged. On that same occasion the whole of the Romney Marsh was flooded and the River Rother changed its course.

Edward I had come to the aid of Winchelsea and had designed a new town on Iham Hill, planned on the gridiron principle of the French *bastides*, which his royal majesty had also ordered built in his duchy of Aquitaine. Stones had been brought from Caen in Normandy and some, indeed, from the ruins of the submerged city, accessible at low tide. Marble for the church had come from West Sussex, timbers for both houses and other buildings from the great oaks of the forest of Anderida. Putting the guide book down, John had thought momentarily that the romantic legends of church bells that ring beneath the sea might well have originated in the 'antient' town of Winchelsea.

The story had continued, telling of repeated raids by the French, of rape and bloodshed, of pillage and arson, of how the great days of the town were over by the end of the fifteenth century when 'the Last Merchant had left'. For the new harbour had silted up and trade had depended on there being a port. Even the support of the religious houses had gone when Henry VIII disolved the monasteries. But there had been a ray of hope. Within the last year or so Huguenot émigrés had started a textile business, manufacturing lawns, cambrics and crepes, which it was hoped would bring renewed prosperity to Winchelsea. Though now, thought John as he turned into the High Street, with war declared, the town must be on its guard. For if ever there was a good spot for an invasion it was the flat coast between Fairlight and Hythe, placing Winchelsea right in the firing line.

Petronilla's Platt, the interestingly named cottage in which the enigmatic Mrs Rose had taken up residence, turned out to be a typical eighteenth-century dwelling, with no sign of its medieval origins. Knocking loudly on the front door, John stood in anticipation, his heart beating faster at the prospect of who would answer – only for his hopes to be dashed. There was nobody at home. Wondering what to do next, John decided on a tour of the town and set off to look at the Strand Gate, an age-old portcullis dating from the thirteenth century, which once had given access to the port. Having inspected this, he proceeded to Back Lane, from whence he had a view of the church's eastern end. And it was just as he was admiring the building's size and splendour that a figure came into sight in the far distance, slowly walking towards him. Instantly, John knew who it was and why he had been sent for above all other members of his profession. The thought of old dark secrets stirred within him and he briefly stepped into the shadow of the church wall, better to observe the creature who was coming his way.

Just as Henrietta Tireman had said, the woman still had that air of beauty about her which, with her inborn grace and charm, the passing years could never take away. Yet there was much sadness in the droop of the shoulders and the carriage of the head, the bearing of one who has seen too much of life and as a result withdrawn to a quiet backwater in which to pass the years left to her.

John could see from where he stood the lovely shock of silver

41

hair which he had always so much admired. This woman might be cowed by all that had happened to her, living in fear of her life from an unknown poisoner's hand, but for all that she was finely coiffed and elegantly presented. As always she wore enamel on her face, attempting to disguise her true age and yet, in a way, drawing attention to it. But the steadfast eyes, though full of despair, were none the less bright as crystal. John's heart went out to the Voice from the Past that she had still not found peace.

He stepped out from the shadows and bowed deeply. 'Don't be afraid, Madam,' he said gently. 'Your summons has been answered. I am John Rawlings, come to serve you as best I can.'

She was so startled that she drew in her breath on a rasp. 'Is it really you?' she asked in a quivering voice.

'Yes, Mrs Harcross, it really is.'

She seized his arm in alarm. 'Oh, don't call me that, I beg you. She is dead, that evil woman. Her hour came long ago.'

This was hardly the place to ask the unhappy creature why she had tried to eradicate all evidence of her past, though it was not difficult for John to guess the reason. Instead he said, 'Then would you prefer me to address you as Mrs Rose?'

She froze. 'How did you know I used that alias?'

'Because I made one or two discreet enquiries about the owner of Petronilla's Platt. You must understand that it is not every day one is delivered a note in the fog. You can hardly blame me for trying to find out a little more about the messenger.'

Mrs Rose relaxed a little. 'No, of course not. I am being foolish. After all, if I can't trust you, Mr Rawlings, who can I depend on?'

'Then shall we go back to your cottage so that you may tell me exactly what is troubling you?'

John's companion grew tense once more. 'No, I cannot rely on the serving girl, Agnes. She comes from the town and, I feel certain, has been primed to find out all she can about me. Let us go into the church. At least it is quiet there.'

So saying, Mrs Rose took the Apothecary's arm and guided him to the gate, then down the path and through the entrance of St Thomas the Martyr, into the hushed and dim interior. Instantly, a sense of great antiquity consumed him – that and something else. There was an air of continuity, as if the medieval craftsmen who had built it had only stepped outside momentarily and would be back at any moment. Their handiwork seemed as fresh as the day it had been carved despite the acts of vandalism inflicted by the fanatical puritans who held sway during the Commonwealth. John, looking to his right, found his eye drawn to the face of the Green Man, that pagan figure of fertility and tree worship, thought by some scholars to be the basis for the legend of Robin Hood, his head planted centrally in the canopy above the tombs that lay beneath.

Taking the Apothecary's hand in her gloved one, Mrs Rose, after glancing all around, led him to the left and down the northernmost aisle, divided in half by a wall with a door in it. Going through this to a pew tucked close to the pulpit, a private place if ever there was one, she sat down. Then she turned her eyes on him, the look in their depths unfathomable.

'One thing before we begin. Swear to me, Mr Rawlings, swear in this holy place, that you will never mention the reason why we are both here.'

'What do you mean?'

'I cannot bear to hear the names that since . . . since Jasper's death . . . I now have come to dread. Swear to me by all that you hold dear that you will not talk about the past.'

'But if I am to discuss your present situation, surely that will be inevitable.'

'No, it will not,' she answered vehemently. 'The facts are, as I told you in my letter, that I am sure I am being slowly poisoned. Yet whether by a friend of Jasper's killers or by a woman who once loved him, and there were so very many, I do not know.'

John sat silently, thinking about her request, wondering how he could possibly comply with it. Beside him, he was horribly aware, Mrs Rose sat trembling with stress, willing him to help her. Yet, if it came to a matter of asking questions how could he agree never to discuss the very situation that had brought the current position about? In the end, though, he could not bear her patent misery a moment longer.

'I promise not to mention, to you at least, all that has gone before,' he said. 'Now, tell me what it is that worries you. How do you know somebody is trying to kill you?'

She looked at him sorrowfully, her eyes full of tears. 'If you will remember I left this country in order to nurse my cousin Ralph, and with him took up residence in Italy. He had gone there for his health, though by that stage no warm climate could help him. He

43

was too eaten up with consumption to last more than a year or two and eventually the poor soul, may God rest him, died in my arms. I was related to Ralph through my mother, my father, if you recall, being a Huguenot weaver. Anyway, Ralph had been left Petronilla's Platt by his maiden sister and he, in turn, thinking to set me up in a modicum of comfort, bequeathed me a small legacy and her cottage. Thus I came to Winchelsea.'

'And?'

'All was well at first. I mingled amongst the people of the town who accepted me as best they could, though a widow on her own is not generally considered quite the thing in polite society.'

John raised a dark brow but said nothing.

'Anyway, after I had been here a month or so, I was given a gift, a cake, which made me violently ill after I ate it.'

The Apothecary stared at her. 'But who gave it to you? Surely you could have raised the matter with them?'

Mrs Rose stared into her lap, where her hands were abstractedly working a handkerchief. 'That is just the point. I do not know where it came from.'

'What on earth do you mean?' John exclaimed, his voice sounding harsher than he had intended.

'I mean that it was left on my doorstep while I was out. Wrapped up very prettily and in a nice basket. Anyway, not suspecting anything, I took it in and had it for supper.'

'And then?'

'During the night I became ill and the physician had to be sent for. Anyway, he purged me and after a few days I recovered and put the matter down to mere coincidence, a chill or something of that sort. Then it happened again. This time a basket of fruit was left on my doorstep.'

'And you ate some of it?'

Mrs Rose, born Elizabeth Tessier, who had once been a woman of importance, a leading actress of her day, for ever enshrined in theatrical history as the creator of Lucy Lockit in the original production of *The Beggar's Opera*, suddenly looked sad and vulnerable.

'Times are hard, Mr Rawlings. I eke out my money as best I can but any gift is welcome, believe me.'

'And did it not occur to you to wonder who your generous benefactor might be?'

'I thought it was somebody connected with the church, which I attend regularly, to pray for Jasper's soul amongst other things, who had seen me and somehow guessed my situation. Someone who was too tactful to approach me openly and offer me charity.'

'I see,' said the Apothecary, concealing his cynicism as the thought went rapidly through his mind that Elizabeth Rose's late husband, the murdered Jasper Harcross, could do with all the prayers for salvation that he could possibly get. 'So the fruit poisoned you as well?' he asked.

'I had a seizure in the middle of the night, just as before.'

'And have any further gifts been left since then?'

'One, a bottle of homemade wine.'

'And what did you do with that?'

'I have kept it untouched.'

John nodded. 'Just as well. I'll be interested to have a look at it. By the way, did you tell the physician your suspicions?'

Elizabeth shook her head, locks of her silver hair rippling beneath her hat. 'No, I am regarded as enough of an oddity as it is. I had no wish to draw even more attention to myself.'

The Apothecary shifted his position, the hard wooden pew uncomfortable beneath him. 'Certainly what you say is very strange. But who could be doing such a thing? How could anyone trace you to this remote corner?'

'Perhaps by pure chance. Perhaps there is somebody living in Winchelsea who knew Jasper, or . . .' – her voice wavered – 'the others.'

'It seems very unlikely.'

'You do not doubt my word, surely, Mr Rawlings? These things happened to me just as I described to you.'

In her vehemence, Mrs Rose's voice had risen in intensity and now reverberated round the walls of the old church, the sound coming back as an echo from the ancient tombs of the long-sleeping dead. And mingling with that hollow noise, John became acutely aware of another. His hackles rose as he realised that he and his companion were not alone in the church of St Thomas the Martyr. Surreptitious footsteps were making their way up the aisle away from them.

He sprang to his feet, simultaneously whirling round to face the door which divided the aisle across. It was closing even as he looked at it. Instantly, John leaped over the back of the pew and plunged

45

down the aisle towards the door, wrenching it open and staring all around him. There was no one in sight, but the Apothecary glimpsed movement in the main entrance. He raced the short distance from where he stood, thrusting his way through the great oak door. But again he was just too late. Whoever had gone out knew the place far better than he did and had instantly found a hiding place. There was nobody to be seen.

'Damnation!' he swore.

'Who was it?' asked Elizabeth, nervously coming up behind him.

'I don't know. They've gone to earth.'

'Could they have overheard what we were saying?'

'It depends on how long they were there.'

She drew herself up and got a grip on her emotions. 'Ought we to try and find the fellow?'

'It could be a woman, you know. And the answer is no. By the time we've searched the grounds they could be halfway home. No, Mrs Rose, a far better idea is for us to return to your cottage and for me to look at that wine bottle of yours.'

'Then follow me, Mr Rawlings,' she said with determination, and set off down the path.

The serving girl whom her employer suspected of gossiping at least was a good worker. A cheerful fire had been lit in the hearth and the smells of cooking pervaded Petronilla's Platt as John and his hostess walked through the front door. The Apothecary raised his brows in surprise and Elizabeth Rose, reading his look, laughed and said, 'You are in the country now, Mr Rawlings. We dine at two o'clock here.'

She was, the Apothecary thought, at her best when challenged. The frightened creature who had whispered to him in the church had vanished with the advent of the intruder. Now something of the spirit of Mrs Jasper Harcross, the death of whose husband John had actually witnessed on the stage of the Theatre Royal, Drury Lane, was coming to the fore. Even her beautiful face, ravaged by time though it might be, seemed brighter and more animated. In fact John was delighted when Mrs Rose said, 'I do hope you will dine with me, my dear friend. There is still much that I want to say to you. I feel that I have rudely monopolised the conversation talking about myself and have asked nothing of you and your dear father.'

'I'd be delighted to accept,' he answered, 'and we can discuss all my news then. But first of all, to business. If you bring the bottle in here and fetch two glasses as well, the girl's suspicions should not be aroused that I've come to examine it.'

'I'll do better than that,' answered Elizabeth, taking his cloak and hat and motioning him to a chair by the fire. 'I'll bring a bottle of claret in with the other. That way she'll guess nothing.'

Holding his hands out to the flames, John stared around him. Though modest in the extreme, Mrs Rose had for all that made Petronilla's Platt cosy. The parlour was whitewashed and beamed and the oak furniture gleamed with polishing. Rag rugs were scattered on the floor and in the cupboard which stood against one wall, the Apothecary could see tea cups and saucers of delicate china. Of the furnishings he could remember from when Elizabeth Harcross had lived in Kensington there was no sign. The poor woman had truly put the past behind her when she had journeyed to Italy.

Candles stood on the mantelpiece, a tinder and flint beside them, and when his hostess returned to the room, bearing a tray which she put down on a small table beneath the window, she lit them. Even though the sun was still shining outside, it gave the room a pleasing air, driving away any lingering shadows.

'Here it is,' said Mrs Rose, and handed John a bottle of a dark red substance together with a corkscrew.

Taking it to the light, he examined the exterior carefully. A label had been tied to the bottle neck which read as follows: 'Damson wine, made by Ourselves in the Year 1754. We Hope this little Gift will bring you Cheer.' Of the donor's identity there was absolutely no indication whatsoever.

'The labels from the other two things,' said John, looking up, 'did you keep them by any chance?'

'The answer is both yes and no. I told you that the cake came in a very pretty basket . . .' He nodded. 'Well, I kept that just as it was. But unfortunately the label on the fruit was destroyed.'

'And what sort of container did that arrive in?'

'It was on a plate, a plate that obviously I kept as I did not know to whom to return it.'

John grinned, and Elizabeth said, 'Oh, you still do that!'

'What?'

'Smile crookedly. I remember that about you clearly. It is one of your most endearing characteristics.'

The Apothecary coloured a little. 'It is just one of those odd things.

'Now, allow me to look at this wine of yours.' John carefully drew the cork and sniffed the contents, holding the neck of the bottle close to his nose. 'Nothing detectable there. Let me try it.'

'Be careful.'

'A few drops won't hurt.' So saying, he poured out a thimbleful and sipped it. 'I can't taste anything untoward. If this is poison it's a very subtle one.'

He drained the glass, Mrs Rose watching every move anxiously. 'Nor is there any aftertaste in the mouth. I wonder what it can be.' He poured himself some more and sipped again. 'No burning sensation. In fact it is very pleasant to take. How very odd.'

'You can discern nothing?'

'Well, it's not one of the Wolf's Banes, that's for sure.'

'How do you know?'

'My tongue and lips would be swollen by now. It could be meadow saffron, I suppose. Though I somehow doubt it.'

'What does that do?'

'Properly compounded it is a good remedy for gout, but it can kill you by choking if given incorrectly. Tell me, did you get any sensation of stifling when you were taken ill?'

Mrs Rose shook her head. 'No.'

John frowned deeply, his mobile eyebrows curving upwards. 'There's obviously going to be no easy solution to this. I shall need to take it to my compounding room and try a few experiments.' He poured out a little more, which he slowly drank.

'Oh, do have a care!' Elizabeth repeated uneasily.

'Don't worry. The moment I feel any discomfort I will stop. If I get into dire straits, my bag of potions is at The Salutation. We can always send the girl for it.'

'Well, if you feel sure.' She sat down and passed John the bottle of claret. 'If you would be so kind as to open this, I'll join you in a glass.'

'Certainly.'

They sat on either side of the fire, the Apothecary studiously sampling the damson wine, Mrs Rose erring on the side of caution and drinking the contents of the other bottle. And slowly the warm and pleasant atmosphere had its soothing effect. If only temporarily, all thoughts of poison and the horrors of the past were forgotten and they chatted and laughed, the hostess's enamelled cheeks becoming quite rosy at the pleasure of the Apothecary's company.

'Tell me,' said John, his thoughts returning to Henrietta Tireman, as they had done several times that morning already, 'about your neighbours. Describe them to me.'

'Well, there's the Squire, Sir Ambrose Ffloote, an extremely noisy baronet who lives in Paradise House.'

'What an exotic name!'

'Isn't it. Not really suitable for him. Then there's Captain Nathaniel Pegram, who lives in Grey Friars.'

'Another interesting title.'

'It's a manor house now but was once a monastery which after the dissolution was sold into private hands. The ruins of the chancel of the chapel stand nearby and are most interesting to visit.'

'And what is he like? Captain Pegram?'

'Shy and retiring. He hardly socialises at all. His wife died many years ago and they say he never recovered from her loss. Apparently, his greatest pleasure is to spend all day in his library.' Mrs Rose paused, then added, 'He's quite a handsome man in his way.'

The Apothecary nodded. 'Obviously something of a recluse. By the way, I met Sir Ambrose on my journey here.' Almost without thinking, he poured himself a little more of the damson wine. 'I can't say I took to him enormously. He's married, I believe.'

'To poor long-suffering little Faith, who is greatly plagued with the headache. Can anyone be surprised? Needless to say, they are childless and pour out all their affection on an aged and decrepit dog which they refer to as The Pup.' Elizabeth Rose threw back her head and laughed, and John joined in uproariously, his suspicion that the wine, far from being poisoned, was of the most potent variety gaining ground with every moment.

'And what of the others? Rector Tireman for example?'

'You've heard of him?' Mrs Rose looked faintly astonished. 'Well, he has two beautiful daughters, one of whom has achieved the triumph of all time. The younger, the fair Rosalind, has managed to get herself betrothed to the Marquis of Rye. There is to be a great wedding in the spring. All of Sussex and most of Kent are talking about it.'

'How did she do that?' asked John, interested.

'I believe she went to his house to act as governess to his young sister. Of course, no sooner did he lay eyes on her than he was at her feet as, indeed, are most members of the male sex.'

'Her sister, Henrietta, was also on the coach with me,' the Apothecary remarked. 'I thought her very pretty.'

'She is, of course, but she pales in comparison with the other. It must be a great misfortune for her constantly to be likened to her sibling.'

'Does the rector have a wife?'

'Yes, most certainly. A *femme formidable*. A big, dominant woman who stands no nonsense. How she gave birth to those two lovely girls I will never know.'

'Why? Is she plain?'

'She is what is called handsome, if you understand me.'

'Yes, I think I do.'

There was silence while both of them stared into the fire. Then John said, 'Is there anyone else, Mrs Rose? Anyone whose circle you touch?'

She looked at him, suddenly very straight-faced. 'Why? Are you thinking that from amongst them must come the person who is trying to kill me?'

John nodded. 'Yes, I'm afraid I am.'

She shuddered. 'But what connection could any of them have with the past?'

'As you said yourself, it could be a random thing. The merest coincidence that one of them knew Jasper or . . .'

'There's no need to say it. Very well, I'll conclude the list. There is Dr Hayman, who attended me when I was ill. He is new to Winchelsea, his predecessor, old Dr Trumble, having fallen off a wagon and broken his neck while under the influence. I'm afraid I know little about him, except that he seems very good at what he does. There is also an apothecary, a Mr Gironde. He makes up various potions for me but I hardly know him socially. His wife asked me to call on her once but I found her inquisitive and intrusive and did not go again. Of course, several other well-to-do people live here but they are merely nodding acquaintances whom I glimpse on Sunday mornings in church.'

'So if I am right and the poisoner is somebody you know, is it your belief that your enemy must be one of the people you've just described?'

Elizabeth's beautiful eyes filled with tears. 'Loath though I am to say it, the answer has to be yes.'

The Apothecary shook his head. 'It is all very strange.' He gave a sudden grin. 'Everything seems shrouded in mystery except for one thing.'

'And what is that?'

'Whoever left this bottle of wine for you had your best interests at heart.'

'What are you saying?'

'I'd stake my reputation that there is not a drop of poison in it. I've been drinking it consistently for the last hour and can feel nothing except the onset of extreme joviality. In short, it is one of the best home brews I have ever tasted and I would very much like to find out who made it so that I can ask them for some more.'

Elizabeth gave him a horrified glance which slowly but surely began to melt as the Apothecary smiled at her. Eventually she smiled too.

'Mr Rawlings, what a risk you took in drinking that. But what you have to say is a great relief to me. It is nice to know that at least one of my neighbours wishes me no ill.'

John stood up and offered her his arm as the maid called from the kitchen that dinner was ready.

'My dear Madam, take my word for it. If there is any who does, I will seek him out.'

And with that assurance he led Elizabeth Rose, once Harcross, in to dine.

Chapter Five

It was evening by the time the Apothecary left Petronilla's Platt and made his way back to The Salutation, a snatch of song on his lips, his gait slightly nautical. His inspection of the labels attached to the anonymous gifts received by Mrs Rose had proved fruitless. Both had been written in different hands. None the less, John had slipped them into his pocket for further investigation in the clear light of day. That done, he had lingered over the port, which a laughing Mrs Rose had seemed only too happy to pour out, begging him to stay for the entire evening. John had thought then what a sad and lonely life she led and what a tragedy that so great a celebrity as Elizabeth had once been should be reduced to such solitary circumstances.

'Next time you come to London,' he had said impulsively, 'you must call on my father. I know he would be delighted to see you.'

Mrs Rose had smiled gently. 'Dear Sir Gabriel. It would be so good to renew my acquaintance with him. But alas I rarely travel to town. My last foray was simply to try and find you, Mr Rawlings. The place holds too many memories for me to be comfortable there.'

'You really must try to shed the past, Mrs Rose. What is done is done. Cast it off as a snake does its skin.'

'Easier said than accomplished, my fine young friend.'

Looking at her face, the Apothecary had decided to let the matter drop. It was perfectly clear that the former actress was not yet ready, if indeed she ever would be, to forget all the terrible things that had gone before. Considering it to be a waste of breath even to try and persuade her, John Rawlings had risen from the table, thanked Elizabeth profusely, kissed her hand and departed.

The evening had turned cold and John was glad to walk through the front door of The Salutation and feel the warmth of the fire in the parlour. Hurrying in, he took a seat in front of the flames and promptly fell asleep, only to dream he was once more travelling by coach with Henrietta, and that the sinister scarecrow, standing so still and so lifelike beside the lonely church, was making the horses rear in their traces with fright. At this, Miss Tireman started to scream and it was to the sound of her terrified cries that the Apothecary woke up.

Somewhere outside in the street a child was weeping, its dismal wails the cause of his awakening. Yet the reassurance that there was a natural explanation to his dream did not come to John. Instead, he sat hunched, his brows drawn together, trying to chase a thought that was as elusive as a will o' the wisp. There had been something wrong about the entire scene he had witnessed through the carriage window; the isolated church, the scarecrow in its lace-trimmed hat, the silently grazing flock, the ruthless moonlight bleaching the landscape. But what was it? What was it the Apothecary had seen that made no sense at all? And then it occurred to him and John let out a small cry, disturbing the man who sat in the chair opposite, a newspaper spread over his face.

'No crops,' the Apothecary said beneath his breath. 'There were no crops.'

'Eh? What's that?' asked the other, lowering his paper.

'I said "There were no crops."' And without further explanation, John shot to his feet and made his way to the taproom, hoping that one of the locals would be able to tell him where that small silent church was located.

Fortune favoured him. The very first man he spoke to responded at once to the Apothecary's sketch of the oddly shaped building, with its long sloping roofs and its weather-boarded bell turret.

'Why that's St Thomas à Becket at Fairfield. Five hundred years old, that is.'

'What can you tell me about it?' asked John, motioning to the serving boy to refill the other man's tankard. 'Does anyone ever worship there? It seems very remote.'

'Well, a few go, from time to time. But there's only a curate to take the service, mind, the vicar being in charge of several parishes and not residing hereabouts, while the curate himself has no parsonage house and has to lodge where he can, poor soul.'

'How do people get there?' John persisted.

'They walk or ride, or when the Marsh is flooded, they row.'

The Apothecary smiled at this quaint mental picture, and his companion added, 'You might laugh, my good Sir, but you can take it from one who knows, when the Romney Marsh goes under water there's no other way. Now, you can answer a question for me. Why are you so interested in the old place?'

'I arrived in Winchelsea from London last night and because of the storm, the post chaise crossed the Marsh instead of going its usual way. I saw the church in the moonlight and it caught my eye so acutely I have a mind to go and visit it. Partly because of its unusual shape.' He did not mention that his real reason was to examine a scarecrow that had no crops to protect.

'Well, they certainly are very quaint, these old Marsh churches. While you're at it, you should go into St Augustine at Brookland; that's about the same age as St Thomas à Becket.'

'You have great local knowledge, if I might say so.'

'The reason is, Sir, I used to be a shepherd on the Marshes many years ago. Know every nook and cranny of them. Well, as much as any man could in a lifetime.'

'And now you've retired?'

'No, not exactly, Sir. I watches sheep over Rye way now. Property of the Marquis. It's not such tricky country as the marshland.'

'I see.' The Apothecary held out his hand. 'I'm John Rawlings, apothecary of Shug Lane, London, by the way.'

'And I'm Roderick. If I can be of any service to you during your stay here, don't hesitate to ask. I live in the third cottage along Back Lane.'

John smiled his most friendly smile. 'Well, there is something, as it happens. But first, would you like another drink? And do you know where I can hire a horse? I'll ride out to Fairfield if it's fine tomorrow.'

Over a further pint of ale, the shepherd revealed that his brother was in the way of doing a little livery work and usually had a horse or two for charter. He also threw in the information that the best route to take was out through Rye, then to cross the Rother on the ferry and follow the road which led north-east.

'There's a sign to Appledore along the way. Stay on that track and you'll see St Thomas on your right. You can't miss it. It'll look a bit more friendly by daylight.'

'I hope so,' John answered cheerfully, but deep inside he shivered at the memory of how very still, and how very lifelike, the dark shape of the scarecrow had been.

Having retired early, the Apothecary rose as dawn tinged the sky

55

with red, just before the sun sailed up effortlessly over the horizon. Then, his usual heroic breakfast consumed, he made his way to the inn yard where a dappled mare was just being led round by Roderick's brother, Tom.

It felt very good, cleansing almost, to be in the saddle again and riding full pelt across the mysterious countryside known as the Romney Marsh. In fact, so fine was it that John took off his hat, cramming it into his saddle bag, and let the wind do its worst with his hair, desperately in need of being shorn as it was. For this late February day heralded the arrival of spring and was as glittering as the one before. The Apothecary felt that he was journeying through a landscape filled with gold as the drainage ditches of the marshland caught the gleam of the sun and reflected it back.

Everywhere he looked were the colours of the burgeoning season, enhanced by the pale blue sky. It was as if the morning had been created for pleasurable adventure and the Apothecary's spirits rose with each passing mile. So much so, that when he saw a sign to the left which said Brookland, he took the track even though it was somewhat out of his way, anxious to look at the church which Roderick had said was so interesting. And as he drew nearer, the Apothecary could see that not only was it interesting but unique, for its belfry stood not on the church but beside it, on the ground. Never having come across such a thing in his life, John tied his horse to one of the rings provided in the church wall and walked round the octagonal wooden structure which, with its conical roof made in three separate parts, resembled three candle snuffers, one above the other. Imagining that the steeple was very old, the apothecary went through the door and stared upwards at the ancient bell cage, supported by beams, thinking of all the generations of bell ringers who had stood on the stages pulling with all their might so that the joyful carillon might ring out over the Romney Marsh.

Having inspected the tower, John made his way into the church through a pair of wooden shutter gates surmounted with spikes, presumably to prevent horses leaping inside during divine service. Instantly, an atmosphere of five hundred years of prayer, of oft-repeated ritual, and of simple unquestioning faith struck him almost tangibly – and with it something else. Despite the fact that the church was deserted – a rapid look round had told him that much – John had the strong impression that he was not alone. Cautiously, his eyes darting over the boxed pews to see if anyone was hiding inside, the Apothecary made his way down the central nave.

And then his eye was drawn to something so mystic and wonderful that he exclaimed aloud and forgot everything else. On the wall of the chapel leading from the aisle to his right was a muted splash of colour, an ancient painting representing the murder of Thomas à Becket in Canterbury Cathedral.

The picture showed the Archbishop kneeling before the altar, his skull already penetrated by the sword of one of the killers. Two others of the quartet of murderous knights could also be seen, their swords held aloft. To Becket's left stood his chaplain, holding the archiepiscopal cross.

His eyes firmly fixed on the mystical painting, John went down the single step into the chapel, then realised why he had felt a presence. A young man in the black clerical garb of a curate was there ahead of him, busily pouring something into the piscina, a bowl standing within a niche used for emptying water used for washing sacred vessels.

It was difficult to say which was the more startled. The man of God leaped into the air, his hands flying to his waist as if he carried a weapon there. John, meanwhile, let out a sharp cry and took a step back, his heart thudding. He just had time to register that the curate had a mop of black curls on his head, even more unruly than the Apothecary's own, before the young man snatched a sober wig out of a concealed pocket and thrust it on his head.

'Bless you, my son,' he intoned.

'Thank you, Father,' John replied solemnly, wondering at the youthful appearance of clergy these days.

'A stranger to this part of the world?' continued the man of the cloth.

'Yes, indeed,' the Apothecary answered enthusiastically, adopting his honest citizen face. 'Doing a small tour of the marshland churches. So very historic.'

'How true, indeed how true. Now, how may I help you? Would you care for a guided inspection of our church?'

John shook his head. 'I would not dream of putting you to the trouble. I can easily find my own way round. I do have one point of interest I would like to raise, though.'

'And what is that?'

'I have heard that the church at Fairfield is tended only by a

Perpetual Curate and has no resident priest. So I would presume that it is not often frequented.'

The Curate narrowed his eyes, which were, John noticed, a vivid shade of hyacinth blue. 'The Perpetual Curate does his best, Sir, but he has a wide area to cover. He attempts to take divine service every Sunday despite certain difficulties. However, our priest is Mr Sopwith who is also Rector of Upper Hardres near Canterbury.'

'A fair distance! How noble of him to sally forth.'

The curate laughed. 'I believe he has visited the parish – once or twice!'

John laughed too, warming to this rather unusual young man. 'So what happens to those who arrive to find the church empty?'

'They ride the short distance here and join this congregation. Tell me, why are you so interested in Fairfield?'

'Only because it seems so remote and lonely a little church. I saw it for the first time the other night and decided to investigate it more closely as soon as I had a chance.'

The curate folded his hands together. 'You will not be disappointed, my son. It is a building as old and historic as this. Strange as it may seem, St Thomas à Becket is waterbound from winter until spring. Indeed, the floods have only just receded, somewhat earlier than usual. Now, may I suggest that you look at our font? It is believed to be from the twelfth century and has carved on it the signs of the Zodiac together with the occupations of the month. Would you like me to accompany you?'

'I wouldn't consider taking you from your duties,' John answered.

'Well, in that case I shall continue.' And the curate stepped over to the large tomb which dominated the chapel and proceeded to dust its marble top.

John, glancing back once, only to discover that the man of the cloth was no longer visible, made his way to the font, dazzled by the artistry of the hands, Norman or even possibly Flemish, which had fashioned such a wonderful thing. Made out of lead, the figures stood out in relief, and the Apothecary found himself looking at Gemini, his own birth sign. Beneath the embracing sign of Castor and Pollux, the occupation was shown as a man on horseback with a hawk. John raised a brow. Was he, then, the hawk, as he strove to bring criminals to justice? Or did the twins represent the dual side of his personality, both lenient and ruthless combined? His eye fell on Janvier. Beneath the sign of a man bearing a pouring water-pot, the two-faced figure of Janus sat at a table feasting, a sceptre in one hand, a drinking horn in the other. As the god of gates and doors, which open both ways, Janus's two faces looked in opposite directions, these representing the old and the new year.

Just like me, the Apothecary thought. Wearing one face to obtain information, the other, secret face, storing it all away. Just for a moment he felt guilty about how often he had been forced to resort to deception, then he thought of the duplicity of a malefactor's mind and conceded that the end justifies the means.

Outside St Augustine's he took a deep breath. Despite the age and holiness of the church, there had been something strange there which had left him feeling cold. So much so that the Apothecary relished the warm sun on his back. Leading his horse round to the mounting block on the right of the porch, he was just about to climb into the saddle when the curate reappeared, bobbing along in his black garb, a hat perched periously atop his ill-fitting wig.

'Ah, my good Sir, are you leaving?' he called cheerily.

'Yes. I must be on my way,' John answered.

'Allow me to hold your mare while you mount.'

'Thank you.'

For a man of God, more used to hymns than horseflesh, he took charge of the creature with great confidence, and also with a pair of very strong brown hands, the Apothecary noticed. In fact the curate himself was tanned, as if he spent a great deal of time outdoors.

Seeing the direction of his companion's eyes, the young man said, 'I'm quite used to horses. I ride from parish to parish, you see. Alas, I have no parsonage of my own.'

'So are *you* the Perpetual Curate?'

'Sadly not. Though I do go where I am called, helping out in cases of illness and so on. A strolling player, in a sense.' He laughed, and the vivid eyes disappeared into creases of amusement.

Once more, John laughed too, liking the man, though at the same time feeling that the cloth was very far from a suitable calling for such a high-spirited individual.

'Well, I'll wish you good-day, Sir.'

'And to you, Sir. Perhaps we shall meet again as we journey round the Marsh.'

'Perhaps,' said John, and rode off.

He left the hamlet of Brookland and turned westwards, picking his way through a maze of drainage ditches and passing little habitation other than the occasional farmhouse. Despite the warm February sunshine, the landscape seemed somehow a little menacing, nothing stirring except for flocks of bleating ewes, scattering as John rode amongst them. So it was, proceeding alone like this, that the Apothecary came to the church of St Thomas à Becket almost from behind, and reined in his horse that he might get his bearings and evaluate the scene by daylight.

Strange and forlorn, the little building, curiously shaped like Noah's Ark, stood lonely and unattended, cut off by floods and battered by storms in the winter, warmed by the sun in spring, the only creatures to visit it regularly the famous Romney Marsh sheep.

St Thomas à Becket had been built on a mound by the craftsman who had created it five hundred years earlier, this, obviously, to raise the small and sacred place above the level of the floods. Walking round it now, John realised that from the church itself the scarecrow was completely invisible, obscured by the ruins of a shepherd's stone hut built on another raised bank. The illusion that the straw man stood close to St Thomas's had been an optical one, created by the moonlight. Tying his horse to a ring in the wall at the back of the church, the Apothecary proceeded on foot.

The ground was squelchy where he trod and it was with some difficulty that John made his way towards the ruined hut being forced at one point to wade through the ditch. Eventually, looking much the worse for wear and with mud to his knees, the Apothecary rounded the corner of the stone shelter and there got his first glimpse of the figure which had so startled him in the deceptive moonlight.

Just as when he had first seen it, the very stillness of the scarecrow, looking for all the world like a man with his back turned towards him, gave John the most eerie sensation. In fact, it was too lifelike to be comfortable with, even in the bright light of day. The clothes it wore were of the finest velvet, superbly cut and fashionable, though by now the elements had drained their vivid colours.

Approaching the scarecrow from behind as he was, the Apothecary was able to take in every detail of the torn and faded claret coat, the elegant tricorne, lace-trimmed and once very stylish. Whoever had created this thing, John thought, had not only found some wonderful garments to dress it in but had also gone to

60

enormous trouble doing so. There were even the remains of ripped hose and breeches upon the short straw legs. Small wonder, then, that it had given him such a fright when he had originally seen it. Taking a deep breath, the Apothecary cautiously circled the straw man, and walked round to look at it from the front.

As he had observed in the moonlight, there was no face, the hat being pulled too far forward to warrant the extra effort of making one. Yet it seemed to John as he stared at the scarecrow in the sunshine that there was a hint of something beneath the tricorne, a small glinting of some white substance like chalk.

The Apothecary stretched out a hand towards the man of straw and even as he did so, a large crow appeared from nowhere and swooped downwards. 'Be off!' John shouted, flapping his arms. The bird hovered for a moment, almost as if it were taking stock of an enemy, then circled and flew away.

Thoroughly unnerved, John repeated the action, gritting his teeth and swiftly plucking the hat from the scarecrow's head.

Hollow eyes stared into his and there was the brilliant gleam of bone beneath the sun. With a cry of pure terror the Apothecary took a step backwards, his gorge rising at the sight of what was revealed. For beneath the hat, still wearing a white wig that made it look utterly grotesque, lay a human skull, a skull which at that moment seemed to be grinning at John Rawlings as if it were greeting an old and long-lost friend.

Chapter Six

The horrific discovery had left him breathless and panting, and it took several minutes of deep breathing and concentrated effort for John to get a grip on himself. As he had so often before, the Apothecary recalled the saying of his old Master that the dead can hurt no one, and fought away his panic by telling himself so repeatedly. Yet still his heart was pounding and his stomach felt as if it had descended to his knees. Fighting off an overwhelming desire to vomit, John sat down on the damp grass and steeled himself for the unpleasant task of examining the body.

The scarecrow had been put in place by, quite literally, being hung upon a crucifix. A humble wooden cross, which had presumably been taken from the church, had been impaled in the ground, the dead man attached to it by the simple means of pushing the cross piece through the sleeves of his full-skirted coat. The head had been held upright by a ribbon which had been attached to the cross, tied at its other end through a cut in the brim of the scarecrow's tricorne, now dislodged by John's tugging at it. With trembling fingers, the Apothecary lifted the white horsehair wig which, with the hat gone, ludicrously crowned the skull. A host of maggots swarmed below, churning and seething in what remained of a dark head of hair. Another wave of nausea swept the Apothecary and he dabbed at his upper lip with the sleeve of his coat.

The dead man's face itself had vanished, only the grinning skull intact after the attentions of the crows and flies. The victim had died with a full set of teeth, John noticed before he staggered away and was violently sick into one of the ditches. He then stood for a moment, mopping his brow with his handkerchief and taking deep breaths, before he returned to his grisly task.

Tentatively, the Apothecary undid the silver buttons of the claret velvet coat, noticing as he did so that it had been sliced neatly through just over the heart and that there were traces of dried blood all around this cut. So the victim had been stabbed with a thin-bladed knife, a dagger most likely, and would have died almost instantaneously. Beneath the coat, a silver waistcoat revealed a similar cut and more blood, and below that a cambric shirt bore the most blood of all. Wishing he had gloves with him, John eased the shirt up and out of the breeches.

Beneath the shirt was a skeletal chest, only that, not an ounce of flesh left anywhere. Slightly relieved that he had not found the body in a state of putrefacation, John took careful note of the nick on the ribs which proved him right. A dagger had definitely entered this unfortunate man's heart and left its mark to prove it. Steeling himself, the Apothecary looked downwards.

Below the knee the legs were completely missing, carried away by the foxes. Above, John saw after delicately lowering the breeches and hose, there were only bones, everything eaten away including the genitals, a bizarre thought to say the least of it. Of the missing shoes there was absolutely no sign and John realised that the impression that the scarecrow had been standing on legs must have been created by the moonlight. The hands, too, had been leaped for and devoured, only the frilled cuff remaining to cover the stumps of the wrist. Wishing he had a hip flask with him, the Apothecary stood silently, taking stock of the situation.

There was no sign of a violent struggle marking the raised bank on which the scarecrow had been positioned, though after several months, to say nothing of the floods, the time John estimated the body must have stood there, it might long ago have disappeared. Yet, he thought, if the crucifix had come from the church, might the house of God yield up anything further? Suddenly certain that there lay the scene of the crime, the Apothecary, his legs still weak from shock, waded through the drainage ditch that separated the ancient building from the grassy knoll on which the scarecrow stood.

On closer inspection, the older John could see the church was. Indeed, the building was clearly medieval, the exterior half timbered, the spaces between the wooden construction filled with laths and plaster. A weatherboarded bell turret reared above, while entry was through an oaken door set in the newly built porch in the north wall. Glad to get away from the scarecrow for a moment or two, the Apothecary made his way into the shadowy interior.

Exposed timbers and arches of wood immediately caught John's eye, lit by weak sunshine coming in through the plain timber-framed windows. Though what little light there was was dimmed by a stud wall running across the whole width of the church in order to support the turret. In medieval times, rushes would have been strewn and the congregation would have either stood or sat on the floor. But to suit eighteenth-century demands, John noticed, a pulpit and pews had been recently installed, the pulpit being particularly interesting because it was of the three deck variety. The lower part of it, consisting of a gated seat, was clearly meant for the parish clerk, a thin man, the Apothecary thought, for anybody stout would get wedged in in such a small space. Above it was another area from which the Perpetual Curate would conduct the main part of the service. Above this again was the third stage, to which the minister would ascend in order to deliver the sermon, usually of prodigious length and ending barely in time for the congregation to get home to dine at three. Because of the amazingly long time involved many families took chamber pots with them into their pews, which both ladies and gentlemen used discreetly while the service continued.

The pews themselves each had a locked door and were square in design, containing benches on which the occupants sat facing one another. Vaulting over the wall of one, John thankfully took a seat and rested quietly in the peaceful silence, letting his thoughts run on.

Could the murder have taken place here, within these very walls? Could there, perhaps, be a clue to the fatal stabbing in this old and holy building? And might there also be an indication as to the identity of the dead man? Much as John had disliked doing so, he had searched the scarecrow's coat pockets, only to find that they had all been bare. Even the waistcoat openings had been empty, the fob watch missing. Whoever had killed him had made sure that the victim's name would remain a mystery. Reluctantly, the Apothecary left the pew and began to search amongst the dim recesses of the little church.

An abandoned cloak lay in the parish clerk's stall, though this, too, had no papers in it, nor the name of the tailor stitched within. There were signs that this last might have been ripped out, for a few loose threads remained near the collar. However, the search for a fight was far less successful, there being nothing other than a few drops of dried blood on the floor by the font, though these could have been caused by anything, John considered, even an innocent nosebleed. Logically he had to admit that if the scarecrow had been dead for some months, any sign of the fight in which he died would have been cleared up by now. Dreading what he had to do next, the Apothecary stepped out into the daylight and gazed around him.

From this angle by the porch, the body was invisible, totally screened by the shepherd's shelter. Small wonder, then, that nobody had seen it or, if they had, recognised it for what it actually was. Yet six months was a long time. Perhaps the scarecrow *had* been observed and simply allowed to remain where it was. But looking for the tailor's name in the cloak had given the Apothecary an idea and now he felt impelled to put it into practice. Hideous though the thought was, John approached the skeleton once more.

The maker's label had been ripped out of the coat, as had that in the horribly foreshortened breeches. But it was just as he was straightening from examining these that the Apothecary caught a glimpse of something protruding from what had once been a fine silk lining, and raised the hem of the coat to eye level. A paper had been stitched inside, there was no doubt of it. A paper that had only become visible as the elements and scavengers tore at the scarecrow's clothing. Taking his herb knife from his pocket, John cut through the remaining stitches and withdrew a sealed document. Breaking the seal, he spread the paper on to the ground in order to study it.

'189 1504 598 2211 1905 500 665 2099,' he read, followed by the cryptic phrase, 'la Grenouille et le Papillon de Nuit'. Then ensued another series of numbers, together with the word 'Winchelsea'.

John stared in astonishment, his brain racing, only able to conclude that he had inadvertently stumbled across some sort of code and wondering how, with all the goodwill in the world, the village constable was going to deal with this extraordinary set of circumstances. And then as he looked at the paper again, the realisation that he had come across some altogether larger game than a straightforward killing for gain or revenge dawned on him. The document stitched into the lining of the scarecrow's coat could be nothing but sealed and coded orders.

The Apothecary stood silently for another few moments, deciding on the best course of action. Then, with great determination, he folded the paper and put it safely in his inner pocket, meanwhile ramming the scarecrow's hat back on its maggot-blown wig. Then having pulled the tricorne well down to hide the skull, John swiftly mounted his horse and went at the gallop back along the road he had come.

'La Gren-oil eh le Pap-pill-yon de Newt', read Joe Jago in an atrocious French accent.

'Extraordinary!' commented the Blind Beak, who sat leaning back in his chair, his black-bandaged eyes tilted towards the ceiling, his hands folded across his stomach, his feet upon a footstool. 'Quite extraordinary.'

'Then come another series of numbers, Sir.'

'Obviously a cipher. Well done, Mr Rawlings. You did absolutely the right thing in bringing this document straight to me.'

'Thank God,' said John. 'My instinct told me so. Yet I kept thinking I ought to inform the constable about the body. Though how on earth he would have sorted it all out, I dread to think.'

'I somehow feel it would have been beyond him. We are a nation at war, Mr Rawlings, and judging by the code the dead man was carrying and the fact that it was concealed in the lining of his coat, I can only presume the victim was a member of what is known as the Secret Service.'

'You mean a spy?'

'Yes, I do.'

The Apothecary gave a sudden laugh. 'I seem to remember you advising me to find myself one, and not that long ago at that.'

Mr Fielding rumbled an answering chuckle. 'Yes, so I did. Well, you appear to have succeeded. But more of espionage in a moment. First, tell me, my friend, how are you getting on with your mysterious visit to Winchelsea?'

'You know about it?'

'Sir Gabriel came here to dine the other evening.'

'Oh, I see. Well, Sir, the mysterious lady turned out to be none other than Elizabeth Harcross, widow of the profligate Jasper. She sent for me in great secrecy because she is under the impression that some enemy from the past is trying to kill her.'

'And are they?'

John frowned. 'Possibly, yes. Anonymous gifts of food and drink are left on her doorstep which she claims are making her ill. However, I sampled a bottle of wine donated in a similar manner and all it did was make me sing.'

Joe Jago cracked a laugh as did the Blind Beak.

'How typical,' said the Magistrate. Then he grew serious. 'None the less, it is a situation that should be watched. What do you intend to do?'

'Return there when you have decided what action you want to take regarding the scarecrow.'

'Um.' Mr Fielding fingered his chin, then turned to his clerk. 'What do you think, Joe? Should we leave our spying friend to the mercies of the village constable?'

'No, Sir. Let's send a couple of Runners to bring him back here. The clothes should be examined, if nothing more. After all, we can give him a burial just as easily as anyone else.'

John's stomach churned. 'His head is in a terrible condition.'

'The Runners can clean him up,' answered the Magistrate cheerfully. 'But before we do anything, we must get this piece of paper to Dr Willes.'

The Apothecary's mobile brows rose. 'Dr Willes?'

Mr Fielding laughed again. 'Should we tell him, Joe?'

The clerk's foxy features vanished in a dried-out riverbed of wrinkles as he grinned scampishly. 'Not all of it, Sir, no.'

Catching their mood, John's crooked smile appeared. 'What don't I know? Who is this Dr Willes?'

The Blind Beak cleared his throat and suddenly looked immensely stern. 'Have respect. We speak of the Decipherer to the King, Sir. A man of great importance whose name you must keep utterly confidential, you understand.'

The Apothecary's jaw dropped. 'I was not aware there was such a post.'

'That is because you are young, my friend. Believe me, there is a Secret Department attached to the Post Office which was founded about the turn of this century and has been functional ever since, its task to open suspect mail and decipher coded messages. That is apart from the Secret Office which falls directly within the jurisdiction of the Secretary of State himself and is responsible for organising the secret agents or spies.'

'I am frankly astounded. Why should there be the need for such things?'

Joe Jago broke in, tapping the side of his nose with his finger. 'To garner information, Mr Rawlings. Governments need intelligence, and they are prepared to pay to get it.'

Mr Fielding shifted the papers on his desk and the other two men turned to look at him. 'I suggest you take your find directly to Dr Willes yourself, Mr Rawlings. It is quite clearly time that you learned something of what goes on behind the scenes. But tell me first, have you breakfasted?'

'Yes, thank you. As I told you, I rode straight from Fairfield to Hastings, a goodish way. But by going hell for leather I managed to catch the two o'clock post chaise. So, having arrived early this morning, I booked a room in one of the inns and got a few hours' sleep and some food before I came here.'

'Very sensible. Then would it suit you to visit Dr Willes immediately? Jago will write a letter of introduction and you can explain to the King's Decipherer exactly how you came across this document.'

'I should be more than delighted. In fact, positively intrigued.'

'Excellent. I shall order you some coffee while Joe puts pen to paper.'

'I think I'd rather take a stroll, Sir. Twelve hours in a coach is enough to give anyone cramp.'

'Indeed, indeed. Come back in half an hour, my friend, and all will be ready for you.'

Emerging into the cold unflattering brightness of London on a February morning, still dressed in the clothes he had worn for the last twenty-four hours and feeling desperately in need of a shave, was hardly the moment to run into the woman for whom John perpetually wanted to look his best. But fate was obviously in quizzical mood, for there she was. Wondering whether to hide in a doorway, but for all that longing to speak to her, the Apothecary hovered like a moth round a flame as Coralie Clive walked in his direction, clearly not yet having seen him.

John's heart beat faster as she drew nearer and he felt his mouth go dry. Then, telling himself not to be a fool, he bowed low, horribly aware that the sleeve of his coat, obviously put under a strain by the marathon ride he had undertaken yesterday, ripped as he did so.

'Good heavens,' said Coralie, her voice rippling with amusement, 'if it isn't Mr Rawlings.'

He felt instantly irritated. 'I had thought we were on first name terms by now, Miss Clive.'

Her green eyes, bright as emeralds and easily as sparkling, gave him an enigmatic look. 'Of course we are. I apologise for being so formal.'

'Then why were you?'

'Because you are such a strange young man.'

'What do you mean?' asked John defensively. 'I studied hard for my profession, I have a shop of my own which is doing very well. I am a model of rectitude. How dare you call me strange!'

Although he was annoyed, laughter was only a breath away, as always with her. In fact every emotion he had for her – love, desire, adoration even – constantly fizzed beneath the surface like a glass of champagne and was just as difficult to control.

She slipped her arm through his. 'I have not seen you for an age, my friend. What have you been up to?'

'Not a great deal, that is until now.'

'Why? What has happened? No, don't tell me. We meet in Bow Street. You are once more involved with Mr Fielding and one of his inquiries.'

John nodded. 'You guess correctly.'

Coralie laughed. 'You look as if you might be.'

He was falling in love with her all over again and the Apothecary took an iron grip on his affections, knowing the extent of her power to hurt him. Indeed, had it not been for Coralie Clive's avowed intent to become as celebrated an actress as her sister, Kitty, John would long ago have proposed marriage.

'I take it from that remark that you noticed I haven't shaved.'

'Something of that sort. Oh my dear, you look a positive ruffian.'

'That's because I am one.'

'How you do surprise me!'

'Do I?' said John, and without another word he kissed her deeply on the mouth, there in Bow Street, in full view of the passing populace.

Mad thoughts went through his mind. Of taking her straight to his home and going to bed with her, of throwing her into a hackney coach and driving to a church where the parson would marry them, of simply offering her his hand and heart for evermore. But John, perhaps to his credit, perhaps not, did none of those things, somehow wanting Coralie to make some gesture indicating that she was as strongly attracted to him as he was to her. Her response to him was warm enough, returning his kisses with ardour, not fighting him off as she so easily could have done.

'Do you care for me at all?' he heard himself whisper.

'Of course I do. I consider you a very dear friend.'

'For God's sake, Coralie,' he answered roughly. 'Please don't mince words. Now that Richmond is off the scene, I thought you might regard me differently.'

She drew away from him. 'The Duke and I were companions, that is all.'

'You mean you didn't sleep with him?'

Now he had made a mistake. Kissing in public might be one thing, but questioning her about a past relationship was another. Coralie positively smouldered.

'How dare you quiz me about what I do? What gives you that right?'

A little light-headed through lack of sleep, the Apothecary answered recklessly, 'The fact that I am totally besotted with you.'

'Besotted?' repeated the actress with contempt. 'Old men are besotted with chitty little girls. Married women are besotted with their husband's apprentices. Couldn't you find a better word to describe what you feel?'

'Oh, for the love of Heaven,' shouted John, losing his patience, 'I adore you. Is that any better?'

'No, it isn't,' stormed Coralie Clive. 'You lust for me, that's the truth of it, John Rawlings. Love simply doesn't enter into it. Good morning to you.' And with that she turned on her high red heel and marched off towards Drury Lane without another word.

John stared after her rigidly retreating back, swore an evil oath and kicked a pile of refuse flying, then stalked back into the Public Office, his face bleached with fury.

And he was in no better frame of mind when he stormed into his home in Nassau Street, banging into the hall and clattering through the house like a tempest.

Sir Gabriel's head appeared over the first-floor banisters. 'Good God, boy, I thought we were under attack. Whatever are you doing?'

'Nothing,' John answered angrily.

'I can only presume that something has gone wrong, judging

71

from the fact that you are back from Winchelsea so soon and that your expression's black as thunder.'

'This face I must see,' said a female voice, and to John's astonishment Serafina de Vignolles, the woman with whom he had once been totally infatuated, her daughter, and John's god-daughter, Italia, toddling beside her, came on to the landing from the first-floor salon.

'My dear friend,' she called down. 'You look so troubled. Whatever has happened to you?'

Milking the situation, the Apothecary cast his features into an expression of deepest gloom. 'What has not!' he answered dramatically.

'That means a woman is involved,' said Sir Gabriel with asperity. 'Come and join us, my son. We are having some champagne prior to dining early for the benefit of Italia.'

'And how is my god-daughter?' said John, running up the last few steps and snatching the child up into his arms.

She was a beautiful little creature, with an abundance of her father's lustrous black hair tumbling in curls on either side of a roses on snow complexion. Little seed-pearl teeth showed when she smiled and her body, secure against John's shoulder, already had the strong supple feel of Serafina's about it.

'I am fine,' answered Italia with composure, and gave the Apothecary a bussing upon his cheek. 'You're very hairy,' she added.

'And that is not the first time I've been told that today,' he replied grimly.

'Has Coralie Clive been misbehaving again?' asked Serafina, looking acute.

'Indeed she has,' said John with feeling, and settling himself by the fire took the glass handed to him by Sir Gabriel.

Suddenly it was very good to be at home again and in the company of those who cared for him, all listening attentively, even the child, to the tale he had to tell.

'So,' said John's father, when his son had finished, 'it seems that you have had a most adventurous time. I can hardly credit that Mrs Harcross has returned and now considers herself to be in danger. Who would want to do such a thing to so lovely a woman?'

'She believes an old friend of Jasper's – or one of the others.' Serafina shook her head. 'I can't agree with her. All the

72

vengeance in that terrible situation was played out long ago. As for Jasper's many women, they have all gone their different ways.'

'You say your spy had a coded message upon him,' put in Sir Gabriel.

'Yes, I am to take it to the King's Decipherer later today.'

'And who might that be?'

'I am not at liberty to divulge. Mr Fielding gave me a name and an address but asked me not to pass it to anyone.'

Sir Gabriel rubbed his thin and elegant hands together. 'What splendid stuff this is. There's nothing better than a good tale of spies in my view. Why, I remember when the Young Pretender marched south in '45, London was full of Jacobite sympathisers. Everybody believed everybody else to be a secret agent for the Bonny Prince. It was all enormous fun.'

'Some people took it very seriously,' the Apothecary answered severely.

'As did I,' Sir Gabriel replied without a flicker.

In this manner they chatted on until, after John had gone to wash, shave and change into clean and more fashionable attire, they went in to dine. Then their amusement came from watching Italia attempting to imitate the eating habits of her elders, even down to the way her mother dabbed her curving lips with a napkin.

'Why, she's as like you as if you had spat her out of your mouth,' said John.

'In manner, yes. In looks I think Italia favours her French ancestry.'

'She already has your elegance.'

'Thank you,' Serafina answered, and shot the Apothecary a look in the depths of which was all the old affection she had felt for him.

Without thinking, John said, 'I wish Coralie were more like you.'

'She really upset you this morning, didn't she?'

'Yes.'

'My son,' put in Sir Gabriel, 'may I give you a little advice?'

'Please do.'

'As best you can, forget that lady. If she cares for you at all she will one day start to realise that acting alone is not enough to satisfy her, then she will come to you and tell you so. If, however, she is not your destined consort, she will turn to someone else

73

when that moment arrives. Therefore, the best thing you can do is let the earth revolve, let time pass, and enjoy life as fully as you can without her.'

'You're right, of course,' said John, with a certain reluctance.

'Indeed he is,' stated Serafina. She looked at her daughter, who was drooping a little. 'Sirs, I must take my leave of you. The effort of behaving impeccably has tired Italia out. My coach is in the mews, John. May my coachman take you to your destination once he has set us down?'

'I suppose that would be in order, provided he does not know upon whom I'm calling.'

'The mystery will remain,' Serafina answered with a smile.

Having been waved off by Sir Gabriel, who had announced his intention of going out to play whist, Serafina slipped her arm through John's in the warmth of the coach's padded interior, while the child sitting on her lap fell straight into a deep sleep.

'My dear, I have something to ask you,' the Comtesse said.

'What is it?'

'Do you think your father still has a *tendresse* for Elizabeth Harcross?'

The Apothecary thought in silence. 'If he has, he gives no sign of it. He is a remarkable man, you know. I think when she disappeared abroad after Jasper was murdered, he positively forced himself to forget her.'

'Oh, that we could all have such self-control.'

Wondering exactly what she meant, John tensed, remembering only too clearly the state of Serafina's marriage when he had first met her. 'There's nothing wrong between you and Louis, is there?' he asked hesitantly.

She sighed. 'Not exactly, no.'

Not satisfied, John added, 'Answer me straightly, Serafina. Has he gone back to his old philandering ways?'

She turned to look at him, her eyes shining. 'No, I am sure that he has not. He has become an excellent father and husband. It is just that he has seemed so preoccupied recently. There is something on his mind, I feel certain of it.'

'Would it help if I had a word with him this evening? I could catch the same early morning coach to Hastings that I did last time.'

Serafina squeezed his arm. 'I would be most grateful if you

74

did. Louis trusts and likes you. If there is anything worrying him I feel certain that you will find it out.'

'If I can be of service,' said John.

The Comtesse kissed him soundly. 'You are so good. I simply can't imagine why I didn't take you for a lover all those years ago.'

If only you had, thought John, as he gazed out of the window and watched the light begin to fade from that eventful day.

Chapter Seven

Having dropped Serafina and her sleeping child at their home at number twelve, Hanover Square, the Comte de Vignolles's coachman, after clipclopping smartly round the quadrangle, turned out of the precinct into Little Brook Street, then went left into New Bond Street, making his way towards that highly fashionable area, still in the final throes of its development, situated behind Berkeley Square. Greatly favoured by the wealthy and powerful, moving out of the city towards the open spaces of Hyde Park, the locality bore the name Mayfair, taking its title from a somewhat rowdy fair which always began on May Day, held annually on a plot of land situated to the east side of the park. Like all events of this nature, the May Fair was a great attraction to the rowdy and the drunk, and John, having visited it the year previously, thought he had never seen such a collection of evil villains and dirty whores amongst those present, and wondered whether the fair could continue much longer, particularly with the influx of such influential people into the area. Indeed, so fine a neighbourhood was this becoming, that the Earl of Chesterfield himself was campaigning to have the public executions which took place at Tyburn, a mere stone's throw away at the corner of Hyde Park, removed elsewhere, and the name of Tyburn Road changed.

Slowing the coach, for Mayfair was not yet familiar to drivers, Louis's coachman drove around Berkeley Square and out into the smart streets of newly-built houses lying at the back of it.

'What address did you say, Sir?' the man called from his box.

The Apothecary looked at the piece of paper John Fielding had given him. 'Twenty-four Hill Street,' he answered out of the window.

'That must be it over there,' and the driver pointed with his whip.

John looked in the direction indicated and his eyes grew wide. A most elegant new mansion, far grander than anything he had imagined would be occupied by a spy, stood imposingly in this street of highly desirable residences. The Apothecary glanced at the paper again but the address was correct.

'Yes, that's it,' he replied.

A footman answered the door and on hearing that the visitor was calling on behalf of John Fielding, showed the Apothecary into a somewhat austere anteroom, hung with pictures of ecclesiastical buildings, including a rather fine painting of St David's Cathedral in Wales. John had just got to his feet to examine this more closely when the servant reappeared.

'My lord will see you now,' he intoned.

The Apothecary stared at him. 'My lord . . . ?' he repeated.

'Follow me, please,' the footman answered, ignoring the visitor's startled expression.

They proceeded across an elegant hall into a stunningly beautiful room.

'Mr Rawlings, my lord,' intoned the footman expressionlessly, and bowed his way out.

John looked around him, amazed by what he saw. Three huge windows, each with a padded seat, draped in gold to match the long and magnificent curtains, looked on to the attractive garden beyond. Above his head, the cornice was picked out in a matching gold, while below it the frieze, though of different design, complemented the colour exactly. But the most exciting element of the room was its shape. For the window wall curved gently outwards, meeting the adjoining walls in a pillar-like configuration which added a pleasing symmetry to the whole effect. This, together with the angled setting of the windows, gave an impression of delicacy and lightness, unequalled by anything John had ever seen.

Modern architecture at its best, the Apothecary thought, and before he could stop himself exclaimed, 'What a wonderful house. Who designed it, if I might ask?'

The man seated behind the desk placed in front of a window, his back to the light so that he appeared in silhouette, looked up from his papers. 'A new young man, a Scotsman, name of Robert Adam. I'm glad you like it. Now, my dear Sir, I believe you have been sent here by Mr Fielding. How may I help you?'

'It's about this document,' said John, fishing in his pocket. And then he stopped speaking and gazed in frank astonishment as the man got to his feet, etched dark against the spring sky behind him, and came round the desk towards his visitor. For a clergyman stood there, a clergyman in black leather gaiters, full-skirted formal coat and waistcoat, both black, and stark white cravat. A very tall clergyman of large build, with a big horse-like face and small observant eyes.

'Oh, I'm sorry, Sir,' John stammered, totally flustered. 'I've obviously made a stupid mistake. I was looking for the King's Decipherer. I've come to the wrong house.'

'Did you want to see Dr Willes?' replied a booming voice.

'Yes, my lord.'

'Then you've found him. I am he whom you seek.'

'You!' exclaimed the Apothecary. 'But Dr Willes is a master spy, Sir.'

'Dr Willes is a decoder,' replied the other severely. 'He cracks ciphers, reduces them to the simplicity of a child's primer. But if that, in your view, is being a spy, then indeed I am one. I am also, but that is merely by the by, Bishop of Bath and Wells. I combine the two callings.'

'Good God!' exclaimed John, wholly astounded.

'Amen to that,' said Dr Willes piously. He extended his hand. 'And you, Sir, who are you? Other than an associate of Mr Fielding's, that is.'

John, still reeling with shock, gave a somewhat jerky bow. 'John Rawlings, my lord, Apothecary of Shug Lane, Piccadilly. It has been my privilege to work with the Principal Magistrate in the past. And now he has sent me here to ask if you might decipher this.' And he handed Dr Willes the document which had been concealed in the lining of the scarecrow's coat.

'Let me see now, let me see,' answered the Bishop, producing some spectacles from an inside pocket. Putting them on, he carried the paper to the light, studying it silently for a moment or two. Then he looked up. 'Where did you get this?'

As best he could, John explained, leaving out no detail.

Dr Willes listened in silence, then said, '189 1504 598 2211 1905 500 665 2099, la Grenouille et le Papillon de Nuit. Well that's fairly straightforward. It's the new French code, only about two months old. They started working on it as soon as war broke out. But we began to decipher it almost as quickly as they invented it, if you know what I mean.'

Stunned, John answered, 'What does it say?'

Dr Willes looked faintly surprised. 'Oh, yes, you'd want to know that, of course. Well, it's direct and to the point.'

'Yes?'

'It reads, "You are ordered to give secret instructions immediately to the British spies, the Frog and the Moth." Then it says, "You will find the pair in Winchelsea. Contact them as arranged."'

'So the dead man was French?'

'Either that or carrying French papers on him. But I would imagine that the former is the case. The Scarecrow, as you call him, was sent over here to awaken two sleepers.'

'By that you mean spies who do little in peacetime except take their money.'

The Bishop's eyes peeped over his glasses at John. 'Precisely, Sir. There are, in my reading of the situation, two of them, both in Winchelsea, perhaps working together, perhaps not even knowing of each other's existence. In any event, the Scarecrow had come over here to give them their orders.'

The Apothecary nodded his head thoughtfully. 'And perhaps one of them objected to that, violently.'

Dr Willes grimaced. 'And did away with the spymaster in order not to obey? Yes, very probably you are right. You will be returning to the Romney Marsh to try to unmask them, I take it?'

'Yes, my lord.'

'Then tread carefully, my friend. Spies are a curious breed.' He laughed suddenly, his big face splitting into a toothy smile. 'I should know, after all.'

'Indeed, you should, my lord,' the Apothecary answered, thinking that the saying about God working in mysterious ways had never been more true than in the case of Dr Edward Willes, Bishop of Bath and Wells, Decipherer to the King, head of the Secret Department and British master spy.

Before they parted company, John and Serafina had arranged that he should call at Hanover Square at seven o'clock that evening in order to visit Louis de Vignolles. So, with an hour or so to spare, the Apothecary hurried to Shug Lane to check that all was well with his shop which, much to his surprise, he found full of customers.

'. . . a perfume of passion,' Nicholas Dawkins was saying to an excited audience of female customers. 'My Master, as fine a scent maker as you'll find in London, albeit he is an apothecary and not a perfumer, mixed it personally from a secret recipe smuggled into this country from Muscovy, while I, his humble apprentice, named it for my Russian ancestors. Ladies, I give you Snow Violets, the fragrance of the Tsars.'

'I'll take a bottle,' called John from the back, and Nicholas had the good grace to blush, while Master Gerard, watching benignly from the doorway of the compounding room, laughed heartily.

There was a slight fluttering as the shop's owner made his way through the throng towards the back room, into which, having patted Nicholas on the back to indicate that he wasn't going to admonish him on the spot, John quietly vanished.

'Well, well,' he said as he went inside.

Master Gerard, who had closed the door to give them privacy, laughed again. 'What a splendid young man that is. Why, in my day, Mr Rawlings, we apothecaries were dry as dust. But now, with people like you and young Nick about, the whole profession is becoming more accessible. And so it should. For if the ladies come in for cosmetics or scents, then they will buy something else and thus our fame will spread.'

John rolled an eye towards the shop. 'What was all that about a secret recipe? Did he compound it himself?'

Old Master Gerard looked flustered. 'I assisted, I assure you. But please don't be angry, Mr Rawlings, not with either of us. It is his enthusiasm that makes Nicholas bend the rules a little.'

'Bend?' John said with a laugh. 'More like buckle! I must have words with him, you know.'

'You won't beat him, will you? It will be punishment enough that you caught him in the act. He so wanted to show you the profit he had made and suggest that you might continue his experiment.'

'My old Master would have beaten me.'

'But you are not the beating kind, Mr Rawlings. You do not have that look about you.'

John shook his head. 'Between the two of you I just don't stand a chance. Just as well that I'm off again tonight. I only get some peace when I am hunting down spies and murderers.' He laughed again to show he spoke in jest. 'And now, Master Gerard, I would much appreciate a brew of tea. I must write to Mr Fielding and tell him the latest turn of events so I'll seize a few quiet moments here.'

He sat down at the scrubbed wooden table and, taking some paper and a pen, copied out the coded message as Dr Willes had dictated it to him before he left Hill Street. This done, John waited for the noise from the shop to subside, then went through the dividing door. Nicholas stood beyond, flushed with a strange mixture of triumph and fear.

'Well?' said John, keeping a card player's face.

'I know I did wrong, Sir. I know I shouldn't have mixed anything in your absence . . .'

'And claimed that it was made by me.'

'And claimed that it was made by you. But I did so want to try this recipe. My grandmother used to make it, you see. It really is Russian . . .'

'Nicholas, stop,' said John, fractionally irritated. 'It *was* wrong of you and I really ought to punish you but this time I am content to leave it at a warning. Namely, do not do such a thing again! I assure you I will not be so lenient if there is another occasion. I am quite happy to compound things with you when I have time, so be content with that. Now, to make up for your transgression, I want you to go round to Bow Street and deliver this note. Then go home and tell Sir Gabriel that I won't be coming back tonight but will go straight to Southwark, then to Hastings early.'

'But who will close the shop? Do you wish to, Sir?'

'Yes, then I'm going to Hanover Square to see the Comte de Vignolles.'

Nicholas frowned. 'Oh, I thought he had gone away.'

'Did you? Why?'

'Because I saw him this morning, catching the York post chaise from the George and Blue Boar Inn in Holbourn.'

'Are you certain of that?'

'Positive, Sir. I was delivering some physick to a lady living in Bloomsbury Square, and I came back to the shop via High Holbourn. And there was the Comte de Vignolles, large as life, setting off for York. I'd swear it was him.'

John looked extremely thoughtful. 'How very interesting. Well, he could hardly get there and back in a day. So presumably all will be made clear this evening.'

'I hope nothing is wrong,' said Nicholas, and his very sincerity would have been enough to have made John forgive him, that is if he hadn't already done so.

Having hired a linkboy and walked with Master Gerard, somewhat

82

infirm of step these days, as far as his house in Hay Hill, John hurried the rest of the way to Hanover Square, his mind already turning over the idea that Louis de Vignolles was not going to be there. Once, long ago, when the Apothecary had first met him, the Frenchman's marriage had been on the verge of collapse. The Comte had had a mistress while Serafina, bored and unhappy, had become the most notorious gambler in London. But since they had been reconciled, the couple had seemed idyllically content, their happiness crowned by the birth of a daughter. Now, though, depressing thoughts assailed the Apothecary and his heart sank low when the footman who answered the door informed him that the Comte was not at home, though the Comtesse awaited her guest in the upstairs salon. Fearing the worst, John climbed the curving stairs and went to join his hostess, who stood before the fire, staring into the flames.

'My dear,' she said, hearing his step and turning round. 'Our plans are thwarted. Louis is not here.'

Deciding to keep Nicholas's story to himself, at least for the time being, the Apothecary answered, 'What a pity. I wonder where he can have got to?'

'I have no idea. He left the house early this morning and did not say what time he would be home. I presumed that he would abide by his usual habit and be here by now.'

'How very strange. And you assure me that there is nothing wrong between you?'

'As best anyone can, yes I do. If anything we have fallen more in love than out of it.'

'I'm delighted to hear it. Serafina, forgive me for being personal but I am only trying to help. Does Louis have any financial worries at all?'

'None that I am aware of. His father left him a great deal of money, all of which has been invested wisely. He visits the Royal Exchange quite often, of course, but there is nothing to suggest things go badly for him there.'

John smiled at the Comtesse and slipped his arm round her shoulders. 'Then perhaps you are imagining that he is behaving strangely.'

She shook her head. 'No, I am not. He is abstracted, preoccupied. there is something on his mind, I know it.'

'Have you asked him what it is?'

Serafina sipped from her wine glass. 'Yes. He denied anything. That is why I am starting to get anxious.'

'But, my dear, if it is not another woman and Louis has no money problems, what can be bothering him?'

'It just occurs to me,' the Comtesse answered slowly, 'that it could be something to do with this wretched war. After all, my husband is French.'

'But his parents were Huguenots and consequently would have no love for their mother country.'

'Louis has never been like-minded. He visited France regularly until hostilities broke out.'

'I see,' said John, accepting the glass his hostess handed him. He chose his next words carefully. 'Perhaps you are right, Serafina. Perhaps he is upset to see two countries, both of which he considers his homeland, in a state of hostility.'

Her eyes glistened in the firelight. 'I think that must be it.'

'Yes,' answered the Apothecary, 'yes, I'm sure you're right.'

But his pictorial memory had already flashed up a picture of himself and the Blind Beak, sitting by another fire, this one in Bow Street, as John Fielding informed him that it was already known that a French spy was working out of London, having successfully infiltrated the ranks of the *beau monde*, amongst whom he dwelled in the guise of a man of substance.

Chapter Eight

This time John avoided temptation and did not visit the parlour of The White Hart, instead going straight to bed and getting a good night's sleep. In fact, with the weather staying fine, the whole journey would have passed off without incident had it not been for the extraordinary coincidence of seeing Dr Florence Hensey at breakfast the following morning.

'My very dear Sir,' said John as he entered the dining room. 'What a surprise to see you here.'

'Likewise, Mr Rawlings. Are you returning from Winchelsea?'

'No. I had to come back on urgent business but now I am making my way there once more. And you?'

'I have one or two affairs to attend to in town, then I too will revisit the coast. Alas the querulous invalid I treat there grows ever more demanding. By the way, I had a letter from Sir Ambrose inviting me to dine. Should you see him could you say that next Friday would be convenient. I have dropped him a note to that effect but never trust the posts.'

'I'll be glad to.'

They breakfasted together in good heart, the doctor explaining that he had arrived in London late and therefore decided to stay at the inn before travelling further. Ever friendly and courteous, he waved John off in the courtyard, shouting to him that he would see him next week. The other passengers, very elderly and dull, glared at the commotion then fell asleep as soon as they left town and woke only for comfort and dining stops. In fact it was a journey of monumental boredom, during which the Apothecary, who normally enjoyed travelling, stared out of the window or read a book.

With nothing to impede its momentum, the flying coach arrived in Hastings twelve hours later, just as the sky began to redden on that early March day. Wondering whether to risk the final push to Winchelsea in the dark, John's better nature overcame him. He had hired Strawberry, the dappled mare, from Roderick's brother Tom, and then must have appeared to have absconded with her.

Though he had stabled the horse in Hastings and written a brief note of explanation there was always the possibility that the letter might not have arrived, leaving the owner frantic with worry about his missing animal. Hoping he would not get lost in the darkness, John saddled Strawberry up and set out.

He headed slightly inland, the sea to his right, and had travelled a fair distance when the mare, normally a very placid animal, suddenly shied at nothing and put her ears forward. With a sixth sense alerting him to danger, the Apothecary reined in and listened. At first all he could hear was his quickened breathing, but then, rumbling like distant thunder, came the sound of cartwheels, many sets of them, making their way down to the coast. Without hesitation, John leaped from the saddle and led the mare into the shelter of a spinney of wind-blown trees. If he was right he was somewhere in the region of the village of Fairlight, with its neighbouring cove. And it was from that cove, so he had heard in The Salutation, that the smugglers loaded contraband from darkened French vessels, lying as close inshore as they dared. Knowing that if he was caught he was as good as dead, the Apothecary stood close to the horse, willing her not to make a sound.

Then something very odd happened. In the distance, presumably from the clifftop, a lantern began to flash on and off in sporadic bursts which John could only imagine must be number sequences. Cursing that it was so dark and that he had no pencil with which to write the numbers down, the Apothecary could do nothing but watch, intrigued that the smugglers were being quite so blatant. If, indeed, smugglers they were, for the sound of cartwheels had abruptly stopped and John imagined the convoy drawing to a rapid halt and watching the lantern, just as he was. Then came another intriguing development. Somebody on horseback passed very close to where he lay hidden, so close that John could have reached out and touched him. But the noise of the plunging hooves had obviously also alerted the signaller, for the flashes of light suddenly ceased, to be swiftly followed by the sound of a horse cantering away before the other rider could reach him. After this came a long period of tense silence, then eventually the carts started up again and continued their journey to the sea.

Trembling with relief, John emerged from the shelter of the spinney and set out for Winchelsea as fast as the dappled mare could take him.

*   *   *

He had never been more relieved in his life to gain the warmth
and welcome of The Salutation. But having downed two excellent
French brandies very fast, the Apothecary still had one further task
to fulfil. Feeling slightly light-headed after his narrow escape, to
say nothing of the alcohol he had just consumed, John returned to
the stables and led out Strawberry, intent on returning her to her
owner that very night.

Truncheons, Tom's home and stableyard, lay within easy walking
distance, a mere stone's throw from St Thomas's Church. So, having
returned the horse to where she belonged, much to the delight of
Roderick's brother, John cut back through the churchyard, only to
stop short and draw behind a tree for the second time that night.
In hushed but bitter tones, a man and a woman were arguing.

'How could you do this to me?' whispered the male voice. 'After
all I have given you and done for you. Why, I was prepared to kill
the . . .'

'Shut your mouth,' hissed his companion. 'You are never to
mention that. Never, do you hear?'

'You evil bitch,' replied the other. 'You are governed by greed
and self . . .'

But he got no further. There was the sound of a stinging blow,
followed by a gasp of pain.

'Not one word more of your insults,' said the woman's voice, its
tone horribly menacing. 'You have as little wish to betray our secret
as I. But betray it I will if ever you speak to me like that again.'

She swept off up the path, passing close to where the Apothecary was hidden. Of average height, her build concealed by an
enveloping cloak, the woman's face was almost entirely hidden
by a sweeping hat, a hat reminiscent of those worn by Henrietta,
John thought with a sinking heart. Yet her perfume was different,
that much he was sure of. With his interest in creating scents, the
Apothecary had long passed the stage where one perfume smelt
very much like another. Henrietta wore a heady blend of hyacinth;
this woman a more exotic spicy mixture. Knowing that it was
the only clue he would have to her identity, John inhaled again
deeply before she passed out of the kissing gate and from his line
of vision.

Then he looked round, only to see that the man, too, had gone,
though the sound of his footsteps still echoed behind him. As did

the sound of the quiet sobs of the spurned lover, as the Apothecary presumed the poor fellow must be.

Living under an assumed name she might be, adopting another personality she may well have done, but Elizabeth Rose, once Elizabeth Egleton, the celebrated actress, was a performer to the very tips of her fingers. And on this particular occasion, with a variety of puzzled expressions, she was playing the role of aggrieved friend to a somewhat unwilling audience of one.

'Imagine my shock,' she was saying, 'when I called at The Salutation only to find that you had gone, without a word, leaving your room just as it had been earlier that morning.'

The Apothecary raised his eyebrows but said nothing.

'I did not know what had happened to you, Mr Rawlings, nor what to think, and indeed I jumped to the worst conclusion. That the poisoner was on your trail and had struck you down.'

'An unjustified fear, for here I am.'

'But how was I to know that?'

'You weren't, but I do feel you should have had more faith in me.'

Elizabeth bridled slightly. 'What do you mean?'

John assumed a dignified expression. 'Have I ever let you down in the past? I think not. I am saddened that you could not trust me, that is all.'

Mrs Rose cast her eyes down but said nothing.

'As it so happened, a discovery on the Romney Marsh sent me back to London post haste, in order that I might confer with Mr Fielding and others in authority. There are dark deeds brewing hereabouts, Madam. You must believe that.'

Beneath her enamel, the actress went very white. 'You mean that I—'

'Not just concerning you,' John interrupted with asperity. 'There are great games afoot. Remember that we are a nation at war.'

Elizabeth Rose looked suitably chastened and the Apothecary relented a little. 'So,' he said in a more kindly tone, 'I have a favour to ask of you. In order that I might mix more freely amongst Winchelsea's polite society, would you object if I passed myself off as your nephew?'

His hostess smiled and momentarily looked amazingly young. 'So there really is something important going on?'

'Yes, there is.'

'A matter of national security?'

'Almost certainly.'

'Then I shall play the part of your aunt with pleasure.' She frowned. 'But if we are going to do this, we must make the story convincing. Mr Rawlings, you will have to leave The Salutation and come and stay here. I have a small back bedroom with a pleasant view which should suit you very well. Furthermore, I will have to call you John.'

'I had always hoped you would one day.'

'Then it's settled. I shall tell the serving girl that we had to keep the fact of being related quiet for a few days but that she can now announce the truth to the world. She'll enjoy spreading that piece of gossip.'

'I'm sure she will. Now, there's one further thing.'

'What is that?'

'In the near future is there to be a public occasion of some sort at which I might meet everyone? It's vital that I get a good look at the town's inhabitants.'

Elizabeth's pale face grew positively animated. 'As luck would have it, there is to be an assembly this very night. Everyone who is anyone is bound to be there because the guest of honour is the Marquis of Rye himself. A fact guaranteed to bring all the little social climbers out in force.'

'Are you going?'

'Not on my own, no.'

'But you would venture forth in the company of your long-lost nephew, would you not?'

'Certainly.'

'Then I shall go straight away and get two tickets. Where are they on sale?'

'At the Town Hall. It has a large saloon set aside for balls and the like. I'm afraid we do not run to Assembly Rooms in Winchelsea.' Mrs Rose smiled a little wistfully.

'I'll call in on my way to settle the bill and collect my bags. Expect me back in an hour. Aunt.'

'Yes, Nephew, I will.'

In good spirits, John left Petronilla's Platt, but no sooner had he set foot into the street than he heard a voice call his name, and light steps come running up behind him. Turning, he was delighted to see that the beautiful Henrietta Tireman had come to join him, her clear eyes fresh in the morning sunshine.

'Why, Mr Rawlings, wherever have you been?' she said. 'I sent a letter to The Salutation inviting you to dine but was told that you had mysteriously departed, leaving all your things behind you.'

'I was urgently called to London and had no time at all to inform anyone.' He bowed. 'I am so sorry if I appeared rude. Am I forgiven?'

'Of course you are.' Henrietta glanced at the front door behind him. 'How are you getting on with Mrs Rose?' she asked in a lowered voice.

'Well, it so turns out that she is my aunt,' John answered, amazing himself yet again at the ease with which he lied.

'Your aunt! But why didn't you say so?'

'I wasn't sure. I suspected but had no proof.' He attempted to look mysterious and clearly succeeded.

'What a strange turn of events,' said Henrietta, shaking her head. She changed the subject. 'Are you by any chance going to the assembly tonight?'

'Yes, I am escorting Aunt Elizabeth. And you?'

'Naturally I am. My future brother-in-law is gracing us with his presence. I could hardly not.'

There could be no mistaking the note of bitterness in her voice and John stole a covert look at her. Momentarily, the crystal-clear eyes had clouded and Henrietta's beautiful mouth had twisted into a line. Deciding to ignore the fact, the Apothecary smiled at her.

'Obviously I have to reserve the first dance for my aunt, but would be most honoured if I could have the second.'

Miss Tireman's good humour restored itself. 'Alas, I have promised that to Dr Hayman. The third is still free.'

'Please mark me down.'

'It will be a pleasure.' She curtsied. 'Well, I must be on my way. My Mama has sent me out to buy some extra feathers for her headdress and will not be best pleased if I keep her waiting. Till tonight, Mr Rawlings.'

'Till tonight,' replied the Apothecary, and made an elaborate bow.

Never believing in travelling unprepared, John had brought with him a truly elegant suit of evening clothes. In fact so elegant that he wondered briefly about the appropriateness of such garments in a town as small as Winchelsea. Then the Apothecary took heart, reassured by the thought that the Marquis of Rye was to be present and that everyone would be dressed within an inch of their life. For a moment he savoured a vivid image of moths whirling through the air as fine garments were heaved out from the back of clothes presses, and waistcoats, heavy with embroidery, which had rarely seen the light of day, were hung on clothes lines and beaten to remove the dust. Then he turned back to his own reflection, adjusted his cravat and secured his wig, before going downstairs to join Mrs Rose.

The lady had made an enormous effort and was wearing a somewhat old-fashioned gown of silver lutestring embroidered with pearls. The very paleness of this ensemble, together with Elizabeth's hair and enamel make-up, succeeded in making her look like an arctic queen of ancient legend, and John would not have been in the least surprised to see that she wore icicles instead of earrings. But in the event, the actress displayed sparkling crystals in her ears, which had very much the same effect.

'You look very beautiful, Aunt,' said John, helping her into a velvet mantle which had seen somewhat better days.

'And you are fine beyond belief. Every woman there will be falling in love with you.'

'That will make a pleasant change,' the Apothecary answered dourly, painfully recalling Coralie Clive's most recent rejection of him.

'Don't be foolish, Nephew,' Mrs Rose answered severely as they stepped out into the street.

There were carriages everywhere. Even though the Town Hall was in easy walking distance of all but the most far flung dwelling, it seemed that every citizen of Winchelsea had dragged some aged equipage from the stable and set his boy to cleaning and polishing it. So bad was the congestion, indeed, that the streets were almost impassable, and John and Elizabeth made far better time on foot than did all those groaning along at a snail's pace.

At the Town Hall itself there was a further bottle-neck as everyone arrived at once and attempted to mount the stairs together. Eventually, though, after a long and patient climb, Mrs Rose and her escort reached the top and were greeted by Sir Ambrose Ffloote, who appeared to have set himself up as official Master of Ceremonies.

'Ha ha, Mrs Rose,' he bellowed. 'You've met up with the young

91

man, I see. He was asking about you on the journey but I was damned if I could remember you name. Memory like a watering can these days.'

She curtseyed charmingly. 'Sir Ambrose, Mr Rawlings is my nephew, as it turns out.'

'Is he by God,' said the Squire, looking puzzled. 'I thought that was somebody else. Ah well.' He turned away to greet the next arrivals.

Elizabeth looked conspiratorial. 'Now, who do you want to meet?'

'Everyone you know. I'll have to find out about the rest by other means.'

'Very well then, we shall start with the Finches, who are standing just over there. She is very rich and therefore considered of some importance.'

They made their way across the room towards the far end where a band of musicians were working up a mild lather in preparation for the exertions yet to come. For at the moment nobody was dancing, presumably waiting for the arrival of the Marquis before allowing themselves to commence festivities.

A fat fair woman, quivering with flowers and gems, was clearly their quarry, but as they drew closer John saw to his amazement that round her stood four more females, all very similar in appearance. A coterie of daughters flanked the redoubtable Mrs Finch, and the Apothecary's heart sank, certain that he would instantly be placed on the mother's list of eligible men.

'My dear Madam,' said Mrs Rose, clearly relishing the role she was playing, 'may I introduce to you my nephew, John Rawlings, who has but recently arrived from London.'

Mrs Finch grew fairer and fatter before the Apothecary's very eyes. 'Honoured Sir,' she said archly, a little bright spot appearing in either cheek, 'I am utterly charmed. Now, let me present my daughters. My eldest, Sophie. Make your curtsey, girl.'

The wretched creature, larger than her mother if anything, bobbed akwardly, not raising her eyes from the floor. John felt so sorry for her that he kissed her hand, then regretted it when she went puce.

'And now my second, Sarah.' Not even blessed with one redeeming feature, another lump bobbed down.

'And my twins, Agatha and Augusta.' These two plump little

madams had extremely knowing expressions which quite shocked John, who considered them far too advanced for their age.

'I do hope that you have some dances free, Mr Rawlings,' said the mother, patting his hand with hers.

'I am partnering my aunt,' John replied swiftly.

'Ah, but she cannot claim such a very handsome young man all the evening,' stated Mrs Finch roguishly. 'Now promise me you will lead one of us out as soon as you are free.'

'Gladly,' the Apothecary replied, and bowed his departure, horribly aware of the mother's heavily ringed hand still clinging to his.

'Best beware,' warned Elizabeth, laughing. 'Mrs Finch is a rich widow and is just as keen to get a husband for herself as she is for her daughters.'

John mopped his brow with his handkerchief. 'Where do they live?'

'In a large mansion right next door to the Town Hall. Yet they came by coach. I saw them.'

'What pretension.'

'It was ever thus. Now, Mr Rawlings, here are three interesting people. The doctor together with Mr and Mrs Gironde, the apothecary and his wife.'

John bowed as Mrs Rose made the formal introduction, studying the trio in the few brief moments while greetings were exchanged. Mr Gironde looked a typical Frenchman, he thought, with mournful dark brown eyes, a large mouth full of formidable teeth, and what appeared to be a bald head beneath his wig, for not a trace of hair was showing anywhere. This was in marked contrast to the doctor who had a mop of marmalade-coloured curls which refused to be tamed by a lump of horsehair. John, who by now desperately needed to visit a barber, felt every sympathy with him. In accordance with all people of his colouring, Dr Hayman ran to freckles, fair brows and lashes, and eyes the colour of sun-ripe gooseberries. The third member of the trio, the inquisitive Mrs Gironde, was very small in stature but to compensate for this had a wildly high coiffure, decorated with imitation birds. This merely enhanced her generally avine appearance, which consisted of bright darting eyes, a beaky nose and underfed sparrow's build. Had she moved forward in a series of hops, John would not have been at all surprised.

'And now for poor little Faith,' Elizabeth murmured.

'Lady Ffloote?'

93

'The very same.'

Around the room had been placed a series of couches and chairs, these intended to accommodate the older ladies and those plainer girls not invited to dance. Seated upon one of them, her head limply supported by a hand, was a faded beauty of yesteryear, these days muted to tones of cream and caramel as regarded her hair and skin. Even her eyes, John thought, looked as if they had once been bright and sparkling but were now reduced to sad little orbs of dullish tan.

With a swish of skirt, Mrs Rose sat down next to her. 'My dear Lady Ffloote, how are you this evening?'

Faith gave the kind of smile that could only be interpreted as brave. 'I'm afraid the headache is plaguing me again.'

'I am so very sorry. Perhaps my nephew might be of some assistance to you.' Lady Ffloote looked perplexed and Elizabeth continued, 'Pray allow me to present him. Mr John Rawlings, Apothecary of London.'

Faith frowned. 'I seem to know that name. Did you not travel to Winchelsea with my husband, Sir?'

'Yes, Lady Ffloote, I did.'

'He seemed much taken with his companions on that occasion. In fact he wants you and Dr Hensey to dine with us.'

'I saw the doctor in London on a brief trip to town. He asked me to tell you that next Friday will be most agreeable.'

'Then you must come too.' Faith looked wan. 'Even if I do not have the strength to join you at table, I am sure you gentlemen will find a great deal to discuss.'

'I trust you will be recovered by then,' John answered. 'But in the meantime I will take the liberty of calling on you to see if I can help cure your pain.'

Lady Ffloote looked wistful. 'Do so by all means. But I must warn you that so far no physician has succeeded.'

'I can but try,' the Apothecary replied cheerfully, then gave a polite bow as a man approached the couch on which the two ladies were seated.

Mrs Rose got to her feet and swept a dramatic curtsey. In fact, John thought, she was becoming more and more the actress with every passing second. Even through her enamel some colour had finally appeared in her cheeks and her eyes had started to sparkle.

'Madam,' said the newcomer, and gave a bow which included a

click of the heels. He kissed Elizabeth's fingers and she glowed, and John, observing this, smiled to himself.

Lady Ffloote, too enfeebled to rise, held out her hand. 'Captain Pegram, how nice to see you here. I thought you did not enjoy such occasions as these.'

'I don't,' the Captain answered honestly. 'In fact I detest them. But the temptation of seeing the future bride and groom proved too great. Put my presence down to idle curiosity.'

He was a tall man with the straight back and military stance of a professional soldier, and the dreamy blue eyes of a scholar, this contrast giving the impression that Captain Pegram was at odds with himself. Remembering Elizabeth's words that though trained for the battlefield the Captain preferred his own company, the Apothecary conjectured that the fellow was probably something of a misfit, and this was borne out by the uneasy way in which Captain Pegram kept glancing round the room, as if he felt out of place in such gawdy surroundings. His hair, what John could see of it beneath an ancient army wig, was brown and inclined to be long. Obviously Captain Pegram wore it tied back when he was at home and did not bother with such fripperies as following fashion. Yet there was something honest and open about him that was difficult to resist. As John was presented by Mrs Rose, he found himself warming to the army officer.

It was at that moment that there was a stir in the doorway and conversation suddenly became hushed. One or two voices could be heard whispering, 'They're here,' and every eye turned towards the entrance. John stared along with everybody else, and found himself frankly amazed at the sight of the couple who had just come in. The man, who could only be the Marguis of Rye judging by the amount of bowing and scraping going on, stood at least six feet tall and carried himself with that inner ease that comes through years of good breeding and privilege. His face, too, bore all the characteristics of a true member of the aristocracy, with its long aquiline nose, thin mouth and dark brilliant eyes. And the features, though inclined to be hawkish, could only be described as arresting. The Apothecary let his eyes wander over the Marquis's clothes, which the aristocrat wore with a negligence which was to be envied, and tried to put an age to the man. Rather to his surprise, John came up with forty, a little old for the future husband of Miss Rosalind Tireman, he would have thought.

But then the Apothecary stopped looking at the Marquis and gave his full attention to the girl on his arm, aware that he was staring as hard as every other red blooded male in the room. For she was more than beautiful, she was exquisite, a fabulous creature, almost inhuman in her perfection. A mass of hair, the colour of spun gold, tumbled round her head, its very wildness attractive. Mermaid's eyes, neither green nor blue but a shade somewhere between the two, were set widely apart in a superbly boned face. Yet though all this loveliness could have been marred had the girl's figure been poor, this, too, was incomparable, small and supple yet with full and shapely breasts. As she walked forward Rosalind glittered with emeralds, clearly a gift from her future husband, which she unconsciously stroked with loving fingers.

'The fair bride?' whispered John to no one in particular.

'Yes,' replied Captain Pegram, and there could be no doubt that his voice came through gritted teeth. Mentally the Apothecary took note, though he said nothing.

The enchanted couple, for that is how they appeared, entered the room and the entire company paid their respects. Stealing a glance while he bowed, John saw that Rosalind's mother, coming in just behind her daughter, adored all the adulation whereas the Reverend Tireman looked decidedly ill at ease. As for Henrietta, bringing up the rear, John could easily understand how much in her sister's shadow she must feel. For to be brought up with someone as lovely as that, to have to live with daily comparisons, must be difficult indeed.

The music for the first dance struck up and sets were formed. Then everyone stood and watched as the Marquis and his fiancée opened the assembly. From nowhere the terrifying Mrs Finch appeared with a wretched young partner and joined the set in which John and Elizabeth found themselves.

'Gorgeous, is she not?' she said to the Apothecary, her eyes following every move Rosalind made.

'Perfectly lovely.'

'So sad for poor dear Henrietta.'

'It can't be easy to have quite so beautiful a sister, though Henrietta herself is very good looking and need have no cause for jealousy.'

Mrs Finch made a little moue as the dance began. 'Oh, it wasn't to their appearance that I was referring.'

John bowed to Elizabeth Rose and they prepared to step off into Portsmouth, a longways dance for eight couples.

'Then what was it?' he asked over his shoulder.

Mrs Finch giggled. 'Why, to the fact that before her sister came on the scene it was Henrietta who was betrothed to the Marquis.'

'Good God!' exclaimed the Apothecary, and went whirling off down the length of the room before he could say another word.

Chapter Nine

It had been a remarkable evening in many senses of the word. First, because John had really enjoyed himself despite the bizarre carnival atmosphere. For underlying all the gaiety, the music, the dancing and the noise, had been his strange conviction that somewhere in the crowded room, the Frog and the Moth had been present, hiding their true identities, laughing and smiling as if they had never contracted to spy for France; as if one, or possibly both, of them, had not stabbed a man to death and hung his body on a crucifix to be eaten away by predators. Because the Apothecary, the more he thought about it, was becoming more and more convinced that the Scarecrow, sent to England to awaken two sleeping spies, must have met his end at the hands of one of them. Why else should an unknown Frenchman be killed in a foreign country where nobody knew him at all?

The other reason why John had found the evening so exceptional was personal. For as he and Henrietta Tireman had met for the third dance, he had felt a welcome glow in his heart which had put an answering smile on his face. With Coralie Clive firmly out of the way, the Apothecary was convinced that he was falling in love.

The admiration in his eyes had brought an immediate response from her. 'Why are you staring at me like that?' she had asked, but almost suspiciously, not with her usual humour.

'Because you look so lovely.'

'Are you serious? Haven't you seen Rosalind?'

John had cast his eyes over to where the Marquis and his beloved sat out from the dancing, taking a cooling drink.

'Yes, of course I have.'

'And?'

'She might be an angel, my dear, but you have a devilish streak which makes you irresistible.'

The words had come from nowhere but he clearly could not have said a better thing. Miss Tireman squeezed his hand warmly as they passed each other in a grand chain. 'Thank you,' was all she said, but her glance was eloquent.

By the time the last dance was called, the Apothecary was in turmoil, wondering how he was going to track down two elusive spies, to say nothing of a killer, and pay court to the rector's daughter simultaneously. Further, the trail leading to the Scarecrow's murderer had gone cold after a delay of several months. It seemed to John, in a rather anxious moment, that he had taken on a task larger than he could handle.

'I wonder if they're here,' whispered Mrs Rose as she and the Apothecary jigged in the centre of their set.

'Who?' John asked, not sure what she meant.

'The poisoner, of course.'

His heart sank even further. He had temporarily forgotten all about the attempts on Elizabeth's life, the reason that had brought him to Winchelsea in the first place. Without meaning to, the Apothecary let out an audible groan.

'What's the matter?'

He shook his head. 'It's just that there are so many games afoot at the moment. I don't quite know how I am going to deal with them all.'

'Perhaps you should send for help,' Mrs Rose suggested sensibly.

'Perhaps I should,' answered John, and decided that the very next day he would write to Mr Fielding.

In the event, there was no need. Early the next morning, just as the Apothecary was struggling out of bed, a boy came up from The Salutation to redeliver a letter to Petronilla's Platt.

'There's post for you,' Mrs Rose called up the stairs.

'I'll be down in a moment,' answered John, and hurriedly washed and shaved, then repeated the process all over again just in case he should meet Henrietta while he was out and about.

He studied the letter over breakfast. It was written in Joe Jago's hand but signed by Mr Fielding, the usual practice for the Magistrate's correspondence.

Dear Mr Rawlings,

   I am Sending this out with the afternoon Post in order that you may receive it by Saturday morning, 10th March. If you do so Please proceed at Once to the Church of St Thomas à Becket, Fairfield, on the Romney Marsh, where two Brave Fellows with a Coach will be waiting to remove the Body of the Scarecrow. They will be accompanied by Joe Jago, who has much to Impart to You. If You have not arrived by Noon they will Proceed without You but in that Event you are to await a Further Message from my Clerk.

Signed, ever your friend,

J. Fielding.

The Apothecary snatched at the watch which his father had given him for his twenty-first birthday.

'God's life, it's nine o'clock already. Aunt Elizabeth' – this for the benefit of the serving maid who was hovering by the door – 'I must run to Truncheons and hire a horse. I have an appointment to keep by twelve.'

The actress responded with great aplomb. 'I'll send the girl while you finish your food. Agnes, go directly to Truncheons and charter a mount for my nephew. Be quick about it.'

'Yes, Ma'am.' And the servant hurried through the front door, removing her apron as she went.

Twenty minutes later John was in the saddle, this time on a dark mettlesome mount with a rolling maddish eye.

'I'll have no trouble from you, my friend,' the Apothecary stated as he put his foot in the stirrup. The horse responded by deliberately moving as John mounted, then proceeded to go like a greyhound with a gale behind it not stopping until they reached the ferry between Rye and East Guldeford, which crossed the wide tidal estuary of the River Rother, taking over men, horses and vehicles heading for the Romney Marsh.

Once across the water, Fairfield was no great distance away, and on this occasion, not stopping to visit Brookland church but half expecting to see the extraordinary young curate on his travels, John covered the miles in excellent time. But for all that the party from London had got there ahead of him. As the Apothecary rounded the bend in the track, he saw the conveyance used by Mr Fielding's Flying Runners, two court officials with a coach ready to leave for any part of the kingdom at fifteen minutes' notice, drawn up as near to the Scarecrow as it could get. He also saw the sun reflect on the foxy red hair of Joe Jago, who

101

did not care for wigs and wore his as little as he could get away with.

'Joe,' called John, and the Clerk turned and waved his arm.

'Mr Rawlings, Sir, how are you?'

'Extremely glad to see you. There is a great deal going on.'

'So I gather.'

'All right, Mr Jago?' called one of the Runners. 'Shall we get the body down?'

'Yes. He needs some work on his head, I understand.'

'He certainly does,' John added with feeling.

'Pass the bucket, George,' came the reply.

'Shall we step into the church, Sir, while they go about their task? The more we keep out of the way of prying eyes the better, I believe.'

'Yes, let's,' John answered, not really relishing having to see the skeleton come down.

They entered the ancient quiet of St Thomas à Becket and sat in one of the boxed pews.

'Now, Mr Rawlings, let's exchange news. Yours first,' said Joe.

'You got my letter telling you what Dr Willes said?'

'We certainly did.' Joe produced a piece of paper from his pocket. 'You are ordered to give secret instructions immediately to the British spies, the Frog and the Moth. You will find the pair in Winchelsea. Contact them as arranged.'

'What does Mr Fielding think?'

'He believes that either one or both of them murdered the Scarecrow. That they either individually or as a team resisted his attempts to awaken them, as the jargon goes, probably near the time of the outbreak of war, which would fit in with the pitiable state of the body.'

'So we are not looking for an outside individual?'

'Unless the Scarecrow fell foul of the smugglers, it doesn't seem very likely to me. I think once we have identified the spies we have found our killer.'

'Talking of that, somebody – though whether it were spy or smuggler I do not know – was signalling with a lantern from the clifftops the other night.'

'How very interesting,' said Joe. 'Ah, well, acting as carelessly as that, he – or she – shouldn't be too difficult to find.'

'That's what you think!' exclaimed John. 'I tell you, Joe, there are several people the spies could be. In fact, Winchelsea is simply swarming with them.' And he went on to describe everyone he had met at the Assembly.

'Are there any other likely candidates, anyone you didn't meet?' Jago asked, scratching his jaw.

'Several people. Quite honestly, Joe, I don't know quite how I'm going to sort it all out. What with that and Mrs Harcross's idea that somebody is trying to poison her.'

'You're still not sure about that, are you?'

'No, to be perfectly honest. The suspect wine was so very good.'

'But perhaps it came from a different donor.'

'That is certainly possible. The labels were not the same.'

'As Mr Fielding said, it is a situation to be watched.'

'Indeed,' said John, not very happily.

'Cheer up, Sir. The Beak has a plan.'

'Which is?'

'Simply put, I am to come to Winchelsea in the role of an official from the Secret Office. I am going to start asking questions about an unknown Frenchman who was here six months ago. This will no doubt provoke some sort of reaction and will, almost certainly, make our sleeping spies nervous. They might then well make a mistake. Meanwhile, you are to work covertly, continuing your pose as Mrs Rose's nephew, an excellent ploy. As such, you may well worm your way into confidences and see more than I do. Between us, we'll flush 'em out, never you fear.'

John was silent, then said, 'So I presume we are to act as if we have never met?'

'We most certainly must.'

'But what about Mrs Rose? She will remember you.'

'For better or worse we must take her into our confidence. If by any chance she is the Moth – I do not exactly see her as a frog, do you? – it will only serve to make her fearful and then she will probably betray herself.'

'But how could Elizabeth be the Moth?' John burst out.

Jago's foxy features looked sly as boots. 'This is war, Mr Rawlings. You must not even trust your own shadow lest it betray you.'

'That is becoming abundantly clear.'

103

There was a shout from outside the church door. 'All done, Sir.'

'Right you are,' called Joe. He stood up. 'Come along, Mr Rawlings. We'll say goodbye here. The Runners will take the Scarecrow back to town, where his remains and his clothes will be examined. The cloak you found told us nothing, by the way. Meanwhile, I shall hire a man with a trap and appear in Winchelsea tonight, under cover of darkness. I shall go straight to The Salutation and book myself a room and in the morning I shall begin my investigations. My plan is that we meet from time to time – I shall get a message to you – to compare notes.'

'And how do you suggest I go about asking questions?'

'Your old ploy of the helpful apothecary, Sir. Now that you have met people it will be *de rigueur*' – Jago pronounced it "dee rigor" – 'for you to call on them.'

'You're right, of course.' John got to his feet. 'I'll leave first.'

'Tell the Brave Fellows I'll be with them as soon as you've gone.'

'Very well.'

He went out into the sunlight, then stopped short, his eyes drawn to the equipage which stood waiting to move off. Through the window, John could see that the Scarecrow sat propped on the seat of the coach like an ordinary passenger, his hat concealing his skull, the stumps of his legs sticking forward, shrouded now by a rug. Beside him sat one of the Runners, while the other was up on the coachman's box. It was one of the most bizarre sights that the Apothecary had ever witnessed and one which was to haunt him for some considerable while to come. So, in this extraordinary manner, the French spymaster was off on his final journey to the grave, something that he had probably not even considered possible when he had left his homeland to come to the Romney Marsh.

'Rest in peace,' whispered John, as he turned the black horse back in the direction of Winchelsea.

As soon as he set foot in Petronilla's Platt, admitted by a terrified Agnes, John knew that disaster had struck. A man's cloak and hat lay on a chair in the small entrance hall and from the bedroom at the top of the stairs came the sounds of a woman in great distress. Without hesitation, the Apothecary threw off his riding coat and hurried up the narrow staircase.

Elizabeth Rose lay on her bed, whiter even than when she wore make-up. A bowl into which she had vomited stood on the floor beside her, and leaning over her anxiously, attempting to spoon some physick down her throat, was young Dr Hayman. He turned as the new arrival came in, quite ready to throw him out, but recognised John instantly.

'What's happened?' asked the Apothecary.

'I think she's been poisoned,' the physician answered shortly. 'According to the girl, your aunt ate some rabbit pie and within about ten minutes was struck down with terrible pain and sickness.'

'I see,' John said grimly. He did not enquire whether the pie had been brought as an anonymous gift, deciding to keep his own counsel for the time being. Instead he put another question. 'When you say Aunt Elizabeth has been poisoned, Dr Hayman, surely you don't mean deliberately?'

The burned orange curls shook. 'I don't know what I mean, to be honest with you. Your aunt has been affected like this twice before.'

'Could it simply be some chronic condition?'

'It's possible, yes. But not producing such violent symptoms, I wouldn't have thought.'

'I'd agree with that.' The Apothecary fingered his chin. 'I suppose it's possible that she has got food poisoning.'

Dr Hayman stood up, his freckled skin flushing a little. 'May I speak to you frankly?'

'Please do.'

'There is something about this that I do not quite like. Twice I have been called to this house to find Mrs Rose in dire straits. It is my opinion, Mr Rawlings, that someone is making an attempt on your aunt's life.'

John hesitated, not quite sure how far to go in taking the doctor into his confidence. Eventually, he said, 'I think she believes as much herself.'

Dr Hayman flushed scarlet. 'So, I wasn't wrong in my suspicions.'

'It would appear not. Anyway, I am here now to keep a wary eye on her.'

There was a groan from Mrs Rose and both men turned back to look at her.

'What have you given so far?' John asked.

'Just an emetic. I want all the poison out.'

'Dr Hayman, she is your patient and it would be intolerable of me to interfere. But would you have any objection if I made my aunt an infusion of thyme? It can be beneficial to the poisoned stomach.'

'Please go ahead. You'll probably find some in her kitchen. If not, go to my surgery. I live in Bear Square, near The Salutation.'

Downstairs, a pale-faced servant looked up anxiously as John appeared. 'What's happening, Sir?'

'Mrs Rose has food poisoning, Agnes. So I'm going to mix an infusion to help her. Have you any dried thyme left from last year?'

'Hanging up there, Sir. Was it the rabbit pie, Sir?'

'Almost certainly. Tell me how my aunt came by it. Was it left on the doorstep?'

'Yes, Sir. Earlier this morning, after you'd gone out.'

'More's the pity. Whyever did she eat it?'

'She said something about not being prey to imagination. Then she read the label and said, "Anyway it's his writing," and she laughed. I didn't know what she was on about so I just gets her some preserve and she had the pie for her dinner.'

'I see.'

'No, you don't,' said Agnes wildly, and burst into tears.

'Heavens, girl, what is it?' asked John, thoroughly alarmed.

She flung herself into his arms, weeping noisily and also extremely damply. The Apothecary extricated himself.

'What have you done?' he demanded, then guessed the answer in a flash. 'You had some of it, didn't you? You helped yourself to what was left over?'

'Am I going to die, Sir?'

'No, of course not. Come with me.'

He led her by the hand, grizzling and howling, to where Dr Hayman held the bowl for Elizabeth.

'Another patient, I'm afraid.'

'She ate some of it,' stated the physician flatly.

'Correct.'

'Give her this.' And Dr Hayman handed John a bottle.

'What is it?'

'A straightforward emetic.'

'Root of Asarabacca?'

106

'Yes. Get a good dose down her.'

'Come along, Agnes,' said John firmly, and dragged the wailing servant back down the stairs and into the kitchen.

An hour later it was all over. Mrs Rose had been declared out of danger and was now sipping John's soothing infusion of thyme, while a pasty-faced Agnes had been sent home on a cart. Before the fire, their booted feet sticking out towards it, sat the doctor and the Apothecary, rapidly consuming brandy, which both of them declared was for medicinal purposes only. Peace had once more fallen over Petronilla's Platt and with it came the opportunity to converse.

'My aunt tells me that you have not been in Winchelsea long,' John remarked, by way of opening gambit.

'Ten months, though it seems like more. I read medicine at Cambridge before then.'

'And how do you find the place?'

'Not easy. The old physician had been much loved, for all that he was usually drunk. I was treated with the customary suspicion, though things are improving now.'

The Apothecary poured Dr Hayman another brandy. 'I suppose like all small towns, the place abounds with rumour and tittle-tattle.'

'Indeed it does,' answered the physician, clearly relishing having a contemporary and a fellow medical man with whom to relax and gossip. 'As you can imagine, it caused a sensation when Rosalind Tireman stole the Marquis from under her sister's nose.'

'Tell me about that.'

Dr Hayman leaned back in his chair and stretched his legs before him. 'Well, the story goes that Henrietta went to the Hall first, some eighteen months ago I'm told, to teach the Marquis's young sister French. Apparently she, Henrietta that is, speaks it fluently. Anyway, Rye, a strange bird if ever there was one and the greatest rakehell in the county, seducing every virgin in a twenty-mile radius when he wasn't gambling his life away, evidently came to his senses and fell madly in love with her. Then a few months later the governess left and Henrietta, some say very foolishly, suggested her sister for the post. And that was that. Poor Miss Tireman found herself cast aside as the Marquis, after taking one look at Rosalind, decided he would do better with her.'

'What a cruel story.'

107

'Isn't it. Henrietta took it very badly, I can assure you.'

'I'm hardly surprised. In fact I am astonished the two women are still speaking.'

'Many people are. I think the rector played a big part in that, begging his elder girl not to make a public show.'

'I see. So what else goes on?'

Dr Hayman winked an eye and his orange hair glowed in the firelight. 'They say that Mrs Finch personally tests out any prospective suitors for her daughters' hands.'

John's eyebrows shot to his hairline. 'Do you mean what I think you mean?'

The physician chuckled. 'Yes, I do. I warn you, one takes one's life in one's hands when one goes calling there!'

'Thank you for the caution. I'll take the greatest care. Do you know anything about Lady Floote? I said I'd call on her about her headaches. Is she a complete hypochondriac?'

'No, she genuinely suffers with migraine. But then who wouldn't, married to him.' Dr Hayman downed another mouthful of brandy. 'He really is a dreadful man. I'm sure he has a mistress some-where.'

'Why do you say that?'

'Because he's never at home. If he's not off to London, he's out and about the county, or walking his terrible dog.' He paused and looked contrite. 'I'm being indiscreet, aren't I? Which is not becoming in a man of my calling.'

'I would imagine,' said John acutely, 'that you often feel rather isolated.'

'Indeed I do. Your coming here is a godsend, quite honestly.'

The Apothecary felt a rush of genuine sympathy. 'As long as I stay, you are most welcome to this house. I am positive I speak for my aunt when I say that.'

'And you must both come and dine with me. As you have gathered, I have no wife, but the serving girl is an excellent cook.'

'I should be delighted. Talking of men who live alone, I was much taken with Captain Pegram. What's your opinion of him?'

'He's something of an oddity. Apparently he left the army because he could not stand the life and does not approve of war. Now he spends most of his time studying and is very learned, I believe.'

'How old is he?'

'About fifty, I imagine. He told me once that he was twenty-five when his wife died and that was some considerable while ago.'

'And he never remarried?'

'No, nor has he taken a mistress, at least that I've heard of. He lives very much as a confirmed old bachelor.'

'How interesting – and how sad. And what about Mr Gironde the apothecary? I take it he is of Huguenot extraction.'

'Yes.'

'My aunt thinks his wife a regular busybody.'

Dr Hayman gave a shout of laughter. 'To hear the gist of our conversation, I could easily imagine that description being applied to us.'

John grinned wryly. 'It might very well. But, Dr Hayman . . .'

'Richard, please.'

'. . . if someone is making an attempt to kill Aunt Elizabeth it is essential that I find out about the local characters.'

The physician nodded, suddenly serious. 'You're quite right, of course. Well, Nan Gironde is a troublemaker, there's no doubt about that. She simulates great friendship for one and all, then proceeds to put the knife in. I don't trust her at all. But Marcel I like. He is a good apothecary and works hard. Inexplicably, he is besotted with her. In his eyes the little shrew can do no wrong.'

'It is often the way. Tell me, is there anyone else my aunt knows who might wish her ill?'

Dr Hayman shook his head. 'She does not have droves of friends. In fact I can't think of anyone else other than the rector and his wife.'

'And what are they like? I saw them at the assembly but wasn't introduced.'

'She is an amazing woman, a *femme formidable*. Quite loud and vulgar for the wife of a cleric, and built like a carthorse. But I suppose she must have been pretty once. How else could she have given birth to two such beautiful girls?'

John shrugged and spread his hands. 'A freak of nature, maybe. There often seems no accounting for such things.'

'Do you really believe that amongst these people we've been discussing there lurks a cruel killer?' Dr Hayman asked seriously.

The Apothecary refilled their glasses, shaking his head slowly as he did so. 'I don't know what to think. But one thing I *do* know,

109

and please don't ask me how, is that Winchelsea, this pretty little
town, contains hidden secrets.'

'In what respect?'

'I am not at liberty to say.'

The physician narrowed his eyes. 'Are you an excise man, Sir?'

John laughed. 'No, I am not. Yet I am well aware that the
smugglers have returned to the Romney Marsh.'

'Not only the Marsh!' Richard Hayman said pointedly, and there
they let the matter drop.

It was late when the doctor left the house and John set about the
task of locking up for the night. Yet even as he prepared to throw
the bolts on the doors he was aware that there was movement in the
darkness outside. Horses with muffled hooves were making their
way up the cobbled streets and, peering through a crack, he saw
that solitary candles stood in the windows of several houses. There
could be no doubt about the cause; the freebooters were making a
delivery. Brandy, tobacco, tea, silks and satins were at this very
moment finding their way into the cellars of the good people of
Winchelsea. Presumably Dick Jarvis, Kit's rascally bastard, was
hard at work even while the Apothecary peered out.

To go outside was dangerous, John knew that well, but the
temptation to get a closer look was so strong that without stopping
even to get a pistol, the Apothecary had slipped through the door
almost before he knew what he was doing. Moving silently, he
stood in the shadows and watched.

It was as he had suspected. Horses with leather shoes on their feet
were pulling laden carts towards various houses. John saw one head
off towards The Salutation, another towards Paradise House, and a
third in what could easily have been the direction of Grey Friars.
So it would appear that the entire town were customers, with one
or two exceptions. He was just about to go back indoors, when a
different sound attracted the Apothecary's attention.

A voice was ringing out in the darkness, a voice speaking too
loudly for its own good, yet one, John thought, that would have
some difficulty in moderating its tone. Interestingly, the voice was
speaking fluent French then translating what it had just heard and
said into English for the benefit of another, someone who spoke
softly and therefore was more difficult to identify. Hardly able to
believe his ears, the Apothecary quietly observed.

A cart was turning in the road, so that it pointed once more towards the sea, and as it did so the moon came out and clearly lit the scene. Driving the vehicle was a figure which looked familiar yet which John could not altogether recognise. Being pulled up into the cart, almost toppling the driver as he strained to help her, was the rector's wife, the fearsome Mrs Tireman. And jumping up beside her, carrying his medical bag and looking decidedly ill at ease, was the man with whom John had just parted company, Dr Richard Hayman himself. Then as the cart crept stealthily down the street, the moon disappeared behind clouds and the Apothecary was alone in the darkness, listening as the sound of the smugglers slowly faded away and all was silence once more.

Chapter Ten

That night John slept with his bedroom door wide open so that he could hear if Elizabeth happened to cry out, but all stayed quiet, and by morning, when he woke and looked in on her, she was in a deep and peaceful sleep, her face quite serene. The Apothecary went downstairs shortly afterwards, only to find that Agnes, tottering around but wearing a bravely defiant expression, had come to work and was making breakfast in the kitchen.

'Good morning,' he called cheerfully. 'Are you feeling better?'

'Yes, Sir. Thank you, Sir.'

'Excellent.' John went into the room and closed the door behind him, taking a seat at the scrubbed wooden table. 'Have you eaten anything yet?'

'No, Sir.'

'Then may I suggest a little bread, and I can make you an infusion if you should still be suffering queasiness.'

Agnes smiled gratefully. 'That would be very kind, Sir.'

'It's no trouble. I was going to prepare some for my aunt, in any event.'

He busied himself alongside her, boiling kettles and pounding thyme leaves, covertly watching the serving girl out of the corner of his eye. Finally, when she seemed sufficiently relaxed to be no longer wary of him, John said, 'Agnes, you told me my aunt said something about *his* writing on the label that came with the pie. Do you know who she was talking about?'

'No, Sir. But the box is still over on the dresser. I'll get it for you.'

A second later it was in his hand and John read the attached note with something approaching amazement. For this was no anonymous gift left in suspicious circumstances. For all the world to see, the donor had written, 'Baked in my kitchens this morning. Please accept this pie with my best wishes, N.P.' So, unless there was someone else with identical initials, it would appear that Captain Nathaniel Pegram had given his friend the present which had poisoned her.

'Is breakfast going to be long?' John asked, well aware that Agnes's eyes were boring into him, willing him to say something.

'Coming now, Mr Rawlings. Sir—' She stopped abruptly.

'Yes?'

'Who *did* send the pie?'

'Surely you know.'

'I can't read, Sir.'

John considered for a few moments, then said, 'Captain Pegram gave it to Mrs Rose, which only goes to show that even in the greatest houses it is possible for bad meat to be used.'

'Bad meat? Is that what it was, Sir?'

'Most certainly.'

'Not poison?'

'Meat that has gone off is a poison in itself. But if you mean the kind of poison deliberately used to kill people, then the answer is no.'

Agnes looked positively downcast and John suppressed a smile. 'Oh, I see,' she said, clearly disappointed that events had turned out not to be as dramatic as she had hoped.

'Good girl.' The Apothecary winked his eye disconcertingly. 'Now take your mistress her breakfast on a tray while I eat mine here. And be sure to tell her that I will come and say goodbye before I go out.'

'Yes, Sir.'

'And take care that both of you stay on a light diet for the rest of the day. A mess of eggs would be just the thing.'

'Very good, Sir.'

The servant appeared so crestfallen that John decided to cheer her up. 'Food poisoning can be fatal, Agnes. Both you and Mrs Rose had a lucky escape. And you can tell your friends I said so.'

The serving girl brightened. 'Oh, I will, Sir.'

'Good,' and with that John fell to eating an enormous breakfast as if he hadn't a care in the world.

Throughout his short walk to The Salutation, the Apothecary gave much thought as to how he was going to engineer a conversation with Joe Jago. To reveal that he knew him would be to ruin the entire plan, yet he felt the urgent need to tell John Fielding's clerk the latest turn of events. The only answer seemed to be to bump into the Magistrate's right hand man and somehow signal that he wished to speak to him alone. But, in the event, the opportunity presented itself without difficulty. Just as John approached the inn, Joe Jago was coming out.

'Good morning, Sir,' said the clerk, a suspicion of a wink about his eye. 'I'm sorry to trouble you but I'm a stranger in town. Only arrived late last night from London. I wonder if you could direct me to the Rectory.' He bowed, his hair blazing in the early sun.

John bowed back. 'Indeed, Sir, I certainly can. I am walking that way myself. If you would care to accompany me, I can guide you to the very door.'

'Splendid,' Joe replied, and rubbed his hands together.

They fell into step and no sooner had they left The Salutation than John launched into a description of all that had taken place, from the poisoned Mrs Rose, to Mrs Tireman and the doctor departing with the smugglers.

Joe listened in silence, then said, 'I've had some further thoughts on the signalling you saw. Did the flashes appear to be a number sequence?'

'Definitely so.'

'Then another visit to Dr Willes may be in order. We must get the latest cipher from him. The Frog and the Moth may be killers but, for all that, one of them appears to have started work already.'

'Yes, damn it. Tell me, what will happen to the Scarecrow now?'

'A physician will examine his skeleton to establish the cause of death.'

'Stabbed through the heart with a thin-bladed implement,' put in John, always slightly irritated when his diagnosis had to be confirmed.

'Quite so,' answered Joe tactfully. 'Then his clothes will go to a tailor to see if he can identify them as definitely being French. After that the Scarecrow will be buried in your own parish church of St Ann's in Soho, where many of his fellow countrymen have been laid to rest.

'Poor thing,' said John, much saddened. 'He probably left a wife and children behind who will never know where he vanished to. Did you know, Joe, that my father disappeared, my real father that is? My mother waited for him to return from London – they were running away to be married – but he did not arrive.

And though she went to look for him, she never found out what happened.'

'One day you must seek him out.'

'Oh, he's quite definitely dead. He would not have let her down otherwise.'

'If you are anything like him, then that is most certainly true,' Joe answered. 'But for the moment let us consider the present problem. I am going calling this morning, starting at the Rectory then proceeding to the richest of them all, Mrs Finch herself.'

'She will eat you alive, my friend.'

'In what way?'

'She'll offer you her honour.'

Joe's face exploded into its customary desert of lines as he roared with laughter. 'A rum doxy, eh? She dances Moll Peatley's jig, I take it?'

'I'm not quite sure what that means but if it's anything like it sounds, the answer is yes.'

'Well,' said Joe, 'if I ain't returned by nightfall you'd better send out a search party, Mr Rawlings.'

'Send out the smugglers more likely. Anyway, you've passed her house. It's the imposing mansion next door to the Town Hall.'

'I noticed it. Grand indeed! Now, we should meet tonight in order to compare notes. Where do you suggest?'

'There's a place called the Roundle to the north-west of the town. It's a deserted area and the Roundle itself, once a watch tower I believe, is rarely visited. Let's rendezvous there.'

'At what time?'

'Ten o'clock?'

'I'll be punctual,' said Joe, and with that he made a sweeping bow and turned into the Rectory, while John set off for Grey Friars.

The house lay to the east of the town, down a pleasant avenue known locally as Friars Walk. Having left the church and other dwellings behind him, the Apothecary strode out, passing through cherry orchards, the trees still in tight bud, on one hand, and pleasant green meadows on the other. With each passing step, John grew more and more envious of Captain Pegram, whose house, whatever it was like as a building, was surely one of the best situated in the county.

The cherry orchards continued, acre after acre of them, and then to the Apothecary's left a lodge house and drive appeared.

Going through the gates, wondering whether he was going to be challenged, John continued on, glad of so fine a day in which to enjoy such a pleasant walk. Then the house came into view and he stopped in his tracks, lost in admiration.

That it had once been an abbey was abundantly clear from the architecture, indeed the choir of the chapel still stood, its lofty and rather beautiful arch making a most attractive ruin. Beyond this, surrounded by its gardens, its orchards and outbuildings, stood the house itself, incorporating into its whole an ancient Chapter House, a cloister range and a gate tower, together with recent wings and what looked from the exterior like the soaring splendour of a Great Hall. Captain Pegram, or one of his forebears, had transformed the entire complex into a domestic dwelling by commissioning a series of corridors to join together this somewhat unsymmetrical group of buildings. The result, triumphantly enough, was a medley of architectural styles which blended together in perfect harmony. Extremely impressed by the size and grandeur of the place, John approached the oak door in the tower and rang the bell.

A servant answered and the Apothecary presented his card, then waited for a few moments before the footman reappeared.

'If you would follow me, Sir. Captain Pegram will see you in the library.'

He set off, John walking immediately behind as the servant opened a door from the Great Hall, which was no more than fifty years old in the Apothecary's estimation. This led them straight into the cloisters, now an internal part of the building and banked on either side with indoor plants. Looking round him, John saw marble pillars contrasting with ornate sixteenth-century perpendicular work, above his head a vaulted roof. To his right and left, what had once been open archways had now been filled with glass, making the place an ideal walkway for inclement days.

At the end of the cloisters lay a stone spiral staircase and having climbed this, the servant knocked discreetly on the door at the top.

'Come,' said Captain Pegram's voice.

'Mr Rawlings, Sir.'

'Tell him to enter.'

And John, who had been shuffling on the landing, went through into an extremely long room, built quite recently above the cloisters themselves, on their very roof in fact. Profusely windowed, it

117

presented stunning views over the sea in one direction and the cherry orchards and fields in the other.

Looking round in undisguised admiration, John saw that between the dozen windows, six on each side, were shelves of books, ranging from floor to ceiling, while at the far end a fire burned brightly in a marbled fireplace, a desk and chair placed in front of it.

'What a room!' the Apothecary exclaimed. 'I envy you this, Sir.'

'I'm glad you like it. My father restored the abbey, you know, and built on all the modern parts, including this library. I've always loved it here; have done ever since I was a child. But he, strangely enough, preferred to live in his other property at Rye. And now, alas, there is no one to inherit except my nephew, and I do not believe he has such a love for the old place as I have.' He motioned John to take a seat on one of the many sofas that stood beneath the windows. 'I was just about to have a sherry, Mr Rawlings. Would you care to join me?'

'I'd be delighted, Captain.'

John's host pulled a bell rope, then sat down at the sofa's other end. 'And how is your aunt today?' he asked conversationally.

The morning light was such that it was difficult to see his face but Captain Pegram's whole demeanour was hardly one of a brutal poisoner. None the less, the Apothecary proceeded with caution.

'As a matter of fact, that is the reason for my call.'

'Oh?' said the captain, clearly surprised.

'To come straight to the point, Sir, she was taken dangerously ill after eating the rabbit pie you gave her.'

'I beg your pardon?'

'She suffered poisoning yesterday, and the only thing she had eaten was the pie that you left on her doorstep. You *did* take her a gift of food, didn't you, Sir?'

'Yes, I sent a servant round with a fresh-baked delicacy. But I can hardly credit what you are saying. I had some of the same with my own dinner and suffered no ill effects. How can this be?'

'The meat must have gone off.'

'Off be hanged!' Captain Pegram shouted angrily. 'My cook comes from France, Sir, and would not stoop to using mouldy ingredients. I find you too free with your accusations, Mr Rawlings. How do you know that was all that Mrs Rose ate yesterday? Were you with her every minute?'

118

Put like that, the Captain's argument had a horrible ring of reason about it. Because of what had happened previously, John had instantly jumped to the conclusion that the pie had been the cause of the trouble. But supposing there *had* been something else, something that he had absolutely no idea about?

'You may well be right, Sir,' he said, his voice contrite. 'I readily agree that I leaped to that inference, namely that it was your gift that was at fault, far too hastily. But there is a reason for that.'

And John told him about the two other occasions on which Mrs Rose had been taken ill.

Nathaniel Pegram stared at him. 'What? Are you trying to tell me that someone is deliberately trying to poison your aunt?'

'I don't know, Sir,' John answered honestly. 'She is certainly very worried about it.'

'I am not at all surprised! But, seriously, who could do such a thing? For you may rest assured that it is not me.'

This time the Apothecary told a lie, remembering his promise to reveal nothing of Mrs Harcross's past. 'I have no idea,' he said.

The Captain looked at him acutely. 'You're lying, aren't you? There's something you haven't told me.'

John nodded his head. 'Yes, there *is* something, but I am pledged not to reveal it.'

Nathaniel Pegram stood up as a servant entered the room with a tray and decanter. 'Put it over there would you, Ridgway. I'll pour.' He turned back to John. 'And this something concerns Elizabeth's past?'

'It does.'

The Captain's voice took on a distant note. 'How strange it is that what has gone before can control us still. To me the events of yesteryear are like a web. Once you are trapped in their cruel mesh the only way out is to cut oneself free.'

'I think she tried to.'

'But the past has caught up with her never the less?'

'So it would seem.'

Captain Pegram stared out of the window, his thoughts obviously going off at a tangent. 'Did you know that I was a soldier who hated fighting?'

John nodded. 'Yes. I had heard.'

'I would go to any lengths to prevent war, or to bring it to a rapid conclusion once it had begun. I abhor the cruel wastage of life that

119

it involves. I loathe the maiming, the destruction, the laying bare of land, the disease and pestilence that follow.' The Captain gestured with his arm towards the Channel. 'Across that strip of ocean, the gallant sailors of France and England are fighting to the death. Yet how many of us can claim not to have the blood of both nations in our veins? My grandmother was French, Mr Rawlings, and there are many in Winchelsea who are of mixed nationality. These are difficult times for such as I.'

The Apothecary did not say a word, a dozen different thoughts presenting themselves simultaneously. Finally he said, 'So what of the current situation, with most of Europe involved? Do you wish this war over quickly?'

'I would see any conflict finished before it had even begun.'

John nodded. 'As would all right-minded men.' He stood up and held out his hand. 'I hope I am forgiven for what passed earlier between us. In no manner did I wish to accuse you, Sir. It was merely worry for my aunt that made me speak as I did.'

Captain Pegram appeared to recollect himself from a daydream. 'Think nothing of it, Mr Rawlings.' He shook John's hand. 'I trust you will keep vigilant, Sir. Your aunt and I have much in common and I would not like to think she might be in danger.'

'I will do my best, be assured of that,' the Apothecary answered, and politely bowed his way out.

The sun was even warmer as he left Grey Friars, cutting through the cherry orchards in order to vary his route home, but John hardly noticed the beauty of that early spring day, his mind was moving so fast.

Of the fact that Captain Pegram was not a poisoner he was absolutely certain. No one could react quite so angrily quite so convincingly had they had anything to conceal. But what other hidden message had Nathaniel been giving him? Were certain people in Winchelsea French sympathisers, was that it? Or was he simply referring to himself? In some oblique manner, had the ex-soldier been trying to tell him that he was prepared to act against national interests in order to stop the war?

John's thoughts turned to other things. What had Mrs Tireman been doing consorting with smugglers and speaking to one of them in fluent French? And where in the name of Heaven did Richard Hayman fit in? Surely the pair could not be caught up in the clandestine world of contraband? Or espionage?

120

The Apothecary stopped in his tracks, staring at the trees but not really seeing them. There were two, no three, strands to this quest. Hidden away in this small and respectable town were not only the freebooters with their nefarious midnight activities, but also a couple of dangerous people, agents for France. And the third skein was that one of them, if not both, was a ruthless killer.

Slowing his pace slightly, he walked on, determined to get some enjoyment out of the delicate day. And it was then that he saw her. Sitting with her back to a cherry tree was the delightful Henrietta Tireman, her face in her hands, crying bitterly.

John hesitated, wanting to go to her but nervous of intruding on her privacy. Yet she must have sensed his presence, for Henrietta lowered her hands and stared at him out of brimming eyes.

'Go away,' she said.

'Why?' he asked, a perfectly sensible question.

'Because I don't want to talk to anyone.'

'Then may I stay if I promise to keep quiet?'

'No.'

'These are not your orchards,' said the Apothecary, and calmly sat down at the foot of the tree adjacent to hers.

'Leave me alone,' wailed Henrietta.

'I haven't touched you.'

'Oh, just be off.' And she wept with renewed vigour.

John sat quietly, longing to take her in his arms but studiously not moving a muscle, and after a few moments, as he stared about him and whistled a tune, became aware that she was darting swift glances in his direction. Nonchalantly he produced an apple from his pocket and started to eat it.

'Mr Rawlings,' said a tremulous voice.

'John.'

'John. May I borrow your handkerchief? I forgot to bring mine.'

'Very foolish when one is going into the woods to cry. Here.'

He got up and crossed the short distance between them, sitting down beside her and applying the handkerchief as if she were a little girl.

'Oh, don't be kind to me,' said Henrietta, and turning towards him wept against his chest, holding on to him tightly as she did so.

Finally she raised a tear-streaked face and looked at him, and

121

John applied the oldest medicine in the world and kissed her, gently, yet with enough fire to show her that a man desired her and thought her lovely.

Henrietta drew away. 'You don't have to do that just because you're sorry for me.'

He took her chin in his hand, his eyes very blue as he looked at her. 'My dear girl, I am not in the least sorry for you. I am deeply attracted to you should the truth be known. But you, if I might hazard a guess, are still pining for his lordship, the Marquis of Rye, wishing you might put back the clock and never let your sister anywhere near him. Am I right?'

A glimmer of a smile appeared. 'Not entirely.'

'There are other things on your mind?'

'One or two.'

'Might I be one of them?'

'You could be.'

'Don't tease me,' said John, and kissed her in earnest.

They had entered the cherry orchard separately. Two hours later they left it together, hand in hand, somewhat dishevelled – and lovers. This last occurrence had taken them both by surprise but had been most definitely by mutual desire and accompanied by a great deal of unabashed affection, if not enacted in the throes of passionate love. Though since the unplanned act of intimacy, both felt even more strongly drawn to the other.

'Can I call on you tomorrow?' John whispered as they stepped from the protection of the trees.

Henrietta's clear eyes gazed into his. 'As a matter of fact Mama has written you a note inviting you to dine. I think she thinks it high time I had another suitor and is in hot pursuit of eligible men on my behalf.'

'She's perfectly right. But will I do?'

Henrietta laughed. 'You will do very well indeed.'

The Apothecary held her at arm's length, gazing at her seriously. 'You don't think I took advantage of you, do you?'

Henrietta looked at him sideways, her old spirit clearly returning. 'I was just about to ask the same of you.'

'Oh, but you did,' said John, lowering his lashes. 'You wicked charmer. My maidenly modesty is all undone.'

'Mine went to the Marquis,' Henrietta retorted.

'How very alliterative,' answered John, and they fell into paroxysms of laughter which seemed to last until they parted company and went their separate ways.

Having returned to Petronilla's Platt to check on Elizabeth Rose and to tidy himself up, John decided to spend the few hours he had to spare before his meeting with Joe Jago in continuing to call on people, the next being Faith Ffloote. Staring at himself in the mirror, noticing the jaunty look in his eye and hoping it would not be visible to the world at large, the Apothecary packed his medical bag with various cures for headache and set forth up the road to visit Paradise House. Much as he had hoped, Lady Ffloote was at home and after just a few moments he was ushered into her presence.

Faith looked up wearily, her eyes dark and dull. 'Oh, Mr Rawlings, how nice of you to call. You have caught me at the very height of an attack, but as it was you I decided to admit you. I am afraid Sir Ambrose is not here. He has business to attend to in Rye.'

Remembering Dr Hayman's theory that the Squire had a fancy woman somewhere, John, who was in a silly mood, suppressed a grin.

'Well, it was you I came to see, Madam. As promised, I have brought some remedies for migraine.'

'Is that what I have, do you think?'

'It would appear so. As your headaches recur so frequently I believe that would be a fair diagnosis. What does Dr Hayman say?'

'He holds that nervous tension may have a great deal to do with it.'

'Are you unduly tense?'

Faith gave a hollow laugh. 'No, of course not. I have everything a woman could wish for. A good home, a loving husband, an adorable dog. He is a good physician but wrong in that.'

'I see.'

'I think it is an illness like any other and that the doctor's theories are too modern for anyone's good.'

'None the less,' said John, 'state of mind does have a role to play with regard to one's physical condition.'

Lady Ffloote, who had been reclining on a couch, sat upright and showed the first sign of spirit the Apothecary had seen since he met her. 'My state of mind is good, I assure you. How could it be otherwise?'

She was very defensive, remarkably so, and John wondered why. Was she trying to give the impression that her marriage was made in heaven? Or was she putting on an act for some other, totally unrelated, reason?

'If you say so, Madam,' he answered primly, and turned to open his bag. At that moment, however, he was interrupted by a loud scratching at the door, at the sound of which Lady Ffloote fairly leaped up and opened it.

'It's The Pup,' she said, her voice dripping sentiment.

John stared towards the opening as an ancient and decrepit dog waddled in on legs stiff and bowed with arthritis, its stomach and privy parts swinging low as it moved. As it proceeded into the room, it huffed, its breath extremely dubious to say the least. It was, without doubt, the most unattractive animal the Apothecary had ever seen.

'Puppy!' cooed Faith. 'Come and greet your Mama.'

The Pup trundled forward, glaring at John with a glazed and rheumy eye as it did so. In no mood to be put upon, he glared back. At this it growled low in its throat.

'Oh, listen,' trilled Lady Ffloote lovingly, 'he's saying how do. Isn't that sweet.'

'Sweet,' echoed John, with feeling.

'There, there, baby,' continued its owner, patting the dog on its flat reptilian head. 'Did I leave you yester night? Did naughty Mama go out then?'

Thinking of the smugglers and their activities, John raised a mental brow but said nothing.

'Now, Boo-Boo,' Faith continued, 'just you sit there at Mama's feet. This nice man has brought Mama some medicine to make her well.'

The Pup bared its teeth and the Apothecary fought off an overwhelming urge to kick it.

'He seems very protective,' he remarked mildly.

'He wouldn't let anyone hurt his mother, would he, precious?'

'Perhaps, then, it might be better if we had the consultation in another room. I would like to examine your head and neck if I may and wouldn't want the dog to think I was attacking you.'

Lady Ffloote looked positively tearful. 'It seems I must leave you,

Boo. We'll go to the salon, Mr Rawlings. The Pup has come into the parlour to take a nap and I couldn't possibly turn him out.'

'No, of course not,' answered John and picking up his bag followed his hostess out of the room to the accompaniment of the horrid animal's rumbles of disapproval.

An examination of Lady Ffloote's cranium and shoulders, something which she very much enjoyed, John could not help but notice, showed that she was indeed very tense. Accordingly, the Apothecary gave her a bottle of compounded juice of mixed daisy flower roots and leaves to sniff up into her nostrils, a great aid to migraine. He also prescribed a lotion of prunel bruised with otto of roses and vinegar with which to bathe her temples. Finally he presented Faith with a potion to remove melancholy: feverfew dried and made into a powder, a well known cure for depression and giddiness.

'Take two drams of this with honey or sweet wine when you get up in the morning, Lady Ffloote. And I will come back and see you in a week's time and find out how you are progressing.'

'Not going so soon, Mr Rawlings, surely. I was about to take a little supper, just soup and a cold collation. Will you not join me?'

'I really ought to return to my aunt.'

Faith laid her hand on his arm. 'Oh don't say no,' she pleaded.

'Well, I . . .'

'Excellent,' she said triumphantly. 'I will go and inform the cook.'

It was an ordeal that John could well have done without. Just for his benefit the table was laid in the dining room, under which The Pup hovered constantly, its muzzle an inch from the Apothecary's knee, its eyes horribly beady. Every time he raised the fork to his mouth it followed what he was doing with a greedy gaze and when he steadfastly refused to give it anything, it growled deep.

In the end he could stand it no longer and said, 'I think your dog is hungry, Lady Ffloote.'

'Oh, is he there? Is he begging? It's all Sir Ambrose's fault. He treats The Pup like a child and feeds him at table. Dear little Boo-Boo, it's difficult to refuse him I must admit.'

John had a strange mental picture of a real child lying on the floor being given scraps by Sir Ambrose. 'Ah,' was all he could bring himself to say.

125

'Will you not stay till my husband gets home?' Lady Ffloote continued 'I know he would like to see you.'

'No, no,' John said, determinedly putting down his napkin. 'I really must go. Aunt Elizabeth will be worrying about me.'

'I'm not surprised, a handsome young creature like yourself. Why, since the Assembly you are the talk of the town. I'm sure Mrs Finch and Mrs Tireman have both picked you out for their daughters.'

On the point of rising, John sat down again. 'How very flattering, though of course I am not in the same league as the Marquis of Rye. Tell me, is he very rich?'

'Well, he is now, though it was a much different story when he was younger.' Faith clearly adored to gossip and launched into her tale with relish. 'At the age of eighteen the Marquis was a profligate gambler and womaniser, money poured through his hands like water. His father, a very different character I can tell you, was forced to rescue him from ruin on more than one occasion. I believe stern words were spoken. Anyway, after the final confrontation between them the young man seemed to pull himself together; indeed I believe he must have taken some form of employment, for money came in on a regular basis. Then his father died, leaving him to bring up his younger half-sister on his own, and this finally forced the Marquis to face reality. And when he met Henrietta, the transformation was complete. He became a reformed character and has been a pillar of rectitude ever since, other than for jilting the poor creature, of course.'

The mention of Henrietta's name brought back memories of the afternoon, and the Apothecary blushed.

'I'm sure she is over it now,' he said with feeling.

Lady Ffloote looked at him sharply. 'I thought you hardly knew the young lady.'

'I don't really. It's just an impression I have.' John stood up and The Pup emitted a low rumble. 'Thank you so much for inviting me. I really must go now.'

'What a shame,' said Faith, her eyes the brightest he had ever seen them.

A quarter of an hour later the Apothecary had managed to extricate himself and was heading briskly for Petronilla's Platt, only to find when he got there that Agnes had returned home and Elizabeth, who had remained in bed, had gone back to sleep.

Putting on a warm topcoat, for the evening had turned chilly, John set off to walk to the Roundle.

It was as dark as pitch outside but he had had the good sense to bring a lantern, the light from which dimly illuminated the way. Stumbling and tripping, the Apothecary set off down the lane lying behind Paradise House, wishing that there could be even one glimpse of moon and stars. Passing the last house on the path, he left civilisation behind him and turned off towards the fields, the lane deteriorating into the roughest track. Bearing right by Joseph's Tree, a local landmark, John headed down the path leading to the windmill, then crossed a stile, dropping the lantern as he did so and extinguishing its flame.

Now he was in the wildest territory of all for the Round Tower, as some called it, stood in a field, these days quite deserted and alone, no longer used for the purpose for which it had been built. Yet Joe must have arrived there before him, for there was a light on in the Roundle, the Apothecary could see it quite distinctly.

With a greeting on his lips, John hurried forward, only to stop dead as a sensation of great danger swept over him. Then a shape loomed up out of the shadows. There was a click as a pistol cocked in the darkness and the Apothecary felt the coldness of the muzzle against his temple.

'One move, you little bastard, and you're a corpse,' said a rough voice.

'Who are you?' asked John, but there was no reply, only a mighty blow to the Apothecary's head which sent him spinning into oblivion, spiralling downwards amongst the whirling stars.

Chapter Eleven

Regaining consciousness was painful, horribly so. With a mighty effort, John opened his eyes, only to close them again rapidly. His head throbbed with such indescribable savagery that even the movement of raising his lids had sent a wave of agony through his entire body. Wondering where he could possibly be and what terrible fate had befallen him, the Apothecary lay very still, willing the hurt to go away.

Beneath him was a hard narrow bed, its mattress sharp with horsehair, its pillow rank with the smell of sweat. In fact so revolting was its stink that if John had had one ounce of energy left he would have thrown it to the floor. But as it was he just lay there, too weak to do anything, his body helpless but his brain slowly beginning to function again.

The last thing he could remember was the sound of the cock of a pistol in the darkness, the blow, then oblivion. That had all happened in the open but now he was inside, most likely the prisoner of whoever had struck him. Bracing himself against the pain, John opened his eyes once more.

He was in a narrow room beneath the eaves, a shaft of moonlight coming through one small window its only illumination. In the dim light, John could make out a broken table with an unlit candle on it, a grimy chamber pot standing beneath. These, other than the bed on which he lay sprawled, were the only furnishings. Very slowly, moving with extreme care, the Apothecary got to his feet, staggering as he did so.

Holding on tightly, he peered out of the window. What view the meagre casement gave revealed nothing but moorland, with no sign of any other form of habitation. Grimly wondering why he was being held captive, John was just about to try the door when he heard voices in the distance and the sound of feet ascending the wooden staircase. Moving as quickly as he could, he lay back on the bed. Beneath the door, the light of a candle was drawing nearer, and the Apothecary could make out the sound of two men speaking in undertones.

'I shall deal with it in my own manner,' one was saying.

'To hell with that,' answered the other contemptuously. 'I know what I'd do with him.'

'Shut your mouth,' the first speaker replied tersely as the door opened. At which John closed his eyes, feigning unconsciousness.

'Merciful God!' the first voice continued, using a noticeably different timbre. 'This poor fellow's wounded. Fetch some warm water and a bandage. He's bleeding from the head.'

'Yes, Your Reverence.' And there was the sound of retreating footsteps.

The candle was set down and the Apothecary felt himself being gently raised as a pair of probing fingers investigated the spot where he had been struck. Groaning theatrically, John lifted his lids.

'He's regaining consciousness, may the Lord be praised,' said the voice, close to his ear.

Squinting into the dimness, John could just make out the dark cloth of clerical habit. 'Who are you?' he asked faintly.

'The Reverend Tompkins,' replied the other, and as he moved into the light the Apothecary saw to his amazement that it was the extraordinary young curate he had encounted in St Augustine's at Brookland.

'I believe we've met before,' John said. 'A few days ago. I was looking around your church.'

'Were you?' The curate peered more closely. 'Why, yes, I *do* remember. You were on your way to Fairfield, were you not?'

The Apothecary nodded weakly. 'Indeed I was. But, Father, where am I now? The last thing I recall was being in Winchelsea. Then someone struck me, with a pistol butt I think. The next I knew I was lying on this bed.'

'My dear man, you're but a mile or so from where we first met You are in The Woolpack, an inn situated within a stone's throw of Brookland Church.'

'But how in Heaven's name did I get here?'

The curate shook his head. 'That I do not know. The landlord found you lying on the Marsh when he went out in his cart about an hour ago. There was no clue as to who put you there. Someone who bears you a grudge, I suppose.'

'But who could have a grudge against me in this part of the world? I am merely staying in Winchelsea and hardly know a soul there.'

Unless, John thought, Mrs Rose's would-be killer believes me to be nearer the truth than I actually am.

There was a knock on the door and the landlord came in with a chipped bowl, a soiled towel and some grubby-looking rags. The Apothecary shuddered.

'Does the wound need a stitch?' he asked the curate, who had started on the business of washing the blood from it.

'I hardly know. I am no expert.'

John looked at the landlord. 'Do you have such a thing as a couple of mirrors?'

The man exchanged a glance with the Reverend Tompkins. 'I might have. Why?'

'Because then I can see for myself just how bad the gash is.'

'And what would you know about such things?'

'Quite a lot. I'm an apothecary.'

The two stared at each other, clearly amazed. 'An apothecary!' exclaimed the curate.

'Yes. Why so surprised?'

'Because you don't really look the part, Sir.'

'Neither do you,' John responded, grinning, then wincing.

The other chuckled, his eyes twinkling. 'Well said. Fetch him the mirrors, Will.'

He seemed very much in command, John thought, for the landlord ambled off to do the curate's bidding without hesitation.

'So you're a man of medicine,' the Reverend Tompkins said, starting to pat the wound dry.

'Yes.' John felt in his inner pocket. 'Unfortunately I have no cards on me but I am John Rawlings, Apothecary, of Shug Lane, Piccadilly, London.'

'And that is all?'

John looked at him in astonishment. 'Yes, of course. Why?'

'Because whoever did this to you obviously thought you were engaged in some other form of business.'

'What do you mean?'

The curate leaned close to him, his wild blue eyes serious. 'My friend, this is smuggling country. It is a fact that free-traders work the Marsh, always have and always will. And Winchelsea, with its wonderful old cellars for storage, provides excellent customers for those who bring goods across the Channel. So my reading of the situation is that one of the fraternity, seeing a stranger in town,

131

made a few enquiries and came to the conclusion that you were an excise man, working under cover as it were.'

Despite his pain, John laughed. 'Nothing could be further from the truth.'

The Reverend Tompkins's vivid gaze grew narrow. 'But you aren't all that you seem, are you? Because if you're here simply to look at churches and visit your aunt, then my intuition ain't worth a tuppeny cuss.'

The Apothecary's eyes tightened in return. 'I don't remember mentioning my aunt to you.'

'Then somebody else must have done. But stick to the point, Sir, do. What have you really come to the marshland for?'

John stared at the Reverend Tompkins, several curious ideas about the man vying for supremacy in his mind. Eventually, the Apothecary grinned as he came to a decision. Lowering his voice dramatically, he whispered, 'To find a spy.'

'A spy!' exclaimed the curate, almost dropping the towel.

'Well two, to be precise. Don't ask me how I know because I have no intention of telling you. Simply trust me that there are two agents of France even now working out of Winchelsea. But I enjoin you to keep that information to yourself if you love your country.'

The curate's startled face grew serious. 'I am a patriot, Sir. Of that I can assure you. But may I ask one question?'

'Certainly.'

'If what you tell me is true would I be correct in believing you work for the Secret Office?'

'In a manner I do. For a branch of it.'

'And you are not connected with the Riding Officers, the excise men, in any way?'

'Absolutely not.'

'Then word shall be put about the Marsh that you must be left in peace to conduct your affairs as you wish.'

'And who will do this, Reverend Tompkins?'

The curate sparkled with intrigue. 'As a man of the cloth I naturally have connections.'

'Oh, I'm absolutely sure you do,' the Apothecary answered, smiling once more.

An hour later, driven by a man in a trap, John was heading for

Winchelsea beneath the dawn sky, his head neatly bandaged by the local physician who had been roused from his bed and brought to The Woolpack, clearly under protest. No stitch had been necessary but an ointment to stop wounds from becoming infected had been liberally applied to the gash, much to the Apothecary's relief.

'So you think I will be safe to pursue my inquiries?' he had asked of the curate as they parted company.

'I feel confident the freebooters will leave you alone when they discover you are not a Riding Officer.'

'Then let it be hoped that word gets round quickly.'

'It will,' the Reverend Tompkins had answered, nodding and smiling.

John had looked thoughtful. 'About your name, Father.'

'Yes?'

'Am I right in thinking it is quite famous round these parts?'

The curate had become vague, his blue eyes veiled. 'Is it? How so?'

'I thought you might have known. It was one of the aliases, or maybe even the real name, of Kit Jarvis, a notorious smuggler, highwayman, and God knows what else, who worked the marshland as an owler in his early days. He was hanged in 1750 for robbing the Chester mail.'

'May God rest his soul,' the man of the cloth had said quietly.

'Indeed, Father, indeed. A strange coincidence is it not, though? And now I really must be on my way.'

John had given a bow which wobbled slightly as his head throbbed with sudden pain.

'Here, let me help you.'

And before he could protest, the curate, with amazing strength, had half lifted the Apothecary into the trap.

'Until we meet again,' he called as the vehicle set off.

'Until next time, Dick,' John had answered, and watched as the curate's look of astonishment turned into a broad grin before he was lost to the Apothecary's view.

Chapter Twelve

At close quarters, John observed with a slight sense of shock, Mrs Tireman was even more redoubtable than she appeared at a distance. Large-framed and broad of hip, her feet and hands matched the rest of her so closely that in some ways she resembled a man, an impression enhanced by her extremely odd make-up. For this afternoon Mrs Tireman was in full enamel, yet with very pink cheeks and heavily rouged lips, while her eyes and brows had been over-darkened with a substance which the apothecary recognised as being imported from China. On her head, much boosted up with false curls, not to mention a mass of frills, furbelows and flowers, Mrs Tireman wore a good sprinkling of Cypress Hair Powder, thus attempting to create an impression of being at the very height of fashion. But all this, combined with her big build, simply served to make her look like a transvestite or, more kindly, a country parson's wife with desperate pretensions to being seen as a member of the *beau monde*.

Also present in the salon of the Rectory, where John, having slept all the morning, was duly keeping his appointment to dine, were Mrs Tireman's two daughters, their beauty almost unreal in comparison with their mother's extraordinary appearance. The company was completed by the saturnine figure of the Marquis of Rye, who sat stretched full length in a chair before the fire. Of the Reverend Tireman himself there was no sign, and John could not help but wonder whether the poor man had taken himself off in order to escape the rigours of pre-dinner conversation.

Having given Henrietta the warmest glance he dared in view of her mother's presence, the Apothecary had let his gaze wander over to her younger sister, the cause of so much grief and distress. That the girl was arrogant beyond belief was clearly evident, every trick of someone totally conceited being played. Rosalind had long since learned to move her head so that her glorious hair picked up and reflected the light with each tiny toss, while her green-blue eyes, the lashes dark around them, gazed on the world serenely, confident that every man living was her adoring slave, and her lips curving into a smile because of it.

Feeling John's scrutiny, finely tuned as she was to every nuance of male attention, Rosalind looked up and directly at him. The smile deepened and the eyes widened guilelessly, a little gleam in their depths that was meant for him to see and him alone. The fact that the Apothecary thought her lovely clearly pleased Rosalind enormously. She was without doubt, John thought, one of the most dangerous young women alive.

A very small sound drew his attention away from his study of this most ravishing of beauties and he realised that Henrietta had observed all that was happening and was biting her lip with consequent anguish. Well aware that Rosalind was still smiling at him, John turned his head to her sister and gave Henrietta a glance, the meaning of which could simply not be mistaken. She gave him a deep unreadable look in return, then smiled. Out of the corner of his eye, the Apothecary saw Rosalind's expression become petulant. However, the vain girl did not let the matter rest there. Rising from her seat, she came to sit next to John on the sofa.

'Where do you live in London, Mr Rawlings?'

'In Nassau Street in Soho, Miss Tireman.'

Rosalind examined her crescent shaped nails. 'Justin has a house in Pall Mall. I hope very much to spend a good deal of time there when we are married, particularly in the winter. I find the cold months so dreary in the country.'

'I am sure that town life will be all the brighter for your presence,' the Apothecary answered blandly.

Rosalind adored the compliment and gave the Apothecary a look aimed at leaving him helpless. It did not succeed.

Meanwhile, the Marquis sat at ease, sipping a dry sherry and staring into the fire. He was, John considered, with his dark looks, black clothes and long, elegant frame, rather like some exquisite insect, a beautiful creature of the night drawn to the brightness of the flames.

'Justin,' Rosalind said, addressing her future bridegroom, her voice rich and sweet as honey, 'when are we going to London? You did promise that it would be very shortly.'

The Marquis ceased his contemplation of the fire. 'I have some business to attend to here, my dear. That should take a week or so. We'll go after that.'

Her lower lip drooped a little. 'I had hoped somewhat sooner.'

Mrs Tireman entered the conversation. 'Now, now, Rosie. You are lucky to have such a beautiful house to stay in when you are in town. Be content I pray you.'

The Marquis smiled fleetingly and deliberately changed the topic. Looking at John, he said, 'Tell me, Mr Rawlings, has your aunt been visited by a certain Mr Jago claiming he is from the Secret Office and asking the whereabouts of a Frenchman, supposed to have visited Winchelsea some eight months ago?'

'Not that I know of, my Lord,' the Apothecary answered truthfully.

'Well he came to see me and I thought it damned impertinent. I hardly knew what he was talking about. No one answering that description called on me, I can assure you. However, he seemed much interested in the fact that my mother was French.'

'A thing that the Marquis and I share in common,' said Mrs Tireman unexpectedly. 'My mama was Claude Vallier from Normandy.'

'Which would explain why you speak the language so well,' the Apothecary replied, his expression innocent.

She shot him a penetrating look from beneath her darkened brows. 'How did you know that, pray?'

'Oh I heard you,' John said vaguely.

'Anyway,' the Marquis continued, 'it seems that we must all be careful. The man is here to snoop, there's no doubt of it.'

'But surely if one has nothing to hide, one has nothing to fear,' said Henrietta, a note of defiance in her voice.

'I wouldn't be too certain,' answered her former lover, not looking at her. 'Men of Jago's type can twist facts very easily.'

'*Was* there a Frenchman here some months ago, then?' John asked ingenuously.

'Yes there was, as a matter of fact,' answered Rosalind. 'He stayed at The Salutation. Only for a few days. Then he left and did not return.'

Killed on the Romney Marsh, John thought. Aloud, he said, 'Surely that was strange, with war declared.'

'It was just before hostilities began.'

The Marquis laughed. 'You seem to recall events very distinctly, my dear.'

'I noticed the fellow because he was so beautifully dressed.'

Or, more likely, because he ogled you and you loved every moment, John reflected cynically.

'Then perhaps you should seek this Jago out and tell him what you remember.'

'That won't be necessary,' said a voice from the doorway. 'He came into church this evening. He will be calling at the Rectory tomorrow.'

Every head turned and words of greeting were exchanged. The Reverend Tireman had arrived home.

He was a sandy sort of man, John observed, his wispy hair, or all that remained of it about the rector's balding pate, a soft ginger shade, as were his bushy brows. Beneath those protuberances, as untamed and sprawling as a nest of spiders, the rector's eyes were the colour of syrup, while his skin was almost dun in tone. Once again, the extraordinary beauty of his daughters seemed inexplicable until the Apothecary remembered their French grandmother and wondered if that might be whom they took after.

'Well, well,' said the reverend gentleman, advancing on John with a beaming smile, 'I don't think I've had the pleasure, Sir.'

His guest, who had risen to his feet, bowed politely. 'John Rawlings, apothecary of London.'

'An apothecary, eh? How interesting. Have you met our local chap, Gironde?'

'Briefly, Sir.'

'You must chat with him. He's very knowledgeable I believe.'

Mrs Tireman rose to her feet. 'Shall we go in to dine? Mr Rawlings, will you take in Henrietta?'

'It will be my pleasure,' John answered, and offered the young lady his arm.

It was not easy to concentrate during that meal, sitting close to the elder Miss Tireman as he was, and consequently beset by passionate feelings every time he looked at her. And yet the Apothecary was acutely aware that there was a pressing need to be alert. With Rosalind's assertion that the Scarecrow had been in Winchelsea on the very eve of war, it was clearer than ever that contact with the Moth and the Frog, or at least one of them, had been made, with disastrous consequences for the spy master. Even now, John was aware, one or both of the secret agents could be sitting at this very table.

He looked round covertly. Mrs Tireman with her awful maquillage and overbearing manner seemed too stupid for a spy, yet she spoke French fluently and her mother had come from that country. Could her connection with the smugglers mean that she was also associated with other equally sinister figures from across the Channel? Equally, the sable-toned rector seemed impossible to suspect, yet the Apothecary had learned long since that the least likely person was often the most guilty. The Tireman women were particularly well turned out for the family of a simple country parson. Had the man of God sold his soul in order to clothe his wife and daughters in style? Or could he be being blackmailed into spying by someone who knew of Mrs Tireman's connection with Dick Jarvis?

Almost unwillingly, John looked at the girl beside him and, as always with his particular personality, shuddered away from the idea that Henrietta could be involved. But had she not gone to the Marquis's household to teach French to his young sister? Did her knowledge of the language stem simply from the fact of having a French grandmother? Or had there been a liaison with a Frenchman at some time in her past? A liaison that had led to her becoming a spy?

Slowly, John turned his eyes to Rosalind, who glowed in the candlelight like a nymph of dawning. She was so totally perfect and so very aware of it that he doubted she had room in her head for another single thought. As far as he could tell, her entire life revolved around her glorious hair, her wonderful eyes, her enticing body, and the art of enslaving men. And even now, feeling him look at her, Rosalind gave him a glance of sublime assurance, her pupils green as the ocean in the dim light. But beauty often masked an ugly heart, the Apothecary knew that well. With looks such as hers there was little doubt that Rosalind had been attracting men since puberty. Had she agreed to become a spy in order that the secret of a past indiscretion should never come to light? Or could avarice alone have been her motive?

Beside her the Marquis fluttered darkly, his hawk face shadowed and closed. Could he, John wondered, peer of the realm though the man might be, have betrayed his country for some reason? And then he remembered Lady Ffloote telling him of the Marquis's early debts and wondered whether Justin had sold out for money at a very different stage of his life and was now too deeply in the abyss to turn back.

139

The Scarecrow almost certainly had been killed in the church then dragged outside and hung upon the wooden cross, a task that would have taken a certain amount of strength. Staring at the women, John considered Mrs Tireman well up to the task. And Henrietta and Rosalind, gorgeous though they looked, were strong young women with the fresh complexions of those who both rode and walked. The Scarecrow had not been a big man, his tattered clothes gave evidence to that. Though it would have required effort, the Apothecary felt certain that either of them could have disguised their crime in the macabre way that was chosen.

Making as if she had dropped something, Henrietta leaned towards him. 'When can we meet?' she whispered close to John's ear.

'Tomorrow,' he murmured, pretending to search the floor.

'In the same place?'

'Yes. At noon.'

'Henrietta, what are you doing?' enquired Mrs Tireman, staring down the length of the table.

'I lost an earring, Mama, but Mr Rawlings has found it for me.'

'I'm sure Mr Rawlings is excellent at discovering things,' Rosalind commented, but though John shot her an enquiring glance she gave him her usual infinite gaze into which he could read absolutely nothing at all.

As before, to risk exposing Joe Jago as an associate was a terrible prospect, but even more terrible was the thought of not catching up with him at all. Therefore, when dinner had ended and John had sat through the usual hour of musical entertainment, he walked out into the dusk and hurried through the back lanes to The Salutation, there to put his head round the door of the various public rooms to see if he could locate Mr Fielding's clerk. Yet again, luck was running with him, for Joe was standing in the taproom, his wig at a rakish angle, his ragged face creased into a smile, consuming ale with the locals and undoubtedly coming by as much gossip as he possibly could. Not quite sure how to handle the situation, the Apothecary went up to the bar and a few moments later felt Joe come and stand beside him.

'Good evening, Sir. Forgive me for intruding but I've been racking my brains ever since you were kind enough to give me directions the other day. You see, I can't help feeling that I know you from somewhere. You don't by any chance come from London, do you?'

John turned to look at him and saw a light eye winking. 'Yes, I do as a matter of fact,' he answered.

'I thought I was not mistaken. I never forget a face. Correct me if I am wrong but do you not own a shop in Shug Lane off Piccadilly?'

'What a phenomenal memory,' the Apothecary replied over-loudly. 'My dear Sir I congratulate you on it.' He wrung Joe Jago heartily by the hand.

'Not quite so good as you might think,' the clerk replied, grinning a great display of teeth. 'I have an aged mama who lives close by. I have to pass your place every time I go and visit her. Small wonder that you were familiar to me.'

He said it so convincingly that John looked at him twice, wondering if it might be true. It had never occurred to him that Joe had parents or any other kind of family, being the type of man who just seemed to be there, permanently arrested in the middle years of his life. Yet this extraordinary individual who spoke cant, the language of the streets, as fluently as standard English, must have come from somewhere.

'Have you really?' John asked, meaning it.

'London is scattered with my relations,' Joe answered, and laughed. 'And now, young gentleman,' he continued, his eyes full of amusement, 'will you allow me to buy you some ale? It is so pleasant to see an acquaintance from town.'

'By all means,' the Apothecary replied, and secured a place for them at a table which stood rather distant from the others, taking his seat on the high-backed settle close by.

'Now,' said Joe in an undertone, putting down the two foaming tankards, 'tell me what happened to you? I waited at the Roundle till late but though much occurred, for that damned foolish fellow's still out there signalling to the Frenchies for all he's worth, you did not appear.'

'I was taken prisoner by the smugglers who clouted me over the head thinking I was an excise man,' John answered, equally quietly. 'In the end I was dragged off to Brookland on the Romney Marsh in order to be interrogated by the head man himself, Dick Jarvis, infamous son of a notorious father. He's little older than I am but has the cheek of the very Devil. He strolls the Marsh dressed as a curate, if you please. What a rogue.' He laughed and removed his wig, delicately feeling the cut that lay concealed beneath.

'You like him,' said Joe, and it was a statement not a question.

'It's difficult not to.'

'Even when he knocks you unconscious?'

'That was one of his henchmen.'

'But his order.'

'Joe, I think he has befriended me,' said John, just above a whisper. 'I believe that he will leave me alone in future. Now, tell me what has been happening to you.'

'I managed to call on most of Winchelsea's worthies, other than for the rector and his family, all of whom were out for the day. Most of them denied seeing a Frenchman or said they couldn't remember that far back, with two exceptions that is.'

'And who were they?'

'Mrs Finch and Captain Pegram.'

The Apothecary chuckled. 'So you braved the lady, did you?'

Joe Jago, man of the people, actually coloured the ripe rich shade of ruby port. 'Yes,' he said non-committally.

John laughed uncontrollably. 'Oh dear me, did she have her wicked way?'

Mr Fielding's clerk put on a dignified countenance, a look that did not sit at all easily on his rugged features.

'I conducted my business formally, Sir.'

'Ha ha,' bellowed John, 'but how did she conduct hers?'

'I thought the lady very amiable.'

'I'll wager she was too,' the Apothecary answered, wiping his streaming eyes.

Joe looked severe. 'Mrs Finch informed me that when out walking with her daughters she was asked the way by an elegant man with a French accent. He told her that he was staying in town at this very inn and also enquired whether she knew where the Marquis of Rye resided.'

John stopped laughing and leant forward. 'Really? How very interesting.'

'Just as I thought. However, the Marquis himself said no such man called on him, denied it emphatically indeed. He's half French, you know.'

'Yes, I do. And so is Mrs Tireman, while Captain Pegram had a French grandmother.'

'Now there's an odd fish.'

'The Captain?'

'Yes. Did you know that his father commanded the Revenue vessel based at Rye and was wounded by your friend Dick Jarvis's blackguardly sire?'

'No, I most certainly did not.'

'Apparently the family was called Pigram in those days but later changed the name for reasons of good taste. Anyway, Captain Pigram the first did not dare leave Rye harbour without the protection of a man-of-war. Three large Calais sloops were constantly waiting to shoot him up if he did. Furthermore, the dastardly Kit together with his gang had the barefaced audacity to board his vessel. Naturally, there was a fight and several crew members were wounded, one of them being stripped of his wig and trousers and made to dance on deck, culls a-leaping with every step and his pizzle swaying in the ocean breeze, no doubt.'

'Did the Captain say that?' asked John, astonished.

It was Joe's turn to laugh. 'Nay, that's just my coarseness. No, the present day Captain Pegram only told me how much he disliked the smuggling fraternity and would have nothing to do with them, though many of the public support them, and at all levels of society too.'

'And what about the Scarecrow?'

'He said that a Frenchman called on him, a very elegantly dressed fellow. He apologised profusely for coming to the wrong house when Captain Pegram received him, said he was looking for somebody else and would be on his way.'

'Did he say who that someone was?'

'Unfortunately no.'

'Damnation! Anything else?'

Joe hesitated. 'I believe the gallant Captain is an admirer of the naked female form.'

'Aren't we all.'

'You are in a very facetious mood, young Sir. I cannot think what Mr Fielding would say.'

The Apothecary composed himself. 'I'm sorry. But even if Captain Pegram does have a lascivious side to his nature how can that have any bearing on the death of the Scarecrow?'

Joe's blue eyes looked steely. 'I am surprised at you, Mr

143

Rawlings. I thought you knew by now that everything has significance when it comes to murder. Perhaps there is something the Captain wants hidden from the world and he was prepared to kill to keep it secret.'

Chastened, John looked down. 'You're right. Tell me what you know.'

'I was alone in his study for a moment or two and it was then that I observed, half hidden in the drawer of his writing desk, a pencil drawing of a beautiful girl, stark naked and with a very knowing expression on her face. I just thought it odd for a man in Captain Pegram's position to have such a thing.'

'Why? He is only human like the rest of us.'

'Indeed he is. Yet there was something provocative about the female's pose. For no reason I got the impression that I was looking at a portrait of his mistress.'

'I still don't see . . .'

Joe Jago played his trump card. 'I believe, Mr Rawlings, that I was looking at a picture of one or other of the Misses Tireman.'

John felt stricken, imagining Henrietta and the Captain together. 'What makes you say that? Have you met the rector's daughters yet?'

'I glimpsed them when they returned from their excursion.'

'My God!' said the Apothecary wretchedly.

'However, when I go to interview them tomorrow I shall know for certain. Meanwhile, Mr Rawlings, nothing can be proved.'

'No, I suppose not,' John answered, trying to rally.

Joe plunged on cheerfully. 'As for the rest, Sir Ambrose Ffloote stared at me as if I were crazed and said he knew nothing of any damned foreigner; his lady pleaded illness in order not to speak to me; Apothecary Gironde and his wife became extremely agitated and swore they hated all Frenchmen as he was a Huguenot. As for the doctor, he says he has so many sick people to deal with he can hardly remember one week from the next, let alone eight months ago.'

'And were they telling the truth?'

'Some of them, I expect.'

'Are our spies amongst Winchelsea's polite society?'

'Definitely, I would say. Only they would have the time and suffcient knowledge of France and the French. I am well aware that working people can act as secret agents but somehow I don't quite see that in a rural community. Anyway, as I told you earlier, somebody is continuing to signal. Tonight we must both watch and note down the number sequences.'

'Shall I meet you?'

'No, we are already being observed by the local gaffers who are not as silly as they look. Let us keep up the pretence of being strangers as long as we can.'

'When shall I talk to you again?'

'Come to The Salutation any evening and wait in the taproom. But if something should go wrong I shall send a note to Mrs Harcross, or ought I to say Rose?'

'Very good.' John got to his feet. 'It is indeed a small world, Sir,' he said loudly. 'I have enjoyed making your aquaintance. I am staying in Winchelsea with my aunt, Mrs Rose of Petronilla's Platt. Do call on me there if you should feel so inclined.'

Joe stood also. 'I am rather busy, Sir, but if I get a moment, I will.' They bowed formally to one another. 'Meanwhile, I bid you farewell.'

'Farewell,' said the Apothecary, and stepped out from the warmth of The Salutation into the cold March night.

It was bitterly cold close to the sea, a high wind lashing in over the waves that could almost freeze a man to death. John stood beside the dappled mare, which he had hired as soon as he had left the inn, shivering violently and hoping that he was not wasting his time and that the signals would be repeated tonight. Further, that he would be able to note them down, unhindered by the activities of smugglers. For it was the sort of night when they might well be active, thick inky cloud obscuring the moon and hiding their dark deeds from the eyes of the Riding Officers.

When in the fifteenth century the sea had receded from the ancient Cinque Port of Winchelsea and the harbour had silted up, the town had become that extraordinary curiosity, a port without water. So now the Apothecary stood icy, deciding that he was not going to wait long on a night like this, on a deserted piece of terrain known as Pett Level, staring out into the blackness waiting for something to happen.

While he kept his freezing vigil his mind drifted as his thoughts ran free and he smiled, alone in the darkness, at the sheer audacity of Dick Jarvis and his not altogether convincing portrayal of an eager young curate. Then John frowned at the notion that Captain Nathaniel Pegram might have a drawing of Henrietta, naked, and wondered, if the man had indeed got such a thing, what the meaning of it might be. For if truth be known, Coralie Clive or no Coralie Clive, John was deeply smitten with the girl he had made love to in the cherry orchard and hated to think of her with anyone else.

At this, the Marquis of Rye came into mind; dark, saturnine and very slightly sinister. Why had the Scarecrow asked Mrs Finch if she knew of the nobleman's whereabouts? And was it the Marquis whom the Frenchman had sought when he had arrived mistakenly at Grey Friars? Going deeply down this path, John hardly noticed when, quite close at hand, no more than a hundred yards away, a light began to flash, its beam directed out to sea.

Hastily dragging his attention back to the moment, the Apothecary drew out the paper and pencil which he had placed in the pocket of his great coat, and started to write.

'2918 386 841,' the sequence ran, the lantern flashing twice, then pausing, then flashing nine times and so on. It meant nothing of course but he painstakingly copied the numbers down. Eventually, with no reply, the sequence was laboriously repeated. Then came an answering flash from a ship close to the shore. '2245 1615 2697,' John wrote, before the lights were abruptly doused.

Nothing stirred in the icy blackness, then suddenly the Apothecary froze as the sound of a horse's hooves drew close. And with that sound, slightly masked by the noise of the trotting horse, there was something else that he could not identify, a strange and rather frightening scrabbling, as if some creature were dragging itself painfully over the sandy terrain. Inexplicably nervous, John waited in the darkness until all had gone quiet, then thankfully headed for home.

Chapter Thirteen

It was with a great deal of curiosity and a strong streak of professional jealousy that John Rawlings drew to a halt outside Marcel Gironde's apothecary's shop and surveyed the premises with an admiring eye, somewhat dazzled by all there was on offer. For not one but *two* bow fronted windows met his envious gaze, the first packed with a thrilling array of exotic containers and jars, all filled with vivid blue liquid, the second with perfume, attractively presented in porcelain bottles, some of which had been painted by hand. Together with the scents were cosmetics, bearing signs showing their country of origin. 'Carmine from the Indies' lay beside a pot of red lip salve, though pride of place in the window display had been given to a dentifrice, described thus: 'Made on the premises from a mixture of coral, Armenian bole, Portugal snuff, Havannah snuff, ashes of good tobacco and gum myrrh. All ingredients well pulverised, mixed, and sifted twice. Rub on the teeth with the fingers.'

Very impressed, John went through the door between the two windows, to the accompaniment of a ringing bell. As he did so Nan Gironde bobbed up from behind the counter.

'Oh good morning,' she gushed. 'Mr Rawlings, isn't it?'

John bowed. 'Yes, Madam. We were introduced at the Assembly the other night. I am staying in Winchelsea with my aunt, Elizabeth Rose.'

The bird-bright eyes regarded him with interest. 'Did she not say that you are an apothecary, Sir?'

'I am indeed. Allow me to present you with my card.'

Mrs Gironde took it, scanning the wording with interest. 'Oh! Shug Lane, eh? A good area indeed.'

'You are familiar with London, Madam?'

'Most certainly. I lived there prior to my marriage. Born and brought up in town, in fact.' She looked wistful. 'I miss the hustle and bustle.' Nan brightened again. 'But there. We have made a thriving business in Winchelsea. People come from as

147

far as Hastings, even beyond, to buy our products. We have the reputation of making the finest cosmetics and scents in the country.'

'Really?' asked John, thoroughly struck by what he was hearing. 'I indulge in perfume blending as well, even though it is frowned upon by other apothecaries who believe I am straying out of my province.'

'Of course, there are *attitudes* wherever one goes,' answered Mrs Gironde, promptly rising in John's estimation. 'That is partly why Marcel lets me compound the scents and cosmetics – under his supervision I might add.'

Thinking of Nicholas Dawkins and Snow Violets, John smiled. 'A very wise move on your husband's part.'

'I heard myself mentioned,' stated a voice from an archway at the back, and Marcel Gironde stepped into the shop from his compounding room.

'My dear Sir,' said John, bowing deep, 'may I say with all sincerity how very much I admire your shop and its range of products.'

'How kind of you. Please let us show you round. Do you have a spare hour?'

John looked at his watch which told him that the time was ten o'clock. 'Yes, I most certainly do. My next appointment is not until noon.'

'Then allow me the pleasure.'

They went along the shelves, looking at bottles and discussing ingredients, then spent a delightful thirty minutes in the back room, examining various simples and talking of their merits and failings. Completely absorbed in his conversation with a fellow practitioner and enthusiast, John almost forgot that he was there to gather information, and it wasn't until Nan announced that it was her turn to show their visitor the perfumery, that the Apothecary recalled the task in hand.

He turned to Marcel. 'I believe you are of Huguenot descent, Sir.'

'Yes, both sets of grandparents fled to London in 1687, after the Edict of Nantes was revoked. My parents were children at the time, of course, but, moving in the same circle, they were introduced, married, and raised a family. I was apprenticed to a town apothecary, also with Hugenot origins, and that is how I met my future wife. She was his niece.'

'And how did you come to live in Winchelsea?'

Nan interrupted. 'My mother moved to Hastings, feeling she needed the sea air for her lungs. We followed to be close by. As I told you, it was a wrench to leave the excitement of London, but I do believe we have made the best of it.'

'You certainly have.'

Nan's beaky face looked animated. 'It is so very nice to speak to another of like mind. Do come and see my section of the shop, Mr Rawlings.'

The way in which the place was set out was clever indeed. A long counter ran almost the entire length of the premises, divided neatly by a wooden partition at its centre. On one side lay Marcel's domain, the shelves behind bearing nothing but physick and pills. On the other were the beauty preparations, the shelves and drawers stacked with perfumes and scents, dyestuffs for the complexion, rouges for the lips and cheeks, blackening for the eyes and brows. Piled amongst these were wash balls and soaps, to say nothing of extraordinary mixtures for cleaning the teeth. Awestruck, John found his eye drawn to a bottle, claiming on its label, 'Elixir of Youth. A Potion for the More Mature'.

'Gracious me,' he said, picking it up. 'What's in it?'

Nan had the good grace to look uncomfortable but Marcel laughed. 'Harmless Pennywort and a few good tasting placebos.'

'I see. Do you sell a lot of the stuff?'

'We have one or two regular customers, mostly from outside. I don't think the ladies of Winchelsea are that concerned about ageing.'

'Some are,' said Mrs Gironde with a knowing smile.

'Yes, a few.'

'But it can't work surely?'

Marcel laughed. 'Oh come now, Mr Rawlings, you know as well as I do that half the cure lies in the belief.'

'Anyway,' chipped in Nan, avine in the extreme at that moment, 'I sell them a complementary paste that smooths out wrinkles, temporarily if nothing more.'

John had to smile despite a certain dislike of what the Girondes were doing, forced to agree that much of what they said was true. 'I suppose as long as the ladies are happy . . .'

'That is precisely how we feel.' Mrs Gironde attempted to look artless. 'And talking of ladies reminds me. I would swear that I know your aunt from somewhere. You see, I was a great theatregoer before I left town. As were all my family. My grandfather went to the first night of all the new plays, never missed one.'

The Apothecary's heart sank. 'Oh yes?' he said politely.

'Well, he was very much taken with the great Mrs Egleton, the one who created the role of Lucy Lockit, and even when he was quite an old man kept a print of her in his bedroom. I grew up with that print, Mr Rawlings. And do you know when I first saw Mrs Rose, I thought the portrait had come to life.'

There was more to be gained by telling the truth, John knew it. 'What a remarkable child you must have been. How very observant,' he said with a humourless smile. 'Aunt Elizabeth was indeed the actress of whom you speak.'

'Well fancy that!' She turned to her husband. 'Just imagine, Marcel, we live in the same town as one of the most famous actresses of all time.' The bright eyes tightened. 'Was she not married to Jasper Harcross, the man who was killed on stage during a performance of *The Beggar's Opera*?'

'Yes, poor lady,' said John sorrowfully. 'The loss of such a devoted husband was very hard for her to bear. That is why she lives here quietly and alone. Here, in the solitude of Winchelsea, she feels she can escape her memories. Therefore, Madam, I would beg you to keep what I have just told you to yourself. My aunt could not tolerate knowing that someone was aware of her hidden sorrow.'

He looked at her shrewdly and saw a momentary flicker of guilt, clearly indicating that she had already started to spread the rumour about Mrs Rose's true identity. Meanwhile, Nan mouthed platitudes. 'No, of course not. Her secret is safe with me. I am the soul of discretion.'

'Naturally,' said John, but his thoughts were racing. Elizabeth might well be right in thinking that her past had caught up with her. Had someone in sleepy Winchelsea once been in love with the beautiful Jasper? Or with the cruel source of his death? It all seemed so improbable that the Apothecary almost abandoned the idea before it had taken hold, and then he remembered that Nan had come from town and there might well be another who had done the same.

Marcel Gironde broke in on his train of thought. 'May I make you some tea, Mr Rawlings?'

John looked at his watch. He had forty-five minutes before he was due to meet Henrietta in the cherry orchard. 'That would be delightful,' he said.

They moved into the compounding room where Nan busied herself with a kettle and a Worcester teapot.

'Tell me,' said the Apothecary, sitting down, 'have you been visited recently by a man called Jago purporting to be from the Secret Office. Apparently he is asking the whereabouts of a certain Frenchman who came to Winchelsea just before the outbreak of war. My aunt was much put out by his questions.'

Marcel rolled his eyes in an extremely Gallic gesture. 'It was terrible. The man seemed fixated with the idea that because of my ancestry I might sympathise with the cause of France. I tried to tell him that I was born here but he seemed unconvinced.'

Mrs Gironde came to the table with the cups. 'He made me so angry that I forbore to tell him there was a man here answering perfectly the description he gave us.'

'*Was* there?' exclaimed John, amazed.

'Oh, yes,' put in Marcel, 'he came into the shop and spoke to me in French, a language in which I am fluent because my parents conversed in it at home.'

'What did he say?'

'Nothing of any interest. In fact most of his conversation was about perfume.'

'Perfume?' John repeated loudly.

'Yes, he wanted to buy a bottle for a friend and asked my advice.'

'And what did you sell him?'

'A blend of my own which I call Evening in Araby.'

'Then what happened?'

'He thanked me, paid, and left. We never saw him again, did we, Nan?'

There was a fraction of a second's pause before she answered, 'Never.'

'May I smell what he bought?'

Marcel stared at the Apothecary narrowly. 'You seem very interested.'

'Well, I am, to be honest. I got the strong impression from my aunt that the man was a French spy, which I find quite fascinating. Did Jago give you the same idea?'

151

'Yes. That's why I kept quiet. I have absolutely no wish to be involved with the Secret Office and their doings. Anyway, this is it.'

He unstoppered a painted bottle and handed it to John, who inhaled deeply. As he had half suspected it was the same exotic mixture that he had smelled in the churchyard on the night when the unseen couple had so bitterly argued with one another. In that case, had she who had administered the stinging blow been known to the Scarecrow? Or was it mere coincidence? Attempting to pursue this line of reasoning, the Apothecary was rudely interrupted by a cooing voice from the shop doorway.

'Bless me, if it isn't Mr Rawlings. Oh, my dear man, I've been trying to find you to invite you to dine with me and my gels. There is so much I have to tell you.' Mrs Finch waved a finger waggishly. 'These are exciting times in Winchelsea indeed.'

'In what way?'

'There's a man here from the Secret Office. Quite a charming individual, considering. He took sherry with me yesterday and I was able to help him with his quest.'

'Really?'

'Yes.' Mrs Finch raised her voice so that the Girondes could hear. 'He is seeking a mysterious Frenchman who was in town some eight months ago and, do you know, when I was out with my daughters I was actually asked the way by a man answering the description he gave. Can you credit such a thing? Of all the people to stop, the stranger chose me.' She laughed archly.

'My, my!' said Nan.

Mrs Finch turned back to John. 'So, Mr Rawlings, when will you grace our humble home with your presence? Would tomorrow be of any use?'

'Alas, no. I am engaged to dine with Sir Ambrose and Lady Ffloote.'

'Then the following day. Oh, do say you will.' She slipped her arm familiarly through his.

John politely but firmly disengaged himself. 'I will have to consult my aunt first. She has arranged all kinds of entertainments for me.'

'*Has* she? I always thought Mrs Rose such a quiet person.'

Nan Gironde let out an audible snigger, at which Marcel shot her a reproving look.

152

'As I was saying,' Mrs Finch continued severely, 'you will be a most welcome guest at any time you care to mention.'

John bowed. 'How very hospitable. I will send word as soon as I have spoken to Aunt Elizabeth.'

Mrs Gironde piped up. 'Have you come for your usual, Molly?'

Mrs Finch looked slightly put out and huffed a little. 'Yes, indeed.'

Nan dived beneath the counter and reappeared clutching a bottle wrapped in tissue. 'Here we are then.'

Molly Finch snatched it, quite pink in the cheeks, and John guessed at once that the bottle contained the famous Elixir of Youth. 'Put it on my account,' she said grandly.

'I will certainly.'

'Then I'll say good-day.'

She swept out, obviously irritated that the Apothecary had witnessed the transaction. He let her get ahead of him by a few minutes, then with a great deal of bowing and thanking, followed in her wake, hurrying along Friars Walk in order not to be late for his meeting with Henrietta.

They were in each other's arms at once, kissing and hugging with a great deal of enthusiasm. Yet even while he made love to her – or at least almost immediately afterwards – the image of Henrietta posing naked for Captain Nathaniel Pegram came to taunt John, who by now was more than a little in love with her and prepared to be desperately hurt at the very thought of such a thing.

Determined to be mature and not mention a word about it, the Apothecary fell straight into the trap when Henrietta said, 'I do hope the Captain doesn't decide to walk through his orchards today.'

'Why?' he asked, immediately defensive.

She stared at him. 'I thought the reason would have been obvious. We are both in a state of disarray.'

Foolishly, John persisted. 'But why him? Why Captain Pegram?'

Henrietta stared all the harder. 'Because these are his grounds. He is more likely to come across us than anyone else.'

'But would that matter to you?'

Miss Tireman drew away from him. 'Of course it would. If I were caught *in flagrante delicto* my reputation would be gone for ever.'

'And that is all?'

153

Henrietta stood up and began to fasten her stays. 'Really, John, what is the matter with you? Wouldn't that be enough?'

The Apothecary pulled on his breeches. 'What I am trying to say is, does it matter if Captain Pegram in particular were to find us?'

She looked at him icily. 'No. Why should it? What are you inferring?'

Realising that he had gone too far, John attempted to retrieve the situation.

'Oh, take no notice of me. I am turning into a jealous lover, that is all. Ignore me and blame the foolishness of youth.'

'How old *are* you?'

'Rising twenty-six.'

'Then you should know better. You lead me by three years, yet behave as if you were still at school.'

She winched the laces of her stays viciously tight and gasped with shock. Despite everything, the Apothecary smiled unevenly.

'I apologise. I hold you in the highest regard, believe me.'

Henrietta loosened the laces a little. 'Do you really?'

'Yes, I do. And somehow I have managed to get it into my mind that you once meant something to the Captain.'

Miss Tireman looked scornful. 'My dear, he is *old*.'

It was out of John's mouth before he could check himself. 'So is the Marquis.'

The stays were pulled so firmly that John's eyes watered at the mere sight of it. Then the hooped petticoat and gown were thrown into position at a speed that defied the human eye. Not stopping to put on her shoes, Henrietta snatched them up, tossed her head in the air, and without a backward glance sped off through the orchards towards the lane, leaving John Rawlings standing in his breeches, mouth open, expression gloomy, daunted yet again by the extraordinarily varied moods of the female sex.

He had returned to Winchelsea with bowed head and slow walk, extremely depressed that he had upset the girl who was beginning to mean so much to him. For now John found it hard to think of Coralie Clive at all, so full of sweet memories of his passionate interludes in the cherry orchards. Yet he was well aware that the time he spent dwelling on Henrietta was time when he was not bending his mind to discovering the identities of the Moth and the Frog, a thought which made him more downcast than ever.

154

Indeed it was with a long face and sad heart that the Apothecary walked through the front door of Petronilla's Platt, only to discover Elizabeth Rose, clearly recovered from her recent ordeal, up and about and baking in the kitchen.

'I never realised you cooked,' he said involuntarily, then took himself to task for yet again being tactless with a member of the opposite sex. Mrs Rose, however, did not seem to mind.

'I don't very often,' she admitted, 'but today I felt like preparing some food that I knew to be free of poison.' Her expression grew serious. 'John, are you any closer to finding out who is doing this to me?'

'Not really, except that I am very certain it isn't Captain Pegram.'

Elizabeth bridled. 'How could it be? The very idea. Nathaniel is a thoroughly decent man.'

The Apothecary made placatory noises, then said, 'But I did discover today that at least one person in Winchelsea is aware of your real identity.'

'And who might that be?'

'Nan Gironde.'

'I might have guessed,' said Mrs Rose in a bitter voice, and sat down suddenly at the kitchen table.

'Why do you say that?'

'Because, as I told you, she is an interfering busybody.'

John nodded slowly. 'None the less, she found out by chance. Her grandfather was a great admirer of yours and kept a print of you in his bedroom. She discovered the truth by the simple means of seeing the resemblance.'

'Be that as it may,' Elizabeth answered with an air of resignation, 'if Nan knows, the entire town knows.'

'I don't think they do – yet. And I may have been able to stop the gossip spreading any further.'

And John brought his hostess up to date with events. She did not look in the least convinced but at least had the good grace to change the subject.

'How is Joe Jago? You told me that he was in town but I must confess I haven't set eyes on him. And what of the spy? Is there really such a person in Winchelsea?'

John shook his head. 'No. There's not one but two of the bastards.'

'*Two!* But how do you know?'

'That I can't tell you, just trust what I say.'

'But who could they possibly be?'

'I have absolutely no idea.'

'But is it a man and a woman? Two men? What?'

Into John's graphic memory flashed a picture of himself concealed in the churchyard, listening to the cruel argument between the unseen couple. 'My instinct tells me they are male and female, though I have no proof,' he said.

'Am I under suspicion?'

'Along with everybody else, yes.'

'Then let me hasten to assure you that I am innocent. Though I may have lived abroad for several years my loyalties lie with this country.'

'I believe you, but I am not the ultimate authority.'

'So who is? Mr Fielding?'

'No, it is a higher command still. The Earl of Holdernesse, who is Secretary of State, is in charge of the Secret Office. While Mr Anthony Todd is head of the Secret Department at the Post Office. Between them the spying activities of this country are co-ordinated and organised.'

'It all sounds rather frightening.'

'It is. Don't let us forget that to spy for the enemy is an act of high treason, and the punishment for that crime is death.'

'And if you catch them that fate will be meted out to two residents of Winchelsea I presume.'

John gave a humourless smile. 'Don't distress yourself, Elizabeth. One of them, possibly both, has already taken a man's life.'

There was silence, broken only by the chirrup of the kettle and the crackle of coal in the stove, then both of them jumped as there came a knock at the front door. From where they sat they heard Agnes plod down the stairs to open it, then Joe Jago's voice rang out loud and clear.

'Is your mistress at home?'

'I'll go and see,' answered the servant and a moment later her plain face appeared round the kitchen door.

'That man's here,' she whispered. 'The one that's going round asking questions.'

'Then show him into the parlour.'

'Yes, Mam,' answered Agnes, round-eyed.

Mrs Rose's voice dropped to a whisper. 'John, is it Joe?'

'Yes, he's here.'

'Oh, bless his good heart. It will be delightful to renew our acquaintanceship.'

They proceeded into the front room to find Mr Fielding's clerk standing with his back to the fire, his light blue eyes full of humour, his red hair glowing in the afternoon sunshine, his lean frame shown to its best advantage in a suit of sombre black. Signalling him to be silent, John stole to the kitchen to make quite sure that Agnes was not loitering in the passageway, then, having instructed her to continue with the cooking, closed both doors. When he returned he winked at Joe, who promptly bowed over Mrs Rose's hand.

'Madam, what a pleasure it is to see you again.'

'A feeling greatly reciprocated even though we first met in such strange circumstances.'

'You will forgive me, I trust, if I ask you one or two formal questions before we socialise?'

'Of course I will. John tells me there is evil work abroad in this town.'

'There is indeed. Now, Mrs Harcross, can you cast your mind back eight months? To the summer, just before war was declared?'

'Indeed I can. I helped Captain Pegram harvest his cherries. It was such fun. Several people came along and we all had jolly picnics together.'

'I wonder if you can recall a stranger who came to Winchelsea round about that time. He was a Frenchman, very elegantly dressed. Apparently he stayed at The Salutation for a day or two.'

'He also visited the apothecary's shop,' John put in.

Joe shot him a surprised look. 'Did he?'

'Yes, I'm afraid the Girondes did not tell you all that took place. Apparently he called there and bought some perfume.'

'Good God!'

'Then he must have had a female friend in the town,' commented Elizabeth. 'That, or one of the spies is a woman.'

The three sat silent for a moment or two, thinking this over, then John said, 'I'd always thought that possible.'

'But who is she?' answered Joe.

'Well, it is not me,' Mrs Rose stated clearly. 'I think John believes that but I want you to do so as well, Mr Jago.'

'I shall do my best, Madam,' the clerk answered solemnly.

'Then that's settled. Now, how may I help you in your search?'

John and Joe Jago spoke together, the Apothecary to say, 'There is a way . . .' the clerk to refuse politely.

'So which of you am I to believe?' Elizabeth asked, acting the innocent for all she was worth. Then not waiting for either to reply, she continued, 'I think I should make it my business to call on all the ladies of my acquaintance and try to find out what perfume they wear. I am quite sure that Mr Rawlings discovered what the Frenchman bought before he was done.'

'I most certainly did. It was Evening in Araby.'

Joe chuckled. 'An exotic scent for a traitorous lady, eh? Yes, Mrs Harcross – er, Rose – do carry out your plan. With your stage abilities it should be easy enough.'

There was the sound of Agnes clomping across from the kitchen, then the door was flung open and her voice called, 'Dinner is ready, Mam.'

Elizabeth turned to Joe Jago. 'Sir, would you care to join us?'

'Gladly, Ma'am,' he replied, and offered her his arm.

In the end, Mr Fielding's right hand man stayed late, warmed by the good company and Mrs Rose's port. But when she had withdrawn to the parlour, leaving the gentlemen to drink and smoke pipes, he leaned across the table to the Apothecary, his eyes suddenly alert.

'As I said to you before, there is nothing to stop her being the Moth, you know. She could easily have been recruited while she lived abroad.'

'I realise that, but one has to take a chance sometimes. Anyway, I trust her. She seems utterly sincere to me.'

Joe smiled his craggy smile. 'Mrs Rose is an actress remember.'

'Then you don't believe her?'

Joe's eyes were suddenly warm. 'On the contrary. I do.' He lit a pipe and looked at John through the curls of blue smoke, his pupils the same hazy colour. 'By the way, Captain Pegram's naked woman *is* Miss Tireman.'

The Apothecary felt physically ill. 'Oh?' he said, his voice a croak.

'Miss Rosalind Tireman. I went to interview the rector and his family this morning. Miss Henrietta, alas, was not available. She had apparently gone for a walk in the orchards. However, that is beside the point. One look at the beautiful younger sister and all was clear. At some time or other the gallant Captain has had her picture drawn – or did it himself!'

''Zounds! What a scandal,' John stuttered, breathless with relief.

'Indeed it is. Now, Mr Rawlings, there is much for you to do. As soon as possible I think you should return to London and show the coded message that was flashed out to sea last night to Dr Willes. Did you get the numbers down?'

'I certainly did.' John delved in his pocket. 'Here. 2918 386 841.'

Joe drew a piece of paper from inside his black coat. 'Yes, the same. It is essential that we get those deciphered fast.'

'I can't go tomorrow,' the Apothecary replied firmly. 'I am engaged to dine with Sir Ambrose Ffloote and feel there is much to be gained from that meeting.'

The clerk rubbed his chin. 'Yes, you're probably right. But the very next day it must be. We are still no nearer a solution. The Moth and the Frog are as far away as ever.'

John looked thoughtful. 'You know, there is one person who still might be able to help us. Someone who roams the Marsh at will and probably sees everything that goes on.'

'And who might that be?'

'Dick Jarvis himself. I think tomorrow morning early I'll ride out to Brookland and leave him a message.'

Joe nodded. 'A very good idea, so long as you're careful and don't fall foul of his henchmen. But don't delay your journey to London too long, Mr Rawlings, whatever the attractions of Winchelsea.' He winked.

Well aware of the clerk's uncanny ability to guess things correctly, the Apothecary gave him an innocent stare. 'I can't think what you mean,' he said as he refilled both glasses of port, smiling at Agnes as she came in to light the candles.

Chapter Fourteen

For once forgoing the pleasure of a large and wholesome breakfast, John Rawlings rose at daybreak, walked briskly through the churchyard to Truncheons, there hired the services of the mild-mannered mare, then set off through the rose pink morning towards Brookland.

As he crossed the River Rother, full of currents and wavelets whipped up by the brisk breeze, the smell of the sea filled his nostrils and John's over-long hair rippled on the wind. Suddenly he felt very alert and alive and ready to meet Dick Jarvis on equal terms. Standing beside his horse, holding her reins, the Apothecary patted Strawberry's flank and she neighed him a greeting, as if she too had caught something of the excitement of that windy early morning.

Once off the ferry, John rode hard and arrived at that most curious of churches with its steeple standing beside it on the ground, while the day was still young. Tying Strawberry to a hitching ring, he went inside, only to find St Augustine's deserted. Undaunted, John strode to the chapel where he had first encountered the curate and left a letter, which he had had the foresight to write the previous evening, lying on the tomb which Dick had been so carefully dusting on the day they first met. Then he set out for St Thomas à Becket at Fairfield, sat down on the mounting block outside, his back to the warmth of the wall, and awaited developments. Sure enough, just under an hour later the Apothecary heard the thud of hooves, and, shielding his eyes against the piercing Spring sunlight, saw a horseman approach.

John stood up and made a bow. 'Good morning, Mr Jarvis,' he called.

'Good morning,' came the answering shout, and a second later the unruly son of an even wilder father slithered out of the saddle and stood grinning before him.

This morning, Dick Jarvis had abandoned his clerical gear and was dressed for sea-going in breeches, boots and a belted jerkin.

161

On his head a scarf tied at the back attempted to constrain the mop of undisciplined black curls without a great deal of success. John thought that the phrase 'a handsome devil' could have been coined for this smiling wind-tanned creature who looked at him as innocently as if he had never broken a law in his entire life.

'I trust I find you completely recovered from your ordeal at the hands of the smugglers,' Dick said, sweeping a low bow.

'Almost,' answered John, fingering the cut on his head.

Dick made a tutting sound. 'One can't be too careful these days. There are so many lawless people about.' He moved his eyes in the direction of the church. 'And talking of that, shall we sit inside for a while? Even in a remote spot like this, one is still within the range of a spyglass.'

John stared round the acres of deserted marshland. 'Are you serious?'

'Very,' answered the smuggler grimly, and taking the Apothecary's elbow resolutely propelled him through the door of the ancient church.

They sat one below the other in the three-tier pulpit, John on the higher level. 'Now,' Dick said briskly, 'I believe you wanted to speak to me.'

'Yes, I most certainly do. I am quite sure that through your network you have heard that a skeleton was discovered here recently, disguised as a scarecrow, and that the remains were subsequently removed to London.'

'Aye, I did hear.'

John looked over the side of the pulpit, his expression earnest. 'Dick, those bones belonged to a French spymaster who was in Winchelsea late last summer, just before war was declared. I told you I was looking for two spies . . .'

'Yes.'

'Well, it is the consensus that one or both of them murdered the man, making them killers as well as traitors.'

Dick looked thoughtful. 'I suppose he was not done away with on the orders of the Secret Office?'

John stared at him. 'What do you mean?'

'That a British agent might have come down to the Marsh and finished him off.'

'I hadn't thought of that.'

'It would be worth checking.'

'You're quite right, it would. But whatever the case, it is my task to find those two spies, code-named the Frog and the Moth, and put an end to their villainous game. That was what I was doing when one of your henchmen crashed a blow to my head. I was watching for the signals that are regularly being flashed from the shore to a watching French vessel. You must have noticed them.'

'I've seen the lights all right. They're coming from a spout lantern. We use them ourselves to alert the French luggers that we're ready.'

'Do you know who's sending the messages?'

'I fear not. Twice I've gone after the bastard and twice he's eluded me.'

'It's a man, then?'

'That I can't swear to. The figure is swathed in a black cloak big as a tent. It could be anyone in there. All I know is that he or she rides a powerful horse and can move like the wind when they have to.'

'I see.' John looked even more earnest. 'Dick, I have to go back to London tomorrow. Can you keep watch for the signals in my absence?'

'I certainly can. I told you, Mr Rawlings, I am a patriot, as was my late father, may he rest in peace. When he first went to Mayfield, a small and somewhat self-important village in Sussex, in the year 1715, Kit Jarvis openly drank in the public inns to Jamie the Rover, the Old Pretender, who had landed in Scotland to try and regain his crown. His very smuggling was a protest against the tax system brought in by the Hanoverian kings.'

The Apothecary's face remained impassive but mentally he grinned.

'Then he became one of the most famous men of his time – smuggler, Riding Officer, highwayman, Bailiff to the Sheriff – there was no end to his talents. And now I intend to emulate him. I will gladly help you in your search for these betrayers of national secrets.'

'I am delighted to hear it. But tell me what you know of the Scarecrow, as we call the dead Frenchman.'

Dick asked one more question. 'How did you discover he was French?'

'He had coded orders stitched into the lining of his coat. Deciphered, they instructed him to contact the two Winchelsea spies, la Grenouille and le Papillon de Nuit, immediately.'

163

'I see. Well, I first saw him go up about August time. I can't remember exactly when it was. I thought one of the church people must have put the Scarecrow there. It never occurred to me that it was a body.'

'But didn't it strike you as odd that he had no crops to protect?'

'Not for a while. Then, of course, I went to look.'

'You examined him?' John exclaimed.

'What was left of the poor bastard. The predators had taken most of him. They left his shoes though. Beautiful, they were. The softest leather and the brightest buckles you ever saw. Fitted me like a glove.'

The Apothecary gazed at him in horror, thinking of the old saying about dead men's footwear. 'And you didn't report your find to the constable?'

Dick pealed with laughter. 'Oh, come now, Mr Rawlings. I would have thought to have heard more sense talked by you.'

John gave a rueful smile. 'So you kept quiet and took the Frenchman's shoes. Then what?'

'I kept a weather eye on him whenever I was round this way. Watched to see if he had any visitors, that sort of thing.'

'And did he?'

'Yes, late one night a woman came.'

'A woman?'

'Yes, she had her nerve too, for it was an eerie sight by moonlight.'

'I know,' John answered with feeling.

'Anyway, she tethered her horse at the church, then clambered over the ditch, went straight up to the poor devil and took something from his coat pocket. Then she turned on her heel and left as fast as she had come.'

'Had you ever seen her before? Did you recognise who it was?'

For the first time during their conversation, Dick frowned and looked uneasy. 'Yes and no.'

'What do you mean?'

'There was something about her I knew, but yet I couldn't call it to mind. The thing is she was in the wrong place, if you understand me.'

'Yes, I do.'

'My only hope is that one day I'll see her again and that I'll know her for who she really is.'

164

'Dick,' said John, remembering the way the skeleton had been stripped of all its possessions, 'please be honest with me. Had you or one of your gang been through his pockets already? Was what the woman took something one of you had left behind?'

The smuggler gave a sheepish grin. 'Aye, Little Harry robbed him, not being a man of scruples.'

'So what didn't interest him?'

'It was a visiting card, that's all. Something even he could make no use of.'

'And whose was it? What did it say?'

'Little Harry is no great reader, being a man of very limited education. But he swore to me that it bore the name of the great man himself.'

'Do you mean the Marquis of Rye?'

'No,' said Dick with a laugh, 'I am referring to that gallant soldier and hater of smugglers, Captain Nathaniel Pegram.'

It would seem that Faith Ffloote had made a determined effort to surround herself with medical advisers, for not only were Dr Hensey and John invited to dine but Dr Richard Hayman had been thrown in for good measure. The female complement was to have been made up by Mrs Finch and her two elder daughters, Sophie and Sarah, who loomed enormous on one of Lady Ffloote's more delicate sofas. However, the eldest Miss Finch had spent the first ten minutes of conversation apologising profusely for the absence of her mother, who was, apparently, laid low with a gastric disorder.

'Perhaps I should go to her,' said Dr Hayman, half rising from his chair.

'No, no,' said Sophie, 'please don't trouble yourself, Sir. Mama gave strict instructions that no one was to call. All she wants, so she says, is a little peace and quiet.'

'There are some members of the female sex,' commented Dr Hensey to nobody in particular, 'who consider it very indelicate to be seen with a stomach disorder.'

'Mother is one of them,' Sophie answered, giving him a tentative smile. She nudged her sister who sat in sullen silence, looking exactly like a Floating Island, that over-sweet dessert made of cream, sack, bread and currant jelly, in a pale yellow hooped petticoat and red satin gown. 'Isn't she, Sarah?' Sophie prompted.

Her sister nodded slowly but said nothing, her eyes fixed on the floor. John, feeling sorry for her, attempted to engage her in conversation.

'Your mother was telling me that she was recently visited by that extraordinary man from the Secret Office. I believe she was able to help him.'

The girl reddened visibly. 'I don't know,' she whispered.

He turned to Sophie. 'Did you meet Mr Jago, Miss Finch?'

'Yes. I thought him most intrusive. He kept asking questions about last summer and a Frenchman.'

Lady Floote chimed in. 'I wouldn't speak to the fellow. I left that to Sir Ambrose. He gave him short shrift I can tell you.'

Knowing what he did, John persisted. 'Your mother informed me that you were stopped in the street by the Frenchman concerned and asked the whereabouts of the Marquis of Rye.'

Sarah went from pink to scarlet and shifted uncomfortably in her place.

'Yes,' said Sophie.

'How fascinating. What did he look like?'

'I can't remember,' the eldest Miss Finch continued, with an expression that suggested she remembered very well indeed.

Sarah spoke for the first time, raising her gaze from the floor to the Apothecary's knees. 'Oh, you do, Sophie. It's naughty to tell fibs. You remarked how dashing and handsome he was. I particularly recall it.'

Sophie appeared to be about to burst with chagrin and Dr Hayman, observing, hastily attempted to calm things down.

'It's strange how memory is different for all of us. I can't remember one week from the next, and told Jago as much.'

Miss Finch threw him a grateful glance but the situation was retrieved by the entrance of Sir Ambrose, who came into the room smelling of the outdoors, The Pup tottering at his heels.

Lady Ffloote adopted her doting expression. 'Has zoo been for a walk, Boo-Boo?'

The dog farted noisily and collapsed in a corner.

'I believe you're over-exercising him, Ambrose. Why, the poor boy has no strength left.'

'Nonsense, m'dear,' answered her husband cheerily. 'There's no such thing as too much walking for a canine. Does 'em good. Keeps 'em fit.' He glanced round the room with a jovial expression. 'Good afternoon everyone. Sorry to keep you waiting. Unavoidably delayed, damme.' Sir Ambrose advanced on Dr Hensey. 'Hensey, how very good to see you. Glad you could be here. I take it you're back in Hastings?'

The physician rose and bowed. 'Yes, indeed. My patient grows ever more exacting. I envisage spending quite some time there before the matter is resolved.'

He was as neat and immaculate as ever, a tidy little man in every respect. Politely, he offered Lady Ffloote his assistance as she rose weakly from her chair.

'Now that Ambrose is here, let us go in to dine. Dr Hayman, if you could escort Miss Sophie, and Mr Rawlings, Miss Sarah.'

The Floating Island wobbled to her feet, clinging to John's arm like a mariner to a rock.

'The joys of youth,' remarked Sir Ambrose inconsequentially as they all progressed towards the dining room.

Much to John's delight, the table had been laid with a great deal of foliage; indeed there was such a thicket of ivy in front of him that he could scarcely see Drs Hayman, Hensey, and Sophie, sitting opposite, let alone communicate with them. This delivered Miss Sarah straight into his clutches and with an empty space to his left, where Mrs Finch would have sat, the Apothecary had virtual freedom to ask her as many questions as he wished.

He put on his most affable smile. 'I'm so intrigued at the thought of a French spy in Winchelsea,' he said artlessly. 'Do tell me what you can about him, Miss Finch. I've always been interested in adventurous things like that.'

She wriggled uncomfortably and kept her gaze on her plate, but at last she spoke. 'What do you want to know?'

'Everything. Was he really very handsome?'

'Yes.'

'In what way?'

'He wore lovely clothes and had big twinkling dark eyes.' The girl suddenly looked up with an air of defiance. 'It was Sophie who thought he was handsome but it was me he passed the note to.'

The Apothecary struggled hard not to drop his knife and fork. 'Passed you a note! What did it say?'

'To meet him that evening by the ruins.'

'What ruins?'

'The old abbey, near Grey Friars.'

'Did you go?'

'Yes, I told Mama I was attending church and slipped out of the house.'

'And was the Frenchman there?'

'Yes, he was.'

'And what did he want?'

Sarah blushed and simpered. 'To see me, of course. He asked if we could be sweethearts. When I said yes, he said it was essential that I introduced him to my mother and, through her, met the cream of Winchelsea society so that he could make a good impression.'

The Apothecary stared at her uncomprehendingly.

'It was part of our pact, to do things for one another.'

'And then?'

The girl's moon-like features took on a dreary expression. 'I never saw him again. I went to our meeting place but he didn't come.' Her bottom lip trembled violently. 'I was upset by that.'

'I'm sure you were. Perhaps he had to go back to France suddenly.'

Sarah shook her head. 'I think some harm befell him. That is why the man with the craggy face is asking all those questions.'

John looked sympathetic. 'Perhaps you're right. Did you tell him about this?'

'No, I didn't.'

'So why choose me?'

'Because I wanted you to know that men do like me. Sophie thinks they don't but I know differently.' She gave the Apothecary what he could only think of as an inviting glance. Terrified, he looked away.

'I'm sure they do,' he said through a fixed smile.

Casting round wildly for help, John flattened the foliage with a slight surreptitious move of his hand. Dr Hensey's jolly rodent eyes came into view.

'I have to return to town tomorrow,' the Apothecary said desperately. 'No chance of you travelling with me, I suppose?'

Much to his surprise, the physician answered, 'There is every chance, my dear Sir. I must spend some time with my London patients lest they think I have deserted them completely, and the fact that you would be my travelling companion is excuse enough. I shall indeed accompany you and will book you a place on the ten o'clock chaise.'

'Splendid.'

Lady Ffloote, who clearly had the hearing of a bat, spoke from her place at the head of the table. 'Not leaving us, gentlemen, surely?'

'Only to return, I assure you, Madam.'

'Then that's as well. You have become quite a part of Winchelsea society, Mr Rawlings. How gratifying to think that our quiet little town is attracting such interesting visitors these days.'

'Starting with the mysterious Frenchman,' answered John, hoping to evoke a response from someone.

'Damned upstart,' said Sir Ambrose, quaffing a great glass of wine.

'I didn't realise you had met him,' commented Dr Hayman, saving the Apothecary the trouble.

'Oh, yes, he called here. No appointment. Said he was looking for the Marquis of Rye.'

A veil lifted in John's brain. So that was the excuse the Scarecrow had used in order to get access to people's houses. But why pick on the Marquis? What had the nobleman done to attract the attention of a French spymaster? Or was it merely because he was a local landowner and known even across the Channel? John felt that once he had the answer to those questions, the whole enigmatic puzzle would start falling into place. Despite Miss Sarah Finch's beady-eyed scrutiny, he spoke.

'What did he say to you, Sir Ambrose?'

Through fronds of fern, the Squire's red-veined face suddenly loomed. 'Not much. Asked a few questions about local people. Said he was thinking of settling in Winchelsea and who were the right folk to know, that sort of thing. Never guessed there was anything rum about the fellow.'

'Did you direct him to the Marquis?'

'Thought I ought to, seeing as he'd asked.'

'Yet Lord Rye denies the man ever called on him.'

Sir Ambrose's tiny eye tensed. 'How do you know that?'

Desperately, John fought to retrieve his error. 'He mentioned it at dinner the other day.'

'I see,' said the Squire, sounding as if he didn't care.

Sophie spoke up. 'For a man who came here but once or twice, the Frenchman certainly caused a considerable stir.'

'I think we'd all have forgotten about him if it hadn't been for the arrival of the man from the Secret Office.'

'I wouldn't,' said Sarah in heartfelt tones.

Florence Hensey asked a sensible question. 'What happened to the Frenchman? Does anybody know?'

There was silence. 'Mr Jago didn't say,' Sir Ambrose answered eventually.

'But is one to presume from all the interest shown that he is dead?'

Sarah let out a heaving sob, much to the embarrassment of the other guests.

'Shouldn't think so,' said the Squire cheerfully. 'Returned to France most likely. Probably come creeping back here one of these days.'

There was another shocked stillness. 'Do you really think so?' asked a woman's voice, John wasn't quite sure whose.

'Yes, I do,' answered Sir Ambrose forcefully. 'Bad pennies like that aren't so easily got rid of, believe you me.'

Recalling only too vividly the wretched skeleton keeping lonely vigil on the Romney Marsh, John said, 'I wouldn't count on it.' But then, fearing he might say something further to reveal his connection with the affair, relapsed into a studied silence.

Chapter Fifteen

He hadn't realised how much he had missed London; dirt, smells, lawlessness, poverty, all of it. All the terrible things that combined to give the capital a unique savage beauty that inexorably drew its children back. John felt his heart beat with an extraordinary excitement as the post chaise approached Southwark and drew into the inn yard where the passengers were to alight.

'We're here,' he said to Florence Hensey, who slumbered at his side.

'Good gracious,' exclaimed the doctor, waking abruptly. 'It seems no time since we stopped to dine.'

In the dim light of the interior, the Apothecary looked at his watch. 'It's nearly eleven. We're running a little late.'

'Never the less, I think I will return home. I have a great deal to do tomorrow morning.'

'As have I. Shall we share a hackney coach?'

'A good idea.'

Having hailed a late carriage still plying for hire, the two men found themselves driven over London Bridge from Southwark, then down through the City to Holbourn where the doctor was dropped at his house in Liquorpond Road, a well-set-up establishment judging from the exterior. As he alighted, Dr Hensey wrung John warmly by the hand.

'When do you plan to return to Winchelsea, my friend?'

'In a few days' time. And you to Hastings?'

'I shall probably remain in town a week or so, unless I get an urgent communication from my patient. But no doubt we shall meet again while we are both in Sussex.'

'Write to me on your return and then come to visit. I think you will find my Aunt Elizabeth interesting.'

'I should enjoy meeting her.' Dr Hensey paused, then said, 'But you must come to dine while you are here. How about the day after tomorrow?'

'It will be my pleasure.'

'Sixteen, Liquorpond Road, shall we say at four o'clock?'

'I'll be there,' answered the Apothecary, and waved as the physician opened the door with a key and disappeared into his house.

It was approaching midnight when John stepped quietly through the door of number two, Nassau Street and whispered to the servant on duty that he would like some tea in the library before he retired for the night.

'But Sir Gabriel is still up,' the footman answered.

'Is he entertaining?'

The man smiled broadly. 'In a sense, Master John.'

Mystified, the Apothecary crossed the hall, then stopped short, his hand on the knob of the library door as there was a sudden burst of song and music.

'Some talk of Alexander and some of Hercules,' sang Sir Gabriel's voice. 'Of Hector and Lysander and such great—' He stopped short as John walked in, his eyes widening in surprise. 'My dear boy! But hush, listen!' He held up a hand.

The music continued, then with a great carillon of bells twelve was struck in a most harmonious and tuneful chime.

'My new toy,' said Sir Gabriel proudly. 'Do you like it?'

Looking round the room, the Apothecary's eye alighted on an imposing longcase clock standing by the wall beside his father's desk. Set in glowing walnut, its delightful dial, depicting a revolving sun and moon, proclaimed that it was made by Windmills of London.

'It plays a tune at every quarter.' And Sir Gabriel raised the hood to show his son the inscription, which read 'The Granadears March'.

'It's magnificent. When did you get it?'

'Last week. I simply could not resist. Besides, I'd had a lucky hand or two at whist.'

'My beloved father, you are incorrigible. But have I really been away that long?'

'So long I can scarce recollect your features.' Sir Gabriel motioned John to take a seat by the fire. 'Now, tell me all your adventures. Have you found the villain who threatens Elizabeth Harcross? And what of the spy? Is he unmasked?'

'The spy comes in the plural, I fear. Apparently there are two people.' And the Apothecary proceeded to tell his father all that had taken place, doing it so thoroughly that The British

Granadears played twice more as the clock struck quarter then half past the hour.

Sir Gabriel steepled his fingers, tapping them together thoughtfully. 'And you have no idea who any of these people might be?'

'Not really. The fact that the Scarecrow bought perfume then tried to make poor suety Sarah introduce him to her mother raises many questions about Mrs Finch. But on the other hand Mrs Tireman was up to no good the night I saw her rush off with the doctor and the smugglers.'

'Um. What of her two daughters?'

'Rosalind is so self-centred, so utterly besotted with herself, that I can't imagine her spending a moment's thought on anything else. As for Henrietta, she's far too lovely to be a spy.' Seeing the cynical lift of Sir Gabriel's eyebrow, John rushed on, 'Yes, I know that is a foolish statement but if you met her you would know what I mean.'

'I take it you find her attractive?' asked his father, ill concealing a smile.

'Very.'

'Then be careful, my son. You tend to lose judgment when your heart becomes involved.'

'I know. I will try to be sensible.'

'Not too sensible, I hope,' Sir Gabriel murmured. In a louder voice, he said, 'And what of the other women?'

'Mrs Gironde I don't altogether trust. I felt she was hiding something, that she knew more about the Scarecrow than she was prepared to admit. As for Faith Ffloote, I find her an enigma. She is one of those sad, dreary little women who are almost impossible to read, permanently hidden in a miasma of migraine.'

'Could either of them be a spy – or a poisoner?'

'Very easily.'

'So who is the Frog?'

'Or indeed the Moth. I don't know. Captain Nathaniel Pegram poses certain questions, one of which involves a nude drawing of Miss Rosalind Tireman.'

'Not a crime in itself.'

'No, but it suggests a certain weakness which might lay him open to blackmail. As regards the Marquis, I'm not sure. There's something odd about the man, and his past is none too savoury, or so I hear. Then, of course, we have the Squire and the rector, two figures from Henry Fielding.'

173

'In what way?'

'Larger than life, caricatures. Particularly Sir Ambrose.'

'Could all that bonhomie be hiding something more sinister?'

'Certainly it could. While the Reverend Tireman is the epitome of a country parson – or so he would have you believe.'

'And what of the doctor and Apothecary Gironde?'

John frowned, framing his answer carefully. 'I rather like them, both of them, particularly Richard Hayman. Yet I observed him dealing with the smugglers in a manner that was not unfriendly. As for Mr Gironde, he has a very thriving business and he knows it. However, he above all has the knowledge to poison Elizabeth.'

'Have you no evidence regarding any of them?'

'Not really. All I can hope for is that soon somebody will make a mistake.'

Sir Gabriel appeared very thoughtful. 'Do you think the poisoning and the spying might be tied in somehow?'

John looked speculative. 'I suppose they could be, if somebody thinks Elizabeth knows more than she does.'

'That might be an idea worth pursuing.'

'It might indeed.'

There was a momentary silence before the clock played its tinkling tune once more.

John stood up, yawning. 'I must get to bed. I've been travelling all day.'

'We'll talk more in the morning,' said Sir Gabriel, and kissed his son fondly on the cheek before he went upstairs.

Like all good apprentices, Nicholas Dawkins rose early and usually had breakfasted and gone from the house before Sir Gabriel had so much as opened his eyes. But this morning, eating steadily through a hearty mound of food, a habit he had caught from his Master, he was amazed to see that very Master walk through the door and join him at table.

'Nicholas, my friend,' said John, shaking him by the hand. 'How are you? And how is the shop?'

The Muscovite shot to his feet, covered in confusion. 'We are both well, Sir. That is, Master Gerard and I. The shop is well, too. I mean business is good.'

'Excellent. Now sit down and finish your meal, and I will join

174

you. Then we'll walk to Shug Lane together and you can acquaint me with all the news – and the gossip.'

Half an hour later, having written a hasty note to Sir Gabriel to say that he would be back that evening, John left the house with Nicholas, both striding out towards Piccadilly, enjoying the morning air.

'Have you see anything of the Comtesse de Vignolles?' the Apothecary asked as they walked.

'Indeed we have, Sir. She has been to the shop and also to Nassau Street enquiring about you.'

The Apothecary gave his apprentice a penetrating look. 'I presume that the Comte was not with her.'

'You presume correctly.'

'Any news of him?'

The Muscovite's russet eyes narrowed. 'I believe, Sir, judging by the lady's manner, that he is still frequently absent.'

'I see. I must make a point of calling on her.'

'I am sure she would welcome it.'

But as things transpired, that was one item on John Rawlings's list of tasks that accomplished itself, for within half an hour of opening the shop in Shug Lane the door was flung wide, the bell pealed loudly, and Serafina de Vignolles, clad from head to foot in a gown the colour of wild orchids, stood in the entrance.

John hurried out from the compounding room where he had been conferring with Master Gerard.

'My dear Comtesse, how wonderful to see you. I was intending to visit.'

'I need to speak to you,' she answered beneath her breath, then said in conversational tones, 'How are you, John? You seem to have been away a long time.'

'A long time indeed. I have missed my friends. Please, Comtesse, step into the back of the shop. I was just about to brew some tea and hope you might join me in a cup.'

Master Gerard came bumbling out, his jocund features one large smile. 'Madam,' he said, bowing. 'Have you a list of requirements?'

'I certainly have, Sir.' And Serafina handed the old fellow a piece of paper with enough items written on it to keep him busy for at least half an hour.

'Well done,' murmured John, and bowed as the Comtesse preceded him into the compounding room.

175

The moment they were alone the Apothecary held her at arm's length to look at her and was disturbed by what he saw. Where other women would have been dark-ringed and watery-eyed, Serafina gleamed molten, and he, knowing her so well, realised that this meant she was at the height of distress. For so strong a female was this elegant racehorse of an individual that only at her lowest moments did she assume such a brilliant and impenetrable veneer.

John cut straight to the heart of the affair. 'I take it this is about Louis?'

'Yes.'

'Is he still disappearing?'

'For days on end. I am beginning to believe that there must be another woman. Either that, or . . .'

'Or?'

'He is involved in something so dark and terrible that he cannot even speak of it. John . . .'

'Yes?'

'Swear to me that you will find out one way or the other and tell me the truth when you do so.'

The Apothecary raised her hand to his lips. 'I swear it,' he said.

Leaving the shop within a half-hour of Serafina's departure, John, seizing a battered umbrella of which he was particularly fond, strode out into the elements. Hurrying down the length of Piccadilly, past the magnificence of Burlington House, the Apothecary turned right into Berkeley Street, then made his way through the splendid surroundings of Berkeley Square. There he turned left and picked his way through the new development to Hill Street, arriving just before the rain started.

Today, the King's Decipherer received his visitor in the Spanish library, another fine example of young Mr Adam's architectural skill, which gained its rather grand name from the Spanish leather wallcovering situated between the bookcases and the fancifully decorated ceiling, or so John was informed as he gaped about him with patent admiration. Yet again, the Apothecary was struck by the harmonious feel to the room, mostly created by its delightful and flowing design. On this occasion a fire had been lit, in front of which Dr Willes sat in a comfortable chair, his gaitered legs resting upon a footstool. He gestured John to take a seat opposite.

'And what do you have for me today, Mr Rawlings?'

'This was a message flashed out to sea to a French vessel, my lord. It was the work of either the Frog or the Moth, I believe.'

The Bishop held out his hand. 'Let me see: 2918 386 841.' He stared at the paper in silence for a while, then crossed to his desk, muttering to himself, and opened a drawer with a key which hung round his neck next to the episcopalian cross. From the drawer he took a leather-bound book with handwritten pages, at which he stared intently. Eventually he said, 'This makes no sense at all.'

'What does it say?'

Dr Willes peered at the Apothecary over his spectacles. 'Quite literally, the French King on foot Admiral Watson.'

John stared. 'What?'

'Precisely. This is either a new code or a cipher within a cipher, if you see what I mean. How very irritating – and how very clever.'

The Apothecary attempted to look intelligent. 'I'm afraid you've left me behind, my lord. What exactly do you mean?'

'That the French have either changed the number sequences so that this means something else entirely, or, more probably, are using a double code, so that French King now stands for something else, and so on. I'm afraid you will have to leave this with me, young man. A new cipher always means many hours of work.'

John rose, looking apologetic. 'I'm very sorry, my lord.'

Dr Willes grunted, his small, close-set eyes glinting at the challenge. 'What a puzzle, eh? Damned Frenchies! Always one step ahead if you give 'em half a chance.'

It was hardly clerical language but John ignored it. 'I'll see myself out,' he said.

But the Bishop merely flapped his fingers at him in dismissal, completely preoccupied with the task in hand and quite clearly already in a world of his own.

Chapter Sixteen

'A new code?' said Mr Fielding incredulously.

'Yes, Sir.'

The Magistrate looked solemn, his strong features settling into hard lines. 'Then we are dealing with two extremely clever people, not only capable of killing but also of highly intelligent espionage. You still have no idea who they are, Mr Rawlings?'

'I think it possible that one is a woman. The fact that a female was seen removing Captain Pegram's calling card from the Scarecrow's pocket could well be significant.'

'And what about the Captain himself?'

'A curious character as I told you.'

'Which doesn't necessarily make him a spy. But could he be the poisoner?'

'I think not. He was highly indignant at the suggestion that his pie was the cause of such severe illness, realistically so in my opinion, and as he pointed out, Mrs Rose could well have taken something else that day. He himself suffered no ill effects from eating it.'

'But she denied that?'

'When I put it to her, yes she did.'

'So you are no further forward with that line of inquiry either.'

John sighed. 'I am sorry. I'm not doing very well, am I?'

'As I have so often said to you in the past, my friend, all the time that you are in Winchelsea, mingling with the inhabitants, listening to their conversation, you are learning. Soon fragments of fact will come together and begin to form themselves into a pattern.'

'I hope they start to do so soon.'

Mr Fielding chuckled and eased the black bandage that covered his eyes. 'By the way, I think you'll be on your own from now on. Jago has decided to return.'

John's heart sank. 'Oh, 'zounds. Why is that?'

'He says in the letter which arrived this morning that he has done all he can. He has interviewed everyone and written down their statements, so now feels there is nothing left to achieve. By

179

the way he has put copies of those statements in a sealed package which he has deposited at your lodging. Joe says to look particularly at those of the Tireman family.'

John's heart sank even further. 'I will.'

'So, Mr Rawlings, it is up to you now.'

The Apothecary felt himself plunged into total gloom. 'I realise that.'

Though the Blind Beak could not see his visitor's face, he obviously read the situation from the sound of John's voice. 'Be of stout heart, my friend,' he said encouragingly. 'Even now I am sure you are aware of something, at the moment just lurking in the back of your mind, that will eventually lead you to the solution.'

John smiled half-heartedly. 'I'll do my best to track whatever it is down. But there is still a question, Sir.'

'And what is that?'

'It was suggested to me by one of the people I talked to' – the Apothecary did not feel it appropriate to inform the principal upholder of the law that he was on amicable terms with the head of a smuggling gang – 'that the Scarecrow might have been killed by a British secret agent. I suppose that is not possible, or is it?'

'I would have thought that if such were the case, word of it would have reached my ears by now. However, an enquiry to the Secretary of State will soon provide the answer.'

'Then, Mr Fielding, there is nothing left for me to do but return to Winchelsea.'

The Blind Beak sat motionless for a while, an old ploy of his. John, who knew this was a sign that the Magistrate was lost in thought, remained silent. Finally, Mr Fielding spoke.

'The couple who argued in the churchyard.'

'Yes?'

'Find them, Mr Rawlings.'

'Were they the Frog and the Moth in your opinion?'

'If not, they will lead you to them, mark my words.' The Magistrate's tone changed completely. 'Now, Mr Rawlings, may I extend you an invitation to dine?'

The Apothecary stood up. 'No, Sir, though I thank you for it. I must get back to my shop and have a brief word with Master Gerard before returning home.'

'And when will you go back to Winchelsea?'

'In a day or two. I feel I ought to spend some time with my father.'

'Quite right. You should indeed.'

John bowed to the Magistrate, even though he could not see his gesture of respect. 'Then I'll take my leave,' he said.

Mr Fielding rose also and patted John Rawlings on the shoulder. 'Good hunting, my friend,' was his reply.

The streets of London were already becoming quiet as the dining hour drew closer and John, hiring a chair for speed alone, reached Shug Lane within twenty minutes. There he found Master Gerard just about to go out to a sick patient, but by delaying him a further quarter of an hour the two apothecaries were able to discuss all the business that was necessary and to exchange cordial greetings, not possible earlier that day. So it was that John was alone as another sedan came to a halt before the shop, out of which stepped his old friend and childhood companion, the Goldsmith Samuel Swann.

'My dear friend,' Samuel greeted him as he loomed into the shop, dwarfing the place with his large and somewhat uncontrolled frame. 'I called at Nassau Street and Sir Gabriel told me you might possibly be here. How fortuitous to find you! I hear that you have been much taken up with a case in Winchelsea. I do hope you will forgive me for not offering my help by going with you but I have been so busy recently with orders.'

The Apothecary smiled to himself, reflecting that his friend's attempts at assistance had sometimes proved more of a hindrance than otherwise, though certainly no one in the world could match Samuel for enthusiasm.

'Of course I forgive you. Indeed, I am pleased that you have so much to do. Are you growing rich?'

Samuel smiled, his jolly face almost split by the size of his grin. 'My situation is improving slowly.'

'You underestimate,' answered John. 'I reckon you'll soon be able to compete with Midas himself.'

Mr Swann guffawed, immensely cheered by this assumption. 'Enough of your jests. I have come to see if you are free to go out this evening.'

'To where?'

'To Stokes's Amphitheatre in Islington Road. There's to be a boxing match. Here.' And Samuel thrust a copy of *The London Journal* into his friend's hand.

John read with interest. 'This present Thursday, being the 23rd of March, will be a complete boxing match by the two following championesses:- Whereas I, Ann Field, of Stoke Newington, ass driver, well-known for my abilities in boxing in my own defence, having been affronted by Mrs Stokes, styled the European championess, do fairly invite her to a trial of her best skill in boxing for ten pounds, fair rise and fall.' To which challenge was printed the following reply: 'I, Elizabeth Stokes, of the City of London, having fought the famous boxing woman of Billingsgate in nine minutes, and gained a complete victory, assure the Stoke Newington ass woman that I will not fail meeting her, and doubt not that the blows which I shall present her with will be more difficult for her to digest than any she ever gave her asses.'

John lowered the paper. 'Do you really want to see this?'

'Yes, indeed I do. Women are such tough little creatures. Always ready for a good mill.'

Remembering the blow which had ended the argument in the churchyard, then thinking of Henrietta's angry exit from the cherry orchard, the Apothecary nodded glumly. 'You're quite right about that. What time does it start?'

'Eight o'clock. We can go by hackney coach.'

'Then come home and dine. My father will enjoy seeing you.'

'And I him.'

In the event, though, Sir Gabriel Kent did more than just eat with his son and his friend, deciding that the occasion bode so well for some lively entertainment that he would accompany them. So it was that Sir Gabriel's carriage drove the three towards the outskirts of London, passing through the turnpike that lay just beyond the Skin Market and the Mad House, which denoted the end of St John's Road and the start of Islington Road. Beyond the tollgate the coachman stopped at The Angel coaching inn in order to join up with other carriages and pass across the fields in a convoy, thus avoiding the unwelcome attentions of the many highwaymen who haunted the open spaces.

To the right of Mr Sadler's Wells, Pleasure Garden and Theatre, and separated from their delightful groves by a thicket of trees, stood Mr Stokes's Amphitheatre. Having paid his shilling entry fee, Sir Gabriel strode in, leaning on his great stick, and immediately the crowd parted before him as in the story of Moses and the Red Sea. John and Samuel, following behind, grinned at one another as the Apothecary's father was shown to a raised seat and offered a cushion for extra comfort. Scrambling into a place beside him, having had to push every step of the way, the two younger men reflected on what it was about Sir Gabriel, other than his commanding height, which always seemed to find him the best spot in the house. However, once seated, the general excitement of the place consumed them and they stopped worrying about the scant respect which they commanded and concentrated on what was going on.

In the centre of the amphitheatre, which had been constructed on the old Roman lines with raised seats all around, stood a wooden platform surrounded by ropes, at the moment totally concealed by bright red curtains, adding an air of anticipation to the proceedings. Meanwhile, the presence of the crowd, which was both noisy and noisome, was becoming more noticeable by the minute. Their sound rose in shrill shrieks, while the stink of sweat, snuff and scent was overpowering. Yet there was a raw excitement to it all, and John felt a surge of love for his fellow creatures, terrible though so very many of them were.

A man, presumably Mr Stokes, stepped up on to the platform and cleared his throat to make an announcement.

'Your lordships, ladies and gentlemen, before the display of feminine fisticuffs which you have all come here to see, allow me to introduce a wrestling match between two well-known champions, the Fighting Quaker and the Welsh Boy.' There was a desultory cheer. 'This will be preceded by a display given by Le Cirque Chinois.' There were several catcalls and boos from those whose only interest lay in prizefighting, but when the curtains parted to reveal six small yellow men with black pigtails, dressed in red trousers and shoes and nothing else, there was a cheer.

Coloured balls flew in the air, tightropes were stretched taut, poles appeared as if by magic and the little men clambered up them, all the while maintaining set serious expressions that never altered. Finally a host of children cartwheeled on to the stage, turning like tiny stars in their tinsel costumes. They ran forward and formed a pyramid up which a dark-eyed tot, no older than three, scrambled and stood like a miniature statue, arms spread wide. Then came the finale as all somersaulted off, whirling faster and faster as the crowd cheered and applauded.

'Excellent,' said Sir Gabriel, clapping his bony hands.

'Bravo,' shouted Samuel, and threw his hat in the air in an enthusiastic manner. John, meanwhile, was relishing London and thinking that despite his love of the open countryside he could never really leave town. His ambition one day to own a house by the river, within striking distance of the capital, perhaps somewhere in Chelsea, took one further step along the path to becoming reality.

The Chinese Circus took a bow and were followed by two enormous men, naked but for loincloths, who ferociously strode on to the platform and glared at one another. John's quirkish sense of humour was much amused by the fact that the Fighting Quaker, nude though he might be wore the tall hat of the Puritans on his head. The Welsh Boy, however, seemed to resent the fact that he had anything on at all and tugged at his covering as if it were in his way, meanwhile pointing at the Quaker's headgear with howls of derision. A second later this mockery proved too much to bear and the Fighting Quaker flew through the air and knocked the Welsh Boy to the ground, then jumped on him with both feet, his hat staying in place throughout this vigorous performance. With a great deal of groaning, the Welsh Boy recovered his equilibrium and proceeded to knock the daylights out of the Fighting Quaker who, despite the punishment he was taking, miraculously still retained his headwear. However, all was resolved when the Quaker seized his opponent round the waist and dashed him to the ground, at which both hat and hair, clearly glued, flew together from his head, revealing a bald man beneath. Amidst a mixture of hisses and laughter, the two wrestlers left the stage.

It was time for the interval and where John and Samuel had to content themselves with oranges, Sir Gabriel, ordering a glass of good canary from a passing trader, actually received one and sipped it with relish.

'Do you think we should wear black and white?' Samuel whispered to his friend.

'It would make no difference,' John answered. 'It's all to do with his manner of conducting himself.'

'I wish I knew the secret,' Samuel replied, his tone a fraction morose. 'I would love to break hearts.'

'Who wouldn't!' said John with feeling.

'Ah! Trouble with Miss Clive I take it?'

'With her and another.'

'Oh! A fair virgin of Winchelsea?'

'Well, fair anyway,' John answered, at which the friends roared with unruly laughter just like the 'prentice lads they had both once been. Sir Gabriel in the meantime raised a high, thin brow but said nothing.

Mr Stokes appeared on the platform once more. 'Your lordships, ladies and gentlemen, the highlight of the evening. The contest between Mrs Stokes, championess of Europe and also my lady wife, and Mrs Field, the ass driver. And first into the ring is the challenger. Please welcome Mrs Field.'

'Good God, poor wretched asses,' murmured Sir Gabriel, as a veritable Amazon of a woman strode down one of the aisles and climbed on to the stage. Six feet if she was an inch and with a mass of wild black hair which sprouted round her head like a demonic halo, Mrs Field also had a formidable moustache and darting black eyes. To frighten further any unfortunate enough to put her out of countenance, she wore black tights and a strange glittering red garment like that adopted by an acrobat.

'Boo,' shouted the audience and Mrs Field raised her clenched fist and shook it at them, strutting about the platform in a highly menacing manner.

'And now,' said Mr Stokes, 'for the defender. I give you Elizabeth Stokes, first-rate fighter of Europe.'

There was a great roar of appreciation as down the aisle tripped a dainty little parcel of womanhood, so delicately made that she resembled a porcelain figurine, complete with long blonde curls and large, angelic china blue eyes.

'God's teeth!' shouted Samuel, loud enough for all the world to hear. 'She won't last five minutes, indeed she won't.'

'Don't be so certain,' answered Sir Gabriel sagaciously.

'What makes you say that?' asked his son.

'Remember David and Goliath, my child. Even the prettiest are capable of delivering a savage punch.'

'Um,' said John, reflecting.

Mrs Stokes, who was clad in pink tights and powder blue costume, a colour combination which made her appear more fragile than ever, stepped tidily into the ring and curtseyed to the audience, who bellowed their approval with one voice. Mrs Field approached to sneer audibly, towering over her opponent in the most unnerving

185

manner, a fact which Mrs Stokes chose to ignore as she removed her cloak and handed it to an assistant.

'At the sound of the bell you will commence,' ordered her husband. 'Ladies, you fight for the sum of ten pounds, fair rise and fall.'

He stepped aside and hit a brass bell with a hammer, at the sound of which Mrs Field flew at her opponent like a tornado, her vast bare knuckles clenched into fists resembling sides of beef. Nimble as a fairy, Elizabeth Stokes stepped to one side so that her antagonist, unable to slow her momentum, crashed into the ropes, clearly knocking the breath from herself. As she stood for a moment, panting, Mrs Stokes stepped forward and delivered a series of short sharp blows to Mrs Field's lumbar region. Furious, the ass woman spun round and swung a fist at the European championess which sent her crashing to the floor, where she sat, momentarily stunned, before scrambling to her feet, agile as a monkey.

So the fight went on, brute force versus speed and dexterity, while those members of the audience fortunate enough to own a watch, glanced at them anxiously, most of them aware that the longest any female boxing bout ever lasted was fifteen minutes.

The tide of fortune changed and it became clear to all that Ann Field's sheer size and stamina were starting to win the day. Fast as Mrs Stokes ducked, then disappeared out of harm's way, she seemed unable to land the punch that would knock her antagonist to her knees, and it was beginning to look as if sheer exhaustion would finally force her to cede victory.

Very disappointed, Samuel leaned across to Sir Gabriel. 'Do you still think Mrs Stokes can win, Sir?'

'One never knows. The battle is not over till it's lost.'

As if echoing this sentiment, the championess of Europe, having just bounded back to her feet again after another felling blow, made a sudden sprint for Ann Field, dived beneath her armpit, and hit the ass woman really hard on the kidneys, a move which caused her eyes to water so much that Ann temporarily lowered her guard and wiped them. At that, Mrs Stokes leaped into the air like a small, determined cannon ball and somehow managed to deposit both her bare fists on to the point of the ass woman's chin. Mrs Field swayed and Elizabeth, displaying a ruthlessness that belied her angelic appearance, promptly smacked her in the solar plexis and, as Ann doubled up, added a clout over the head which brought her crashing down like a felled oak. As one man, the audience rose and cheered and threw money into the ring which Mrs Stokes, with much kissing of her hand and graceful acknowledgment, scooped up and dropped down the front of her costume. The prostrate ass woman, meanwhile, was dragged off the platform by two burly assistants and Mr Stokes raised his wife's hand on high to shouts of 'The winner'. Then, to thunderous applause, the triumphant championess left the ring, waving and smiling as she did so.

Sir Gabriel stood up. 'Most enjoyable. And there's a moral in it, is there not?'

'That David always brings Goliath down?' John asked, not quite certain.

'More likely, never trust a determined little female,' put in Samuel, and they all laughed.

Having once more fallen into company with his enthusiastic childhood companion, John found himself conversing with and enjoying Samuel's society right up to the time of his departure for Winchelsea. Accordingly, the two friends shared a hackney coach to Liquorpond Road, from where the Apothecary, after dining with Dr Hensey, intended to make his way to The White Hart and on to Hastings, and Samuel to his lodgings in Little Carter Lane. But as chance would have it the physician answered the door himself and seeing Samuel about to depart, insisted that he come in and join the dinner party. Thus the three men sat down to a meal in an atmosphere of spontaneous conviviality.

John was more than surprised to find that the doctor lived alone, having formed the opinion, based on no particular evidence, that he was a married man. But a tactful question elicited the fact that Dr Hensey's wife, a beautiful woman to judge by her portrait, who had borne the elegant name of Veronique, had died of fever in her early twenties.

'And you never thought to remarry, Sir?' asked Samuel, who liked to get to the heart of things and was not known for an abundance of tact.

'No, no,' the physician answered sadly. 'At the time I decided to devote myself to my patients and my other interests. And now I am far too busy, life being what it is.'

'What do you make of the man Jago and all his questions about

187

a mysterious Frenchman?' asked John, changing the subject and treading hard on Samuel's foot under the table.

'Well, I heard you ask about him the other night at Sir Ambrose's,' Dr Hensey answered cautiously, 'but to be honest with you that was the first I knew of such a thing. What is it all about? And why are you so interested? Surely the fellow has nothing to do with you?'

Realising he had made the most enormous error and was throwing suspicion on his own role, the Apothecary tried desperately to think of something clever to say, but while he sat swallowing hard, Samuel rose magnificently to the occasion.

'Oh, that's typical of John,' he replied merrily. 'Loves a mystery, does my friend. Has done ever since he was a boy. He'll go on and on until someone comes up with a good theory. So humour him, Dr Hensey, do.'

The dapper little man's eyes twinkled and suddenly he was all smiles. 'Oh, I see. Well, Mr Rawlings, I thought that some present on that occasion knew more than they were going to tell.'

Mentally wiping his brow, John brightened. 'Really? Who for example?'

'Miss Sophie and Miss Sarah to name but two.'

'What about the Squire?'

Dr Hensey shook his head. 'Too stupid, if you'll forgive my frankness. If he had been in secret contact with the Frenchman he would have said so, straight out. As it is, I believed his story that the man called on him without an appointment.'

Samuel guffawed. 'Real silly arse, is he?'

The Doctor laughed and nodded. 'Very much so.'

'So who do you think this Frenchman could have been?' asked John, plucking up courage to return to the fray once more.

'As the Secret Office are investigating him, I presume a spy,' Florence answered drily.

'But why choose Winchelsea?'

'Because that was where his contact was, I imagine.'

'I wonder who it is,' said John, with just the right note of ingenuous fervour in his voice.

'That,' answered the doctor pessimistically, 'we shall probably never know.'

The friends left the house in Liquorpond Road far later than they had intended, having sampled some excellent French brandy and drunk rather more of it than they should. Having bowed several times and thanked Dr Hensey profusely for his hospitality, John and Samuel stepped out into the street to hire a hackney coach only to find that the weather had changed and it was now pouring with rain. There was not a soul in sight, nor a conveyance for that matter, and the Apothecary shivered at the bare discomfort of the unfriendly evening.

'Let's run to the corner,' said Samuel. 'There might be a hackney up there.'

So they set off, sprinting over the slippery cobbles, splashing into puddles which wet them to the knees. It was at that moment that they heard another pair of feet behind them and a second later were overtaken by a dark young man, running like a racehorse, and bellowing 'Hackney, hackney,' at the top of his lungs. Much to John's annoyance, a carriage promptly appeared and slithered to a halt right beside the runner who deftly leaped inside, his feet barely touching the step.

'Oy!' bellowed Samuel, and, 'Stop that!' yelled the Apothecary.

The stranger stuck his head out of the window and said in one of the broadest Irish accents John had ever heard, 'Sure, and wasn't I securing it for you as well. Would you care to share, gentlemen?'

'Yes, we would,' Samuel replied truculently.

'Thank you,' added his friend in a more conciliatory tone.

'Then jump in.' And the door was opened by a small, quite neat hand, allowing them to climb aboard.

The rich voice continued in the darkness. 'Allow me to introduce myself. Lucius Delahunty of Dublin, at your service, gentlemen.'

'John Rawlings.'

'Samuel Swann.'

'And where might you good people be heading?'

'To The White Hart in Southwark. I'm catching the morning post chaise to Hastings,' John answered.

'Well glory be to God on high!' exclaimed Mr Delahunty. 'If that isn't the king of all coincidences. That's where I'm heading m'self.' He chuckled infectiously. 'I may as well cut through all formality as we're destined to be in each other's company for so many hours. Just call me Lucius, all of Dublin does.'

Shaking his head in bewilderment at the number of people heading for the Sussex coast these days, the Apothecary replied, 'Then you must use my first name too.'

189

'Oh, be assured I will, John. You may wager your very life on it.'

And with that rather odd turn of phrase, Mr Delahunty burst into song as they headed off in the direction of London Bridge.

Chapter Seventeen

Even the miserable old woman with a face like a fig was laughing by the time the four occupants of the post chaise disembarked at their journey's end, such was the effect of the sparkling company of Lucius Delahunty. John, whose acquaintance with the fellow had started somewhat inauspiciously, to say the least, found himself warming with each passing mile to the sheer charm of this inhabitant of the Emerald Isle, and by the time they reached The Swan coaching inn at Hastings was inviting Lucius to visit him in Winchelsea.

The Irishman stared, thunderstruck. 'Well, now, if that isn't an even greater coincidence. Winchelsea is *my* destination, saints bless us all.'

It was the Apothecary's turn to stare. 'But why are you going there? It's such a dull little town. Nothing ever happens.'

Which would be true if it weren't for the spies, the smugglers, and the poisoner, John thought.

Lucius grinned. 'You might well ask such a question. But the fact is, my friend, I'm an artist. Yes, seriously. I've even sold a painting or two in my time. So I'm going to set up my easel and daub away, then hope I can sell a few of the finished products to the local inhabitants.'

'Rather a strange choice of location, if I might say. Rye is far more picturesque.'

'Ah, but I met a girl from Winchelsea once, name of Molly Malone. Irish as they come but living in England with some old relative or other. You wouldn't happen to know her by any chance?' John shook his head. 'Oh, that's a terrible shame. Maybe she's moved on. After all, it was four years ago.'

'So you're going there to look for her?'

'Well, hardly that. Let's just say I had hoped to combine a bit of pleasure with business.'

Lucius stretched, clearly glad to be out of the confines of the carriage, and John thought that he was very much the Celtic type

191

of Irishman with his long black hair and deep blue eyes. It was believed by many people that those particular looks came from the shipwrecked sailors of the Spanish Armada, driven ashore on to Ireland's West coast, though others again said that that theory was only folklore, that none of the Spaniards had survived the ordeal. The Apothecary kept an open mind on the subject, finding it hard to believe that not one of the mariners had lived on, spirited into the community by a willing local girl, there to vanish from prying eyes. And Lucius for sure had a certain exotic style which seemed to speak of an interesting ancestry.

The Irishman looked at his watch. 'Great God in the evening, if it isn't ten o'clock. The rain must have delayed us. Well, I'm booking in here. What about you, John? Shall we have a few drinks before we retire?'

It was too tempting, particularly as the downpour, widespread throughout the south of England, had only just stopped and the night was damp and unappetising.

'Yes, I'm your man. We can travel on to Winchelsea early in the morning.'

Handing their luggage to a lad, the two men proceeded inside, warming their hands at a welcoming log fire which burned in an inglenook in the ancient hostelry's hallway, then making their way into the guests' parlour, crowded with people at this particular moment, a confusion caused by the fact that the stage coach and another chaise had all arrived at the inn at roughly the same time. With not a seat to be had, John and Lucius leaned against the bar and quaffed ale, looking about them at the varied but cheerful company. And then the Apothecary's eye was caught by a familiar figure, sitting quietly in a dark corner, slightly hunched in his cloak, his hat pulled well down in a clear attempt not to be recognised.

'It can't be,' John whispered to himself.

'What?' asked the Irishman, overhearing.

'Nothing. It's just that I think I've seen someone I know.'

'Is that unusual?'

But the Apothecary did not answer, craning his neck to check that the fellow really was who he thought. Then the man moved, pouring himself another glass of wine from the bottle before him, and there could be no further doubt. Louis de Vignolles, of all the unlikely people in the world, was also in The Swan at Hastings that night.

John stood silently, wondering what to do next. If his suspicions were correct and the Comte truly was the mysterious French spy who had cleverly managed to conceal himself amongst London society, would it be better to challenge him with the fact, or to await developments? Then the Apothecary thought of Serafina, of his future relationship with her and of all the trouble and heartache it would cause if he were falsely to accuse her husband. Knowing that he must add observing Louis's movements to all the other tasks he had to fulfil, John grimaced.

He must have sighed as he did so, for Lucius said, 'I assume it is. Who are you looking at?'

'That man over there, the one with the hat over his eyes. His wife thinks he's up to no good and now I discover him in a place where he shouldn't be.'

'Could he not have come to Hastings on business?'

'It's possible I suppose, but not very likely.'

'What does she suspect him of, infidelity?'

'That, or something more sinister.'

'What do you mean?' asked Lucius, his blue eyes widening.

'We're a nation at war, remember,' hinted John.

Lucius reacted like a hound sniffing a scent. 'Jesus and Joseph, you're not talking spies are you?'

Regretting that he had even uttered, the Apothecary said, 'I don't know, possibly I suppose. But it is more likely a case of *cherchez la femme*.'

'Do you want me to get talking to him and find out? I've the gift of the gab, you know.'

John smiled. 'You certainly have at that . . .'

But he got no further. Behind him came the sound of a chair scraping back on the flagstones and footsteps rapidly making for the door. The Apothecary wheeled round just in time to see Louis vanish into the hall.

'He must have noticed me. Wait here,' John ordered, and went off in hot pursuit, only to find that the Comte had broken into a run and was already through the entrance leading on to the street. Taking to his heels, the Apothecary ran after him.

Once away from the lights of the inn, all was darkness. A thick pall of cloud obscured the moon, and the inhabitants of Hastings obviously cared little about illuminating their walkways. A flickering torch stuck in a bracket above a row of shops was all that threw a feeble glow over the cobbles. Wondering in which direction to go, John stood still for a moment, listening, and above the sound of his own panting breath came the noise of footsteps retreating up an alley. Without hesitation, the Apothecary set off in pursuit.

The lane climbed steeply upwards, not an easy ascent, and then split into two mean twittens. Gasping, John paused at the fork, then rushed along the right-hand one, but the only sign of life was a large cat which stared at him with glittering green eyes. Even as he retraced his steps, the Apothecary knew that it was too late, that the slight delay would have given Louis de Vignolles the time he needed to make his escape. Cursing under his breath, John set off back to The Swan, only to jump with fear as a man's shape materialised out of the darkness.

'Louis?' the Apothecary gasped.

'No, no, 'tis Lucius,' answered a reassuring voice. 'I thought you might like a bit of a hand if it comes to a mill. I'm quite useful with m'fists, you know.'

The Apothecary laughed with relief. 'So I can imagine. No, there'll be no fighting. I lost him in the darkness.'

'Well in that case there's only one thing to do,' replied the Irishman,

'And what is that?'

'Go back to the inn and down a few bumpers.'

So saying, Lucius Delahunty threw his arm round John's shoulders and together they made their way back to The Swan.

Despite the copious amounts of wine and spirits they had consumed the night before, the two young men were up early the next morning to hire a man with a trap to take them on the last leg of their journey. John, as ever, had eaten a trencherman's breakfast, but to his astonishment had witnessed the Irishman eating even more.

Reading his look of admiration, Lucius had said, 'I usually don't have any more till m'dinner, except for a few snacks while I'm out painting.'

'A man after my own heart. I'm a great believer in a good start,' John had answered.

And now, stomachs comfortably full, they sat in the back of the trap with their belongings, including the Irishman's painting equipment, jogging along the road leading them to Winchelsea.

An hour later they had not only arrived but Lucius had obtained Joe Jago's old room at The Salutation, even though he was blissfully unaware of the fact. Having arranged to meet his new friend later that evening, John proceeded to Petronilla's Platt, there to deposit his bag and check on the health of Elizabeth Rose, who was much cheered by a bottle of Snow Violets which the Apothecary had brought her as a gift from his shop.

'Has anything of excitement happened in my absence?'

'Yes, two things. I have discovered that the following ladies own a bottle of Evening in Araby: Mrs Finch, Miss Rosalind Tireman, though not Henrietta . . .'

'No, I've never smelled it on her,' John answered reflectively.

Mrs Rose shot him an astonished stare but made no comment. 'Together with Lady Ffloote,' she added.

John was silent, remembering the whispered conversation in the churchyard and the strong scent of perfume that had filled his nostrils at the time.

Mrs Rose, misunderstanding his lack of response, emphasised the point. 'The Frenchman, the Scarecrow, bought a bottle for an unknown woman. Therefore the Moth must be among the three I have just mentioned.'

'Not necessarily. Perhaps there is someone who keeps a bottle concealed.'

Elizabeth looked extremely puzzled. 'Then how are you going to find out?'

'By sniffing all and sundry,' said John, and laughed. 'Tell me the other news.'

'The Marquis and Rosalind have announced the date of their wedding. It is to be next month, in the middle of April.'

'Isn't that rather quick?'

'Well, they had always said it would be in the spring, but it seems that Rosalind is anxious to move to London, declaring loudly that she is bored to sobs with this dreary little town.'

'That girl needs a good talking to.' John thought a moment, 'Is she *enceinte* do you think?'

'I wondered, but I truly believe not. I don't see her allowing her figure not to look its absolute best on her wedding day.'

'But what about the preparations?'

'The Marquis has a horde of servants, my dear. A few weeks more or less will make little difference to them.'

195

John fingered his chin thoughtfully. 'Very interesting. Thank you for the information. And now, Elizabeth, if you have no objection, I must be on my way. I have some calls to make.'

She nodded. 'I am sure you do.'

'And your health? Has it held up while I've been away?'

'Perfectly. You need not worry on that score.' Mrs Rose laughed. 'But then I have taken to throwing away any gifts that have been left for me.'

'A wise precaution,' John answered seriously. 'A very wise precaution indeed.'

Captain Pegram today received his visitor in the beautiful gardens that stretched out behind Grey Friars, rolling on until they, too, disappeared into yet another cherry orchard. Seated on a stone bench, enjoying the late March sunshine, though having taken the precaution of dressing warmly against the wind, the military man read a newspaper, his sight enhanced by a pair of spectacles which he wore perched on the end of his nose. This gave him rather a sweet, endearing look which John found hard to equate with a man who kept a sketch of Rosalind Tireman, stark naked, in his desk drawer. However, knowing that appearances were the most deceptive thing in the world, the Apothecary soon steered the usual pleasantries round to the subject he actually wanted to discuss.

'I hear that the Marquis of Rye and his betrothed are to be married next month,' he said, beaming a smile at his host.

'Yes, so I believe,' answered the Captain, stony faced.

'I must confess that secretly I rather envy the bridegroom. Rosalind really is one of the most beautiful women alive. Don't you think so, Sir?'

'Yes, I suppose I do,' came the unhelpful reply.

'Oh, I had thought you were an admirer of Miss Tireman's, in a purely aesthetic way, of course.'

'What gave you that impression?' asked Nathaniel, colouring up.

The Apothecary decided to take the bull by the horns. 'I thought I glimpsed a drawing of her when I was in your study the other day,' he answered.

The Captain's complexion became livid. 'Do you visit people just to pry, Sir?'

'Oh I wasn't prying,' John answered, assuming the most innocent expression from his range of suitable faces. 'Your desk drawer happened to be open. I could not help but see.'

Captain Pegram clearly wrestled with two alternatives, denial or an excuse. He decided on the latter. 'It was drawn from my imagination,' he said falteringly. 'I've always prided myself on being something of an artist.'

'And what more lovely a subject! The naked female form can be most inspiring.'

The Captain loosened his cravat. 'Yes, indeed.' He looked around him uncomfortably, as if hoping for divine intervention, then said, 'If you would excuse me, Mr Rawlings. I apologise for cutting short your visit but I have just recalled some urgent business I must attend to. Please forgive me.'

And with that the poor man was off.

John stared after him, his face sad. He had never enjoyed snooping into people's private affairs in order to get at the truth, yet was very aware that it was a necessary evil. Furthermore, there was something pathetic about the military man's obvious obsession with Rosalind Tireman, besotted with her as he quite clearly was. Dwelling on the misery of unrequited love, the Apothecary put on his hat and walked off slowly in the direction of the cherry orchard, an idea that had crept into his mind beginning to take shape as he did so.

Strangely, Lucius Delahunty did not appear at the arranged meeting place in the parlour of The Salutation, nor was he anywhere in the town, at least as far as John could see when he strolled about looking for him. Presuming from this conspicuous absence that the Irishman must have discovered the whereabouts of the missing Molly Malone, John went back to Petronilla's Platt, changed into black clothes, said goodbye to Elizabeth, and went out under cover of darkness, quietly heading off towards Grey Friars.

Tonight there was a moon, lighting the old Abbey from behind, so that its black silhouette was etched starkly against the deep indigo sky. Like this, the house looked even bigger, almost palatial, and John felt dwarfed and intrusive, and also somewhat nervous, as he took up his hiding place beneath one of the trees that gave protective shade to the lawn in summer. In doing so, the Apothecary was well aware that he left the front door unobserved, yet he was counting on the fact that if the Captain went out of the house, as John had a

197

strong suspicion he might well do, it would be secretly, using one of the entrances that led into the garden.

As he waited in the stillness, disturbed only by the rustling of nocturnal animals and the hoot of a distant owl, John considered his idea. Had Nathaniel Pegram's passion for the rector's daughter led him down a more sinister path, causing him to spy for a foreign power in order to shower her with the gifts the girl so clearly craved? Had a longing to compete with the Marquis, a desire to be seen to be as wealthy and as influential as the nobleman, persuaded the Captain to enhance his not inconsiderable fortune and spy for France? Or did the Frog lie elsewhere, in some less obvious guise? Could the Rector, or Mr Gironde, Sir Ambrose, or even the Doctor be responsible for wiping out the Scarecrow? And what of the Moth? Was she the mysterious woman who had removed Captain Pegram's card from the dead man's pocket. Or was that merely a blind? Was the Moth not female at all? Could it be a man who, like his name, was a creature of the night, moving stealthily through the darkness to achieve his wicked objectives?

Lost in thought like this, it took John several seconds to realise that a door at the back of the house had opened, very furtively and slowly, and that a dark shape, just recognisable as the Captain, was coming into the garden, his only light a lantern held high in his hand.

John shrank against the trunk of the tree as Nathaniel turned, looked round carefully, then strode off in the direction of the stables. Praying that his quarry was not intending to ride to his rendezvous, the Apothecary hurried after him, flitting from shadow to shadow to maintain cover. Fortunately, luck favoured John, and the Captain passed to the left of the stabling block, then disappeared into the leafy arches of the cherry orchards. Now pursuit became hard as twigs snapped beneath the Apothecary's feet and his vision was impaired by burgeoning foliage. Several times, Nathaniel stopped and listened, as if aware that somebody trailed him, each occasion forcing John to freeze where he stood, his heart thudding madly. But somehow he managed to escape detection and follow Captain Pegram through the grove where the Apothecary and Henrietta had made love, then on again, still protected by the trees, till at last he came out close to St Thomas's, hardly having gone along the lanes at all. With one final burst of speed, the Captain made for the campanile which stood near to the church, and hurried inside. As closely as he dared, John hovered by the oak door of the entrance, thankfully left ajar, listening.

The person he had arranged to meet had obviously got there first because a woman hissed in a voice that the Apothecary did not recognise, 'I told you I never wanted to see you again.'

'But sweetheart . . .'

'Don't call me that!'

'Very well. Anyway, it's about the picture of . . .' Captain Pegram lowered his tone and even though John could guess what he must be saying, the rest of the sentence was lost to him.

'Then destroy it,' the woman said clearly.

'I can't bring myself to.'

'You must, for all our sakes.'

The Captain's voice dropped again and John took a step forward in order to try and catch what was said next. Unfortunately, as he did so he must have brushed against the wall, dislodging a rotting brick which crashed to the ground and disintegrated into several fragments. From inside the campanile came a profound silence.

'What was that?' whispered the woman, her voice sibilant.

'Shush,' Nathaniel answered, and John heard him creep towards the door, his feet echoing slightly on the stone floor.

Slithering round the wall, the Apothecary hovered in the shadows, listening as the Captain come out of the tower and looked round. 'Who's there?' he called.

John remained motionless, then a second later heard Nathaniel's quiet breathing as he, too, started to walk round the square shaped campanile. There was nothing for it but to run, which he did, taking off at considerable speed in the direction of The Salutation where he could lose himself in the crowd.

Behind him, the Apothecary was aware of the woman screaming as she realised that something had gone wrong, then he heard her hurry through the churchyard and away. Tempted though he was to turn and stare, John did not dare risk a second's pause but plunged on through the darkness, aware that the Captain was almost upon him. Then came another moment of sheer luck. There was a shout, followed by a heavy thud, and Nathaniel went sprawling over a low gravestone, gasping for air, clearly winded.

Despite all his training to go to the aid of those in difficulties, John continued his headlong flight and did not stop until he reached the end of the street in which the inn was situated where, seeing one or two people strolling about, he slowed his pace and joined the throng, proceeding in a slow and deliberate fashion towards The Salutation.

'Great God in the evening, if you aren't out of breath,' said a familiar voice.

'Lucius, for the love of heaven, walk with me as if nothing has happened,' John muttered.

The Irishman looked down the length of the street. 'So who is it you're trying to avoid? Would it be a tall fellow, red in the face and gasping like a goldfish?'

'Yes.'

'And would he be having a pistol in one hand and a sword in the other?'

'If you say so.'

'He's staring in our direction.'

'Well, don't stare back.'

'Who is he, for the love of the Lord?'

'One Captain Nathaniel Pegram.'

Lucius whistled through his teeth. 'Well, well. I see.'

'Why do you say it like that? Do you know the name?'

'I've heard it somewhere,' the Irishman answered thoughtfully. 'Though I'm damned if for the life of me I can remember where.' He brightened up. 'Bumpers, my rogue. Bumpers all round.'

'Yes,' answered John, thankful to be going inside. 'Bumpers it is.'

Chapter Eighteen

The papers left by Joe Jago made fascinating reading. Long before Elizabeth Rose had stirred, John got out of bed, dressed, and took the packet of correspondence down to the kitchen, where he sat warming himself by the stove, drinking tea and absorbing the documents that Mr Fielding's Clerk had prepared for him. A letter from Joe in a flowing hand that seemed completely out of character with such a rugged individual, accompanied copies of the statements.

My dear Mr Rawlings, Your Servant, Sir.
    Allow me to draw to your attention, Sir, the fact that the other Members of Winchelsea's Polite Society to whom I have Spoke can, for Reasons that will soon be Obvious, be excluded from Suspicion of causing the Death of the Scarecrow. Two were Abroad at the Time, the Others too Infirm for Reasons of Health or, in one Case, Fatness, to be Suspected. I pray you, Sir, in the other Regard, to cast your Eye upon the Statements of the Tiremans in Particular.
    I remain, Sir, your most Humble and Obedient Servant,
    J. Jago

John read all the statements, noticing the differing way in which people told their tale. Whereas Mrs Finch positively gloated over the fact that the Frenchman had asked her for directions, her daughter lied most blatantly about her liaison with the man, claiming that she had hardly been aware of him. In contrast, the Marquis of Rye's statement was curt to the point of rudeness, as was Sir Ambrose's, who ranted on about 'damned foreigners' and very little else. The two Girondes' account was a falsehood from start to finish, Lady Ffloote's declaration was conspicuous by its absence, and Dr Hayman's story of events was vague to the edge of evasiveness. Captain Pegram, on the other hand, admitted quite freely that the Frenchman had called on him and repeated their conversation almost

201

word for word. But it was most certainly the Tiremans' statements that stood out, having such an air of negativity about them that John instantly became suspicious. According to the Rector and his family they had seen nothing, met nobody, and appeared to be unable to understand why they were being questioned at all. Which, as John knew was at odds with Rosalind's admission of having noticed the Frenchman because of his beautiful clothes. Henrietta's description of incidents appeared to have been dictated by an empty-headed flap with a pea where her brain should have been. In fact it was all too guileless to be real.

Sighing heavily, the Apothecary put the papers down, wishing that he had parted with the elder Miss Tireman on better terms, that the days when he had not seen her had not weighed so heavily on him, that she had replied to the letter he had written before he left for London. Giving in to a severe bout of depression, the Apothecary picked at his breakfast, for once leaving most of it, then went quietly out of the house without waking Elizabeth Rose.

It was still early and there were few people about. Determined to try and retrieve something from the wreckage of the previous night's fiasco, John beat a determined path to the campanile and went inside, hoping that Captain Pegram's unseen companion might have left some clue to her identity. But there was nothing to be seen. The flagstone floor was bare of everything but bird droppings. Scowling, the Apothecary set out to retrace the route that the scurrying footsteps had taken.

If his hearing had been correct, the woman had run up the path that came out close to Paradise House. Moving swiftly, John started to walk the same way, and it was then that he saw it, lying on the ground like a dead bird. Stooping, the Apothecary picked the object up, then his heart sank as he recognised it. With its bobbing feathers and sweet little furbelows, it was the hat that Henrietta Tireman had worn on the day that he first met her.

'Oh no!' John groaned aloud.

But wish to deny it as he might, it was quite clear from its general state of dampness that the hat had been lying on the path all night. Thrusting it into his pocket, the Apothecary turned his steps back towards Petronilla's Platt, more to give himself somewhere to sit and think quietly for a while than for any real need to return.

Yet it was as well that he did go back, for as he came through the door Elizabeth called out, 'John, is that you?'

'It is.'

'A letter has arrived. It is on the dining room table.'

'Thank you. The post boy's very early today.'

'It was delivered by a rough looking individual driving a cart.'

One of Dick's henchmen, thought John, and broke the seal with interest.

The writing was clear and neat for the bastard son of a notorious smuggler, and John was seized by the idea that the rascally Kit Jarvis had seen to it that his progeny had been given a good education. In fact the more he thought about it the more likely it seemed, particularly in view of Dick's ability to pass himself off as a curate when he so desired.

My Friend,

I have found a Spyglass near Fairfield Church with a French Maker's Name on It. I believe It to be the Property of the Scarecrow. If you want to take Possession of It meet me at St Augustine's, Brookland, this Day at Two O'Clock.

Signed by a Patriot, R. Jarvis, who has the Honour to remain Your Loyal Servant

Glad to have something to do other than ask perpetual questions, John was just heading out of the front door for Truncheons livery stable, when the post boy arrived at a fast trot and thrust more correspondence into his hand. Seeing yet another letter for him, the Apothecary opened it where he stood and realised with a great rush of pleasure that it was from Henrietta.

Dear Mr Rawlings,

I received your Recent Communication and have Consequently decided to accept Your Apology. There is Much that I would Say to You. Please meet Me in the Cherry Orchard after Dinner at Five O'Clock.

John was filled with an enormous sense of joy, then he remembered the bedraggled hat in his pocket and his spirits slumped again. Further, there was the delicate matter of timing his appointments. To get from Dick to Henrietta in two hours flat was not going to be easy. Putting Elizabeth's letters on the table, the Apothecary called out that he was off and hurried to the stables to hire the fast dark horse with the untrustworthy eye.

One breathless hour later, John Rawlings arrived in Brookland, feeling in need of rest and refreshment. His evil mount had, once again, thundered to a halt on the very banks of the river, threatening to tip his rider into the water, had fidgeted throughout the ferry ride, then had gone off like a tempest and had only been persuaded to stop by the sight of a horse trough, where it had put its head down so low to drink that it was all John could do not to slither the length of its equine neck. Fearing the worst, the Apothecary had dismounted at this stage and led the creature the rest of the way to The Woolpack.

It wasn't only John's own thirst that had dictated this stop at a hostelry instead of going straight to Brookland Church, rather it was the notion that he might find Dick there ahead of him. For if he were to be back with Henrietta by five, an assignation he did not wish to miss for a variety of reasons, he must be early for everything else. However, The Woolpack was empty, and the Apothecary, having downed a draught of ale, was just about to take his leave when a familiar voice boomed from the doorway.

'Great God in the noontide,' said Lucius Delahunty, 'if it isn't yourself.' And in came the Irishman, a bag containing pots and brushes on one shoulder, his easel on the other.

'Lucius!' John exclaimed. 'I didn't realise you travelled so far afield when you go painting.'

'Oh, I go everywhere and anywhere there might be some custom. How now, landlord.'

'Yes?' grunted the surly individual who had helped hold John prisoner.

'What would you say to a new inn sign in return for a guinea or two and some sustenance?'

'I'd say be off, you Irish tinker.'

'How very unchristian of you, Will,' remarked a reproving voice, and Dick, in his guise as the Reverend Tompkins, bobbed his way into the inn, all black hat and clerical clothing. Seeing John ahead of him, he gave a grin and a jerky bow.

'Mr Rawlings! This is indeed a surprise.' The unruly blue eyes flicked over Lucius, then looked straight at the Apothecary and in their depths asked a question. John gave an almost imperceptible shake of his head.

Dick smiled at the newcomer. 'Allow me to introduce myself, Sir. The Reverend Tompkins, curate of this and other parishes. I travel around, you know.'

'Lucius Delahunty,' said the Irishman, bowing deep, his long black hair falling forward over his cheekbones as he did so. 'I'm a bit of a traveller m'self. Come to this part of the world to do a spot of painting and see something of the countryside.'

'Actually,' added John, with a wink, 'he's here in search of a young woman by the name of Molly Malone. The man's an incurable romantic at heart.'

'Splendid,' answered Dick. 'May I buy you something to drink, Sir?'

'I never say no to an offer like that, Reverend.'

'Two jugs of ale and a simple sherry for myself, Will,' Dick ordered, every inch the kindly young curate. 'And if I were you I would seriously consider the offer of a new inn sign. The one you have now is barely discernible.'

'If you say so, Your Reverence,' growled the landlord, glaring at Lucius.

'Oh, I do indeed.'

They took their drinks to a long wooden table, big enough to seat a dozen. In his mind's eye John imagined the smugglers sitting round it, discussing their latest run and laying plans for the next, the air thick with pipe smoke and the smell of sweat and sea.

'I've a mind to go and paint the church of St Thomas à Becket at a place called Fairfield,' Lucius announced. 'I've been told it's very old and picturesque and is surrounded by floods from winter to spring. I thought I might use what imagination the Lord gave me and show the place rising out of the waters like an arm bearing Excalibur.'

'How poetic,' said Dick enthusiastically. 'I think you should, Sir. Why, I might even buy a painting like that myself.'

'Would you now, Reverend?'

'Yes, indeed.'

'Then consider it done.' Lucius finished his ale. 'I'll be on my way directly.' He paused as if remembering something, then said, 'I heard the strangest rumour in an alehouse in Winchelsea and I just wondered if there might be any truth in it.'

'What was it?' asked Dick, looking benign yet at the same time suddenly cautious.

'That a skeleton was found near St Thomas's dressed up as a scarecrow. But that now it's vanished, though nobody seems to know where.'

The smuggler paused, clearly unsure how to respond. 'Er . . .' he began.

John chimed in, 'It's true enough. A man *did* die nearby, possibly trapped by the floods.'

'Who was he, do you know?'

'A stranger to these parts, apparently. Nobody could identify him.'

'But what was he doing rigged up like a bird scarer?'

'That part of the story is probably fiction. I never saw anything and I am in and out of St Thomas's Church quite regularly,' Dick said with the sort of air that suggested words spoken by the clergy are beyond question.

'It never ceases to amaze me how gossip spreads,' Lucius answered as he hoisted his bag and easel on to his shoulders.

'Alas, it is the way of this sinful world,' Dick replied mournfully. 'And where may I find you, my son, to collect my painting?'

'I'm staying at The Salutation in Winchelsea, Reverend. But I'll write to you care of St Augustine's when it's ready.'

'No,' said Dick hastily, 'I roam about too much for that. Better to send a letter here to The Woolpack. The landlord will always keep it for me if I am on a parochial visit.' He smiled engagingly.

'It's been a pleasure meeting you,' said Lucius, bowing somewhat akwardly, weighed down as he was with his painting gear.

'Likewise.'

'Goodbye, my friend,' called John. 'I'll see you later this evening perhaps.'

'Sure and I'll be sending a search party if you don't come.'

'Farewell and God bless you,' said Dick, but as soon as the Irishman was out of the door the smuggler turned to John hastily. 'Is the fellow all that he says he is?'

'Yes, I think so. Why shouldn't he be?'

'It's just that I wondered what he was doing at Brookland.'

'Painting, as you saw for yourself.'

'Yes, but why *here*?'

'Because the countryside is beautiful, in its own harsh way.'

'And how would he know that?'

John grew impatient. 'For Heaven's sake, Dick, stop being so suspicious. First me and now Lucius. We're not all of us revenue men in disguise. Let the poor chap paint in peace.' He pointedly changed the subject. 'Now show me the telescope.'

Dick fished in the pocket of his cassock and produced a small folding spy-glass which he elongated and put to his eye.

'A very fine model. Where did you find it?'

'Hidden in the grass, near where the Scarecrow had been placed. See, the maker's name.' Dick pointed. 'Henri Varonne, Rue St Louis, Ile de la Cité, Paris.'

'And it doesn't belong to any of your fraternity?'

'They've all got their greedy eyes on it, but the answer is no. There's something else too, John.'

'What's that?'

'There are initials engraved just here.' He pointed again. 'Can you see them?'

The Apothecary nodded. 'G.D.L.T. The Scarecrow's?'

The smuggler smiled. 'More than likely in my opinion, unless the Frenchie stole the spyglass, that is.'

'Remember he was elegantly dressed and could afford to buy perfume for a lady. I should imagine he had money enough and would have considered robbery beneath him.'

'You're probably right. I'll mention the initials to the French free-traders, see if anybody recognises them.'

'Dick,' asked John, 'you say you are a patriot yet you continue to smuggle in French goods despite the fact that we are at war with France.'

'That,' answered the smuggler grandly, 'is business, which is a completely different matter.'

The Apothecary shook his head. 'There's no logic in that.'

'There is to me,' said Dick Jarvis with such finality that John knew the subject was closed.

Chapter Nineteen

The very sight of Henrietta, looking so pale and somehow so vulnerable, tore at John's heart-strings. She stood beneath the dusky cherry trees, a forlorn figure, and yet again the Apothecary thought that had he been the Marquis of Rye nothing would have induced him to drop such an adorable creature in favour of her glittering sister.

'I'm here,' he called out quietly, not wanting to startle her.

Henrietta turned and gave the Apothecary a smile that warmed his soul. In love with him she might well not be, but it was abundantly clear that she not only held John in the highest regard but was truly delighted to see him. Without saying a word, he opened his arms and had the pleasurable sensation of feeling her snuggle into them.

'I'm sorry about leaving you as I did,' she whispered.

'I shouldn't have said such a cruel thing about the Marquis. It's only that I'm jealous of the man.'

Henrietta laughed. 'There's no need to be. He marries my sister next month.'

'But I have the strangest feeling that you still care for him.'

'Well, put it out of your mind, John. What is done, is done.'

The Apothecary held her at arm's length and looked into her face. 'It would be very easy to fall in love with you, you know.'

'I could say the same.'

'Shall we do it then, just to see what happens?'

Henrietta gave a rather sad smile. 'Perhaps just a little more caution might be in order.'

'Why? I hate caution. To hell with it,' answered John, and kissed her.

And then all the old magic came back and they were safe in each other's embrace, forgetting everything else while they experimented with the delights of lovemaking. Yet it was as he held her close to him, delighting in her nearness, that the Apothecary noticed that Henrietta was wearing a different perfume. And one sniff of it was enough to tell him that it was Evening in Araby, the scent which the Scarecrow had bought for a woman unknown. But John cast such suspicious thoughts from his mind as he and Henrietta mingled delightfully. Yet afterwards, as they lay quietly in the darkening orchard, the Apothecary remembered the hat and knew that whatever the consequences he must ask Henrietta how it had come to be dropped on the path leading to Paradise House.

It was as they were leaving the shelter of the trees, heading for Friars Walk and the homesteads of Winchelsea, that John finally produced the dishevelled piece of headgear from his pocket and handed it to the girl he was falling in love with.

'Is this yours?' he said, regretting the abruptness with which the words came out.

Henrietta looked at him in surprise. 'Yes. Where did you find it?'

'On the path in the churchyard.'

She looked at him in amazement. '*Did* you? I wonder how it got there.'

'I thought you might be able to tell me.'

Henrietta narrowed her eyes. 'Are you accusing me of something?'

'No, not at all. It's just that I interrupted Captain Pegram in conversation with a woman in the campanile of St Thomas's. I rather thought the hat belonged to her.'

Miss Tireman drew away from him. 'Oh, so that's it! Now I'm meeting Nathaniel clandestinely. I see!'

John stopped dead in his tracks, pulling Henrietta to a halt as well.

'No, you don't see. Not one tiny little bit. I care for you, you foolish girl. I'm not accusing you of a thing. All I want is for you to tell me how your hat came to be dropped in the churchyard and I will be satisfied.'

Henrietta gave him a mercurial smile. 'I'm afraid I can't do that.'

'Why not?' asked the Apothecary, astonished.

'Because I don't know. You see that hat has been missing quite some while. I must have gone out in it, then left it somewhere. But though I made enquiries at all the places I usually visit, nobody had seen it. This is the first time I've set eyes on it for about a fortnight.'

'Is that the truth?'

'Of course it is,' Henrietta answered snappishly. 'Are you accusing me of lying now?'

'No, of course not. Please don't look so angry.'

'Well, I *am* angry. First you infer that I'm Captain Pegram's mistress, then that I'm an out and out falsifier.'

'I didn't mean to,' John said wretchedly. 'It's just that there was something odd about the way that hat was dropped. I can't help wondering if somebody is trying to incriminate you.'

'Incriminate? But who would do that? And why?'

'I've no idea, but, Henrietta, listen to me. There are a lot of odd things happening round here, things that don't bode well. I beg you to be on your guard.'

'Against whom?'

'Of that I have no idea. Just be careful, that's all. And if you believe yourself to be in any kind of trouble, come to me at once.'

'I don't understand any of this. What are you hinting, John?'

'We are a nation at war, my dear. Just remember that.'

Henrietta tightened her gaze once more. 'Are you a spy by any chance?'

The only really good answer the Apothecary could think of giving was, 'You must believe what you want to.' And after that he insisted that the matter was dropped so that they could walk home in some sort of harmony.

All congenial feelings were instantly swept away as the Apothecary put his key in the door of Petronilla's Platt. From where he stood he could hear Agnes shrieking, while above this racket rose the sound of Elizabeth groaning and heaving in the most terrifying fashion. Without waiting even to remove his cloak, John sprinted into the kitchen, the place from which all the rumpus was coming.

The former actress lay sprawled supine across the kitchen table, her enamelled face like a death mask. But though she was retching, no vomit had come up, and she was slipping rapidly into unconsciousness as whatever had poisoned her took hold of her system. Agnes, meanwhile, eyes popping with fear, was rushing about wringing her hands, clearly incapable of doing anything to help.

'Fetch a pail,' ordered John, then rushed upstairs to snatch his bag of physicks and potions, hurriedly mixing up a compound of powdered root of Asarabacca with some crushed thyme, the whole

211

contained in a concoction of the liquid achieved by boiling damask roses and sugar in water, of which the Apothecary always carried a supply.

The serving girl appeared with a bucket, looking slightly less terrified now that John had returned and taken command of the situation. 'Will this do, Sir?' she asked in a whisper.

'Yes, yes. Hold it by Mrs Rose's head. I am going to try and make her sick.'

'Is she poisoned again, Sir?'

'Yes. More anonymous gifts of food, I suppose.'

'Not that I know of, Sir.'

In the middle of spooning emetic down Elizabeth's throat, John looked up. 'What's that?'

'There ain't been no food or drink left here, leastways while I've been about.'

'So what has your mistress eaten today?'

'Nothing, that's just the point. She complained of feeling a little delicate this morning and had nought but a pot of tea. And there weren't nothing wrong with that because I had a cup from the same brew and I'm all right. Anyway, Mrs Rose felt ill at dinner-time and so told me to eat it all up, which I done. That's how I'm certain she can't have had anything bad, do you see.'

John nodded. 'Unless she took something you know nothing about.'

Agnes shook her head vigorously. 'I don't think so, Sir. When Mrs Rose is poorly she fasts.'

A thought flashed through John's mind. 'So is your mistress ill very often? Other than for the bouts of poisoning, I mean.'

'Quite a bit.'

'And what form does the malaise take?'

'Headaches and stomach cramps.'

The Apothecary nodded but was unable to pursue his questioning, for at that precise moment Elizabeth heaved violently as the emetic began to work. Half an hour later, barely conscious and ghastly white, she was sufficiently recovered to be put to bed, where John left her in the charge of Agnes, who held grimly on to the bucket, just in case.

It was then that the Apothecary began his search, starting with the actress's dressing table, where lotion and potions jostled side by side. Pulling out corks and removing tops, John cautiously sniffed everything, then delicately tasted the pills, before moving on to the medicine chest where he repeated his actions. Finally, a smile spread over his face and he removed one particular bottle, tasted its contents, then placed it in his pocket.

'Agnes, can you stay another hour?' he called to the servant.

'I can, Sir. Though I expect my mam will be worried.'

'I'll write her a note explaining why you are late.'

'That'll be no good. She can't read.'

'Then I promise to be as quick as I can. It's just that I have to go out for a while and Mrs Rose is too frail to leave on her own.'

'Don't dilly dally whatever you do, Sir. I don't want to get my father's belt.'

'I promise to run there and back.'

And with that pledge, the Apothecary left the house at double-quick time and rushed through the darkness towards his destination.

Chapter Twenty

By night the two bow-fronted windows of Mr Gironde's apothecary's shop were almost as attractive as they were by day. Using lantern light in an extremely subtle way, with cleverly placed mirrors reflecting their illumination, the attractive and exotic contents were clearly displayed to passers-by and even John, despite his hurry, paused momentarily to admire the prettily packaged goods before he pealed the bell.

The Girondes lived over their shop in a three-storey house, the ground floor of which was completely taken up by their emporium. Consequently, it took some while for footsteps to descend the staircase, then come through the shop, but eventually the door was opened with a great deal of chain rattling. A small round-faced serving girl stood there, grander than Agnes by far by reason of the smart white apron and mob cap that she wore.

'Good evening, Sir.'

'Good evening. Are your master and mistress at home?'

'Madam is within but Sir has gone out. Who shall I say is calling?'

John handed over his card with a flourish.

The girl peered at it, clearly having trouble with reading the print. 'Is that Mr Rolling?'

'Rawlings, actually.'

'If you will wait, Sir, I'll check whether Madam is receiving.'

But she needn't have worried. A series of light steps could be heard and the next second Mrs Gironde flew down the stairs, greeting John like a long-lost friend.

'My dear Sir, how pleasant indeed to see you. Mrs *Rose*' – she emphasised the word almost with a wink, presumably indicating that she had kept the secret of Elizabeth's true identity to herself – 'told me that you had recently returned to town and I had no idea that you were back with us. What a pleasant surprise. Do, pray, come to our private rooms.'

She turned to ascend the stairs but John said, 'If I may I would rather linger in your shop a moment.'

Mrs Gironde looked slightly surprised but made a little movement expressing flattered delight. 'Why, of course. I remember how much you admired it the other day. Is there any particular product you wanted to look at?'

'Yes,' answered John silkily. 'Would it be possible for me to examine your Elixir of Youth?'

Nan giggled girlishly. 'Not for yourself, surely?'

The Apothecary twitched his brows. 'In a way, yes.' And he drew out the bottle which he had concealed in his pocket. 'This belongs to Aunt Elizabeth,' he went on. 'I found it amongst her cosmetics. It's my guess that she took some this morning and that it very nearly killed her.'

'What are you saying?' demanded Mrs Gironde furiously.

'That this mixture has not been properly compounded and, I would hazard a guess, neither was the one that Mrs Finch bought recently. The other night she could not attend Lady Ffloote's dinner party because of sickness. It's my contention, Madam, that you are slowly poisoning the older ladies of the town with this wretched concoction.'

Nan's face hardened. 'That is a very serious accusation, Sir.'

'It is indeed. Tell me, Mrs Gironde, is the preparation of the elixir your province? Do you, with no medical training at all, make up this noxious brew?'

'Well, I . . . er . . .'

'I see. At least it's as well that your husband is not responsible. Now, I believe you said the main ingredient was pennywort.'

'Yes.'

'And where do you gather your simples?'

'In the marshlands. Pennywort thrives in watery places.'

John's voice was like the cut of a razor. 'Water pennywort has another name, did you realise that?'

'No.'

'It is also called sheep's bane. And do you know why?'

Mrs Gironde shook her head.

'Because it kills any unfortunate enough to graze on it. Just as it kills human beings. The only pennywort safe to use is that which grows on walls. Through your ignorance and your husband's laziness, you have embarked on a campaign of systematic destruction.'

Nan looked at him with an expression of utter horror. 'Is that the truth?'

'Of course it is. If I were to report this to the Worshipful Society of Apothecaries I believe that stern action would be taken against Marcel Gironde.'

She clutched his arm beseechingly. 'Oh, do not do so, I beg you. We have built up a good business here. I don't know what he would do if it were jeopardised in any way.'

John paused, considering the matter, then said, 'If I agree to remain silent there will be certain conditions attached.'

'I will fulfil them all. I could not bear our livelihood to be threatened.'

'Very well. First I want you to destroy all the bottles of this elixir that you have left, and burn the water pennywort you use for compounding. Then go to your customers first thing tomorrow morning and tell them that you are no longer selling the product and somehow persuade them to part with their old supply. After that I want you to promise me you will never dispense again. You are not an apothecary, Mrs Gironde, and you must no longer act as if you are one. Then . . .' John paused for effect.

'Yes?'

'I want you to tell me all about your dealings with the mysterious Frenchman who came here last summer. I think you lied when you told me you never saw him again after he left this shop. Your hesitation gave you away. I suspect that you are concealing information which is vital to the national interest.'

Mrs Gironde sat down rather hard on a chair kept for infirm customers and covered her face with her hands. Unimpressed, John watched her. 'Well?' he said eventually.

'It shall be as you say,' she muttered. 'I shall destroy everything tonight and tomorrow I will go in search of all the elixirs already sold.'

'Here is Mrs Rose's.' And John banged the bottle down on the counter, furious that this pretentious little woman should have endangered life by her arrant ignorance. 'Now tell me about the Frenchman. And if you omit anything you leave me no option but to go to your husband with the entire story.'

She looked up fearfully. 'Oh, no, no! He is a good man and

hardworking. I couldn't bear him to learn the depths of my foolishness. What happened was this. The Frenchman murmured to me while Marcel was in the compounding room that he found me beautiful and chic. He asked me to meet him by the mill.'

'And you went? Wasn't that highly dangerous with a man you didn't know?'

Mrs Gironde gave a light laugh. 'He was a man of honour, one could tell.'

'So honourable that he also had a secret tryst with Miss Sarah Finch, bamboozling the poor girl with promises of love. In return for meeting her mother and thus gaining entrée to Winchelsea society, I might add.'

Nan turned from a bird to a wasp. 'I don't believe you.'

John shrugged. 'Ask her for yourself. You'll be seeing Mrs Finch tomorrow morning, no doubt.'

'I can hardly believe that Gerard was like that.'

'Gerard? Was that what he was called?'

'So he told me.'

The initials on the telescope were G.D.L.T., John thought. So at last the Scarecrow had a name.

'Did he give you his surname?'

'No.'

'Then what did you and he talk about.'

Mrs Gironde had the good grace to blush crimson.

'I see. So the amorous little beast didn't waste much time on conversation I take it. Tell me, what did he want, other than the obvious, that is?'

He was being unbelievably blunt, John knew, but he still felt furious with her and at that moment had no compunction about what he said.

'He asked me about the ladies of society and whether I would introduce him into their circle.'

'Did he mention any particular names?'

'Lady Ffloote, Mrs Tireman and her girls, Mrs Rose.'

'Did he now? How very interesting.'

Nan Gironde looked at him with much distress. 'You won't breathe a word to Marcel, will you?'

John shook his head. 'No, provided you keep your side of the bargain.'

'I swear to you.'

'Did Gerard say anything else?'

'Funnily enough, he asked me if I knew where the Marquis of Rye lived.'

'He seemed quite preoccupied with that. I wonder why.'

'Perhaps they are connected in some way. After all, the Marquis has French blood.'

'There's a link somewhere,' John murmured to himself. 'But what the devil is it?' He turned to Mrs Gironde. 'Is that all? Or is there something else you have to tell me?'

'Not really. After we parted company that day I never saw him again.'

'And the woman he bought the perfume for, you have no inkling who it was?'

'None at all, but then neither did he.'

'What?'

'He said he was buying it for a lady he had never met but whom he wanted to impress favourably. I asked him what age this woman might be, but he replied that he was not sure of that either. Eventually we decided on Evening in Araby as likely to appeal to all ages.'

'How intriguing.'

'Was Gerard a spy?' Nan asked timidly.

'Oh yes,' John answered ruthlessly, rubbing a final bit of salt into her wounds. 'You consorted with the enemy Mrs Gironde, remember that.'

The redness drained from her cheeks. 'Believe me, I will.'

The Apothecary consulted his watch. 'I must leave you. Mrs Rose is still very ill and the girl needs to get home but won't leave until I return.' He moved to the door.

Nan whispered after him, 'I will try to make amends. Thank you for treating me so fairly.'

It was on the tip of John's tongue to say that he would have far preferred to wring her neck but he maintained his calm exterior and strode out in dignified silence.

Feeling very guilty about keeping Agnes waiting, the Apothecary ran all the way back to Petronilla's Platt, only to discover that Elizabeth, paler than he had ever seen her, was fast asleep in bed, while Agnes slumbered in the chair beside her. Quietly waking the serving girl, John led her downstairs.

'I'm sorry I took so long.'

Her pasty face looked up at him. 'I'll get the belt, I know it.'

'No you won't. I'll walk back with you and explain.'

'Oh, would you, Sir?'

'Of course. Let me just check Mrs Rose again.'

But Elizabeth was in a deep sleep that seemed set to go through to morning. Feeling that Agnes's need was even greater than the invalid's, John headed off with her through the darkness, their only light a pair of lanterns.

Before he had gone even a quarter of a mile, the Apothecary found his thoughts turning to the extraordinary cipher he had delivered to Dr Willes, wondering what it could possibly mean and whether the King's Decipherer had managed to crack it yet. Then, just as if John had conjured them up by some strange magic power, from the headland at Pett came a series of flashing lights.

'What's that?' exclaimed Agnes, pointing.

'Probably the smugglers,' John answered tersely, grabbing his pencil and a piece of paper from his pocket, watching the number of flickers and making a mental note before he wrote them down.

'1027 1991 1637 1695,' he said aloud.

'Whatever does it mean?' asked Agnes.

'God knows. Listen, my girl, you are to say nothing about what we've observed, not even to the mistress.'

'Oh, I won't, Mr Rawlings,' the servant replied excitedly, and by the light of his lantern, John saw that plain, dumpy Agnes was more animated and alert than he had ever seen her.

Chapter Twenty-One

It seemed to the Apothecary that no sooner had he laid his head on the pillow and closed his eyes than he was awoken again by a violent knocking on the front door. Startled, he sat bolt upright, then ran downstairs in his nightshirt and wrestled with the locks. Dr Richard Hayman, fully dressed, stood in the doorway, the light of a fitful moon revealing that he was sweating profusely and seemed in a considerable state of agitation.

'There's a ship aground at Pett Level,' he said, 'caught on the sandbank. To make matters worse, it's French.'

'What?'

'There are men wounded. Somebody went to fetch the Riding Officers from Rye and there's been a pitched battle on the beach. It's total confusion and God alone knows what's going on. We need all available help. Can you come and tend the injured?'

'Give me a moment to look at Aunt Elizabeth and get dressed, then I'll be with you.'

'I've got my carriage outside. I thought it would save time.'

Ten minutes later they were seated in the doctor's trap and heading for the coast as quickly as the horse would go.

'Tell me again what happened,' said John, who had barely got the gist of events.

'I don't know exactly. All I can say is that this is nothing to do with the smuggling fraternity. A frigate with French troops aboard obviously came in too close to land and got stuck fast on the sandbank. What they were doing here nobody seems to understand.'

Remembering the flashing signals, John said, 'I wonder.'

'What's that?'

'Whether they were to rendezvous with an English spy.'

'It's possible, I suppose.'

'Anyway, who sent for the Riding Officers?'

'Someone with quick wits and an even quicker horse. He must have noticed French uniforms on an English beach and gone like the wind.'

'Who could it possibly have been, do you suppose?'

'We might learn more later.'

They were approaching the shore and John strained his eyes in the darkness, trying to make out signs of the fighting. This particular bit of the coast was well loved by smugglers, mostly because the beaches at Fairlight Glen and Cove were accessible to carts. Pett Level itself was also popular, a flat expanse of water meadows criss-crossed by drainage ditches, frequently flooded by the sea which lapped at the shingle beach just below it. And it was on this beach that the Apothecary first made out the signs of what had happened. Marooned on a sandbank from which, presumably, it would have floated away with the tide, was a French frigate. Its occupants, a troop of soldiers, had rather foolishly come ashore, perhaps tempted by the sheer devilment of making such a landing. Now several of them lay on the shingle, dying or dead, victims of the Revenue men, the Riding Officers, who must have come from Rye at speed after someone sounded the alarm.

The French, too, had scored some hits. Several of the English were being tended by those who had come to the beach to see for themselves what had been going on. And staring about him as he and Dr Hayman abandoned the trap and proceeded the rest of the way on foot, John saw to his total astonishment that the *beau monde* of Winchelsea, as he liked to think of it, had turned out in force, even the sickly Lady Ffloote feebly attempting to bind a cut head with a white cotton rag.

Crouched amongst the young Frenchmen, the Apothecary noticed with a wry smile, were Mrs Finch and her four dumpling daughters, all causing more problems than they were relieving. Mrs Tireman, on the other hand, was speaking to a French officer fluently in his own language, clearly acting as an interpreter. Her husband, meanwhile, was tending to the dying, trying to ease the passing of all, regardless of race or religion and obviously very moved by the whole experience. Needless to say, though Henrietta gallantly staunched wounds, the beautiful Rosalind was sitting on a camp stool, swaying with faintness. Her future husband, dark and morose as ever, was hefting into the air those unable to walk and carrying them to where they could be tended by the medical men, of whom there were two present, Marcel Gironde and surprisingly, Florence Hensey. The Squire, acting in an advisory capacity and bellowing incomprehensible instructions, had brought The Pup, which slithered over the shale with scrabbling claws, breathing noisily. Mrs Gironde, who had been nursing a wounded soldier, looked apologetic when she felt John's eyes on her. Captain Pegram, clearly harking back to his early training, was supervising the taking of prisoners, marching those who were still standing into the custody of the Dragoons.

'Let's to it,' said Richard, and fell to his knees amongst the wounded, grabbing for his medical bag as he did so.

There was something immensely satisfying about the whole effort, and John knew that he was not alone in feeling it. There was an element of excitement in the air, created by the fact that the enemy had come so close and then turned out to be nothing more than a bunch of frightened boys. The leathery old officers who had charge of them chatted away together, obviously not caring a cuss about being captured, as long as they could smoke their pipes and take a pull from bottles of brandy.

'War!' said John, with a cynical laugh.

'The aftermath!' answered a voice at his side, and the Apothecary glanced over to see that Dr Hensey had come to work beside him, putting a sheep's gut stitch into a wounded Frenchman's arm.

'How on earth did you get here, Sir? The last I saw of you was at that delightful meal in London.'

'My patient in Hastings took a turn for the worse and I travelled down to the coast shortly after you. Strangely, I was spending the night at The Salutation, having dined long and late and rather too well with Mrs Finch and her girls, when the cry went up that a French ship had run aground and there were casualties. I hastened here in the dear lady's carriage.'

John raised his eyebrows but said nothing.

'And what a strange affair it turns out to be. First, why should the frigate have come so close inshore? Second, who told the Riding Officers that the French had landed?'

The Apothecary shook his head. 'I have no idea. It is all very odd.' He looked round for his next patient and saw that the line of bodies had been finally cleared, the dead put in a cart for disposal, the living into another for removal either to prison or hospital. Down by the shoreline, Dr Hayman was washing his hands in the sea, while Apothecary Gironde was putting away his collection of physicks and ointments. Noticing for the first time that he was covered in blood, John also made his way to the water.

A voice called out from the distance. 'Good people, if you can undertake a journey of five miles or thereabouts, I invite you all to a late supper with me. I feel you need some reward after your labours of tonight.'

It was the Marquis of Rye, standing on a small round rock, his arms raised to draw attention to himself. Etched dark against the ocean, his black figure looked like that of a bird, or even an insect, the cloak hanging from his shoulders rippling in the manner of wings.

Richard Hayman turned to his colleague. 'Will you go?'

'Yes, I think so. It will be interesting to see the future home of the fair Rosalind.'

'Exactly my reaction.' The doctor gave a bow which looked strangely out of place on the battle-scarred seashore. 'I can't thank you enough, John, for your help. There has obviously been some savage fighting here.'

'A sharp reminder of what might happen if the French tried to invade in earnest.' The Apothecary looked the physician squarely in the eye. 'Richard, talking of enemies in our midst, something has been bothering me for quite some while and I feel I have to ask you about it.'

'Yes?'

'That night after my aunt was last taken ill . . .'

'What of it?'

'Shortly after you left the house, the smugglers made a drop of goods, serving practically every citizen of Winchelsea as far as I could make out. I looked out of the window and saw you and Mrs Tireman going off on a cart with them and have puzzled about it ever since.'

'Oh, that! There was a sailor with fever aboard a French lugger. Dick Jarvis asked the rector's wife to translate his symptoms into English and I went along to tend the fellow.'

'And neither you nor she minded that you were assisting an enemy?'

'A suffering human being is simply that to me. I care not whether he be French, English, Eskimo. Do you?'

'Certainly not. I was merely curious, that is all.'

'I am not a traitor if that is what you're thinking.'

'What is a traitor?' answered John reflectively. 'To the side for which he fights he is a hero.'

And his thoughts flew to Gerard the Scarecrow, who had come to England to do his duty, and flirt with a few ladies besides, and had ended up stabbed through the heart by a murderer.

'Come on,' said Marcel Gironde, hurrying up to join them at their ablutions in the sea. 'The Marquis is leaving.'

With the strange feeling that this night would bring much that was unknown to the surface, John turned his back on the water and started to walk inland.

The Marquis of Rye's home, Ravenhurst Park, had been built in the reign of William and Mary, a warm red-bricked building of eleven bays and three storeys set in its own rolling parkland, with sheep grazing in the meadows surrounding the glorious gardens. They stood in the moonlight beneath the spreading trees, raising their heads as the convoy of carts and carriages wound up the drive. For it seemed that everyone had accepted Justin's invitation to supper. Indeed, John counted at least half a dozen conveyances in front of Dr Hayman's trap.

During the journey he had told the medical man the cause of Elizabeth Rose's mysterious bouts of poisoning.

'And you say you are not going to report the Girondes for malpractice?'

The Apothecary shook his head. 'I would prefer not to, dog eating dog and all that.'

Richard Hayman let out a neighing laugh. 'Can you imagine eating that ghastly hound of Sir Ambrose's? Did you see it lumbering round the beach, getting in the way?'

'Yes,' said John, and at that moment an odd idea was born.

The doctor, not noticing his companion's silence, continued to laugh, then became serious. 'You are quite certain you have frightened Nan Gironde off? You don't think she'll start compounding again once your back is turned?'

'To make doubly sure I'll tell her that you know everything. That should stop her for good and all.'

'And what about him?'

'He is innocent, of the poisoning at least.'

'What do you mean by that?'

'I'm not quite sure,' answered the Apothecary.

The carriage in front, in which travelled the five large Finches and an extremely squashed Dr Hensey, began to slow, and, peering

225

out of the window, John saw that the head of the procession had drawn to a halt before an imposing front door. Instantly, even at this hour of the night, servants appeared as if by magic and began helping the visitors and leading the conveyances round to the stables. The Apothecary jumped down, balancing on the trap's high step, and Richard swung off the driving seat and handed the reins to an hostler. Then they both gazed in open admiration as they stepped through a fairly unpretentious entrance hall into a further larger hall. Here the feeling was Italianate, for a marble staircase, broad and gracious, curved upwards from a distinctive black and white flagged marble floor. Just ahead of him, John saw that Rosalind had revived and had taken up her position alongside her betrothed, charmingly welcoming the guests.

It was like some bizarre carnival, he thought, with all these different people, brought together by a potential disaster, going through the motions of a harlequinade. It occurred to him at that moment that the Frog and the Moth had to be present. If Joe Jago were right and the other members of Winchelsea's society could be ruled out as suspects for one reason or another, then the two French spies were in the midst of this company. John stared upwards as the visitors began to climb the stairs towards the first-floor saloon.

Captain Pegram led the way, gallantly escorting both Miss Sophie and Miss Sarah Finch. Behind them walked the two younger girls, giggling and casting the eye at an extremely handsome footman of eligible age. Following behind came their mother, her arm most determinedly thrust through that of Dr Hensey.

A few steps below them climbed Sir Ambrose and Faith Ffloote, she dragging her feet, much weakened by all that had gone before. As for her husband, he was much put out of countenance by the fact that the Marquis had refused The Pup house room and had insisted the dog went to the stables.

'Just 'cause the feller's got wolfhounds,' the Squire was muttering beneath his breath.

Much subdued, Mrs Gironde, studiously avoiding the gaze of both the Apothecary and Dr Hayman, climbed the stairs beside her husband. Marcel, on the other hand, positively glowed with satisfaction, and John hazarded a guess that he had never set foot in Ravenhurst Park before and probably might never do again, and thus was relishing every moment.

The Reverend Tireman and his wife, however, walked with the

226

kind of negligent gait that assured the world they were regular
visitors to these exalted premises and were so used to them that
they were now beyond noticing the splendour of the surroundings.
At least, John considered, the wife gave this impression very
strongly, though the rector still seemed to have the cloud of
death hanging over him, having eased the passing of so many
men on this extraordinary night.

There was a sound at John's elbow and he turned to see Henrietta,
looking rather pale, her clear eyes distinctly cloudy. The Apothecary
bowed low. 'Madam,' he said, and offered her his arm, which she
swiftly took.

'I can hardly believe this invitation,' she said in a low voice
as they ascended the stairs together, Richard Hayman immediately behind.

'Why is that?'

'It seems such an extraordinary thing to do, to give a supper party
following such a harrowing event. I wonder if Justin has taken leave
of his senses.'

'I doubt that. More probably he felt the spirit of camaraderie
which we all experienced, working as a team on that beach. By
the way, do you know who went for the Riding Officers?' he added
casually.

'I have no idea.'

'How can I find out?'

'By asking the Captain of Dragoons. Look, he's just coming
in.'

And John stared down into the marble hall to see a tall man
in military uniform making his way inside. The Dragoon saluted
smartly when he saw Henrietta and called out, 'Good evening, Miss
Tireman.' She curtseyed in response and the Apothecary felt a pang
of jealousy.

They had reached the top of the stairs and followed the throng into
a stately saloon dominated by a fully lit chandelier which gleamed
with a thousand candles, their reflection in the huge gilt-framed
mirrors enhancing the crimson wallpaper and the wonderful windows looking out over the sleeping park.

'Magnificent,' said John.

'I'm glad you like it,' answered a voice at his ear, and there was
the Marquis, dressed in black and scarlet, looking over his guests
with an enigmatic eye.

227

Servants must have toiled up another, invisible, staircase while the company was assembling, for elegant silver-topped jugs of wine and glasses of gleaming crystal had been laid out, and there were clear signs of activity in the dining room which led off the saloon. Taking a glass from a liveried footman, the Rye coat of arms emblazoned on his coat, John drank deep, thinking he had earned his reward. Then he saw that Captain Pegram was approaching, a somewhat sheepish expression on his face. Remembering the scene in the campanile, the Apothecary adjusted his features into a mask of inscrutability.

'Mr Rawlings,' said Nathaniel, hopping from one foot to the other in obvious embarrassment.

'Sir.' John bowed civilly.

'I am sorry I had to leave you so abruptly when you called the other day. A pressing engagement.'

The Apothecary adopted a puzzled expression, as if he could not quite recall the incident. 'Now, let me see . . . Ah, yes. We were discussing the merits of Miss Rosalind's portrait at the time, were we not?'

The Captain frowned. 'Yes. I told you then and I tell you now. I drew that picture from my imagination. But, damme, it's none of your damnable business anyway. I can have portraits of whomsoever I like in my own house.'

'As long as they don't lay you open to blackmail,' John answered quietly.

'And what do you mean by that, Sir?'

'Merely that some unscrupulous person, knowing that you possessed such a thing, might threaten to reveal you to the Marquis. My advice to you would be to destroy it,' the Apothecary added, echoing the words he had heard spoken in the campanile.

But who had uttered them? Had the formidable Mrs Tireman, desperate to protect her daughter's honour in view of her forthcoming marriage, resorted to threatening the Captain? Or had Henrietta lied about losing her hat? Had she, perhaps to protect the Marquis rather than her sister, begged him to destroy the picture? Or could the beautiful bride, terrified of losing her great match, have been the woman in the bell tower? Or, John thought, could another female, perhaps a new and jealous mistress, have insisted that Nathaniel get rid of the revealing drawing?

The Apothecary looked round the room. Mrs Gironde, who had

willingly gone to flirt with a total stranger, the Scarecrow, might well be having an adulterous affair. And he supposed, though without much conviction, that even Faith Ffloote could possibly do likewise. The only person he could safely discount, even though John believed he had detected a certain penchant for the Captain in her, was Elizabeth Rose, who had been fast asleep in her cottage at the time. Or had she? Just because she had retired for the night by the time the Apothecary returned from The Salutation didn't actually prove a thing.

'My lords, ladies and gentlemen, supper is served,' intoned a voice, and the Marquis, Rosalind shimmering on his arm, led the way into the dining room where a cold collation had been prepared and a seat had been laid at the enormous table for all those present.

Justin sat at the head with Mrs Tireman on his right and Lady Ffloote on his left, obviously showing his respect to the older ladies. Rosalind meanwhile took her place at the table's foot, flanked by her father and Sir Ambrose. John found himself seated halfway down, Mrs Finch on one side, Henrietta on the other, the Captain of Dragoons beyond her.

John, rather familiarly, leaned across his lady love, bowing his head and extending a hand. 'Sir, may I take the liberty of introducing myself? John Rawlings, an apothecary from London. I was present on the beach tonight. Tell me, what do you think of such a remarkable happening?'

The Captain of Dragoons bowed and shook the offered fingers. 'Grant, Sir. Matthew Grant. A most extraordinary occurrence, I agree.'

'Is it your belief that the French frigate got on to the sandbank accidentally? Or do you think she was signalled in?'

Captain Grant shook his head. 'It seems very unlikely that a crew of experienced sailors would run aground accidentally. I rather think they responded to a signal.'

'But who could possibly give such a thing?'

'An English secret agent trying to trap them, perhaps, or else somebody very foolish.'

'I hadn't considered that,' John replied truthfully. He turned both ideas over in his mind, then asked, 'Who rode to Rye and aroused the Riding Officers?'

'Well, I didn't see the chap personally but I was told that it was a dark, youngish man with a strong accent of some kind.'

Lucius, thought the Apothecary.

'What happened exactly?'

'He went to the Customs House and told them there had been a French landing on the beach at Pett Level. Fortunately they believed him. The Riding Officers called out the Dragoons and we went off in force.'

'And the man?'

'Went without giving his name.'

Henrietta joined in. 'What an odd thing to do.'

'It wouldn't surprise me at all if he didn't have something to hide,' answered Captain Grant, gazing at her in what John could only think of as an extremely forward manner.

'What do you mean, Sir?'

'That he was an English secret agent wishing to remain anonymous.'

'How very exciting!' Henrietta answered, clasping her hands together.

The Apothecary sat in silence, thinking that the Captain was probably right, that no honest citizen would vanish into the night having delivered a message of such great importance. And this train of ideas reminded him of the French master spy supposedly in their midst, and the extraordinary appearance of Louis de Vignolles in Hastings. Making a decision that after a few hours' sleep he would return there to try and seek out the Comte, the Apothecary concentrated instead on preventing the dashing Captain of Dragoons from monopolising the entire conversation, to say nothing of Miss Henrietta Tireman and her beautiful eyes.

The party did not break up until long after dawn, indeed the younger, more resilient people stayed on and had breakfast, somewhat to the annoyance of the exquisite Rosalind, John thought. Her beauty looked as fresh and flawless after a night without sleep as it did at any other time but there was a kind of irritation about her, as if she could no longer be bothered to entertain those members of the lower orders who were filling her intended bridegroom's house. Like many who had risen higher that the social strata in which they had been born, the younger Miss Tireman had developed into an arrant little snob.

Finally, though, the guests congregated in the half moon of the carriage sweep, waiting while the conveyances were brought round from the stables. And it was just at that moment, as he was preparing to mount the high step into the trap, that John saw a familiar figure making its way up the drive on horseback.

'Good morning, Lord Rye,' called a cheery voice.

'Good morning,' the Marquis called back, raising his eyebrows in surprise.

The figure drew closer and dismounted, leaving his easel and paints attached to the saddlebag. Then he bowed.

'I'm a painter, my Lord. In the area to execute whatever commissions I am given. I thought you might like a picture of your house . . .'

Then he stopped dead as Rosalind stepped forward and took her betrothed by the hand.

'. . . or of this beautiful woman, here. Great God in the dawning, but isn't she perfection.'

'Lucius,' said John, aware that the Marquis was starting to frown.

The Irishman's head swivelled. 'Holy Mary, but if it isn't yourself.' He gazed round the group, all of whom stood staring at him as if he were a freak at a fair. 'Lucius Delahunty, ladies and gentlemen, artist to the gentry and nobility. Well, Sirs, which of yous would like your portrait painted?'

'I think, Mr Delahunty,' said Justin, regaining his humour, 'that you should leave these good people alone for the moment. They have endured rather a long and difficult night. But if you would be so kind as to step inside, I most certainly would like to see some samples of your work.'

'Gladly, my Lord,' Lucius answered promptly. He bowed low. 'What the devil have you been up to?' he whispered to the Apothecary as he straightened up.

'I think perhaps you know,' John muttered back.

An angelic expression of innocence crossed the Irishman's face. 'Now how, my friend,' he answered with a broad wink, 'could I possibly do that?'

So saying and with another sweeping bow and a wave to the assembled onlookers, Lucius Delahunty followed the Marquis and Rosalind into the gracious confines of Ravenhurst Park.

Chapter Twenty-Two

All John could think of was going to bed for a few hours and sleeping off the effects of such a remarkable night, but this was not to be. Just as Richard Hayman dropped him at the door of Petronilla's Platt, the post boy came trotting down the empty street, handing the Apothecary a letter bearing the seal of the Public Office in Bow Street. John broke it, unrolled the paper on which the letter was written, and surveyed the contents.

> Sir,
>   I write to You on a Matter of some Urgency and under the Instruction of the King's Decipherer. That Learned Gentleman requests Your Presence in London as soon as it is Convenient for You to Travel. In the Profound Hope that You will be Able to Comply,
>   I remain, Sir, Your Obedient Servant,
>   J. Fielding

'Oh no!' John groaned aloud.

But there was no escaping the fact. He had been summoned and that was that. Feeling decidedly the worse for wear, John quietly let himself into the house only to find that Agnes was bustling and banging about, singing very loudly as she did so.

'Agnes!' he remonstrated.

She jumped. 'Oh, Sir, you startled me. Don't worry, the mistress *is* awake. I've just taken her a mess of eggs and a cup of chocolate.'

The Apothecary thought it sounded an unappetising combination but gave the simple soul a grateful smile none the less. 'That was very thoughtful. Perhaps you might enquire if I could see her before I go.'

Agnes's plain face fell. 'Are you off again, Sir?'

John sighed. 'Yes, alas.'

'When are you leaving?'

233

'In the next thirty minutes or so. There's a post chaise departing from Hastings at noon but I want to get there early and have a look round.'

And see if there's any sign of Louis de Vignolles, he thought.

'I'll tell Mrs Rose, Sir.'

In her days as a great actress, the former Mrs Egleton had no doubt received many an admirer déshabillé, but now she pulled a shawl round her shoulders as John went into her bedroom.

'Well,' he said, without preface, 'I've found the poisoner.'

She sat erect, biting her lip with sudden strain. 'Who was it? Not Cap—?'

'No, not Captain Pegram. He may be up to all sorts of things but poisoning is not one of them.'

'Then who—?'

John shook his head. 'Not who, my dear, but *what*.'

Mrs Rose looked thoroughly perplexed. 'Could you explain that?'

'The poison was contained in the Elixir of Youth, Mrs Gironde's special brew. She's no apothecary and was using an ingredient dangerous to human life. So, Elizabeth, every time you tried to make yourself look younger you succeeded instead in making yourself ill. Anyway, I think all's well that ends well. Silly Nan is by now thoroughly nervous and is sworn to retrieve all existing bottles and make no more. I think I'll have to do the ladies of Winchelsea a service and bring them some of my wrinkle cream, a perfectly harmless substance that might even work.'

Elizabeth frowned. 'Then who left those gifts on my doorstep?'

'Probably people who genuinely wanted to help you, Nathaniel Pegram for one. It was all a terrible coincidence.'

'Then I fetched you down from London for nothing.'

'On the contrary. Had I not come the Scarecrow might still be keeping his lonely vigil and the activities of the Frog and the Moth would have continued unchecked.'

'Are you any nearer knowing who they are?'

'I have a notion about one of them but the other remains as big a mystery as ever.'

'Are you going to tell me who it is?' Elizabeth asked, her eyes brightening.

'No,' John answered firmly. 'I most certainly am not.'

*   *   *

One hour later he was in Hastings, alighting at The Swan, the coaching inn at which he would pick up his conveyance to town. Having time to spare, the Apothecary strode into the parlour in which he had first seen Louis, only to find that it was almost empty, only a few travellers sitting there, waiting to journey on as he was. Having ordered a drink, John sat down to consume it and also to think.

Despite the fact that he was completely exhausted, his brain seemed to be working sharply. If Louis were staying in Hastings, John considered, and knew that he had been recognised, the chances were high that he would have moved on to another hostelry in order to escape further attention. And an enquiry from the serving girl confirmed that there were two other large coaching inns, serving differing destinations, in the town.

'I should try The Maiden's Head and The Lamb and Flag, if I was you,' she said, giving John an impudent look.

'Thank you,' he answered, tipping her, then went on his way, having left his bag in the girl's care.

The Lamb and Flag was indeed large and splendid, and also full of a great many noisy children, all of whom seemed to be travelling to Deal. Making a mental note never to go there, the Apothecary proceeded on, only to discover that The Maiden's Head was situated a fair distance from the town, overlooking the sea. By now he felt utterly exhausted and was glad to go into the travellers' parlour and take a seat.

One thing he had not been prepared for was the fact that the Comte was sitting on a settle directly opposite him, reading a newspaper. Collecting himself, John took a mouthful of brandy, then said in a quiet voice, 'Don't run away Louis, please. I haven't come here to harm you in any way. I just want to find out what is going on. Serafina believes that you are having an affaire. Is that true?'

The Comte de Vignolles's hands trembled slightly as he lowered the newspaper and looked to see who was addressing him. Then he scowled.

'John, damn you! Why are you such an interfering busybody? I could hardly believe it when you came into The Swan the other night. You, of all people, in Serafina's thrall as you once were.'

'What difference does that make?'

'Only the fact that for her sake you'd worry the matter like a dog a bone. Anyone else might have accepted the fact that I was visiting the sea for a few days. But not you, my friend. Not you.'

'In that case, why not tell me what you *are* doing here? I shall not breathe a word, not to your wife or anyone else, I can assure you of that.'

Louis's scowl deepened. 'It's not another woman, that much I will swear to.'

'No, I never thought it was.' John leaned forward. 'Shall I tell you what I believe?'

'Please do.'

'I think you're engaged on work concerning the national security of the country to which you owe allegiance.'

The Comte gaped and the Apothecary knew that he had gone to the heart of the matter. 'You cunning little bastard,' Louis gasped.

John looked grim. 'My friend, I beg you to cease this folly. The authorities know all about you. It will only be a matter of time before they come to arrest you.'

De Vignolles stared uncomprehendingly.

'Listen, they could hang me for a traitor for telling you this, but I heard it from Mr Fielding himself. Louis, for the love of God, stop now, or you leave me no alternative but to inform.'

The Comte's gaze constricted. 'What exactly did the Blind Beak say to you?'

'That there is a known French spy, someone acceptable to London society, working in our very midst, and that he has been doing so for some while.'

De Vignolles's dark eyes suddenly glinted. 'And you say they have no idea who the man is?'

'It is only a matter of time before they find out. Oh, Louis, I'm begging you. For the sake of Serafina and your child, stop now, before it is too late.'

'And if I do, you would agree not to betray me?'

'It may be treacherous but you and I have known each other a very long time.'

Louis suddenly burst out laughing and, leaning across, ruffled John's hair with his hand. 'What a peculiar creature you are! Listen, you clever little apothecary, you've worked it out but come to the wrong conclusion. I'm on your side. I was approached by the Secretary of State – Serafina has gambled with him in the past

236

– and asked if I would help track down the French spy of whom you've just spoken. Naturally, I had to give a Bible oath of secrecy, which I have just broken in order to tell you this.' The Comte de Vignolles crossed himself.

John stared, then drank his brandy in a gulp. 'You are . . .' He lowered his voice. 'You are a secret agent on the *British* side?'

'Of course I am. I was born here, remember. I adore visiting France, but I owe it no fidelity whatsoever.'

'So how can we reassure your wife that you are not keeping a mistress somewhere?'

'You did not swear a pledge, did you?' asked Louis, still laughing.

'No.'

'Then I thought the answer would have been obvious.'

The Apothecary recovered his equilibrium. 'But why are you here? In Hastings?'

The Comte inclined forward. 'Because he's in this area,' he whispered.

'How do you know?'

'Signals are going out from the hill above the town. Once I nearly caught the fellow in action but he just managed to elude me.'

'Someone is signalling from Winchelsea as well, using a most extraordinary code. So extraordinary, indeed, that a French frigate ran aground the other night.'

'Perhaps the signaller is a British agent in disguise.'

'Somehow I don't think so,' said John, and grinned.

The next hour passed splendidly, with a great deal of brandy being consumed. In such quantities, in fact, that the Apothecary hired a man with a trap to take him the short distance to The Swan. Then, having booked a place on the post chaise to London and got aboard, he promptly fell asleep, woke to dine, then slept again and did not wake till the carriage's midnight arrival in the city. There, with no hackney coaches to be seen and the hour being late, John booked a room at The White Hart, went to bed and slept till morning, waking much invigorated and ready for the day.

His first call was to Bow Street where Mr Fielding was just preparing to go into court. Having arranged to come back at a later hour, the Apothecary proceeded to Dr Willes's house in Hill Street, only to find that the Bishop was still in Bath and would not be back until evening. This left him with three choices; to go home, to go to his shop, or to see Serafina. And she, being the nearest and also in great need of reassurance, was John's first choice.

Cutting across to Berkeley Square, the Apothecary made his way down Bruton Street, then into Conduit Street, and finally up Great George Street and into Hanover Square, where the de Vignolles resided at number twelve.

It being one of those strange mornings, John rang the bell only to discover that the Comtresse and her daughter were out taking the air. But as he turned to go he saw them coming out of the garden that stood in the centre of the square and hurried across to join them. Each adult taking one of Italia's hands, they walked back and sat on a stone seat beneath a budding tree.

'My dear, this is such a pleasant surprise. I had no idea you were back in town,' Serafina said with a smile, watching as Italia wandered off to play Battledore and Shuttlecock by herself.

'I returned from Hastings late last night. Listen, my friend, I saw Louis there.'

The Comtesse's smile vanished. 'I wondered where he was. Oh, John, he's been missing for a week, making some ridiculous excuse about visiting an aunt. It's all too terrible. My heart is breaking.'

'Then mend it,' said the Apothecary crisply. 'There is no other woman I assure you.'

'Really?' John nodded and Serafina burst into sobs of relief, saying in a muffled voice, 'Then what the devil is he doing?'

The Apothecary wiped her tears with his handkerchief. 'Sweetheart, be calm, for what I am about to tell you is a great secret which you must never divulge.'

She stared at him moistly. 'He's not a spy, is he?'

'Yes, of course he is. But for England not France. He has been sent to Hastings to track down the French master spy who has infiltrated London society.'

'Is that true?'

'Every word, I swear it.'

Serafina flung herself into John's arms, weeping harder than ever. 'Oh Louis, Louis,' she sobbed. 'How could I ever have mistrusted you?'

John felt his patience stretch itself a little thin. 'Come now Serafina, it is pointless wasting your energy on self-recrimination. Better by far to invite me to your home and let me talk over my hunt for the two spies with you. I need your fine brain, I really do.'

As always with a woman of such powerful character, the Comtesse instantly responded, straightening her back and wiping away her remaining tears.

'Of course, I will do all that I can to help. If Louis is contributing his all, then so must I. Come Italia, we are going indoors now. Your nursemaid will bring you out later.'

So saying, the three of them crossed the road and entered number twelve. John making his way to the spacious upstairs drawing room while Serafina saw to her child. He was staring out of the window at the gardens when the Comtesse came back in, and turned to smile at her.

'Did you know you are still beautiful, even when you weep?'

'No, I did not. You are an idle flatterer,' Serafina answered severely. 'Now, how may I help you?'

'If I describe all the people who could possibly be the Frog and the Moth, will you pick them out for me?'

'I don't know that I can do that, but I will certainly try.'

'Very well.' They sat down in opposite chairs and the Comtesse rang the bell for refreshments. 'Do begin,' she said.

'Well, to start with the highest, there is the Marquis of Rye. A strange dark fellow, who has decided to marry beneath him. He was betrothed to his sister's teacher, Henrietta, but fell in love with *her* sister, Rosalind, instead.'

'How very cruel. But why should he spy for France?'

'When he was young he was an inveterate gambler and spend-thrift. He could have signed up with the enemy then in return for money and now be too far enmeshed to get out. And he also has French blood.'

'I see.'

'Then there's Captain Nathaniel Pegram, a most extraordinary chap. He, too, is in love with Rosalind who, by the way, is a ravishing beauty, but whether this passion was ever consummated I am not certain. However, the Captain has probably had a mistress recently because one night I heard him arguing with a woman about a picture he drew of Rosalind in the nude.'

'Did she pose for it?'

'I don't know. He says not.'

'What kind of woman is this Rosalind?'

'Unbelievably vain, and also unbelievably self-seeking. Like an ambitious butterfly.'

239

Serafina pealed with laughter. 'What a wonderful description. Tell me about the rest.'

'Next on the social scale comes Sir Ambrose Ffloote, who likes to be known as the Squire.' And John gave a rather brilliant word portrait of the man, which he rounded off by saying, 'He is so awful that he is almost likeable, if you understand me.'

'I have heard a saying that people grow like their dogs. Does the Squire resemble The Pup?'

'In a way, yes. They both huff and fart about the place.'

Serafina laughed once more. 'His wife is magnificently long-suffering, I take it?'

'Very, but interestingly she let slip that she was out one night when the smugglers were abroad in Winchelsea. I have never had the chance to ask her about it but it certainly means that she does not live as sheltered a life as she likes to make out. It also indicates that she is not as feeble as she would like to pretend.'

The Comtesse nodded. 'I don't like the sound of her at all. Nor of her husband. They seem highly suspicious to me, both of them. As for Rosalind, she is clearly a social climber of the very worst kind. Now tell me about the rest.'

'There are three professional men, the doctor, the rector and Apothecary Gironde.'

'Are they beyond reproach?'

'Most certainly not. Dr Hayman admits quite freely to consorting with smugglers, while the rector is the father of the fair Rosalind, and for a country clergyman manages to keep his family in quite some style.'

'Perhaps the Marquis gives him money to help out.'

'And there again, perhaps not. Do the funds to keep his wife and daughters in the latest fashions come from France I wonder?'

Serafina spread her hands. 'Go on.'

'Mr Gironde is also very odd. He lied to Joe Jago about meeting the Scarecrow but confessed to it quite openly to me. Furthermore, his wife is a bundle of trouble.'

And John told the Comtesse about the poison in the Elixir of Youth, and about Nan Gironde's indiscretion with the French spymaster.

'Did it go to the ultimate?' Serafina asked, wide-eyed.

'Heaven alone knows. The profligate swine seems to have made very free with his pendulum whilst in Winchelsea. He tried to seduce the fattest girl in town in return for meeting her mother.'

'Her mother? Why?'

'Because Mrs Finch is very wealthy and knows everybody. She also delights in young men, or so rumour has it.'

'Might she spy for France in return for a regular supply?'

'Of boys do you mean?' Serafina nodded. 'Indeed she might.'

'They all sound highly dubious to me. Who have you left out?'

'Mrs Finch's other daughters, two of whom are rather young, though extremely forward for their age.'

'And the others?'

'The eldest sister, Sophie. Another large girl longing for attention. And Sarah, whom the Frenchman tried to seduce.'

'They both sound extremely vulnerable and ripe for any kind of adventure, even spying. Is there anybody else?'

'Mrs Tireman, the Rector's wife. She is a *femme formidable*. Very masculine in a way. She had a French mother and is bilingual. How she could have given birth to two such exquisite girls is difficult to imagine.'

'You are referring to Henrietta and Rosalind?'

'Yes, I am.'

'Tell me about the jilted one.'

'She, too, is very beautiful, yet not considered as lovely as her sister, though I prefer her looks,' John answered gallantly.

Serafina stared at him acutely but said nothing.

'She is also something of a mystery. There have been two odd incidents in the churchyard and even though she denies it I still feel she might have been involved in one of them.'

And John described the conversation in the campanile, together with the incident of the argument between the unseen couple, the argument which had ended in a slap and tears.

Serafina sat up very straight. 'And the man said he was prepared to kill?'

'Yes.'

'And the words "our secret" were mentioned?'

'They were.'

'Then those two people are probably the spies,' Serafina said with a flourish, echoing Mr Fielding.

'I'm not so sure,' answered John, as he went over the words again and put them into another context.

241

'Anyway, tell me why you suspect Henrietta.'

'It was to do with her hat – and her perfume.'

'You smelt her perfume. You must have been very close to her,' said Serafina, her fine eyes gleaming.

'I was close enough,' John replied, and smiled at the memory.

Two hours later he had got as far as Bow Street, and was sitting in Mr Fielding's cosy salon on the first floor, having very much the same sort of conversation as the one he had just had with the Comtesse de Vignolles.

'So,' said the Blind Beak. 'You think you know who one of the spies might be?'

'Yes,' answered John, and told him who and why.

'I agree. It is often an apparently inconsequential memory that gives the game away. So there's one identified. But who is the other?'

'I'm still not sure, though I believe the choice is narrowed down to three people.'

The Magistrate nodded, then sat in silence, quite motionless, his old ploy. Finally he said, 'Mr Rawlings, you must bring Dick Jarvis and Winchelsea's *beau monde* together. Though he may not be aware of it, he knows who the other spy is.'

'I think you're right. But how do I do it?'

'Announce that you are leaving the town, then give a party to say farewell. Ask everyone to it and somehow infiltrate Dick.'

'But most of them know him. They are all his customers.'

Mr Fielding rumbled his melodious chuckle. 'People see what they want to see. Let me make a suggestion.'

John listened, his smile growing broader as he did so. 'What an excellent plan. I will do exactly as you say,' he said eventually.

'Splendid,' answered the Magistrate, and raised his voice to call down the stairs. 'Joe, come up, will you? Mr Rawlings is here and I think a toast is in order. Can you bring some champagne and glasses?'

'Certainly, Sir,' came the shouted reply.

A moment later the Clerk appeared, bearing what was required.

'A toast,' announced Mr Fielding. 'To the unmasking of the Frog and the Moth.'

'Indeed,' chorused John and Joe, and clinked their glasses together.

Chapter Twenty-Three

Having dined early with the Blind Beak and his family, John Rawlings made his way back to Hill Street by hackney coach and this time found that the Bishop of Bath and Wells had returned from preaching in Bath Abbey and was once more in his London residence. Working, too, for as John was shown into Dr Willes's beautiful study he saw the master spy seated at his desk with reams of paper spread out in front of him. The Bishop looked up as his visitor came into the room, pushing his spectacles down his nose and peering at John over the top of them.

'Ah, Mr Rawlings,' he said, 'how kind of you to respond to my call. There is much that I would say to you.'

He got up and sat down in a chair by the fire, motioning the Apothecary to do the same.

'Pray take a seat. Let us not stand upon ceremony.' The Bishop cleared his throat. 'Please do not take offence at what I am about to say next.'

'I assure you I won't,' answered John, thoroughly puzzled and wondering what was coming.

'You see, the fact of the matter is that I found the code you brought me last time impossible to decipher. I tried every variation with it but its meaning still remains a mystery. Therefore I am bound to ask, did you copy it down correctly? Is it possible that you could have made a mistake?'

God's life, thought John, instantly doubting himself. 'At the time I believed it to be accurate,' he said cautiously. 'Though like the rest of mankind, I am fallible, of course.'

Dr Willes steepled his fingers. 'To err is human.'

'But,' the Apothecary added, 'there was a second set of signals, given only the other night. I saw those in the presence of a witness. I am absolutely convinced that I put those down properly.'

The Bishop's horse face grew longer. 'Ah,' he said. 'May I see them?'

'Yes, my lord. It was my intention to send them to you in a letter but your summons forestalled me.'

He handed the rather crumpled piece of paper to Dr Willes, who readjusted his spectacles and stared at it intently. There was silence and then the Bishop let out a quiet sigh.

'Another piece of nonsense?' asked John tentatively.

'Not quite so bad, indeed good sense all but for the last word. Listen to this. Frigate Approach Coast Dance.'

John stared askance. 'Well, that is strange indeed. For a French frigate ran aground on a sandbank at Pett Level the night those signals were flashed. Are we dealing with someone so cunning that he is luring the enemy into danger?'

The Bishop echoed the words of Captain Grant. 'Or someone so silly that he had not properly learned the cipher?'

'What do you mean, my lord? Don't secret agents carry the ciphers on them?'

Dr Willes let out a neighing laugh. 'Bless you, no. It would be far too dangerous. The code might so easily fall into enemy hands should they be apprehended. No, the rule for French and English spies alike, and for any other nationality come to that, is to learn the ciphers by heart.'

'Isn't that rather difficult?'

'It takes a very clever mind.' The Bishop hesitated. 'My son, are you prepared to take an oath of secrecy?'

'Yes, my lord, I am.'

'Then I am going to take the unusual step of showing you some of the ciphers. Then you will see their complexity for yourself.'

So saying, Dr Willes went to a panel in one of that lovely room's curving walls and pressed a hidden switch which slid back to reveal a shelved cupboard. From one of the shelves, the Bishop took a sturdy iron box with a magnificent lock. Taking a key from his watch chain, Dr Willes undid it and John's astonished stare took in a mass of parchments.

'Now you must swear on the Bible that you will tell no one what you see tonight, and that includes even Mr John Fielding himself.'

Saying this, the Bishop snatched an important looking, red-bound copy of the scriptures from his desk and in a voice sufficiently solemn to quell a restive congregation in Bath Abbey, swore John to secrecy. Then he unrolled the parchments and let the Apothecary look. He gazed astonished. Under the heading *Cipher – 1757* was written alphabetically practically every word in the English language, together with alternative endings, to say nothing of the names of all the countries in Europe complete with their heads of state and other important personages. Beside each word was a number code, showing how it could be transmitted or written by figures alone. It was the most comprehensive thing John had ever seen and even he, used to study as he was, blanched at the thought of having to learn it all.

'Why is it in English if this is the French cipher?' he asked over his shoulder.

'Because, in company with most lazy Englishmen, the majority of secret agents employed by France cannot speak French.'

'How typical!'

Putting the parchment on the desk and drawing it close, the Apothecary looked up 'frigate' and saw 1027. Running his finger down the column, he came to 'approach', which was 1991. Close to it, however, lay the word 'apprise'. Suddenly ceased by an idea, John looked up 'dance', 1695, then saw that the word 'danger' was not far away.

'My Lord,' he said excitedly, 'is it possible that this inept spy of ours was trying to say "Frigate Apprise Coast Danger"?'

The Bishop leant over his shoulder. 'Um. Yes, it might be so. If he'd half learned what he was supposed to know by heart there could be a strong possibility that he's been sending out the wrong messages.'

John grinned. 'Perhaps we should let him go on. He's doing so much good for our side.'

'Do you know who it is?' asked Dr Willies sharply.

'I think I do, but one can never be certain until the challenge is made.'

'And you are going to do that?'

'Yes.'

'Then be careful. He or she will probably be armed.'

'I'll choose my moment, I promise you.'

The Bishop said unexpectedly, 'You are a very bright young man, Mr Rawlings. It really has been a pleasure to know you.' He made a small stiff bow whilst still maintaining his dignity.

'The delight has been entirely mine, my lord,' the Apothecary answered, and went away still pondering the unlikely fact that

one of God's most highly annointed should also have felt himself called into that most clandestine of posts, the King's Secret
Decipherer.

Paying only the briefest of visits to his shop and Sir Gabriel, John
risked the exhaustion that comes with too much travelling and
journeyed back to Hastings that very night, taking a fast chaise
that only stopped to change horses and to allow its passengers
to relieve themselves, which they had to do at the roadside,
including the ladies. Fortunately, the Apothecary's travelling companions were both male and, like him, slept most of the way, so
any embarrassment caused by matters of delicacy simply did not
occur. Arriving in Hastings in the early light, John immediately
hired a man and trap and thus appeared at Petronilla's Platt,
unshaven and bleary eyed, just as Elizabeth Rose was finishing
her breakfast.

She looked startled. 'My dear John, I hadn't expected to see you
back so soon.'

'It really was just a flying visit. Yet much good has come
out of it.'

'Did you see Mr Fielding?'

'I certainly did. Which reminds me. I am thinking of giving an
assembly to return various amounts of hospitality I have received
here in Winchelsea.'

Mrs Rose looked slightly surprised. 'Why? Are you going to
leave us?'

'Soon, yes.'

'But what about the Frog and the Moth?'

'I hope to conclude my business with them fairly swiftly.'

Elizabeth's arched eyebrows rose. 'I did not know you had made
such rapid strides.'

'I haven't, not completely that is.'

'Anway,' the former actress replied, 'you can't go just yet. You
have received an invitation to the Marquis's wedding.'

'Have I? How suprising.'

'Not at all. He added your name to mine believing you to be my
nephew. Will you come?'

'I most certainly will. So in that case, time clearly being of the
essence, I had better proceed with arranging my soirée.'

Mrs Rose looked about her doubtfully. 'I think Petronilla's

Platt might prove somewhat small if you want to have several guests.'

'I shall hire the saloon in the Town Hall,' the Apothecary answered grandly. 'And the services of a chef to prepare the collation.'

'La, la,' answered Elizabeth, laughing. 'And will you be inviting all the young ladies of the town?'

'Of course I shall,' John answered, and suddenly realised how hard it would be to leave Winchelsea while Henrietta Tireman still lived there.

The sound of Lucius Delahunty's voice was audible in the street outside The Salutation. 'Let every man's glass be filled,' he was bellowing. 'I've got a splendid commission, not only to paint Lord Rye's home but also his lovely bride.' There was a cheer and a somewhat obscene drunken shout.

'That'll be enough of that,' Lucius continued. 'I'll propose her health, so I will. Gentlemen, I ask you to raise your glasses to that great beauty, Miss Rosalind Tireman.'

The same drunken voice called out, 'One guinea, that's what I'd pay, just to spend one hour in her bed.' At which an affray broke out, John could hear it distinctly, together with Lucius shouting, 'A mill, by God! How I love a good mill!' Hurrying into the taproom, the Apothecary saw Captain Pegram down on the floor, punching the guts out of a farm labourer, while Lucius was swinging his fists at someone else.

'Captain, please,' shouted John, attempting to drag the struggling Nathaniel from his adversary. 'Let me be,' the military man answered brokenly, and the Apothecary saw to his dismay that the Captain was fighting drunk.

'Great God at nightfall,' the Irishman roared at John, 'it's yourself. Now what a moment to come into a hostelry. Do you have a sense for a mill?'

'I have a sense that these two will kill each other if we don't stop them,' John answered implacably. 'Give me a hand, will you.'

Lucius promptly stopped punching what appeared to be a perfectly innocent bystander and flung himself bodily on to the Captain, who groaned as all the air was knocked from him.

'Carry him outside. Now,' John ordered, and between them the two men picked Captain Pegram up by his wrists and ankles and hoisted him into the cold afternoon air.

'Would you look at that,' Lucius said, fingering his jaw and laughing. 'Anyone would think the poor bastard's in love with the girl.'

'He is,' John answered shortly.

'Well, may the Lord be praised. I didn't know that.'

'Neither do I, for sure,' the Apothecary said with a rueful grin. 'But I'm just about to find out. You go back inside. I'll get him home.'

'His carriage is round in the yard. I requested all the gentlemen of town to celebrate my recent success, and you would have been top of the list, old friend, had I but known that you were returned from London.'

'Thanks for the invitation. I'll join you later,' John answered, turning to the Captain who was now being violently sick beneath a tree.

'Come on, Sir,' he called. 'I'll take you home. I don't want you getting into any more scrapes.'

'I won't have her insulted,' Nathaniel answered thickly, wiping his mouth.

'You made that obvious,' John answered mordantly. 'Now, sit down on that stump a moment while I go and get your carriage.'

Five minutes later they were on their way. Between them, the Captain's coachman and the Apothecary had managed to heave Nathaniel into his, leaving the window open in case of accidents.

'I've never seen him so bad,' said the driver, shaking his head and clucking his tongue.

John decided to take the most tremendous chance. 'Ah well,' he said with a sigh, 'Miss Rosalind's wedding is only a few weeks away now.'

The coachman shot him a penetrating glance. 'I didn't know he'd told anyone.'

'I'm a medical man,' the Apothecary answered, as if that explained everything.

'But even doctors can't mend broken hearts,' the driver answered pithily, then climbed on to his box and cracked his whip.

Captain Pegram had reached the weeping stage and by now had started to sob in earnest. 'I can't help myself,' he moaned, more to himself than to his fellow passenger. 'I still love her, God help me. I would kill for her, you know.'

'I don't think that will be necessary,' John answered crisply. 'It seems to me that Miss Tireman has a very rosy future ahead of her.'

The Captain ignored him and continued his monologue. 'She was still a child when I fell in love with her. Only fifteen years old and as beautiful as if she'd just stepped out of a morning rose. Of course, I acted like a man of honour. Nothing took place between us until . . .'

'Yes?' said John, agog.

'Until . . .' Captain Pegram's head fell forward and he let out a mighty snore.

''Zounds and 'zounters!' the Apothecary exclaimed angrily, certain that he had been on the brink of an important revelation. 'Until when, man?'

But Nathaniel had lost consciousness, deep down in a drunken sleep from which it appeared he would not be surfacing for several hours.

'Damnation!' John swore, realising only too well that he might never have such an opportunity to talk freely with Captain Pegram again.

The party, which had obviously been in full swing for several hours, was just beginning to show signs of flagging when he returned to The Salutation. Several people had gone and only Lucius, together with Marcel Gironde and Sir Ambrose Ffloote sat together on a settle, still quaffing ale.

'John,' called the Irishman delightedly, as the Apothecary walked into the taproom. 'Come and join us.' His wild blue eyes were blazing and his grin was huge, but he seemed very far from tipsy. Like so many men of his nation, Lucius was clearly well able to hold his drink.

'Gladly,' said John, bowing to the two others before taking his seat.

'How is the Captain?' the Irishman continued.

'Unconscious. His servants carried him indoors and his valet was about to undress him when I left.'

Lucius winked a marvellous eye. 'Oh, the troubles we inflict on ourselves, eh? Women and all.'

'Women and all,' John echoed with feeling.

The Irishman banged his tankard down on the table. 'I'm tired of all this ale. Let's move on to some decent wine.'

Marcel shook his head, standing up, his words slurring very slightly. 'Thank you, no. I must return to my beloved wife. There is much to be done this day and the dinner hour approaches,' he added enigmatically.

The Squire, however, remained where he was. 'No point in my going. Faith has got one of her migraines again and won't eat a thing.'

'Well, I'm dining here,' Lucius announced. 'Why don't you two good people join me?'

The generosity was typical of him but John said, 'Provided we all pay our own way, that sounds a very good suggestion.'

'Hear, hear,' chortled Sir Ambrose, clearly delighted to be able to extend this enjoyable social occasion.

'I'll accede to your wishes if it's the only way of keeping your company,' Lucius answered cheerfully, and the three of them made their way into the dining parlour.

Three hours later they were still at table, the Irishman and Sir Ambrose having consumed a great deal of wine and port. John, though, had drunk little, having such a feeling about him that his time in Winchelsea was drawing to its conclusion, and that he must bring the signalling spy to book within the next day or two, or risk losing him or her for ever. With this idea uppermost in his mind, the Apothecary planned to take the horse, Strawberry, out as soon as it was dark and scour the clifftops, riding as far as Hastings if need be in pursuit of whoever had lured the French frigate on to the sandbank.

'You're not drinking much,' Lucius commented, observing closely but at the same time pouring himself a large glass of Old Tawny.

'I want to keep a clear head tonight,' John answered.

'Why?' asked Sir Ambrose, rolling a tiny eye.

'Paperwork,' the Apothecary answered vaguely.

'No point,' the Squire stated baldly. 'Life's too short. Eat, drink and be merry, that's my motto.'

'I agree with you but on this occasion I intend to be abstemious.'

'As you wish.' Sir Ambrose refilled his glass, muttering under his breath.

John presumed that the inaudible words were bound to be imprecations against those lily-livered enough not to get blind drunk at six o'clock on a late March afternoon, and thought what an old fool the man was. But the Squire surprised him.

'Ought to be getting back,' he said, downing his port in one. 'I've been away in Rye since I last saw you, Rawlings, and The Pup will have missed me. Care to walk with me?'

'I certainly would.'

'Weaklings,' said Lucius, with a cheery wave. 'I'll have to finish the bottle m'self.'

'I'm sure you'll manage,' John answered, and gave the Irishman a conspiratorial wink before following Sir Ambrose out of the dining room.

Outside, it was a cold evening and the two men walked briskly towards Paradise House.

'Not going home yet?' the Squire asked, surprised.

'No, I thought I'd hire a horse from Truncheons and go for a ride. I need a bit of exercise after so much travelling.'

'Care to come in for a minute? I know Faith would like to see you, if she's up, that is.'

'Just for a moment,' John answered, The Pup holding a fearful fascination for him.

The dog was asleep, however, and did not stir as they went into the living room, where it lay sprawled before the fire.

'Always misses me terribly,' Sir Ambrose whispered. 'Lives for me, does that animal. Puppy, Puppy,' he called. 'Papa is home.'

The Pup slowly opened a rheum-laden eye, licked its festering chops, farted, and went straight back to sleep.

'Papa's home,' the Squire bellowed again, applying the boot. 'Get up, damn you.'

Most half-heartedly, The Pup staggered to its feet, wagged a feeble tail, then crashed to the floor again and closed its eyes.

'Out of sorts,' Sir Ambrose said morosely.

'Yes,' answered John, hardly able to control his mirth.

'Well, Faith ain't around. Want a brandy, Rawlings? Keep out the cold.'

'No, thank you, Sir Ambrose. I'd better get on with my ride or I can see myself deciding against being so foolhardy.'

'Planning to go far?' the Squire asked, reaching for the decanter.

251

'Just to Rye and back. Nothing too ambitious.'

'Very wise. Goodnight, young man. I'll think of you as I warm my feet.'

From Paradise House to the livery stables was just a few yards, and John set off to hire the mild-mannered Strawberry from its somewhat surprised owner.

'Riding tonight, Sir? There's a rough wind.'

'Just getting a bit of activity after sitting in a chaise too long. I'll bring her back in a couple of hours.'

'Very good, Mr Rawlings.'

It was a fool's errand, John thought, as he set off. The signalling spy might well remain within doors tonight. On the other hand his French masters could easily be trying to reach him after the fiasco of the grounded frigate, now impounded by the British navy and therefore lost to the war effort. Quite deliberately, John turned not to Rye but in the other direction, and cantered along towards Pett Level and Fairlight, his cloak billowing out behind him in the chill March wind.

He had not gone far when he heard other hooves at his back, though whether deliberately following or just coincidentally there he could not know. Taking no chances, John led the mare into a rough wooden shelter, for shepherds he supposed, and stood there quietly, peering out. A horseman went by, wearing neither hat nor wig, his hair flying out in a dark streak behind him. A few minutes later there followed another, this one with a tricorne pulled well down. With a familiar pricking of his thumbs John led Strawberry from their hiding place and went in pursuit at a quiet trot.

And then from out at sea, quite a fair way out, the Apothecary noticed, came a series of flashes: 54 902 659, he saw. Instantly John's visual memory recalled the pages of parchment that Dr Willes had shown him. Surely 54 had been 'come' and 902 'in'? But what was 659? John frowned and creased his brow with effort and then it came to him. It stood for one of those words with multiple endings and could mean from, frost – or frog! That was it then: 'Come in, Frog.' The French wanted to have words with the secret agent who had clumsily lost one of their ships for them!

John dismounted and led his horse by the reins so that the noise of his approach would be minimal. But even as he advanced, a spout lantern began to flash from only a few hundred yards away.

252

John counted nine flickers and then the light abruptly and rather shockingly went out.

'You bloody old fool,' said a low voice in French. 'What the devil do you think you're playing at?'

'Don't understand your lingo,' came the reply.

The voice spoke again, this time in English. 'I'll give you lingo,' it said.

Cocking his pistol, John stepped out of the darkness. 'Sir Ambrose Ffloote,' he said. 'I am arresting you on behalf of the Public Office, Bow Street, on a charge of high treason, and possibly murder.'

'Christ!' exclaimed the Frenchman and was on to his horse and off into the night before the Apothecary had so much as a chance to look at his face.

The Squire stared at John, frozen to the spot. Then he, too, leaped into his saddle with an agility born from years of riding to hounds. 'Damn you!' he shouted. 'Damn you, John Rawlings! Spying, maybe. But murder – never!' And, raising his pistol, he took careful and deliberate aim.

Chapter Twenty-Four

There could be little doubt that the people John had hired to decorate the smaller of the two Saloons in the Town Hall had done a splendid job. Early spring flowers and greenery had been brought in and arranged in a rather wild abandoned manner, giving the air of a country ball. Candles shone everywhere, there were red hangings at the window, and the floor gleamed with beeswax. Food of the most delicious kind – succulent meats, tempting salads, crystal syllabubs and swaying jellies – was set on a table in an alcove, and there was a warming punch to combat the effects of the chilly March night.

John, finely dressed in cinnamon satin, a dark green waistcoat embroidered with violets and heartsease, all picked out in silver, looked fit to grace a London ballroom, as did Elizabeth Rose, in a new gown of lilac lutestring with pearl decorations. Awaiting their guests, they toasted one another as they took a drink to keep out the cold.

'To your coming back to us, safe and sound,' said Mrs Rose.

'To your gracious hospitality,' John replied. 'And to still being here.'

He had saved himself from the Squire's bullet, well aimed though it had been, by throwing himself flat on the ground, and in so doing had lost his quarry. Sir Ambrose had ridden off with a start of two minutes or so, and though John might have caught him up on the dark horse, on gentle Strawberry he stood no chance. The silliest spy of all had vanished into the night and, presumably, across the Channel in a fishing boat, for neither hide nor hair had been seen of him since.

In a way the Apothecary had been glad. Archetypal country squire though Sir Ambrose was, there had still been something likeable about the man, unfunny jokes and xenophobic attitudes into the bargain. But, of course, he had not been xenophobic at all. In fact, despite being too dense to learn the cipher, he had been quite clever. For who would have suspected him, of all people, of being a French sympathiser?

255

Picking up John's train of thought, Elizabeth said, 'I wonder if poor little Faith will put in an appearance.'

'I think she well might,' John answered. 'I suspect her of being far more lively when Sir Ambrose is not around.'

'Then let us hope he will never return.'

'If he does he faces the rope. They hang traitors.'

Elizabeth shivered. 'Just like they hanged Jasper Harcross.'

Wishing he had not said what he had, a call from the doorway came as a great relief to the Apothecary, instantly lightening the mood.

'John, my friend, how are you?' said a voice with a delightful French accent. 'How very kind of you to invite us from London. May I present my young cousin, Olivier?'

'Of course,' answered the Apothecary, bowing, then warmly embraced the couple who were entering. 'Serafina, Louis, how wonderful to see you.' He turned to the person with them and bowed once more. 'My dear Sir, I am delighted to meet you.'

'And I, Sir, and I,' answered Dick Jarvis, and gave a salutation fit for a prince.

His hair had been cut short so that a fashionable white wig with rolled curls over the ears sat easily upon his head. Dick had also been shaved so that not a whisker dared be seen upon his handsome countenance. Dressed in a black and crimson suit fashioned in the very latest mode, the smuggler's bastard looked every inch a gentleman of quality and knew it.

Amused, the Apothecary said, 'I always reckoned that your father had seen to it you received a good education.'

To which Dick surprisingly replied, 'My mother came from good stock, Mr Rawlings. Sir Percy Bellingham of Goudhurst was her brother.'

'Well, well. Kit Jarvis moved in exalted circles indeed.'

Dick smiled. 'He lived and loved recklessly, and sowed his seed the same.' He became serious. 'But let us not speak of him. For this evening I am Olivier de Vignolles, cousin of the Comte and his delightful Comtesse. Now remind me again, what is it I am to do?'

'You are to act the part so convincingly that even your regular customers will merely think that you bear a startling resemblance to Dick the smuggler and nothing further.'

'And then?'

'I want you to identify the woman who removed Captain Pegram's visiting card from the Scarecrow's pocket. Then it will be up to me to decide whether she did so in order to protect herself or the Captain, or perhaps even a third party.'

Dick nodded. 'But you want nothing made public at this stage?'

'Nothing at all.' John lowered his voice to a whisper even though Serafina and Louis were deep in conversation with Elizabeth. 'Have you heard about the Squire's disappearance?'

'Oh, yes, even though you said nothing my wild boys knew all about it next day. Anyway, he's skipped. Guineas changed hands and Little Harry took him across to France.'

The Apothecary smiled cynically. 'What price patriotism now?'

Dick grinned disarmingly. 'I told you Little Harry had no scruples. This proves it.'

There was the sound of feet on the stairs and John raised a finger to his lips. 'A great pleasure to meet you, Sir,' he said loudly, then turned to greet the new arrivals.

Mrs Finch and her girls, large in white satin, had come in a body, and were looking decidedly more cheerful, all of them, having set their eyes on the supposed Olivier. There was a great deal of saluting and bowing and low curtseys were dropped, from which Miss Sarah in particular had difficulty in rising. To add to the authenticity of his role, Dick had adopted a French accent, and helped her up with a great many Gallic exclamations. The musicians, three of them, that being the total sum John could afford to hire, struck up a merry air and the atmosphere became extremely festive.

Supported on either side by the Girondes, Faith Ffloote came into the saloon sniffing at a bottle of salts. Yet there was a liveliness in her eye that John had not seen before and which spoke volumes about her state of mind. He bowed and kissed her hand.

'It was good of you to come, Lady Ffloote. Your husband's sudden departure must have been a terrible shock.'

'He eloped, Mr Rawlings, let's not mince words. I always thought he had a fancy piece in Rye. And now I have been proved right.'

John nodded, having told no one other than Elizabeth – and Mr Fielding by letter – the true reason for Sir Ambrose's abrupt departure. In that way poor Faith could continue to hold up her head in society, for other than the Frenchman present that night, whoever he might have been, there had been not one witness to what had actually taken place.

257

'If that is the case then you are better without him, Madam,' the Apothecary answered seriously, and Lady Ffloote bowed her head in agreement.

A roar of laughter came from below and Lucius Delahunty, hair tied back in a bow and looking immensely smart in emerald green, bounded into the room accompanied by Richard Hayman. The Irishman bowed to the assembled company, then saw Dick.

'Why, Reverend . . .' he began, his tone startled.

John cut across him. 'Lucius, may I present Olivier de Vignolles. He is the cousin of a very old friend of mine.'

The Irishman's flaming blue eyes looked into his and there was the momentary hint of a wink. 'My dear Sir,' Lucius said promptly, 'it really is an enormous pleasure.'

'Likewise,' Dick answered with dignity.

The Apothecary turned away, then felt his heart beat faster at the sound of Mrs Tireman's booming voice as its owner mounted the stairs with her party. The very thought that Henrietta was about to come into the room was enough to excite and exhilarate him, and John knew that leaving her was going to be almost an impossibility.

With these latest arrivals the company was at full complement, only the puzzling Captain Pegram missing, and the Apothecary made a small speech of welcome in order that everyone could start dancing.

'My Lord, ladies and gentlemen, do not stand on ceremony, I beg you. This assembly is by way of thanking you all for being so kind to me during my stay in Winchelsea. So please let us dance and take refreshment without further ado. Thank you.' At this the guests formed themselves into two sets, each one of an even number, Faith Ffloote wistfully sitting out as she had no partner, and the musicians struck up The Dumps.

'So this is goodbye?' said Henrietta, her eyes suspiciously brilliant.

'No, it isn't,' answered John, as he led her into the centre. 'Whatever happens, whatever lies ahead, I'll come back for you.'

'That sounds rather ominous.'

'Does it? I'm sorry. It's just that I want you to know that though my time in Winchelsea may be up, my time with you is most definitely not. In other words I am on the brink of falling in love with you.'

'Only on the brink?' she said, and laughed, all her old humour suddenly restored.

The dance progressed, and though one or two people shot Dick Jarvis a curious glance no one queried that the graceful young man with the French accent was anyone other than who he said he was.

The conjuror's illusion, thought John. As Mr Fielding had said, people will see what they think they see.

About halfway through the evening, just as most of the guests had taken a seat in order to have supper, Captain Pegram appeared, very pale but perfectly sober. He immediately sought out Mrs Rose and sat with her while they both took refreshments, making her laugh and look young and happy.

I wonder, thought John.

Dick, he noticed, was wandering round the room, meanwhile, chatting to every lady in turn, to each of them pitching the same yarn about owning and breeding horses, then asking their views on the equine species and whether they rode, and if so to what distance. Intrigued, John, in his role as host, went to join him.

'No, I can't pretend I ride at all,' Mrs Finch was saying. 'Of course I did as a gel but nowadays I prefer the comfort of a carriage. Now my daughters are fine horsewomen, every one of 'em. Sophie rides for miles, don't you, Sophie?'

'Yes, Mama,' answered the hapless female.

Looking at the girth of the four young Finches, John could only imagine they must mount Shires, and pitied any other breed that would have to carry them any distance at all.

Good actor that he was, Dick was also smiling rather widely and the Apothecary guessed that he shared the same thought. 'Charming,' the smuggler said, his accent very broad. 'One day you must come and see my stables, dear ladies.'

'Oh, yes,' they chorused, and Mrs Finch made a moue and hid behind her fan.

Mrs Tireman, immensely wigged this night, came to join the group and immediately addressed Dick in French. John's heart sank, not having anticipated anything like this, but either the smuggler's education had been first rate or he had picked up the language during his many years of trading with that country. Whatever the explanation, he answered her fluently, even cracking a joke which made her laugh.

'Damme, but you do remind me of someone,' she said, still in her mother's tongue.

'As you do me, Madam,' Dick countered. 'I believe it must be that famous actress Peg Woffington.'

Mrs Tireman's eyes almost vanished into the depths of her smile. Girlishly, she hit his arm with her closed fan. 'Oh, you flatterer, you.'

'That is who I must remind you of,' Dick continued charmingly, 'the Devil himself.'

The rector's wife laughed all the more.

'Come, Olivier,' said John, 'allow me to present you to the rest of the ladies.' He bowed to Mrs Tireman and Mrs Finch. '*Mesdames*, if you will excuse us.'

Taking Dick by the elbow he propelled him firmly to where Mrs Rose sat, now joined by Faith Ffloote, who had gained colour during the course of the evening and actually appeared to be enjoying herself.

'Lady Ffloote, Mrs Rose, Captain Pegram, may I present to you the cousin of my friend Louis, Olivier de Vignolles.'

Mrs Rose held out her hand for a kiss and said, 'We've already met but I remain charmed.' Lady Ffloote, after peering somewhat suspiciously, suddenly became kittenish and giggled as Dick paid her the same courtesy. Captain Pegram, probably the only person in Winchelsea who did not deal with the smugglers, accepted Dick at face value and gave him a somewhat military bow.

'Olivier breeds hundreds of horses,' said John, elaborating.

'I really must take up riding again,' Faith said with a sigh. 'I used to ride like the wind when I was young but of recent years my health has not been all that it should be. My husband rode well, of course, but he's eloped. Gone off with a dolly-mop from Rye.'

To his credit, Dick's face did not move a muscle. 'Really?' he answered. 'Then more fool him.'

Lady Ffloote was clay in his hands. 'What an amiable young person,' she commented to the room in general. 'You really must call on me.'

'Alas, I return to London tomorrow,' the smuggler answered with a sigh.

'Oh, boo!' said Faith, looking the most human John had ever seen her.

'And now,' the Apothecary put in, 'I would like to introduce you to the Marquis of Rye, who has kindly graced my gathering with his presence.'

'My Lord,' said Dick, bowing till his wig scraped the Marquis's shoe, 'Olivier de Vignolles, at your service.'

Justin smiled indulgently and indicated his beautiful future bride, who adorned his arm charmingly. 'Rosalind, my dear, this is Mr Rawlings' friend's cousin, Olivier de Vignolles.'

'To be in your presence is a gift,' Dick replied with a Gallic roll of his eyes.

She laughed and held out her hand. 'And what do you do, Monsieur?'

'I breed horses on my estates in Warwickshire,' he replied, his fingers waving to indicate enormous acreage. 'Do you ride, at all?'

The Marquis answered for her. 'There is only one finer horsewoman in the county and that is Rosalind's sister, Henrietta.'

'Our mother is also very good,' his betrothed added. 'We all of us take after our French ancestress who was, if legend is to be believed, the greatest equestrienne in Normandy.'

'Do you ride out over the marshlands?' Dick asked.

'Everyone does,' Justin answered. 'Don't they, Mrs Gironde?'

'I've had to learn to do so,' she said tentatively. 'I often carry out my husband's deliveries for him, you see. And if he is using the carriage I have no alternative but to go on horseback when I visit the more remote houses and farms.'

'My wife is a superb rider,' put in her husband, joining the group.

'So it would seem that every lady here has ridden at some time or another,' Dick commented. 'Excellent. All the better for my stud farms.'

'You have more than one?' asked Rosalind.

'Several,' Dick replied exuberantly, and spread his arms wide.

They had gone home, all of them. The musicians had been paid and had left, the chef and his assistants had cleared away the remains of the cold collation. Even Louis and Serafina, John's special guests, had made their way back to The Salutation, leaving only the Apothecary and Dick Jarvis to walk back through the silent streets towards Petronilla's Platt.

'Was she there tonight?' John said. 'The woman who searched the pockets of the Scarecrow?'

261

'Yes,' the smuggler said solemnly.

'And was it . . . ?' He mentioned a name.

Dick looked at John in amazement. 'How did you know?' Then he saw how white his friend had gone in the moonlight. 'This hurts you, doesn't it?' he asked.

'Very much.'

'I am so sorry, but how *did* you know?'

'There were various pointers along the way.'

'All leading to her?'

John sighed very heavily. 'Yes, all leading to her.'

Chapter Twenty-Five

The day of the Marquis of Rye's wedding dawned merry as a marriage bell. March may have come in like a lion but now it had given way to April, with soft breezes taking the place of cutting winds and the air full of the scent of daffodils and sweet spring flowers still in bud.

John, who had been back to London to consult with the Blind Beak, had returned with Joe Jago, now once again resident in The Salutation, and the promise of the Flying Runners, two Brave Fellows ready with a coach to go anywhere in the kingdom at fifteen minutes' notice, should the occasion demand it. Yet even he, heavy with the import of all that must be done, did not get up as early as Elizabeth Rose, formerly both Egleton and Harcross, who rose at daybreak and put on a new gown of ice blue velvet and a hat brimming with flowers, especially made for the occasion. Later, while John was still putting the final touches to his toilette, Captain Pegram came to fetch her in his carriage and escort her to St Thomas's in Winchelsea, where the wedding was to take place, telling her that she looked beautiful and making her smile more than she had done for a long time.

The marriage of the Marquis was a great occasion and the entire county of Sussex had turned out. Not just those gentry folk fortunate enough to be on the list of guests, but also all the people who had worked for Lord Rye or his father and who owed them their livelihood. They came from miles away, pouring into Winchelsea, either on foot or horseback, and waited outside the church in a mood of ever increasing jollity, watching for the great moment when the bride and groom should appear.

The Marquis came first, dressed from head to toe in lavender and pink, his witness, an old friend from school days whom nobody knew, sitting beside him as the Rye coach, rather an old-fashioned affair with the coat of arms emblazoned on the door, drew up at the church and allowed the bridegroom to alight. A great cheer was raised from all his workers who threw rose petals, saved and stored from the year before, along his path into the solemnity of the church.

The guests were arriving in droves by now, and all those people with whom John had become so familiar, hurried into St Thomas's shadowy interior, dressed within an inch of eternity. The Girondes were there, bearing bottles of salts lest anyone should faint; Lady Ffloote made a dignified entrance on the arm of Dr Richard Hayman and brought a small cheer from the onlookers; the Finches, all five of them, overflowing in gowns the various colours of a rainbow, arrived by carriage and made much of alighting and walking into church. Captain Pegram escorted Mrs Rose; John, resplendent in a damson coloured suit with a waistcoat of silver, walked in just behind them; Joe Jago, in sombre black, shadowed his footsteps, then went to sit at the back of the church where anyone, invited or otherwise, was free to sit and observe the proceedings. Last in before the bridal party was that free spirit Lucius Delahunty, who also took his place at the rear, portrait painter to the Marquis but not yet established enough to have an invitation.

Last of all to enter before the bridal party itself came Mrs Tireman, clad from head to foot in puce pink and gold, a hat upon her head fit to turn mortal man to stone should he gaze upon it. Then, as she took her seat in the front pew, a quiet fell over the whole congregation, waiting for that wonderful moment when the bride would enter the church. But even before she came they knew that Rosalind was drawing near. A great huzzah went up from all the retainers standing outside and there was the sound of a group of musicians. The bride was marrying in the old style, with fiddlers, trumpets and all.

Everyone rose and every eye turned to the door. Then there was a great gasp as the golden beauty came into view. Rosalind wore white, with coloured ribbons tied as true lovers knots upon her sleeves, her glorious hair loose about her shoulders, a wreath of fresh flowers on her brow. Beside her walked her father, in full clerical regalia, behind, again in the old tradition, two boys bearing sprigs of rosemary and her sister, Henrietta, clad in tawny, carrying garlands of flowers and leaves.

To a wild peal of bells, Rosalind walked down the aisle to where the Marquis of Rye awaited her, an expression of such adoration on his face that those sentimental members of the crowd wept to see it.

At last she stood beside him at the altar and the Marquis's chaplain, who was to conduct the ceremony that day, began with the familiar old words, 'Dearly beloved, we are gathered here together today in the sight of God . . .' His voice flowed on, a soft, harmonious discourse with no discordant sounds, until at last it came to that most telling moment when a silence fell over the entire church and no one dared so much as cough.

'. . . that if anyone knows of any just cause or impediment why these two may not be joined together in holy matrimony, let him speak now or for ever hold his peace.'

There was the usual hush, during which John's heart sank into his shoe, and then very slowly and deliberately Joe Jago rose from his place at the back.

'I do,' he said, and his voice seemed to ring down the corridors of time.

The chaplain looked thoroughly flustered and goggled at Mr Fielding's clerk, devoid of speech. Eventually, he managed to stutter, 'And what might that be?'

'It is, Sir, that a member of the wedding party is about to be placed under arrest on a charge of high treason and murder.'

The Marquis whirled round, his dark face livid with fury. 'Explain yourself, man.'

Joe Jago cleared his throat. 'I'm sorry, my Lord, I have here' – he tapped his pocket – 'a warrant for the arrest of . . .'

But he got no further. Acutely aware that another figure had risen at the back, John, up to that moment too wretched to stare, turned to gape, as did every other member of the congregation.

'I'll save you the trouble,' drawled Lucius Delahunty, his voice more Irish than it had ever sounded before. 'Rosalind Tireman is a murdering bitch.'

There was a gasp as the import of the words sank into the minds of the listeners, then following on like a wave of the sea came a loud explosion. A scream cut through the petrified silence which ensued and John, along with everybody else, watched in horror as Rosalind, a red patch appearing at the breast of her wedding gown, slumped to her knees before the altar and then fell sideways to the floor.

'So die all traitors and enemies of France,' said Lucius in perfect French, then he ran from the church without looking back.

A spell was broken and as John rose to his feet, torn between helping the wounded and giving chase to her assailant, he saw

265

that Dr Richard Hayman had already leaped several pews and was kneeling beside the bride, tending her where she lay in the Marquis's arms. Without hesitation, he set off in pursuit of Lucius.

The Irishman was just about to mount the fast dark horse from Truncheons but he paused, one foot in the stirrup as John hurled himself the distance between them. He bowed.

'Lucien de la Tour at your service, Sir. Father, French; mother, Irish. The Scarecrow, as you call him, alias Gerard de la Tour, was my cousin and a good man, albeit a little weak with the ladies. He came over to waken the Frog and the Moth, who had signed their allegiance to France in return for money many a year ago. As you now know, the Frog did his poor best. But the Moth, too enraptured with gaining even more money and a title into the bargain, killed my cousin rather than do her forsworn duty. That is why the evil bitch had to die.'

'But Lucius . . .' said John, lost for words.

'Sorry, my friend,' answered the other. 'I really am very fond of you. Great God on a wedding day, I should be killing you but sure as hell I'm not going to do so.' And with that he swung a gloved fist which crunched on to the Apothecary's chin, hard as a flat iron, and the sunshine of that glorious April day turned black.

The mists cleared slowly to reveal two anxious faces peering into his. One, the familiar craggy visage of Mr Fielding's right-hand man, the much-loved Joe Jago. The other, the neat little countenance of Dr Florence Hensey, applying cold compresses and salts as if his professional reputation depended on it.

'Ah, my dear Mr Rawlings,' he said, as John's lids flickered. 'Thank God you are coming back to us. That was a very nasty blow you received at the hands of that ruffian.'

Despite all the horror he had witnessed, to say nothing of an extremely painful jaw, the Apothecary gave a brief crooked smile. 'Lucius Delahunty, what an all-out rogue. What happened to him?'

Joe's light blue eyes twinkled. 'He escaped. The Flying Runners arrived a little too late to apprehend any villains – they lost a wheel in Lamberhurst! – and he was clean out of sight by the time they came.'

'Do you think he will get back to France?'

Joe tapped the side of his nose. 'Did you not tell me that he got on particularly well with the Reverend Tompkins?'

The Apothecary smiled. 'Well, if Dick's somewhat dubious patriotism troubles his conscience I am certain Little Harry will have no such qualms.'

The clerk looked at him quizzically. 'You bear Lucius no grudge, do you?'

'No. He was doing his duty as he saw it and avenging his cousin's murder.'

'Quite so,' said Dr Hensey. 'We must all act as our sense of decency dictates.'

John looked at the doctor properly as the dark shadows finally retreated. 'I didn't realise you were in the church today, Sir.'

'I did not have an invitation, of course, but being in the area I was determined to see the ceremony. However, my patient in Hastings was more querulous than ever and I arrived somewhat late. I stole into the back to watch and found myself sitting almost behind Mr Delahunty.'

'What happened exactly?'

'He simply stood up, drew a gun, and shot the unfortunate Miss Tireman dead.'

The Apothecary went very white. 'So he killed her? I wasn't sure.'

Florence Hensey looked oddly matter-of-fact. 'She died within seconds. He hit her clean through the heart.'

'Just as she stabbed the Scarecrow. A dark revenge indeed.'

Joe broke the mood. 'Most of the wedding guests have gone to Grey Friars where Captain Pegram is acting as host. Just before she departed, Mrs Rose told me to look after you. Can I fetch you anything, Mr Rawlings?'

'Brandy for shock,' suggested the doctor. 'I think I might join you. It has been a most terrible day for us all.'

'It certainly has,' said Joe with feeling.

John collected himself. 'But what of Henrietta? Is she safe? Where did she go?'

The two older men exchanged a glance. 'She is comforting the Marquis,' said Joe quietly, and not so much from the words themselves but in the way that they were said to him, John knew that all between him and the beautiful girl with whom he had so nearly fallen in love, was lost.

Chapter Twenty-Six

One week after the dramatic shooting of a lovely bride standing at the altar, ready to take her vows with the Marquis of Rye, seven people, two of whom had known her and two more who had spent an evening in her company, sat down to dine in the exquisite first-floor salon of Sir Gabriel Kent. Present were the host himself, his son, the Comte and Comtesse de Vignolles, Elizabeth and John Fielding and Joe Jago. Yet this was not an occasion for frivolity and hearty laughter, in fact the conversation was subdued throughout the meal itself. And when it was over, the Blind Beak, who sat at the head of the table while Sir Gabriel occupied the foot, cleared his throat and said, 'I believe the time has come when we must ask you to tell us the whole story, Mr Rawlings.'

The Apothecary nodded. 'As you wish, Sir, though I may ask for Joe's help in the middle.'

'By all means,' said the clerk, his light eyes somewhat sad, knowing how wretched his young friend had been when he had said his final farewell to Miss Tireman.

'Well, as you all know by now,' John began, 'I was summoned to the Romney Marsh by a mysterious woman who begged me to help her. Much intrigued, I arrived in Winchelsea only to discover that the lady was the former Mrs Jasper Harcross, now living under the assumed name of Rose. She declared that someone was making attempts on her life and that the poison was being adminstered by means of gifts of food and wine left on her doorstep. It is apparently quite the custom for the more prosperous to donate anonymous presents for the needy of the parish.'

'A charming idea,' said Serafina, while Elizabeth Fielding chorused, 'How kind.'

'Indeed, yes. Though it presented me with many worries at the time. However, to go back a little, on the journey to Winchelsea, which was diverted through the marshlands because of storms, we passed a remote and tiny church, close to which, quite incongruously, stood a scarecrow. A most realistic one, for it gave me a great sense of fear when first I saw it. Eventually I went to investigate why a scarecrow should be standing in a place with no crops. Then I discovered the skeleton, now at rest in a churchyard in London. Inside his coat was stitched a coded message which, when deciphered, revealed that the dead man was a French spymaster who had come to England to awaken two sleeping spies, the Frog and the Moth.'

Mr Fielding came in. 'It was then that I asked Joe Jago to go to Winchelsea in an official capacity and assist Mr Rawlings in his hunt for the two French agents. For it seemed certain, particularly when we discovered through the Secret Office that no English spy was involved, that one or other of them was also a killer. Joe.'

The clerk took up the tale. 'Posing as an agent of that Office I obtained statements from one and all, realising as I did so that Mr Rawlings's task was well nigh impossible. Many of the residents lied, some embroidered the truth, others seemed to know nothing. However, many interesting facts *did* emerge. First and foremost, that the Scarecrow, as we had nicknamed the dead man, seemed fixated with contacting the Marquis of Rye and also with meeting the *beau monde* of Winchelsea. I concluded from this that the Marquis might well be personally implicated and, possibly, a lady of quality as well. Second, Mr Rawlings discovered that two ladies of the town, one young, the other not so fresh, had indulged in flirtations with our lecherous spying friend. Third, while visiting Captain Pegram I saw, partly concealed in a half open drawer, a sketch of Miss Rosalind Tireman in the nude.'

'And what conclusion did you draw from that?' asked Sir Gabriel, his deep sapphire ring flashing splendidly as he moved his hand.

'Either that she and he were somehow involved together, or simply that he lusted after her,' Joe answered.

John spoke up. 'That fact made me suspect the Captain at once. His behaviour was extremely strange to say the least of it. However, we progress too rapidly. Other equally odd facts were emerging. Some of which seemed quite inexplicable.'

'Such as?'

'A contact who frequents the Romney Marsh . . .'

Mr Fielding rumbled his tuneful laugh. 'Come now, Mr Rawlings, don't mince words. It was Dick Jarvis the smuggler, wasn't it?'

'Yes, Sir. I'm afraid it was. The man declares he is a patriot and I suppose, according to his lights, he is. Anyway, he provided the very interesting piece of information that in the dead of night the skeleton was visited by a woman who removed Captain Pegram's visiting card from the corpse's pocket.'

There was a silence, then 'Why?' asked Serafina.

'To obliterate evidence of a link between the Captain and the dead man, which might inadvertently reveal her identity, I presume.'

'But how?'

'If the Captain should be suspected of being a spy, the authorities would have been at liberty to search amongst his papers for ciphers and so on. I can only presume that Rosalind feared that her naked portrait, the one that she was so anxious he should destroy, would be found if that happened.'

'So was she the woman?' asked John's father.

'I thought at first it was Henrietta Tireman,' the Apothecary answered slowly.

'Why was that?'

'Because she was strong and had told me she could ride well. And, further, I found her hat on the church path after I had overheard Captain Pegram conversing with an unknown woman. But probably most of all because she had been in love – and still is – with the Marquis of Rye, whom I suspected of being involved.'

'Did you think she was the Moth?' asked Louis.

'No, I thought that was Lord Rye himself.'

'Why?'

'Because of his misspent youth. I wondered whether he had become a spy in order to pay his debts and that now, for fear of blackmail, he was too deeply enmeshed to escape. There was another thing, too. The Scarecrow's obsession with meeting him. Now, of course, we know it was to get to Rosalind but at the time it seemed to me it was the Marquis that the spy was after. Mistakenly, the Scarecrow visited Captain Pegram, thinking, or so I believe, that such a grand house must belong to nobility. And indeed Nathaniel admitted, more openly than anyone else, that the Frenchman had called on him. It was on that occasion that the Scarecrow must have been given, or at the very least acquired, Captain Pegram's visiting card. Anyway, there was one other odd thing that happened round about that time. I overheard a couple arguing in the churchyard, quite bitterly and cruelly. The woman wore a strong scent but other than that I could not identify her. The man, who seemed in despair, was equally anonymous. Then there emerged the fact that

271

the Scarecrow had bought a bottle of Evening in Araby, a perfume blended by Apothecary Gironde, for an unknown woman. Was it all the same female, I began to wonder.'

'Go back a little,' requested Sir Gabriel. 'Did you believe Miss Tireman to be the woman in the churchyard? Miss Henrietta, that is?'

'Not at the time. But later, when I overheard the other altercation, the one I mentioned to you. I did.'

'For what reason?' asked Joe Jago.

'As I told you, I found Miss Henrietta's hat lying on the path near where the argument had taken place and, on another occasion, I smelled Evening in Araby on her.'

'I see,' said the clerk, and John felt absolutely certain that he did!

'Then came a conversation with Serafina, during which we discussed the various people involved. She was convinced that the anonymous couple who had fallen out so bitterly were the Frog and the Moth, but in that she was wrong. Yet in a way what the Comtesse said led me further along the path. You see, I believe that Captain Pegram knew that the Moth had been contacted by the Scarecrow. I believe that, desperate for help, she went to her former lover and he, still besotted, assured her that he would kill the Frenchman if necessary. However, she relieved him of that task by doing so herself, probably in a moment of fury.'

'But how did you manage to identify the Frog?' asked Louis, leaning forward intently.

'In relation to discovering the identity of the Moth, that was really quite simple. One night, when I was watching one of the spies signalling to a French ship – I wasn't sure which spy it was at that stage – I heard a sound that half frightened me out of my wits. It was a strange scrabbling, clawing noise, as if some awful monster were roaming the seashore. Then, when a French frigate ran aground on a sandbank, completely misled by an incorrect signal, I heard the sound again.'

'And what was it?' asked Elizabeth Fielding, intrigued.

'A dog.'

'What?'

'I said a dog.' John laughed. 'Sir Ambrose and Lady Ffloote owned – still do, I suppose – a wretched old hound which they will insist on calling The Pup. The poor thing seemed in a constant state of exhaustion, and now I know why. The Frog took the wretched creature with him when he went on his signalling missions, probably said that he was off to give it exercise. Anyway, the sound I heard was its claws scrabbling on the shale. That train of thought together with the sheer stupidity that the Frog demonstrated at every turn, convinced me that the spy could be nobody but Sir Ambrose.'

There was general laughter and a smattering of applause. John inclined his head, then looked directly at Louis de Vignolles.

'There is one thing about that night which still remains unexplained. A dark man with a strong accent informed the Riding Officers at Rye that the French had landed at Pett Level. At the time I thought it had to be Lucius but now, of course, I realise it couldn't have been.'

Louis gazed at him, his expression blank. 'How strange. It must have been somebody patrolling the shoreline. But who would do such a thing in the middle of the night?'

'Who indeed?' answered John, and raised a cynical eyebrow.

'Enough of that,' put in Serafina, hiding a secret smile. 'Tell us how you discovered the identity of the Moth.'

'As I said, I spent a while believing it to be the Marquis. However, the more I mulled the various ideas over the more a picture of a vain and greedy person kept coming into my mind, a person who would stop at nothing in order to reach the pinnacle of society and have money to burn. Now the people of the town may be odd but there was only one who answered that description in my mind, the fabulously beautiful Rosalind. When he was drunk, Captain Pegram *almost* told me the story of his love affair with her when she was very young – and he very rich! Once, probably twice, I had heard him in bitter argument with an unidentified female. And on the second occasion she actually ordered him to destroy 'the picture'. That made me feel certain that the field was narrowed to either one of the three Tireman women or a new and jealous mistress, for who else would care so much about a compromising portrait?

'The dropped hat gave me food for thought. But what easier than for a sister to appropriate another sister's headgear? Then there was the perfume, Evening in Araby, which Apothecary Gironde sold to the Scarecrow for an unknown lady. Rosalind owned such a brand but Henrietta smelled of it. Isn't it a fact that sisters frequently borrow one another's cosmetics?'

Mr Fielding spoke again. 'So you had no physical clues, only the character portrait of someone cruel enough to kill in order not to obey an early commitment to spy for France and thereby risk losing their wealth and social position?'

'There was just one piece of evidence, Sir,' answered John. 'Acting on your advice, I introduced Dick Jarvis into society, masquerading as Louis's cousin and dressed as a gentleman of quality. He came to my farewell assembly and there he identified Rosalind as the woman who had removed the card from the Scarecrow's pocket.

All that night I wondered whether she was protecting Captain Pegram or acting for herself by not wanting the Captain's name to be associated with the victim in any way. But in the end only she, wretched and jealous girl that she was, seemed to meet all the qualities, if one can use that word, the murderer displayed. Then I realised that I had described her as a butterfly to Serafina and that the French for moth is Papillon de Nuit. But still I wasn't totally sure, not until the moment when the second French spymaster, Lucius Delahunty, alias Lucien de la Tour, a rogue who managed to deceive me utterly, killed her, just as she had murdered his own cousin.'

'But who,' asked Elizabeth Fielding, 'was poisoning Mrs Harcross?'

John smiled ruefully. 'No one. She was doing it to herself. The poor woman, along with several others I might add, was taking something called the Elixir of Youth, prepared by Mrs Gironde without the supervision of her husband. Not knowing any beter, the silly soul was picking and compounding the wrong simples, with the result that she was slowly poisoning the entire middle-aged female population of Winchelsea.'

'What did you do?'

'I told her to stop it at once – and she did!'

'What a sad and extraordinary tale,' said Sir Gabriel slowly.

'Very sad,' echoed John, and just for a moment he looked utterly downcast.

Joe Jago cleared his throat noisily. 'Tell everyone about the post script, Mr Rawlings.'

The Apothecary smiled again. 'A small and disreputable smuggler called Little Harry arrived at Petronilla's Platt just before I left. He gave me a bag of money and a letter—'

'What did it say?' interrupted Elizabeth.

'I'll read it to you.' John produced a paper covered with exuberant handwriting from his inside pocket. '"Greetings to my old companion, John Rawlings. I beg you, my friend, for the sake of the hours that we have spent jovially together to provide a headstone for my cousin with the enclosed guineas. Let it read, 'Gerard de la Tour, 1727 – 1757, who died in the service of his country.'" It was dated three days after Rosalind's fatal shooting and the address was merely given as "En route à Paris".'

'So Lucius definitely escaped?'

'Yes.'

'And the headstone?'

'The order is already in train,' said Sir Gabriel. 'I have taken the liberty of adding a fleur-de-lys to it, unpatriotic though some might think it.'

'Two more things,' said Serafina, looking very puzzled. 'The first is, why did Rosalind do it? How did a country parson's daughter come to be spying for France?'

'Her grandmother was French and I presume, though I don't know for certain, that she spoke the language fluently, as did Henrietta. After all, that is how the Tireman family became involved with the nobility. Henrietta went to teach the Marquis's sister French, then, very foolishly, introduced Rosalind to the household when the governess left. I say foolishly because by this time he had asked Henrietta to marry him, only for the Marquis to abandon her in favour of her more beautiful sister.'

'Poor thing,' said Elizabeth Fielding sympathetically.

John looked very pinched indeed. 'All's well that ends well,' he answered bitterly. 'I am told that Lord Rye has now seen the error of his ways and that Henrietta is restored in his affections.'

'John,' said Sir Gabriel, his voice gentle. 'I am still not quite clear. Did Rosalind agree to spy in return for money?'

'I believe so, yes. Simply for the sake of her own vanity and perhaps, too, to ensure she landed a wealthy husband. I always thought how well dressed and fashionable the Tireman family was. In fact at one time I thought the rector might be spying in order to cope with the cost of clothing them. However, it seems the girls supported themselves. Henrietta obviously earned extra by teaching, but her sister had other, darker ways.'

Serafina nodded. 'So who is the French spy who has infiltrated London society and whom Lou – I mean the Secret Office –

275

is so desperately seeking? Which one of your suspects is he, John?'

The Apothecary gave a shrug worthy of a Frenchman. 'That I have not been able to discover, my dear. We will simply have to wait and see,' he said.

Historical Note

John Rawlings, Apothecary, was born circa 1731, though his actual parentage is somewhat shrouded in mystery. He was made Free of the Worshipful Society of Apothecaries on 13 March, 1755. On that occasion he gave his address as 2, Nassau Street, Soho, thereby linking himself irrefutably with H.D. Rawlings Ltd., Soda Water Manufacturers, who were based at the same address over a hundred years later.

It might surprise some readers to know that at the time of the Seven Years War the secret service in this country was extremely well organised. It was roughly divided into two sections, the Secret Office and the Secret Department. The Secret Office came directly under the control of the Secretary of State, who funded it. It was the duty of this office to run the secret service, whose function it was to obtain information for the government. It employed spies in Britain to detect plots, and abroad to discover the designs of foreign powers. The Secret Department was part of the Post Office and was founded as early as 1718, though it is possible that the Department had existed before then in a slightly different form. During the Seven Years War the Secretary of State, the Earl of Holdernesse, would instruct Anthony Todd, head of the Post Office, to open any mail that he considered might be suspect. Anything written in code or cipher was then immediately taken to Dr Edward Willes who, unbelievably, combined the roles of Bishop of Bath and Wells and Secret Decipherer to the King. Ciphers, of course, are as old as time and are still used today. Interestingly, the Secret Department was not disbanded until the middle of the nineteenth century. The Secret Office, however, though now called the Secret Service, still flourishes.

During my researches I not only found Dr Willes but also a French spy who lived amongst London society and was eventually caught by the Secret Department. For the moment I intend to keep his identity secret in the hope that one of these days he might return! Meanwhile all I can say is 2729 386 1285.